Richard Morris

Early English Alliterative Poems

Richard Morris

Early English Alliterative Poems

ISBN/EAN: 9783337395513

Printed in Europe, USA, Canada, Australia, Japan

Cover: Foto ©Andreas Hilbeck / pixelio.de

More available books at **www.hansebooks.com**

Early English Text Society.
Original Series, 1864.—No. I.

Early English Alliterative Poems,

in the

West-Midland Dialect

of the

Fourteenth Century.

COPIED AND EDITED FROM A UNIQUE MANUSCRIPT IN THE LIBRARY OF THE BRITISH MUSEUM, COTTON, NERO A x.

WITH AN

INTRODUCTION, NOTES, AND GLOSSARIAL INDEX.

BY

RICHARD MORRIS,

AUTHOR OF "THE ETYMOLOGY OF LOCAL NAMES," EDITOR OF "LIBER CURE COCORUM," AND RICHARD HAMPOLE'S "PRICKE OF CONSCIENCE," MEMBER OF THE COUNCIL OF THE PHILOLOGICAL SOCIETY.

[Third Reprint, 1896.]

LONDON:
PUBLISHED FOR THE EARLY ENGLISH TEXT SOCIETY,
BY KEGAN PAUL, TRENCH, TRÜBNER & CO., LIMITED

MDCCCLXIV.

Price Sixteen Shillings.

Early English Text Society.

Committee of Management.

Director: DR. FREDERICK J. FURNIVALL, M.A.

Treasurer: HENRY B. WHEATLEY, Esq.

Hon. Sec.: W. A. DALZIEL, Esq., 67, Victoria Road, Finsbury Park, N.

Hon. Sec. for America: Prof. F. J. CHILD, Harvard Coll., Cambr., Mass., U.S.A.

Lord ALDENHAM, M.A.
Prof. E. KÖLBING, Ph.D.
S. L. LEE, B.A.
Rev. Prof. J. E. B. MAYOR, M.A.
Dr. J. A. H. MURRAY, M.A.
Prof. NAPIER, M.A., Ph.D.
EDWARD B. PEACOCK, Esq.
Rev. Prof. WALTER W. SKEAT, Litt.D.
Dr. HENRY SWEET, M.A.
Dr. W. ALDIS WRIGHT, M.A.

(*With power to add Workers to their number.*)

Bankers: THE UNION BANK OF LONDON, 2, PRINCES STREET, E.C.

The Early English Text Society was started by Dr. Furnivall in 1864 for the purpose of bringing the mass of Old English Literature within the reach of the ordinary student, and of wiping away the reproach under which England had long rested, of having felt little interest in the monuments of her early language and life.

On the starting of the Society, so many Texts of importance were at once taken in hand by its Editors, that it became necessary in 1867 to open, besides the *Original Series* with which the Society began, an *Extra Series* which should be mainly devoted to fresh editions of all that is most valuable in printed MSS. and Caxton's and other black-letter books, though first editions of MSS. will not be excluded when the convenience of issuing completed Texts demands their inclusion in the Extra Series.

During the thirty-three years of the Society's existence, it has produced, with whatever shortcomings, an amount of good solid work for which all students of our Language, and some of our Literature, must be grateful, and which has rendered possible the beginnings (at least) of proper Histories and Dictionaries of that Language and Literature, and has illustrated the thoughts, the life, the manners and customs of our forefathers.

But the Society's experience has shown the very small number of those inheritors of the speech of Cynewulf, Chaucer, and Shakspere who care two guineas a year for the records of that speech. "Let the dead past bury its dead," is still the cry of Great Britain and her Colonies, and of America, in the matter of language. The Society has never had money enough to produce the Texts that could easily have been got ready for it; and many Editors are now anxious to send to press the work they have prepared. The necessity has therefore arisen for trying whether more Texts can be got out by the plan of issuing them in advance of the current year, so that those Members who like to pay for them by advance Subscriptions, can do so, while those who prefer to wait for the year for which the volumes are markt, can do so too. To such waiters, the plan will be no injury, but a gain, as every year's Texts will then be ready on the New Year's Day on which the Subscription for them is paid.

The success of this plan will depend on the support it receives from Members, as it is obvious that the Society's printers must be paid half or two-thirds of their bill for a Text within a few months of its production. Appeal is therefore made to all Members who can spare advance Subscriptions, to pay them as soon as they get notice that the Texts for any future year are ready. In 1892, the Texts for 1893 were issued; in 1893, those for 1894 and 1895; those for 1896–8 will be ready in 1896.

The Subscription to the Society, which constitutes membership, is £1 1*s.* a year [and £1 1*s.* additional for the Extra Series], due in advance on the 1st of January, and should be paid either to the Society's Account at the Head Office of the Union Bank of London, Princes Street, London, E.C., or by Cheque, Postal Order, or Money-Order to the Hon. Secretary, W. A. Dalziel, Esq., 67, Victoria Road, Finsbury Park, London, N., and crost "Union Bank of London." (United-States Subscribers must pay for postage 1*s.* 4*d.* a year extra for the Original Series, and 1*s.* a year for the Extra Series.) The Society's Texts are also sold separately at the prices put after them in the Lists.

Early English Alliterative Poems.

PREFACE.

The following poems are taken from a well known manuscript in the Cottonian collection, marked Nero A x, which also contains, in the same handwriting and dialect, a metrical romance,[1] wherein the adventures of Sir Gawayne with the "Knight in Green," are most ably and interestingly described.

Unfortunately nothing can be affirmed with any certainty concerning the authorship of these most valuable and interesting compositions. The editor of "Syr Gawayn and the Green Knight" considers that Huchowne, a supposed[2] Scotch *maker* of the fourteenth century, has the best claims to be recognised as the author, inasmuch as he is specially referred to by Wyntown as the writer of the *Gret gest of Arthure* and the *Awntyre of Gawayne.*

I do not think that any certain conclusions are to be drawn from the Scotch historian's assertion. It is well known that more versifiers than one during the fourteenth century attempted romance composition in the English language, having for their theme the knightly deeds of Arthur or Sir Gawayne. These they compiled from French originals, from which they selected the most striking incidents and those best suited to an Englishman's taste for the marvellous. We are not sur-

1 Edited by Sir Frederic Madden for the Bannatyne Club, under the title of "Syr Gawayn and the Grene Knyȝt," and by me for the Early English Text Soc., 1865.

2 Wyntown nowhere asserts that Huchowne is a Scotchman.

prised, then, at finding so many romance poems treating of the exploits of the same hero, and laying claim to be considered as original productions. In Scotland, Huchowne's works might no doubt have been regarded as the standard romances of the period, but that they were the only English *gests* is indeed very doubtful.

The Early English alliterative romance, entitled the *Morte Arthure*, published from a manuscript in Lincoln Cathedral by Mr. Halliwell,[1] is considered by Sir F. Madden to be the veritable *gest of Arthure* composed by Huchowne. An examination of this romance does not lead me to the same conclusion, unless Huchowne was a Midland man, for the poem is not written in the old Scotch dialect,[2] but seems to have been originally composed in one of the Northumbrian dialects spoken *South* of the Tweed.[3]

The manuscript from which Mr. Halliwell has taken his text is not the original copy, nor even a literal transcript of it. It exhibits certain orthographical and grammatical peculiarities unknown to the Northumbrian dialect which have been introduced by a Midland transcriber, who has here and there taken

[1] Edited for E. E. T. Soc. by Rev. G. G. Perry, M.A.

[2] This is evident from the following particulars:—

I. In old Scotch manuscripts we find the guttural *gh* (or ȝ) represented by *ch*; thus, *aght*, *laght*, *saght*, *wight*, are the English forms which, in the Scotch orthography, become *aucht* (owed), *laucht* (seized), *saucht* (peace), *wicht* (active). It is the former orthography, however, that prevails in the Morte Arthure.

II. We miss the Scotch use of (1) *-is* or *-ys*, for *-es* or *-s*, in the plural number, and of possessive cases of nouns, and in the person endings of the present tense indicative mood of verbs; (2) *-it* or *-yt*, for *-ed* or *d*, in the preterites or passive participles of regular verbs.

III. There is a total absence of the well-known Scotch forms *begouth* (began), *sa* (so), *sic* (such), *throuch*, *thorow* (through). Instead of these *bigan*, *so*, *syche*, *thrughe* (*thurgh*) are employed. See Preface to Hampole's Pricke of Conscience, pp. vii. viii.

[3] This is shown by the frequent employment of *-es* as the person ending of the verb in the present tense, plural number. The corresponding Southern verbal inflexion *-eth*. *never* occurs; while the Midland *-en* is only occasionally met with in the third person plural present, and has been introduced by a later copyist. There are other characteristics, such as the predominance of words containing the A.S. long *a*; as *hame* (home), *stane* (stone), *thra* (bold), *walde* (would), etc.; the frequent use of *thir* (these), *tha* (the, those), etc.

the liberty to adapt the original text to the dialect of his own locality, probably that one of the North Midland counties, where many of the Northumbrian forms of speech would be intelligible.[1]

A comparison of the Arthurian romance with the following poems throws no light whatever upon the authorship of the poems. The dialect of the two works is altogether different, although many of the terms employed are common to both, being well known over the whole of the North of England. The grammatical forms (the best test we can have) in the poems are quite distinct from those in the *Morte Arthure*, and of course go far to prove that they do not proceed from the pen of the same writer.

The Editor of "Syr Gawayn and the Green Knight" acknowledges that the poems in the present volume, as now preserved to us in the manuscript, are not in the Scottish dialect, but he says "there is sufficient internal evidence of their being *Northern*,[2] although the manuscript containing them appears to have been written by a scribe of the Midland counties, which will account for the introduction of forms differing from those used by writers beyond the Tweed."

Now, with regard to this subsequent transcription of the poems from the Scotch into a Midland dialect,—it cannot be

[1] The peculiarities referred to do not appear to be owing to the copyist of the Lincoln manuscript (Robert de Thornton, a native of Oswaldkirk in Yorkshire), who, being a Northumbrian, would probably have restored the original readings. The non-Northumbrian forms in the Morte Arthure are—1. The change of *a* into *o*, as *bolde* for *balde*, *bote* for *bate*, *one* for *ane*, *honde* for *hande*, *londe* for *lande*; 2. *they*, *theyre*, *them*, *theym*, for *thay*, *thaire*, *tham*; 3. *gayliche*, *kindliche*, *semlyche*, etc., for *gayly*, *kindly*, *seemly*, etc. (the termination *lich*, *liche*, was wholly unknown to the Northumbrian dialect, being represented by *ly* or *like*); 4. *churle*, *churche*, *iche*, *mache*, *myche*, *syche*, *wyrche*, etc., for *carle*, *kirke*, *ilk*, *make*, *mykelle*, *swilk*, *wyrk*, etc.; 5. infinitives in *-en*, as *drenschen*, *schewenne*, *wacchenne*, etc.; 6. the use of *eke*, *thos*, for *als* (*alswa*), *thas*; 7. the employment of *aye* for *egg*. The former word *never* occurs in any pure Northumbrian work, while the latter is seldom met with in any Southern production.

[2] The poems are *Northern* in contradistinction to *Southern*, but they are not Northern or Northumbrian in contradistinction to *Midland*.

said to be improbable, for we have abundant instances of the multiplication of copies by scribes of different localities, so that we are not surprised at finding the works of some of our popular Early English writers appearing in two or three forms; but, on the other hand, a comparison of the original copy with the *adapted transcriptions*, or even the reading of a transcribed copy, always shows how the author's productions have suffered by the change. Poetical works, especially those with final rhymes, of course undergo the greatest amount of transformation and depreciation. The changes incident upon the kind of transcription referred to are truly surprising, and most perplexing to those who make the subject of Early English *dialects* a matter of investigation.

But, in the present poems, the uniformity and consistency of the grammatical forms is so entire, that there is indeed no internal evidence of subsequent transcription into any other dialect than that in which they were originally written. However, the dialect and grammatical peculiarities will be considered hereafter.

Again, in the course of transcription into another dialect, any literary merit that the author's copy may have originally possessed would certainly be destroyed. But the poems before us are evidently the work of a man of birth and education; the productions of a true poet, and of one who had acquired a perfect mastery over that form of the English tongue spoken in his own immediate locality during the earlier part of the fourteenth century. Leaving out of consideration their great philological worth, they possess an intrinsic value of their own as literary compositions, very different from anything to be found in the works of Robert of Gloucester, Manning, and many other Early English authors, which are very important as philological records, but in the light of poetical productions cannot be said to hold a very distinguished place in English literature. The poems in the present volume contain many passages which, as Sir F. Madden truly remarks, will bear comparison with any similar ones in the works of Douglas or Spenser.

I conclude, therefore, that these poems were not transcribed from the Scotch dialect into any other, but were written in their own West-Midland speech in which we now have them.

Mr. Donaldson, who is now editing for the Early English Text Society the Troy Book, translated from Guido di Colonna, puts forward a plea for Huchowne as its author, to whom he would also assign the *Morte Arthure* (ed. Perry) and the Pistel of Sweet Susan.[1] But Mr. Donaldson seems to have been misled by the similarity of vocabulary, which is not at all a safe criterion in judging of works written in a Northumbrian, West or East Midland speech. The dialect, I venture to think, is a far safer test. A careful examination of the Troy Book compels me to differ in toto from Mr. Donaldson, and, instead of assigning the Troy Book to a Scotchman, say that it cannot even be claimed, in its present form, by any Northumbrian south of the Tweed; moreover, it presents no appearance of having been tampered with by one unacquainted with the dialect, though it has perhaps been slightly modernised in the course of transcription.

The work is evidently a genuine West-Midland production,[2] having most of the peculiarities of vocabulary and inflexions that are found in these *Alliterative Poems.*[3] I feel greatly inclined to claim this English Troy Book as the production of the author of the *Alliterative Poems*; for, leaving out identical and by no means common expressions, we find the same power of

[1] Printed by Mr. D. Laing in his "Inedited Pieces," from a MS. of Mr. Heber's. Other copies are in the Vernon MS., and Cotton Calig. A. ii.; the latter imperfect.

[2] Other specimens of this dialect will doubtless turn up. Mr. Brock has found a MS. in British Museum (Harl. 3909) with most of the peculiarities pointed out by me in the preface to the present work, and I believe that this dialect was probably a flourishing one in the 13th century. See O.E. Homilies, p. li.

[3] (1) *en* as the inflexion of the pres. tense pl., indic. mood of verbs; (2) *s* in the second and third pers. sing. of verbs; (3) *ho* = che; (4) *hit* = its; (5) *tow* = two: (6) *deȝter* = daughters, etc.

description,[1] and the same tendency to inculcate moral and religious truths on all occasions where an opportunity presents itself.[2]. Without dwelling upon this topic, which properly falls to the Editor of the Troy Book, it may not be out of place to ask the reader to compare the following description of a storm from the Troy Book, with that selected from the present volume on pp. 14 and 18.

A TEMPEST ON ÞE SEE.

There a tempest *hom* toke on þe torres hegh:—
A *rak* and a royde wynde rose in *hor* saile,
A myst & a *merkenes* was mervell to se;
With a *routond* rayn ruthe to be-holde,
Thonr*et*[3] full *throly* with a thicke haile;
With a leuenyng light as a *low* fyre,
Blas*et* all the brode see as it bren wold.
The flode with a felle cours flow*et* on hepis,
Rose uppon rockes as any *ranke* hylles.
So wode were the waghes & þe wilde *ythes*,
All was like to be lost þat no lond hade
The ship ay shot furth o þe *shire waghes*,
As qwo clymbe at a clyffe, or a clent[4] hille.
Eft *dump* in the depe as all drowne wolde.
Was no *stightlyng* with stere ne no stithe ropes,
Ne no sayle, þat might serue for *unsound* wedur.
But all the buernes in the bote, as *hom* best liked,
Besoght unto sainttes & to sere goddes; (p. 65)

A STORME ON THE SE.

All the company enclin*et* cair*yn* to ship;
Cach*yn* in cables, knyt up *hor* ancres,
Fesit vp *hor* sailes in a sad hast;
Richet þere rapes, rapit unto see.

[1] See p. 36, ll. 1052–1066; p. 37, ll. 1074–1089; pp. 161-162, ll. 4956–4975.

[2] See pp. 25, 26 (Jason's unfaithfulness); pp. 74, 75, ll. 2241–2255; p. 75, ll. 2256–2263; p. 69, ll. 2267–2081; p. 158, ll. 4839–4850; p. 189, ll. 4881–4885; p. 165, ll. 5078–5086, etc.

[3] In the Harl. MS. 3909, nearly all the p. part. and preterites end in *-et* (*-ut* and *-et* occur in Romances ed. by Robson).

[4] This seems to furnish an etymology for *Clent* Hills, Worcestershire—*brent* is the term employed in Alliterative.

Hokit out of hauyn, all the hepe somyn,
Hade bir at hor bake, blawen to þe depe;
Sailyn forthe *soberly*, somyn but a while,
Noght fyftene forlong fairly to the end.
. . . .
When sodenly the softe aire *unsoberly* rose;
The cloudis overcast, *claterrit* aboute;
Wyndes full wodely *walt* up the ythes;
Wex *merke* as the mydnighte mystes full thicke:
Thunret in the *thestur throly* with all;
With a *launchant laite* lightonyd the water;
And a *ropand* rayne *raiked* fro the heuyn.
The storme was full stithe with mony stout windes,
Hit *walt* up the wilde se vppon wan hilles.
The ffolke was so ferd, that *on flete* were,
All drede for to drowne with dryft of the se;
And in perell were put all the proude kynges.—(p. 150.)

The poems in the present volume, three in number, seem to have been written for the purpose of enforcing, by line upon line and precept upon precept, Resignation to the will of God; Purity of life as manifested in thought, word, and deed; Obedience to the Divine command; and Patience under affliction.

In the first poem, entitled by me "*The Pearl*," the author evidently gives expression to his own sorrow for the loss of his infant child, a girl of two years old, whom he describes as a

Perle plesaunte to prynces paye
Pearl pleasant to princes' pleasure,
To clanly clos in golde so clere
Most neatly set in gold so clear.

Of her death he says:

Allas! I leste hyr in on erbere
Alas! I lost her in an arbour,
Þurȝ gresse to grounde hit fro me yot
Through grass to ground it from me got.—(p. 1.)

The writer then represents himself as visiting his child's grave (or arbour) in the "high season of August," and giving way to his grief (p. 2). He falls asleep, and in a dream is carried toward a forest, where he saw rich rocks gleaming gloriously, hill sides decked with crystal cliffs, and trees the leaves of which were as burnished silver. The gravel under his feet was "precious pearls of orient," and birds "of flaming hues" flew about in company, whose notes were far sweeter than those of the cytole or gittern (guitar) (p. 3). The dreamer arrives at the bank of a stream, which flows over stones (shining like stars in the welkin on a winter's night) and pebbles of emeralds, sapphires, or other precious gems, so

> þat all the loȝe lemed of lyȝt
> *That all the deep gleamed of light,*
> So dere watȝ hit adubbement
> *So dear was its adornment.*—(p. 4.)

Following the course of the stream, he perceives on the opposite side a crystal cliff, from which was reflected many a "royal ray" (p. 5).

> At þe fote þer-of þer sete a faunt
> *At the foot thereof there sat a child,*
> A mayden of menske, ful debonere
> *A maiden of honour, full debonnair;*
> Blysnande whyt watȝ hyr bleaunt
> *Glistening white was her robe,*
> (I knew hyr wel, I hade sen hyr ere)
> *(I knew her well, I had seen her before)*
> At glysnande golde þat man con schore
> *As shining gold that man did purify,*
> So schon þat schene an-vnder schore
> *So shone that sheen (bright one) on the opposite shore;*
> On lenghe I loked to hyr þere
> *Long I looked to her there,*
> þe lenger I knew hyr more & more
> *The longer I knew her, more and more.*—(pp. 6, 7.)

The maiden rises, and, proceeding along the bank of the stream, approaches him. He tells her that he has done nothing but mourn for the loss of his Pearl, and has been indeed a "joyless jeweller" (p. 8). However, now that he has found his Pearl, he declares that he is no longer sorrowful, but would be a "joyful jeweller" were he allowed to cross the stream (p. 8). The maiden blames her father for his rash speech, tells him that his Pearl is not lost, and that he cannot pass the stream till after death (p. 10). The dreamer is in great grief; he does not, he says, care what may happen if he is again to lose his Pearl. The maiden advises him to bear his loss patiently, and to abide God's doom (p. 11). She describes to him her blissful state in heaven, where she reigns as a queen (p. 12). She explains to him that Mary is the Empress of Heaven, and all others kings and queens (p. 13). The parable of the labourers in the vineyard[1] (pp. 15–18) is then rehearsed at length, to prove that "innocents" are admitted to the same privileges as are enjoyed by those who have lived longer upon the earth (p. 18). The maiden then speaks to her father of Christ and his one hundred and forty thousand brides (p. 24), and describes their blissful state (p. 26), She points out to him the heavenly Jerusalem, which was "all of bright burnished gold, gleaming like glass" (p. 29). Then the dreamer beholds a procession of virgins going to saluto the Lamb, among whom he perceives his "little queen" (p. 33). On attempting to cross the stream to follow her, he is aroused from his dream (p. 35), laments his rash curiosity in seeking to know so much of God's mysteries, and declares that man ever desires more happiness than he has any right to expect (p. 35).

The second poem, entitled "*Cleanness,*" is a collection of Biblical stories, in which the writer endeavours to enforce Purity of Life, by showing how greatly God is displeased at every kind of impurity, and how sudden and severe is the punishment which falls upon the sinner for every violation of the Divine law.

After commending cleanness and its "fair forms," the author relates (I.) The Parable of the Marriage Feast (p. 39); (II.)

[1] Matthew, chapter xx.

the Fall of the Angels (p, 43); (III.) The wickedness of the antediluvian world (p. 44),

> He watȝ famed for fre þat feȝt loued best
> *He was famous as free that fight loved best,*
> & ay þe bigest in bale þe best watȝ halden
> *And ever the biggest in sin the best was held;* (p. 45.)

(IV.) The destruction of mankind by the Flood. When all were safely stowed in the ark,

> Thenne sone com þe seuenþe day, when samned wern alle
> *Then soon came the seventh day when assembled were all,*
> & alle woned in þe whichche þe wylde & þe tame.
> *And all abode in the ark (hutch), the wild and the tame.*
> Þen bolned þe abyme & bonkeȝ con ryse
> *Then swelled the abyss and banks did rise,*
> Waltes out vch walle-heued, in ful wode stremeȝ
> *Bursts out each well-head in full wild streams,*
> Watȝ no brymme þat abod vnbrosten bylyue
> *There was no brim (stream) that abode unburst by then,*
> Þe mukel lauande loghe to þe lyfte rered
> *The much (great) flowing deep (loch) to the loft (sky) reared.*
> Mony clustered clowde clef alle in clowteȝ
> *Many a clustering cloud cleft all in clouts (pieces),*
> To-rent vch a rayn-ryfte & rusched to þe vrþe
> *Rent was each a rain-rift and rushed to the earth;*
> Fon neuer in forty dayeȝ, & þen þe flod ryses
> *Failed never in forty days, and then the flood rises,*
> Ouer-walteȝ vche a wod and þe wyde feldeȝ
> *Over-flows each wood and the wide fields;*
>
> . . . .
>
> Water wylger ay wax, woneȝ þat stryede
> *Water wildly ever waxed, abodes that destroyed,*
> Hurled in-to vch hous, hent þat þer dowelled
> *Hurled into each house, seized those that there dwelt.*
> Fyrst feng to þe flyȝt alle þat fle myȝt
> *First took to flight all that flee might,*
> Vuche burde with her barne þe byggyng þay leueȝ
> *Each bride (woman) with her bairn their abode they leave,*
> & bowed to þe hyȝ bonk þer brentest hit wern
> *And hied to the high bank where highest it were,*

& heterly to þe hyȝe hilleȝ þay [h]aled on faste
And hastily to the high hills they rushed on fast;
Bot al watȝ nedleȝ her note, for neuer cowþe stynt
But all was needless their device, for never could stop
Þe roȝe raynande ryg [&] þe raykande waweȝ
The rough raining shower and the rushing waves,
Er vch boþom watȝ brurd-ful to þe bonkeȝ eggeȝ
Ere each bottom (valley) was brim-ful to the banks' edges,
& vche a dale so depe þat demmed at þe brynkeȝ
And each dale so deep that dammed at the brinks.—(pp. 47, 48).

The ark is described as "heaved on high with hurling streams."

Kest to kyþeȝ vncouþe þe clowdeȝ ful nere
Cast to kingdoms uncouth the clouds ful near,
Hit waltered on the wylde flod, went as hit lyste
It tossed on the wild flood, went as it list,
Drof vpon þe depe dam, in daunger hit semed
It drove upon the deep dam, in danger it seemed,
With-outen mast, oþer myke, oþer myry bawe-lyne
Without mast, or mike,[1] *or merry bow-line,*
Kable, oþer capstan to clyppe to her ankreȝ
Cable or capstan to clip to their anchors,
Hurrok, oþer hande-helme hasped on roþer
Oar or hand-helm hooked on rudder,
Oþer any sweande sayl to seche after hauen
Or any swinging sail to seek after haven,
Bot flote forthe with þe flyt of þe felle wyndeȝ
But floated forth with the force of the fell winds.
Wheder-warde so þe water wafte, hit rebounde
Whither-ward so (as) the water waft, it rebounded,
Ofte hit roled on-rounde & rered on ende
Oft it rolled around and reared on end,
Nyf our lorde hade ben her lodeȝ-mon hem had lumpen harde
Had our Lord not been their (pilot) leader hardship had befallen them.—(p. 49.)

(V.) The Visit of Three Angels to Abraham (p. 54).

(VI.) The destruction of Sodom and Gomorrah (pp. 64, 65), including a description of the Dead Sea, the tarn (lake) of traitors (p. 66).

[1] See Glossary.

(VII.) The invasion of Jerusalem by Nebuchadnezzar (p. 71), and the captivity of Judah (p. 74).

The following is a paraphrase of the fourth and fifth verses in the twenty-fifth chapter of the second book of Kings.[1]

Þenne þe kyng of þe kyth a counsayl hym takes
Then the king of the kingdom a counsel him takes,
Wyth þe best of his burnes, a blench for to make
With the best of his men a device for to make;
Þay stel out on a stylle nyȝt er any steuen rysed
They stole out on a still night ere any sound arose,
& harde hurles þurȝ þe oste, er enmies hit wyste
And hard hurled through the host, ere enemies it wist,
Bot er þay at-wappe ne moȝt þe wach wyth oute
But ere they could escape the watch without,
Hiȝe skelt watȝ þe askry þe skewes an-vnder
High scattered was the cry, the skies there under,
Loude alarom vpon launde lulted was þenne
Loud alarm upon land sounded was then;
Ryche, ruþed of her rest, ran to here wedes,
Rich (men) roused from their rest, ran to their weeds,
Hard hattes þay hent & on hors lepes
Kettle hats they seized, and on horse leap;
Cler claryoun crak cryed on-lofte
Clear clarion's crack cried aloft.
By þat watȝ alle on a hepe hurlande swyþee
By that (time) was all on a heap, hurling fast,
Folȝande þat oþer flote, & fonde hem bilyue
Following that other fleet (host), and found them soon,
Ouer-tok hem, as tyd,[2] tult hem of sadeles
Over-took them in a trice, tilted them off saddles,
Tyl vche prynce hade his per put to þe grounde
Till each prince had his peer put to the ground;
& þer watȝ þe kyng kaȝt wyth calde prynces
And there was the king caught with crafty princes,

[1] "4. And the city was broken up, and all the men of war fled by night by the way of the gate between two walls, which is by the king's garden: (now the Chaldees were against the city round about:) and the king went the way toward the plain.
"5. And the army of the Chaldees pursued after the king, and overtook him in the plains of Jericho: and all his army were scattered from him."

[2] Immediately.

& alle hise gentyle for-iusted on Ierico playnes
And all his nobles vanquished on Jericho's plains.—(pp. 71, 72.)

(VIII.) Belshazzar's impious feast (pp. 76–80), and the handwriting upon the wall (pp. 80, 81).

In þe palays pryncipale vpon þe playn wowe
In the palace principal upon the plain wall,
In contrary of þe candelstik þat clerest hit schyned
Opposite to the candlestick that clearest there shone.
Þer apered a paume, with poyntel in fyngres
There appeared a palm with a pointel in its fingers,
Þat watȝ grysly & gret, & grymly he wrytes
That was grisly and great, and grimly it writes,
None oþer forme bot a fust faylaynde þe wryst
None other form but a fist failing the wrist
Pared on þe parget, purtrayed lettres
Pared on the plaister, pourtrayed letters.
When þat bolde Baltaȝar blusched to þat neue
When that bold Belshazzar looked to that fist,
Such a dasande drede dusched to his hert
Such a dazzling dread dashed to his heart.
Þat al falewed his face & fayled þe chere
That all paled his face and failed the cheer;
Þe stronge strok of þe stonde strayned his ioyntes
The strong stroke of the blow strained his joints,
His cnes cachcheȝ to close & cluchches his hommes
His knees catch to close, and he clutches his hams,
& he with plat-tyng his paumes displayes his lers[1]
And he with striking his palms displays his fears,
& romyes as a rad ryth þat roreȝ for drede
And howls as a frightened hound that roars for dread,
Ay biholdand þe honde til hit hade al grauen,
Ever beholding the hand till it had all graven,
& rasped on þe roȝ woȝe runisch saueȝ
And rasped on the rough wall uncouth saws (words).

(IX.) The story of Nebuchadnezzar's pride and its punishment (pp. 84, 85), and the interpretation of the handwriting by Daniel (p, 86).

[1] ? feres.

(X.) The invasion of Babylon by the Medes (pp. 87, 88).

Baltaȝar in his bed watȝ beten to deþe
Belshazzar in his bed was beaten to death,
Þat boþe his blood & his brayn blende on þe cloþes
That both his blood and his brains blended on the clothes;
Þe kyng in his cortyn watȝ kaȝt by þe heles
The king in his curtain was caught by the heels,
Feryed out bi þe fete & fowle dispysed
Ferried out by the feet and foully despised;
Þat watȝ so doȝty þat day & drank of þe vessayl
He that was so doughty that day and drank of the vessels,
Now is a dogge also dere þat in a dych lygges
Now is as dear (valuable) as a dog that in a ditch lies.—(p. 88.)

The third poem, entitled "*Patience,*" is a paraphrase of the book of Jonah. The writer prefaces it with a few remarks of his own in order to show that "patience is a noble point though it displease oft."

The following extract contains a description of the sea-storm which overtook Jonah:—

Anon out of þe norþ est þe noys bigynes
Anon out of the north east the noise begins,
When boþe breþes[1] con blowe vpon blo watteres
When both breezes did blow upon blue waters:
Roȝ rakkes þer ros with rudnyng an-vnder
Rough clouds there arose with lightning there under,
Þe see souȝed ful sore, gret selly to here
The sea sobbed full sore, great marvel to hear;
Þe wyndes on þe wonne water so wrastel togeder,
The winds on the wan water so wrestle together,
Þat þe wawes ful wode waltered so hiȝe
That the waves full wild rolled so high,
& efte busched to þe abyme þat breed fysches
And again bent to the abyss that bred fishes;
Durst nowhere for roȝ arest at þe bothem.
Durst it nowhere for roughness rest at the bottom.
When þe breth & þe brok & þe bote metten
When the breeze and the brook and the boat met,

[1] Eurus and Aquilo.

Hit watȝ a ioyles gyn þat Ionas watȝ inne
It was a joyless engine that Jonah was in,
For hit reled on round vpon þe roȝe yþes
For it reeled around upon the rough waves.
Þe bur ber to hit baft þat braste alle her gere
The bore (wave) bear to it abaft that burst all her gear,
Þen hurled on a hepe þe helme & þe sterne
Then hurled on a heap the helm and the stern,
Furste to murte[1] mony rop & þe mast after
First marred[2] many a rope and the mast after.
Þe sayl sweyed on þe see, þenne suppe bihoued
The sail swung on the sea, then sup behoved
Þe coge of þe colde water, & þenne þe cry ryses
The boat of the cold water, and then the cry rises;
ȝet coruen þay þe cordes & kest al þer-oute
Yet cut they the cords and cast all there-out.
Mony ladde þer forth-lep to laue & to kest
Many a lad there forth leapt to lave and to cast,
Scopen out þe scaþel water, þat fayn scape wolde
To scoop out the scathful water that fain escape would;
For be monnes lode neuer so luþer, þe lyf is ay swete
For be man's lot never so bad, the life is aye sweet.—(p. 93.)

The writer, in concluding the story of Jonah, exhorts his readers to be "patient in pain and in joy."

For he þat is to rakel to renden his cloþeȝ,
Mot efte sitte with more vn-sounde to sewe hem togeder.
For he that is too rash to rend his clothes,
Must afterwards sit with more unsound (worse ones) to sew them together. (p. 104.)

This brief outline of the poems, together with the short extracts from them, will, it is hoped, give the reader stomach to digest the whole. It is true that they contain many "uncouth" terms; but this will be their highest merit with the student of language, as is shown, by Dr. Guest's testimony, that they are "for several reasons curious, and especially so to the philologist."[3] To those readers who do not appreciate the importance

[1] ? = to-marte.
[3] History of English Rhythms, vol. i. p. 159.

of such a very large addition to the vocabulary of our Early Language as is made by these treatises, let Sir Frederic Madden's opinion of their literary merit suffice. That distinguished editor says, of the author's "poetical talent, the pieces contained in the MS. afford unquestionable proofs; and the description of the change of the seasons, the bitter aspect of winter, the tempest which preceded the destruction of Sodom and Gomorrah, and the sea storm occasioned by the wickedness of Jonas, *are equal to any similar passages* in Douglas or Spenser."[1] Moreover, as to the hardness of the language—inasmuch as the subject matter of the poem will be familiar to all who may take up the present volume, the difficulty on the word-point will not be such as to deter the reader from understanding and appreciating the production of an old English poet, who—though his very name, unfortunately, has yet to be discovered—may claim to stand in the foremost rank of England's early bards.

The Editor of the present volume has endeavoured to do justice to his author by giving the text, with some few exceptions, as it stands in the manuscript.[2] The contractions of the scribe have been expanded and printed in italics, a plan which he hopes to see adopted in every future edition of an early English author.

The Glossary has been compiled not only for the benefit of the reader, but for the convenience of those who are studying the older forms of our language, and who know how valuable a mere index of words and references sometimes proves.

In conclusion, I take the present opportunity of acknowledging the kind assistance of Sir Frederic Madden and E. A. Bond, Esq., of the British Museum, who, on every occasion, were most ready to render me any help in deciphering the manuscript, in parts almost illegible, from which the poems in the present volume are printed.

[1] Syr Gawayn, ed. Madden, p. 302.

[2] Wherever the Text has been altered, the reading of the MS. will be found in a foot-note.

REMARKS UPON THE DIALECT AND GRAMMAR.

Higden, writing about the year A.D. 1350, affirms, distinctly, the existence of three different forms of speech or dialects, namely, Southern, Midland, and Northern;[1] or, as they are sometimes designated, West-Saxon, Mercian, and Northumbrian. Garnett objects to Higden's classification, and considers it certain "that there were in his (Higden's) time, and probably long before, five distinctly marked forms, which may be classed as follows:—1. Southern or standard English, which in the fourteenth century was perhaps best spoken in Kent and Surrey by the body of the inhabitants. 2. Western English, of which traces may be found from Hampshire to Devonshire, and northward as far as the Avon. 3. Mercian, vestiges of which appear in Shropshire, Staffordshire, and South and West Derbyshire, becoming distinctly marked in Cheshire, and still more so in South Lancashire. 4. Anglian, of which there are three sub-divisions—the East Anglian of Norfolk and Suffolk; the Middle Anglian of Lincolnshire, Nottinghamshire and East Derbyshire; and the North Anglian of the West Riding of Yorkshire—spoken most purely in the central part of the mountainous district of Craven. 5. Northumbrian," spoken throughout the Lowlands of Scotland, Northumberland, Durham, and nearly the whole of Yorkshire.

Garnett's division is based upon peculiarities of pronunciation, which will be found well marked in the *modern* provincial dialects, and not upon any essential differences of inflexion that are to be found in our Early English manuscripts.[2]

The distinction between Southern and Western English was not at all required, as the Kentish Ayenbite of Inwyt (A.D.

[1] Polychronicon R. Higdeni, ap. Gale, p. 210, 211. See Garnett's Philological Essays, p. 43, and Specimens of Early English, p. 338.

[2] It is to be regretted that Garnett did not enter upon details, and give his readers some tests by which to distinguish the "five distinctly marked forms."

1340) exhibits most of the peculiarities that mark the Chronicles of Robert of Gloucester (Cottonian MS. Calig. A. xi.) as a Southern (or West-Saxon) production. The Anglian of Norfolk, Lincolnshire, and Nottinghamshire may be referred to one group with the Mercian of Lancashire, as varieties of the Midland dialect.

A careful examination of our early literature leads us to adopt Higden's classification as not only a convenient but a correct one.

There is, perhaps, no better test for distinguishing these dialects from one another than the verbal inflexions of the plural number in the present tense, indicative mood.

To state this test in the briefest manner, we may say that the Southern dialect employs *-eth*, the Midland *-en*, and the Northumbrian *-es* as the inflexion for all persons of the plural present indicative :[1]—

	Southern.	Midland.	Northern.
1st pers.	Hop-*eth*.	Hop-*en*.	Hop-*es*. (we) hope.
2nd „	Hop-*eth*.	Hop-*en*.	Hop-*es*. (ye) hope.
3rd „	Hop-*eth*.	Hop-*en*.	Hop-*es* (they) hope.

It is the constant and systematic employment of these inflexions, and not their occasional use that must be taken as the criterion of dialectical varieties.

In a pure specimen of the Southern dialect, we never find the Northumbrian *-es*. We do occasionally meet with the Midland *-en*, but only in those works written in localities where, from their geographical position, Southern and Midland forms would be intelligible.[2] We might look in vain for the Southern plural *-eth* in a pure Northumbrian production, but might be more successful in finding the Midland *-en* in the third person plural; as, "thay *arn*" for "they *ar*," or "thay *er*."

[1] In English works of the fourteenth century the *-en* of the Midland, and the *-es* of the Northumbrian is frequently dropped, thus gradually approximating to our modern conjugation.

[2] We are here speaking of works written in the thirteenth and fourteenth centuries.

In a work composed in Lincolnshire, Nottinghamshire, or Lancashire, we should be sure to find the occasional use of the Northumbrian plural *-es.*[1]

The inflexions of the verb in the singular are of value in enabling us to discriminate between the several varieties of the Midland dialect.[2] The Southern and Midland idioms (with the exception of the West-Midland of Lancashire, Cheshire, etc.) conjugated the verb in the singular present indicative, as follows :—

1st pers.	hope	(I) hope.
2nd ,,	hop-*est*	(thou) hopest.
3rd ,,	hop-*eth*	(he) hopes.

The West-Midland, corresponding to Garnett's Mercian, instead of *-est* and *-eth* employs the inflexions that are so common in the so-called Northumbrian documents of the ninth and tenth centuries :—

1st pers.	hope	(I) hope.
2nd ,,	hop-*es*	(thou) hopest.
3rd ,,	hop-*es*	(he) hopes.

The Northumbrian dialect takes *-es* in all three persons; but mostly drops it in the first person.

The peasantry of Cheshire and Lancashire still preserve the verbal inflexions which prevailed in the fourteenth century, and conjugate their verbs in the present indicative according to the following model :—

	Singular.	Plural.
1st pers.	hope	hopen.
2nd ,,	hopes	hopen.
3rd ,,	hopes	hopen.

Inasmuch as the poems in the present volume exhibit the

[1] Robert of Brunne, in his "Handlyng Synne," often employs it instead of *-en*, but only for the sake of the rhyme.

[2] The Midland dialect is a very difficult one to deal with, as it presents us with no uniform type; and, moreover, works written in this idiom are marked by Northern or Southern peculiarities, which have led many of our editors altogether astray in determining the locality of their composition.

systematic use of these forms, we cannot but believe that they were originally composed in one of those counties where these verbal inflexions were well known and extensively used. We have to choose between several localities, but if we assign the poems to Lancashire we are enabled to account for the large number of Norse terms employed. It is true that the ancient examples of the Lancashire dialect contained in Mr. Robson's Metrical Romances,[1] the Boke of Curtasye,[2] and Liber Cure Cocorum,[3] present us with much broader forms, as *-us* for *-es* in the plural number and possessive case of nouns, *-un* for *-en* in the plural present indicative mood, in passive participles of irregular (or strong) verbs, *-ud* (*-ut*) for *-ed* in the past tense and passive participle of regular (or weak) verbs, and the pronominal forms *hor* (their), *hom* (them), for *her* and *hem.*[4]

These forms are evidence of a broad pronunciation which, at the present time, is said to be a characteristic of the north-western division of Lancashire, but I think that there is good evidence for asserting that this strong provincialism was not confined, formerly, to the West-Midland dialect, much less to a division of any particular county. We find traces of it in Audelay's Poems (Shropshire), the Romance of William and the Werwolf,[5] and even in the Wickliffite version of the Scriptures.

Formerly, being influenced by these broad forms, I was led to select Cheshire or Staffordshire as the probable locality where the poems were written; but I do not, now, think that either of these counties ever employed a vocabulary containing so many Norse terms as are to be found in the Lancashire dialect. But although we may not be able to fix, with certainty,

[1] Published by the Camden Society, 1842.

[2] Edited by Mr. Halliwell for the Percy Society.

[3] Edited by me for the Philological Society, 1862.

[4] *-us* and *-ud* for *-es* and *-ed*, as well as *hom*, *hor*, do occasionally occur in the MS. containing our poems.

[5] The Romance of William and the Werwolf is written in the West-Midland dialect as spoken probably in Shropshire.

upon any one county in particular, the fact of the present poems being composed in the West-Midland dialect cannot be denied. Much may be said in favour of their Lancashire origin, and there are one or two points of resemblance between our poems, the Lancashire Romances, and Liber Cure Cocorum, that deserve especial notice.

I. In Sir Amadace,[1] lxviii. 9, there occurs the curious form *miȝtus=miȝtes=mightst.*[2] As it appears only once throughout the Romances we might conclude that it is an error of the scribe for *miȝtest*, but when we find in the poems before us not only *myȝteȝ=myȝtes* (mightst), but *woldeȝ=woldes* (wouldst), *coutheȝ=couthes* (couldst), *dippteȝ* (dippedest), *travayledeȝ* (travelledst), etc., we are bound to consider *miȝtus* as a genuine form.[3] In no other Early English works of the fourteenth century have I been able to find this peculiarity. It is very common in *the Wohunge of Ure Lauerd* (xiiith cent.). See O.E. Homilies, p. 51. The Northumbrian dialect at this period rejected the inflexion in the second person preterite singular, of regular verbs,[4] and in our poems we find the *-es* often dropped,

[1] Robson's Metrical Romances, p. 54, l. 9.

[2] *Woldus=woldes=wouldst*, appears in Audclay's poems (in the Shropshire dialect of the fifteenth century), p. 32, l. 6.

[3] The so-called Northumbrian records of the ninth and tenth centuries frequently use *-es* instead of *-est*, in the 2nd pers. preterite of regular verbs, *e.g.*,

ðu *forcerdes usic on-bec*=Thou turnedst us hindward.—(Ps. xliii. 11.)

ðu *saldes usic*=Thou gavest us.—(Ps. xliii. 12.)

ðu *bi-bohtes folc* ðin *butan weorðe*=Thou soldest thy folk without price.—(Ps. xliii. 12.)

ðu *ge-hiowades* me & *settes* ofer me hond ðine=Thou madest me and settest over me thy hand.—(Ps. cxxxviii. 5.)

ðu *ðreades* ða ofer-hygdan=Thou hast rebuked the proud.—(Ps. cxviii. 21.)

Ic ondeto ðe fader drihten heofnes forðon ðu *gedeigeldes* ðas ilco from snotrum & hogum & *ædeaudes* ða ðæm lytlum=I thank thee, O father, Lord of heaven and earth, because thou hast hid these things from the wise and prudent, and hast revealed them unto babes.—(Matt. xi. 25).

[4] Þou *torned* us hindward.—(Early English Nn. Psalter, xliii. 11.)

Þou *salde* þi folk.—(*Ibid.* xliii. 12.)

Þou *meked* us.—(*Ibid.* xliii. 20.)

Þou *made* me and set þi hand over me.—(*Ibid.* cxxxviii. 5.)

Þou *snibbed* proude.—(*Ibid.* cxviii. 21.)

so that we get two conjugations, which may be called the inflected and the uninflected form.

	Inflected.	Uninflected.	
1st pers.	hopede	hoped	(I) hoped.
2nd ,,	hopedes	hoped	(thou) hopedest.
3rd ,,	hopede	hoped	(he) hoped.

Originally the inflected form may have prevailed over the whole of the North of England, but have gradually become confined to the West-Midland dialect.

II. The next point of resemblance is the use of the verb SCHIN OR SCHUN=schal=shall. It is still preserved in the modern dialect of Lancashire in combination with the adverb *not*, as schunnot[1]=shall not. The following examples will serve to illustrate the use of this curious form:—

"—— þay *schin* knawe sone,
Þere is no bounté in burne lyk Baltaȝar þewes."[2]
(B. l. 1435.)
"& þose þat seme arn & swete *schyn* se his face."[3]
(*Ibid.* l. 1810.)
"Pekokys and pertrikys perboylyd *schyn* be."[4]
(Liber Cure Cocorum, p. 29.)
"For þer bene bestes þat *schyn* be rost."[5]—(*Ibid.* p. 34.)
"Alle *schun* be draȝun, Syr, at þo syde."[6]—(*Ibid.* p. 35.)
"Seche ferlies *schyn* falle."[7]—(Robson's Met. Rom. p. 12, l. 4.)

III. Nothing is more common in the present poems than the use of *hit* as a genitive=its, which is also found in the Lancashire romances.

[1] I am informed by a Shropshire friend that it prevails in his county under the form *shinneh*.

Win=will, in *winnot*, *wunnot*=will not, is still heard in the West-Midland districts. It is found in Robson's Romances and in Liber Cure Cocorum.

[2] They *shall* know soon there is no goodness in man like Belshazzar's virtues.

[3] And those that seemly are and sweet *shall* see His (God's) face.

[4] Peacocks and partriches parboiled *shall* be.

[5] For þer are beasts þat *shall* be roasted.

[6] All *shall* be drawn (have the entrails removed), Sir, at the side.

[7] Such marvels *shall* happen.

"Forþy þe derk dede see hit is demed ever more,
For *hit* dedeȝ of deþe duren þere ȝet."[1]—(Patience, l. 1021.)
"And, as hit is corsed of kynde & *hit* coosteȝ als,
Þe clay þat clenges þer-by arn corsyes strong."[2]
(*Ibid.* l. 1033.)

"For I wille speke with the sprete,
And of *hit* woe wille I wete,
Gif that I may *hit* bales bete."[3]
(Robson's Met. Romances, p. 5, ll. 3, 4.)

The present dialect of Lancashire still retains the uninflected genitive:—

"So I geet up be strike o' dey, on seet eawt; on went ogreath tilly welly coom within two mile oth' teawn; when, os tha dule woud height, o tit wur stonning ot an ale heawse dur; on me kawve (the dule bore eawt *it* een for me) took th' tit for *it* mother, on woud seawk her."[4] (Tummus and Meary).

Thus much for the dialectical peculiarities of our author. The scanty material at our disposal must be a sufficient excuse for the very meagre outline which is here presented to the reader. As our materials increase, the whole question of Early English dialects will no doubt receive that attention from English philologists which the subject really demands, and editors of old English works will then be enabled to speak with greater confidence as to the language and peculiarities of their authors. Something might surely be done to help the student by a proper classification of our manuscripts both as to date and place of composition. We are sadly in want of unadulterated

[1] Wherefore the dark dead sea it is called ever more.
For *its* deeds of death endure there yet.

[2] And as it is cursed of kind and *its* properties also,
The clay that clings thereby are corrosives strong.

[3] I will speak with the spirit,
And of *its* woe will I wit (know),
If that I may *its* bales (grief) abate.

[4] So I got up by break of day and set out; and went straight till I well nigh came within two miles of the town, when, as the devil would have it, a horse was standing at an ale-house door; and my calf (the devil bore out *its* eyes for me) took the horse for *its* mother, and would suck her.

specimens of the Northumbrian and East-Midland idioms during the twelfth and thirteenth centuries. There must surely be some records of these dialects in our university libraries which would well repay editing.[1]

GRAMMATICAL DETAILS.

I. Nouns.

(1) *Number.*—The plurals generally end in *-es* (*eȝ*), *-s*. *Yȝen* (eyes), *trumpen* (trumpets), are the only plurals in *-en* that occur in the poems. In Robson's Metrical Romances we find *fellun* (fells, hills,), *dellun* (dells), and *eyren* (eggs), in Liber Cure Cocorum. The plurals of *brother, child, cow, doȝter* (daughter), are *brether*, *childer, kuy*, and *deȝter*.

(2) *Gender.*—The names of inanimate things are in the neuter gender, as in modern English. The exceptions are *deep* (fem.), *gladnes* (fem.), and *wind* (masc.).

(3) *Case.*—The genitive singular (masc. and fem.) ends in *-es* (*-eȝ*), *-s*, but occasionally the inflexion is dropped; as, "Baltaȝar thewes," the virtues of Balshazzar.[2] If "*honde* myȝt," "*honde* werk," "*hellen* wombe," are not compounds, we have instances of the final *-e* (*en*) which formed the genitive case of *feminine* nouns in the Southern English of the fourteenth century.

In the phrases "*besten* blod" (blood of beasts), "*blonkken* bak" (back of horses), "*chyldryn* fader" (father of children), "*nakeryn* noyse" (noise of nakers), we have a trace of the genitive plural *-ene* (A.S. *-ena*).

II. Adjectives.

(1) *Number.*—The final *e*, as a sign of the plural, is very frequently dropped. *Pover* (poor), *sturn* (strong), make the

[1] Three specimens of the East-Midland dialect have come to light since writing the above. Harl. MS. 3909; Troy Book, ed. Donaldson, E. E. T. Soc.; The Lay-folks Mass-Book, ed. Simpson, E. E. T. Soc.

[2] In the romance of "Syr Gawayn and the Grene Knyȝt" we find "*blonk* (horse) sadele," "*fox* felle" (skin). In *blonk* an *e* has probably been dropped.

plurals *poveren* and *sturnen*. In the phrase, "þo syȝteȝ so *quykeȝ*"[1] (those sights so living), the *-eȝ* (=*-es*) is a mark of the plural, very common in Southern writers of the fourteenth century, and employed as a plural inflexion of the adjective until a very late period in our literature.

The Article exhibits the following forms:

SINGULAR		PLURAL.
Masc.	Fem.	
The.	tho.[2]	tho.

This forms the plural *thise* and *thes* (*these*). *That* is always used as a demonstrative, and never as the neuter of the article; its plural is *thos* (those).[3] The older form, *theos*=*these*, shows that the *e* is not a sign of the plural, as many English grammarians have asserted.

(2) *Degrees of Comparison.*—The comparative degree ends in *-er*, and the superlative in *-est*.

Adjectives and adverbs terminating in the syllable *-lyche* form the comparative in *-loker* and the superlative in *-lokest*; as, positive *uglyche* (=ugly), comp. *ugloker*, superl. *uglokest*. The long vowel of the positive is often shortened in the comp. and superl., as in the modern English *late*, *latter*, *last*.

Positive.	Comparative.	Superlative.
Brade (broad),	bradder,	braddest.
Dere (dear),	derrer,	derrest.
Lyke (like),	lykker,	lykkest.
Swete (sweet),	swetter,	swettest.
Wayke (weak),	wakker,	wakkest.
Wode (mad),	wodder,	woddest.

The following irregular forms are occasionally met with:

Fer (far),	ferre (fyrre),	ferrest.
Heȝe (high),	herre,	heȝest (hest).

[1] The feminine form is seldom employed. [2] The Northumbrian plural article is *tha*.
[3] The Northumbrian corresponding form is *thas*.

Positive.	Comparative.	Superlative.
Neȝe (nigh, near)	nerre,	nerrest (nest).
Sare (sore),	sarre,	sarrest.
Forme (first),		formast.
Mikelle (great),	mo	most.
Yvel, ill (bad),	wers (worre),	werst.

Numerals.—*Twinne* and *thrinne* occur for two and three. The ordinal numbers are—

first (fyrste), the forme,	sexte,
secunde, that other, tother,	sevenþe,
thryd, / thrydde,	aȝtþe,
	nente,
furþe,	tenþe, / tyþe.
fyfþe,	

The Northumbrian numerals corresponding to *sevenþe, aȝtþe, nente, tenþe*, are *sevend, aghtend, neghend, tend.* The Southern forms end in *-the*, as *sevenþe, eiȝteoþe, nyþe, teoþe* (*tyþe*).

III. Pronouns.

In the following poems we find the pronoun *ho*, she, still keeping its ground against the Northumbrian *scho.*[1] *Ho* is identical with the modern Lancashire *hoo* (or *huh* as it is sometimes written), which in some parts of England has nearly the same pronunciation as the accusative *her.*

The Northumbrian *thay* (they) has displaced the older Midland *he*, corresponding to the Southern pronoun *hii, hi* (A.S. *hi*. *Hores* and *thayreȝ* (theirs) occasionally occur for *here.*[2] The genitives in *-es*, due no doubt to Scandinavian influence, are very common in Northumbrian writers of the fourteenth century, but are never found in any Southern work of the same period.

[1] *Scho* occurs *once* in the present poems.

[2] *Youreȝ* (yours) sometimes takes the place of *youre* in the romance of "Sir Gawayne and the Grene Knyȝt."

Hit is frequently employed as an indefinite pronoun of all genders, and is plural as well as singular. It is, as has been previously shown, uninflected in the genitive or possessive case.

Me in Southern writers is used as an indefinite pronoun of the *third* person, and represents our *one*, but in the present poems it is of all persons, and seems to be placed in apposition with the subject of the sentence corresponding to our use of myself, thyself, himself, etc.; as,

"*He* swenges *me* þys," etc. = He himself sends this, etc.[1]
"Now sweȝe *me* þider swyftly" = Now go (thou) thyself thither swiftly.[2]
"*He* meteȝ *me* þis good man" = He himself meets this good man.[3]

Sturzen-Becker ("Some Notes on the leading Grammatical Characteristics of the Principal Early English Dialects, Copenhagen, 1868") thinks that I have been led astray with regard to this use of *me*, which he says is nothing more than the *dativus ethicus*.

The *me* in these examples may be merely an expletive, having arisen out of the general use of the dative ethicus, but the context does not satisfy me that it has the force of a dative. Dr. Guest (Proceedings of Philolog. Soc., vol. i. p. 151–153, 1842-1844) has discussed this construction at some length, and he carefully distinguishes the dative of the 1st person from the indeterminate (or indefinite) pronoun *me* = Fr. one. He says that in Old Frisian the indefinite pronoun has two forms, *min* and *me*, "the latter of which seems to be always used as a suffix to the verb, as *momme*, one may; *somme*, one should," etc. "The same construction was occasionally used in our own language, and it no doubt gave rise to those curious idioms which are noticed by Pegge in his "Anecdotes of the Eng. Lang.," p. 217. This writer, whose evidence to a *fact* we may avail ourselves of, whatever we think of his criticism or his scholarship, quotes the following as forms of speech then prevalent among the

[1] Page 92, l. 108. [2] Page 91, l. 72. [3] Syr Gawayn, l. 1932.

Londoners: "and so says *me* I;" "well what does *me* I;" "so says *me* she;" "then away goes *me* he;" "what does *me* they?" Here it is obvious that *me* is the indeterminate pronoun, and represents the *subject*, while the personal pronoun is put in apposition to it, so that "says *me* I" is equivalent to "*one says, that is I,*"[1] These idioms are not unknown to our literature.

(1) 'But as he was by diverse principall young gentlemen, to his no small glorie, lifted up on horseback, *comes me a page* of Amphialus, etc.' Pembr. Arcad. B. iii.

Other idioms, which have generally been confounded with those last mentioned, have the indeterminate pronoun preceded by a nominative absolute.

(2) '*I*, having been acquainted with the smell before, knew it was Crab, and—*goes me* to the fellow, who whips the dogs,' etc. Two Gent. of Verona, 4. 4.

(3) '*He thrusts me* himself into the company of three or four gentlemanlike dogs under the Duke's Table.' *Ib.* See B. Jons. Ev. Man in his Humour, 3, 1.

Johnson considers the *me* in examples 2 and 3 to be the oblique case of the first pers. pron., and treats it as "a ludicrous expletive." It is difficult to say how he would have parsed example 2 on such a hypothesis.

With these instances of the use of *me* (indef. or reflexive), the reader may compare the following:

(1) "Suche a touche in that tyde, *he* taȝte (Gauan) hym in tene
And *gurdes me*, Sir Gallerun, evyn grovelonges on grounde."
(The Anturs of Arther at the Tarnewathelan, p. 22.)

(2) There at tho dore he (the Fox) cast *me* downe hys pack.
Spenser's Shep. Cal. ed. Morris, p. 460, l. 243.

Cp. *Cut me*, i. Hen. IV. Act 4. Sc. 4; *steps me*, Ib. Act 4, Sc. 3; *comes me, runs me.* Ib. Act 3, Sc. 1.

(3) "Juno enraged, and fretting thus,
Runs me unto one Æolus."
(Virgile Travestie, 1664.)

[1] I would say that *says me I*=I myself say.—R.M.

The indefinite *me* = one is not uncommon in Elizabethan writers. Cf. "*touch me* his hat;" "*touch me* hir with a pint of sack," etc.; "and *stop me* his dice you are a villaine" (Lodge's Wit's Miserie).

The following table exhibits the declension of the personal and relative pronouns:—

SINGULAR.

Nom.	I,	thou,	he	ho,	hit.
Gen.	My, myn,	thy, thyn,	his,	hir, her,	hit.
Dat.	Me,	the,	him,	hir, her,	hit.
Acc.	Me,	the,	him,	hir, her,	hit.

PLURAL.

Nom.	We,	ȝe,	thay,	hit.
Gen.	Oure,	yor, youre,	her (here), hor,	hit.
Dat.	Vus (=uus),	yow, you,	hem, hom,	hit.
Acc.	Vus (=uus),	yow, you,	hem, hom,	hit.

Nom.	Who (quo).
Gen.	Whose (quos).
Dat.	Whom / Wham (quom).
Acc.	Whom / Wham (quom).

IV. Verbs.

Infinitive Mood.—The *-en* of the infinitive is frequently dropped, without even a final *-e* to mark its omission. Infinitives in *-y*, as *louy* (love), *schony* (shun), *spotty* (spot, defile), *styry* (stir), *wony* (dwell), occasionally occur, and probably owe their appearance to the author's acquaintance with Southern literature.[1]

Indicative Mood.—The final *e* often disappears in the first and third persons of the preterite tense, as I *loved*, he *loved*, instead of I *lovede*, he *lovede*.

[1] *Schonied* occurs for *schoned*. No Southern writer would retain, I think, the *i* in the preterite.

The -*en* in the plural of the present and preterite tenses is frequently dropped. The pl. present in -*eȝ* occasionally occurs.

Imperative Mood.—The imperative plural ends in -*es* (*eȝ*), and not in -*eth* as in the Southern and ordinary Midland dialects.

Participles.—The active or imperfect participle ends in -*ande*[1] and never in -*ing.*

The participle passive or perfect of regular verbs terminates in -*ed*; of irregular verbs in -*en.* Occasionally we find the *n* disappearing, as *bigonn-e, fund-e, runn-e, wonn-e,* where perhaps it is represented by the final -*e.*

The prefix -*i* or -*y* (A.S. -*ge*) occurs twice only in the poems, in *i-chose* (chosen), and *i-brad* (extended); but, while common enough in the Southern and Midland dialects, it seems to be wholly unknown to the Northumbrian speech.

The verb in the West-Midland dialect is conjugated according to the following model:—

I.—Conjugation of Regular Verbs.

INDICATIVE MOOD.

PRESENT TENSE.

Singular.	Plural.
(I) hope,	(We) hopen.
(Thou) hopes,	(ȝe) hopen.
(He) hopes,	(Thay) hopen.

PRETERITE TENSE

(I) hopede[2] (hoped),	(We) hopeden,
(Thou) hopedes (hoped),	(ȝe) hopeden.
(He) hopede[2] (hoped),	(Thay) hopeden.

IMPERATIVE MOOD.

Hope (thou).	Hopes (ȝe).

[1] Garnett asserts that the present participle in -*ande* is "a *certain criterion* of a Northern dialect subsequent to the thirteenth century." It is never found in any Southern writer, but is common to many Midland dialects. Capgrave employs it frequently in his Chronicles. It is, however, no safe criterion by itself.

[2] The final *e* is often dropped.

PARTICIPLES.

Imperfect or Active.	Perfect or Passive.
Hopande.	Hoped.

II.—Conjugation of Irregular Verbs.

INDICATIVE MOOD.

PRESENT TENSE.

Singular.

(I) kerve,	renne,	smite,	stonde.
(Thou) kerves,	rennes,	smites,	stondes.
(He) kerves,	rennes,	smites,	stondes.

Plural.

(We) kerven,	rennen,	smiten,	stonden.
(ȝe) „	„	„	„
(Thay) „	„	„	„

PRETERITE TENSE.

Singular.

(I) carf,	ran,	smot,	stod.
(Thou) carve,	ranne,	smote,	stode.
(He) carf,	ran,	smot,	stod.

Very frequently the *e* in the second person is dropped,[1] as in the Northumbrian dialect, but we never meet with such forms as carves (= carvedest), rannes (=ranst), smotes (=smotest), etc.

Plural.

(We) corven,	runnen,	smiten,	stonden.
(ȝe) „	„	„	„
(Thay) „	„	„	„

PASSIVE PARTICIPLES.

Corven,	runnen,	smiten,	stonden.

The Northumbrian dialect does not preserve any separate form for the preterite plural, and this distinction is not always observed in the present poems.

[1] In *The Wohunge of Ure Lauerd* the *e* is constantly omitted.

TABLE OF VERBS.

A.—SIMPLE ORDER.

		Present.	Preterite.	Passive Participle.
Class I.		Hate,	hatede,	hated.
Class II.	(*a*)	Bede (offer),	bedde,	bed.
		Dype (dip),	dypte,	dypt.
		Kythe (show),	kydde,	kyd.
		Lende,	lende,	lent.
		Rende,	rende,	rent.
		Sende,	sende,	sent.
	(*b*)	Clothe,	cladde,	clad.
		Dele (deal),	dalte,	dalt.
		Lede,	ladde,	lad.
		Leve,	lafte,	laft.
		Rede (advise),	radde,	rad.
		Sprede (spread),	spradde,	sprad.
		Swelt (die),	swalte,	——
		Swette (sweat)	swatte,	——
		Threte (threaten),	thratte,	thrat.
Class III.		Byye (buy),	boȝte,	boȝt.
		Bringe,	broȝte,	broȝt.
		Cache (catch),	caȝte,	caȝt.
		Lache (seize),	laȝte,	laȝt.
		Reche (reck),	roȝte,	——
		Reche (reach),	raȝte,	——
		Selle,	solde,	sold.
		Worche (work),	wroȝte,	wroȝt.

B.—COMPLEX ORDER.

DIVISION I.

	Present.	Preterite.	Passive Participle.
Class I.	Bere (bear),	ber,	born.
	Bete (beat),	bet,	beten.

	Present.	Preterite.	Passive Participle.
	Breke (break),	brek,	broken.
	Chese (choose),	ches (chos),	chosen.
	Cleve (cleave),	clef,	cloven.
	Ete (eat),	ette (*for* et),	eten.
	Forȝete (forget),	forȝet,	forȝeten.
	Frese (freeze),	fres,	frosen.
	Gife (give),	gef,	given, geven.
	Heve (heave),	hef,	hoven.
	Ligge (lie),	leȝ,	leyen, leȝen.
	Lepe (leap),	lep,	lopen.
	Nemme / Nimme (take),	nem (nam),	nomen.
	Schere (shear),	scher,	schorn.
	Slepe (sleep),	slep,	slepen.
	Speke (speak),	spek,	spoken.
	Stele (steal),	stel,	stolen.
	Swere (swear),	swer,	sworen.
	Wepe (weep),	wep,	wopen.
	Wreke (avenge)	wrek,	wroken.
Class II.	Falle,	fell,	fallen.
	Fonge (take),	feng,	fongen.
	Growe,	grew,	growen.
	Hange, honge,	heng,	hangen, hongen.
	Knowe, knawe,	knew,	knawen, knowen.
	Schape (make),	schep,	schapen.
	Walke,	welk,	walken.
	Wasche,	wesch,	waschen.
Class III.	Drawe, draȝe,	droȝ,	drawen,
	Fare (go),	for,	faren.
	Laȝe (laugh),	loȝ,	laȝen.
	Stande, stonde,	stod,	standen.
	Slaye,	slow, slew,	slayn.

	Present.	Preterite.	Passive Participle.
	Take,	tok,	tane, tone.
	Wake,	wok,	waken.

DIVISION II.

Class I.	Biginne,	bigon,	bigonnen, bigunnen.
	Breste,	brast, borst,	brusten, bursten.
	Climbe,	clamb, clomb,	clumben.
	Drinke,	dronk, drank,	drunken, dronken.
	Finde,	fand, fond,	funden.
	Fiȝte,	faȝt, feȝt,	foȝten.
	Helpe,	halp,	holpen,
	Kerve (cut),	carf,	corven.
	Melte,	malt,	molten.
	Renne (run),	ran,	runnen.
	Ringe,	rong,	rungen, rongen.
	Singe,	song, sang,	sungen.
	Steke,	stac,	stoken.
	Sterve (die),	starf,	storven.
	Werpe (throw),	warp,	worpen.
	Win,	wan, won,	wonnen, wunnen.
	Ȝelde (yield),	ȝald,	ȝolden.
Class II.	Bide (abide),	bod,	biden.
	Bite,	bot,	biten.
	Drive,	drof,	driven.
	Fine (cease),	fon,	——
	Glide,	glod,	gliden.
	Ride,	rod,	riden.
	Rise,	ros,	risen.
	Schine,	schon,	——
	Slide,	slod,	sliden.
	Smite,	smot,	smiten.
	Trine (go),	tron,	——

	Present.	Preterite.	Passive Participle.
Class III.	Fly,	fleȝ, flegh, flaȝ,	flowen.
	See,	seȝ, segh, syȝ,	seen.
	Stiȝe, steȝe,	steȝ	——

Anomalous Verbs.

Can,	pret.	couthe.	Schal,	pret.	scholde, schulde
Dare,	„	dorste.	Thar,	„	thurte.
May,	„	miȝte.	Wote,	„	wiste.
Mot,	„	moste.	Wille,	„	wolde.
Oȝe (owe),	„	oȝte.			

Schal (shall) in the second person singular is *schal* or *schalt;* so, too, we occasionally find *wyl* for *wylt.*

The present plural of *schal* is *schul, schulen,* or *schyn.*

The verb *to be* is thus conjugated :—

INDICATIVE MOOD.

PRESENT TENSE.	PAST TENSE.
Singular.	
(I) am.	(I) was, watȝ.
(Thou) art.	(Thou) was, watȝ.
(He) is, bes, betȝ.	(He) was, watȝ.
Plural.	
(We) arn, are, ar.	(We) wern, were.
(ȝe) arn, are, ar.	(ȝe) wern, were.
(Thay) arn, are, ar.	(Thay) wern, were.

The verbs *be, have, wille,* have negative forms; as, *nam*=am not; *nar*=are not; *nas*=was not; *naf*=have not; *nade*=had not; *nyl*=will not.

The following contractions are occasionally met with: *bos*= behoves; *byhod*=behoved; *ha*=have; *ma*=make; *man*=make (pl.) *matȝ* (*mas*)=makes; *ta*=take; *tatȝ* (=*tas*)=takes; *tane, tone*=taken.

V. Adverbs.

Ths Norse forms *hethen*, *quethen* (*whethen*),[1] and *thethen*, seem to have been known to the West-Midland dialect as well as the Saxon forms *hence* (*hennes*, *henne*), *whence* (*whennes*), *thence* *thennes*), etc*t* The adverbs *in-blande* (together), *in-lyche* (alike), *in-mydde* (amidst), *in-monge* (amongst), are due, perhaps, to Scandinavian influence.

VI. Prepositions.

The preposition *from* never occurs in the following poems; it is replaced by *fro*, *fra* (Northumbrian), O.N. *frá*.

VII. Conjunctions.

The conjunction *if* takes a negative form; as, *nif*=if not, unless.

[1] "Syr Gawayn and the Grene Knyȝt."

DESCRIPTION OF THE MANUSCRIPT USED IN THE PRESENT VOLUME.[1]

COTTON MS. NERO A. x. A small quarto volume, consisting of three different MSS. bound together, which originally had no connection with each other. Prefixed is an imperfect list of contents in the hand-writing of James, the Bodley Librarian.

The first portion consists of a panegyrical oration in Latin by Justus de Justis, on John Chedworth, archdeacon of Lincoln, dated at Verona 16th July, 1468. It occupies thirty-six folios, written on vellum, and is the original copy presented by the author.

The second portion is that we are more immediately concerned with. It is described by James as "*Vetus poema Anglicanum, in quo sub insomnii figmento multa ad religionem et mores spectantia explicantur,*" and this account, with some slight changes, is adopted by Smith and Planta, in their catalogues; both of whom assign it to the fifteenth century. It will appear, by what follows, that no less than four distinct poems have been confounded together by these writers.

This portion of the volume extends from fol. 37 to fol. 126, inclusive, and is written by one and the same hand, in a small, sharp, irregular character, which is often, from the paleness of the ink, and the contractions used, difficult to read. There are no titles or rubrics, but the divisions are marked by large initial letters of blue, flourished with red, and several illuminations, coarsely executed, serve by way of illustration, each of which occupies a page.

1. Four of these are prefixed to the first poem. In the first the Author is represented slumbering in a meadow, by the side of a streamlet, clad in a long red gown, having falling sleeves, turned up with white, and a blue hood attached round the neck.

[1] Taken with some few alterations from Sir F. Madden's "Syr Gawayn."

In the second the same person appears, drawn on a larger scale, and standing by the stream. In the third he occurs nearly in the same position, with his hands raised, and on the opposite side a lady dressed in white, in the costume of Richard the Second's and Henry the Fourth's time, buttoned tight up to the neck, with long hanging sleeves. Her hair is plaited on each side, and on her head is a crown. In the fourth we see the author kneeling by the water, and beyond the stream is depicted a castle or palace, on the embattled wall of which appears the same lady, with her arm extended towards him.

The poem commences on fol. 39, and consists of one hundred and one twelve-line stanzas,[1] every five of which conclude with the same line, and are connected by the iteration of a leading expression. It concludes on fol. 55*b*.

2. Then follow two more illuminations; in the first of which Noah and his family are represented in the ark; in the second the prophet Daniel expounding the writing on the wall to the affrighted Belshazzar and his queen. These serve as illustrations to the second poem, which begins at fol. 57, and is written in long alliterative lines. It concludes on fol. 82.

3. Two illuminations precede, as before; one of which represents the sailors throwing the prophet Jonas into the sea, the other depicts the prophet in the attitude of preaching to the people of Nineveh. The poem is in the same metre as the last, and commences at fol. 83.

It is occupied wholly with the story of Jonas, as applicable to the praise of meekness and patience; and ends on fol. 90.

4. The Romance intitled *Sir Gawayne and the Grene Knyȝt* follows, fol. 91. Prefixed is an illumination of a headless knight on horseback, carrying his head by its hair in his right hand, and looking benignly at an odd-eyed bill-man before him; while from a raised structure above, a king armed with a knife, his queen, an attendant with a sabre, and another bill-man scowling looks on. Here and elsewhere the only colours used are green, red, blue, and yellow. It ends on fol. 124*b*., and at

[1] A line, however, is missing from the MS. on fol. 55*b*. See page 15.

the conclusion, in a later hand, is written "Hony ſoit q̃ mal pene," which may, perhaps, allude to the illumination on the opposite page, fol. 125, representing the stolen interview between the wife of the Grene Knyȝt and Sir Gawayne. Above the lady's head is written:

Mi mind is mukel on on, þat wil me noȝt amende,
Sum time was trewe as ston, & fro schame couþe hir defende.

It does not appear very clearly how these lines apply to the painting. Two additional illuminations follow; in the first of which Gawayne is seen approaching the *Grene Chapel*, whilst his enemy appears above, wielding his huge axe; and in the second Sir Gawayne, fully equipped in armour, is represented in the presence of king Arthur and queen Guenever, after his return to the court.

The third and concluding portion of the Cotton volume extends from fol. 127 to fol. 140*b*, inclusive, and consists of theological excerpts, in Latin, written in a hand of the end of the thirteenth century. At the conclusion is added *Epitaphium de Ranulfo, abbate Ramesiensi*, who was abbot from the year 1231 to 1253, and who is erroneously called *Ralph* in the *Monasticon*, vol. ii. p. 548, new ed.

CONTRACTIONS USED IN THE GLOSSARY.

The letters A. B. C. refer severally to the poems, entitled by me, "The Pearl," "Cleanness," and "Patience."

A.S. Anglo-Saxon.
Dan. Danish.
Du. Dutch.
E. English.
O. E. Old English.
Prov. E. Provincial English.
N. Prov. E. } North Provincial English.
N. P. E. }
Fr. French.
O. Fr. Old French.
Prov. Fr. Provincial French.
Fris. Frisian.
G. Doug. Gawin Douglas's Æneid, published by the Bannatyne Club, 2 vols.
Ger. German.
Goth. Gothic.
Icel. Icelandic.
Jam. Jamieson's Scottish Dictionary.
K. Alex. King Alexander, Romance of (Ed. Stevenson).
Met. Hom. Metrical Homilies (Ed. Small).
O.N. Old Norse.
O.S. Old Saxon.
Prompt. Parv. Promptorium Parvulorum (Ed. Way).
Sc. Scotch.
O. Sc. Old Scotch.
S.Sax. Semi Saxon.
Sw. Swedish.
O. Sw. Old Swedish.
Town. Myst. Townley Mysteries.
T. B. Troy Book (Ed. Donaldson).

THE PEARL.

I.

Perle plesaunte to prynces paye,
To clanly clos in golde so clere,
Oute of oryent I hardyly saye,
Ne proued I neuer her precios pere,
So rounde, so reken in vche araye,
So smal, so smoþe her sydeȝ were.
Quere-so-euer I Iugged gemmeȝ gaye,
I sette hyr sengeley in synglure;
Allas! I leste hyr in on erbere,
Þurȝ gresse to grounde hit fro me yot;[1]
I dewyne for-dolked of luf daungere,
Of þat pryuy perle with-outen spot.

Description of a lost pearl (i.e. a beloved child).

The father laments the loss of his pearl.

[1] ? got.

Syþen in þat spote hit fro me sprange,
Ofte haf I wayted wyschande þat wele,
Þat wont watȝ whyle deuoyde my wrange,
& heuen my happe & al my hele,
Þat dotȝ bot þrych my hert þrange,
My breste in bale bot bolne & bele.
ȝet þoȝt me neuer so swete a sange,
As stylle stounde let to me stele,
For-soþe þer fleten to me fele,
To þenke hir color so clad in clot;
O moul[2] þou marreȝ a myry mele.
My priuy perle with-outen spotte,

He often visits the spot where his pearl disappeared,

and hears a sweet song.

Where the pearl was buried there he found lovely flowers.

[2] ? mould.

Þat spot of spyseȝ myȝt nedeȝ sprede,
Þer such rycheȝ to rot[1] is runnen;
Blomeȝ blayke & blwe & rede,
Þer schyneȝ ful schyr agayn þe sunne.
Flor & fryte may not be fede,
Þer hit doun drof in moldeȝ dunne,

Each blade of grass springs from a dead grain.

For vch gresse mot grow of grayneȝ dede,
No whete were elleȝ to woneȝ wonne;
Of goud vche goude is ay by-gonne.
So semly a sede moȝt fayly not,
Þat spryngande[2] spyceȝ vp ne sponne,
Of þat precios perle wyth-outen spotte.

[Fol. 39b.]

In the high season of August the parent visits the grave of his lost child.

To þat spot þat I in speche expoun
I entred in þat erber grene,
In augoste in a hyȝ seysoun,
Quen corne is coruen wyth crokeȝ kene.

Beautiful flowers covered the grave.

On huyle þer perle hit trendeled doun,
Schadowed þis worteȝ ful schyre & schene
Gilofre, gyngure & gromylyoun,
& pyonys powdered ay by-twene.
Ȝif hit wat; semly on to sene,

From them came a delicious odour.

A fayr reflayr ȝet fro hit flot,
Þer wonys þat worþyly I wot & wene,
My precious perle, wyth-outen spot.

The bereaved father wrings his hands for sorrow,

Bifore þat spot my honde I spenn[e]d,
For care ful colde þat to me caȝt[e];
A denely dele in my hert denned,
Þaȝ resoun sette my seluen saȝt[e].
I playned my perle þat þer watȝ spenned
Wyth fyrte skylleȝ þat faste faȝt[e],
Þaȝ kynde of kryst me comfort kenned,
My wreched wylle in wo ay wraȝte.

falls asleep upon the flowery plot,

I felle vpon þat floury flaȝt[e],
Suche odour to my herneȝ schot;

and dreams.

I slode vpon a slepyng slaȝte,
On þat prec[i]os perle with-outen spot.

[1] P rote,

[2] The MS. reads *sprygande*.

II.

Fro spot my spyryt þer sprang *in* space,
My body on balke þer bod *in* sweuen,
My goste is gon in godeȝ grace,
In auenture þ*er* meruayleȝ meuen;
I ne wyste in þis worlde quere þ*at* hit wace,
Bot I knew me keste þ*er* klyfeȝ cleuen;
Towarde a foreste I bere þe face,
Where rych rokkeȝ wer to dyscreuen;
Þe lyȝt of hem myȝt no mon leuen,
Þe glemande glory þat of hem gle*nt*;
For wern neu*er* webbeȝ þat wyȝeȝ weuen,
Of half so dere adubmente.

In spirit he is carried to an unknown region,

Where the rocks and cliffs gleamed gloriously.

[Fol. 40*a*.]

Dubbed wern alle þo downeȝ sydeȝ
W*ith* crystal klyffeȝ so cler of kynde,
Holte-wodeȝ bryȝt aboute hem bydeȝ;
Of bolleȝ as blwe as ble of ynde,
As bornyst syluer þe lef onslydeȝ,
Þat þike con trylle on vch a tynde,
Quen glem of glodeȝ agaynȝ hem glydeȝ,
Wyth schym*er*y*n*g schene ful schrylle þay schynde.
Þe grauayl þat on grou*n*de con grynde
Wern p*re*ciou*s* perleȝ of oryente;
Þe su*n*ne bemeȝ bot blo & blynde,
In respecte of þat adubbement.

The hill sides were decked with crystal cliffs.

The leaves of the trees were like burnished silver.

The gravel consisted of precious pearls.

The adubbemente of þo douneȝ dere
Garten my goste al greffe for-ȝete
So frech flauoreȝ of fryteȝ were,
As fode hit con me fayre refete.
Fowleȝ þ*er* flowen in fryth *in* fere,
Of flau*m*bande hweȝ,[1] boþe smale & grete,
Bot sytole stry*ng* & gyt*er*nere,
Her reken myrþe moȝt not retrete,
For quen þose bryddeȝ her wyngeȝ bete
Þay songen wyth a swete asent;

The father forgets his sorrow. He sees birds of the most beautiful hues, and hears their sweet melody.

[1] Or *hiweȝ*.

So grac[i]os gle couþe no mon gete
As here & se her adubbement.

So al watȝ dubbet on dere asyse;

No tongue could describe the beauty of the forest.

Þat fryth þer fortwne forth me fereȝ,
Þe derþe þer-of for to deuyse
Nis no wyȝ worþe þat tonge bereȝ.
I welke ay forth in wely wyse,
No bonk so byg þat did me dereȝ,

All shone like gold.

Þe fyrre in þe fryth þe feier con ryse,
Þe playn, þe plontteȝ, þe spyse, þe pereȝ,
& raweȝ & randeȝ & rych reuereȝ,
As fyldor fyn her b[o]nkes brent.

The dreamer arrives at the bank of a river,

I wan to a water by schore þat schereȝ,
Lorde! dere watȝ hit adubbement!

[Fol. 40b.]

The dubbemente of þo derworth depe

which gave forth sweet sounds.

Wern bonkeȝ bene of beryl bryȝt;
Swangeande swete þe water con swepe
Wyth a rownande rourde raykande aryȝt;

In it, stones glittered like stars [1] ? As. in the welkin on a winter night.

In þe founce þer stonden stoneȝ stepe,
As glente þurȝ glas þat glowed & glyȝt,
A[1] stremande sterneȝ quen stroþe men slepe,
Staren in welkyn in wynter nyȝt;
For vche a pobbel in pole þer pyȝt
Watȝ Emerad, saffer, oþer gemme gente,
Þat alle þe loȝe lemed of lyȝt,
So dere watȝ hit adubbement.

III.

His grief abates, and he follows the course of the stream.

The dubbement dere of doun & daleȝ,
Of wod & water & wlonk playneȝ,
Bylde in me blys, abated my baleȝ,
For-didden my [dis]tresse, dystryed my payneȝ.
Doun after a strem þat dryȝly haleȝ,
I bowed in blys, bred ful my brayneȝ;
Þe fyrre I folȝed þose floty valeȝ,

Þe more strenghþe of ioye myn herte strayneȝ,
As fortune fares *þer* as ho frayneȝ,
Wheþ*er* solace ho sende oþ*er* elleȝ sore,
Þe wyȝ, to wham her wylle ho wayneȝ,
Hytteȝ to haue ay more & more.
More of wele watȝ i*n* þat wyse
Þe*n* I cowþe telle þaȝ I tom hade,
For vrþely herte myȝt not suffyse
To þe tenþe dole of þo gladneȝ glade;

No one could describe his great joy.

For-þy I þoȝt þat paradyse
Watȝ þer oþ*er* gayn þo bonkeȝ brade;
I hoped þe water were a deuyse
By-twene myrþeȝ by mereȝ made,
By-ȝonde þe broke by slente oþ*er* slade,
I hope[de] þ*at* mote merked wore.

He thought that Paradise was on the opposite bank.

Bot þe water watȝ depe I dorst not wade
& eu*er* me longed a more & more.

The stream was not fordable.

[Fol. 41*a*.]

More & more, & ȝet wel mare,
Me lyste to se þe broke by-ȝonde,
For if hit watȝ fayr þ*er* I con fare,
Wel loueloker watȝ þe fyrre londe.
Abowte me con I stote & stare
To fynde a forþe, faste con I fonde,

More and more he desires to see what is beyond the brook.

Bot woþeȝ mo i-wysse þ*er* ware,
Þe fyrre I stalked by þe stronde,
& euer me þoȝt I schulde not wonde
For wo, þer weleȝ so wy*n*ne wore.
Þe*n*ne nwe note me com on honde
Þat meued my mynde ay more & more,

But the way seemed difficult.

More meruayle con my dom adau*n*t;
I seȝ by-ȝonde þat myry mere,
A crystal clyffe ful relusau*n*t,
Mony ryal ray con fro hit rere;
At þe fote þ*er*-of þ*er* sete a fau*n*t,
A mayden of menske, ful debonere;
Blysnande whyt watȝ hyr bleau*n*t,

The dreamer finds new marvels.

He sees a crystal cliff,

at the foot of which, sits a maiden clothed in glistening white.

(I knew hyr wel, I hade sen hyr ere)
As glysnande golde þat man con schere,
So schon þat schene an vnder schore;

He knows that he has seen her before.

On lenghe I loked to hyr þere,
Þe lenger I knew hyr more & more
 The more I frayste hyr fayre face.
Her fygure fyn, quen I had fonte,
Suche gladande glory con to me glace,
As lyttel byfore þerto watȝ wonte;

He desires to call her but is afraid,

To calle hyr lyste con me enchace,
Bot baysment gef myn hert a brunt,

at finding her in such a strange place.

I seȝ hyr in so strange a place,
Such a burre myȝt make myn herte blunt
Þenne vereȝ ho vp her fayre frount,
Hyr vysayge whyt as playn yuore,
Þat stonge myn hert ful stray atount,
& euer þe lenger, þe more & more.

IV.

[Fol. 41b.]

More þen me lyste my drede aros,
 I stod ful stylle & dorste not calle.

So he stands still, like a well trained hawk.

Wyth yȝen open & mouth ful clos,
I stod as hende as hawk in halle;

He fears lest she should escape before he could speak to her.

I hope þat gostly watȝ þat porpose,
I dred on ende quat schulde byfalle,
Lest ho me eschaped þat I þer chos,
Er I at steuen hir moȝt stalle.
Þat gracios gay with-outen galle,

His long lost one is dressed in royal array—decked with precious pearls.

So smoþe, so smal, so seme slyȝt,
Ryseȝ vp in hir araye ryalle,
A prec[i]os pyece[1] in perleȝ pyȝt.
 Perleȝ pyȝte of ryal prys,
Þere moȝt mon by grace haf sene,

She comes along the stream towards him.

Quen þat frech as flor-de-lys
Doun þe bonke con boȝe by-dene.
Al blysnande whyt watȝ hir beau uiys,

[1] MS. looks like *pyete*.

Vpon at sydeȝ & boun*d*en bene
Wyth þe myryeste margarys at my deuyse,
Þat eu*er* I seȝ ȝet with myn yȝen;
Wyth lappeȝ large I wot & I wene,
Dubbed with double perle & dyȝte,
Her cortel of self sute schene,
W*ith* p*re*cios perleȝ al vmbe-pyȝte.

Her kirtle is composed of 'sute,' ornamented with pearls.

A pyȝt coroune ȝet wer þat gyrle,
Of mariorys & non oþ*er* ston,
Hiȝe pynakled of cler quyt perle,
Wyth flurted flowreȝ perfet vpon;
To hed hade ho non oþ*er* werle,
Her here heke[1] al hyr vmbe-gon;
Her semblau*n*t sade, for doc oþ*er* erle,
Her ble more blaȝt þen whalleȝ bon;
As schorne golde schyr her fax þe*n*ne schon,
On schyldereȝ þat legh*e* vnlapped lyȝte;
Her depe colo*ur* ȝet wonted non,
Of p*re*cios perle i*n* porfyl pyȝte,

She wore a crown of pearls.

Her hair hung down about her.

[1] In the MS. it is *lere leke.*

Her colour was whiter than whalebone.

Her hair shone as gold.

The trimming of her robe consisted of precious pearls.

[Fol. 42*a*.]

Pyȝt watȝ poyned & vche a he*m*me,
At honde, at sydeȝ, at ouerture,
Wyth whyte perle & non oþ*er* ge*m*me,
& bornyste quyte watȝ hyr uesture.
Bot a wonder perle w*ith*-outen we*m*me,
In myddeȝ hyr breste watȝ sette so sure;
A ma*n*neȝ dom moȝt dryȝly de*m*me,
Er mynde moȝt malte i*n* hit mesure;
I hope no tong moȝt endure
No sau*er*ly saghe say of þat syȝt,
So watȝ hit clene & cler & pure,
Þat p*re*cios perle þ*er* hit watȝ pyȝt,

A wonderful pearl was set in her breast.

Pyȝt in perle þat p*re*cios p[r]yse.
On wyþ*er* half wat*er* com dou*n* þe schore,
No gladder gome heþen i*n* to grece,
Þ*en* I, quen ho on bry*m*me wore;
Ho watȝ me nerre þen au*n*te or nece,

No man from here to Greece, was so glad as the father, when he saw his pearl on the bank of the stream.

My Ioy for-þy watȝ much þe more.
Ho profered me speche þat special spyce,
The maiden salutes him.
Enclynande lowe in wommon lore,
Caȝte of her coroun of grete tresore,
& haylsed me wyth a lote lyȝte.
Wel watȝ me þat euer I watȝ bore,
To sware þat swete in perleȝ pyȝte!

V.

The father enquires of the maiden whether she is his long-lost pearl,
"O perle," quod I, "in perleȝ pyȝt,
Art þou my perle þat I haf playned,
Regretted by myn one, on nyȝte?
Much longeyng haf I for þe layned,
Syþen into gresse þou me aglyȝte;
Pensyf, payred, I am for-payned,
& þou in a lyf of lykyng lyȝte
In paradys erde, of stryf vnstrayned.
and longs to know who has deprived him of his treasure.
What wyrde hatȝ hyder my iuel vayned,
& don me in þys del & gret daunger?
Fro we in twynne wern towen & twayned,
I haf ben a Ioyleȝ Iuelere."
[Fol. 42b.]
That Iuel þenne in gemmyȝ gente,
Vered vp her vyse with yȝen graye,
Set on hyr coroun of perle orient,
& soberly after þenne con ho say:
The maiden tells him that his pearl is not really lost.
"Sir ȝe haf your tale myse-tente,
To say your perle is al awaye,
Þat is in cofer, so comly clente,
As in þis gardyn gracios gaye,
Here-inne to lenge for euer & play.
She is in a garden of delight, where sin and mourning are unknown.
Þer mys nee mornyng com neuer here,
Her were a forser for þe in faye,
If þou were a gentyl Iueler.
Bot Iueler gente if þou schal lose

þy ioy for a gem*m*e þat þe wat*ȝ* lef,
Me þynk þe put *in* a mad porpose,
& busye*ȝ*[1] þe aboute a raysou*n* bref,
For þat þou leste*ȝ* wat*ȝ* bot a rose,
þat flowred & fayled as kynde hyt gef;
Now þur*ȝ* kynde of þe kyste þat hyt con close,
To a perle of prys hit is put *in* pref;
& þou hat*ȝ* called þy wyrde a þef,
þat o*ȝ*t of no*ȝ*t hat*ȝ* mad þe cler;
þou blame*ȝ* þe bote of þy meschef,
þou art no kynde Iueler."

The rose that he had lost is become a pearl of price.

The pearl blames his rash speech.

A Iuel to me þen wat*ȝ* þys geste,
& iuele*ȝ* wern hyr gentyl sawe*ȝ*"
"I-wyse," q*uod* I, "my blysfol beste,
My grete dystresse þou al to-drawe*ȝ*,
To be excused I make requeste;
I trawed my perle don out of dawe*ȝ*,
Now haf I fonde hyt I schal ma feste,
& wony wit*h* hyt in schyr wod schawe*ȝ*,
& loue my lorde & al his lawe*ȝ*,
þat hat*ȝ* me bro*ȝ*[t] þys blys ner;
Now were I at yow by-*ȝ*onde þise wawe*ȝ*,
I were a ioyfol Iueler."

The father begs the maiden to excuse his speech, for he really thought his pearl was wholly lost to him.

[Fol. 43*a*.]

"Iueler," sayde þat gem*m*e clene,
"Wy borde *ȝ*e men, so madde *ȝ*e be?
þre worde*ȝ* hat*ȝ* þou spoken at ene,
Vn-avysed, for soþe, wern alle þre,
þou ne woste in worlde quat on dot*ȝ* mene,
þy worde byfore þy wytte con fle.
þou says þou trawe*ȝ* me *in* þis dene,
By cawse þou may wit*h* y*ȝ*en me se;
Anoþ*er* þou says, *in* þys countre
þy self schal won wit*h* me ry*ȝ*t here;
þe þrydde, to passe þys wat*er* fre,
þat may no ioyfol Iueler.

The maiden tells her father that he has spoken three words without knowing the meaning of one.

The first word.

The second.

The third.

[1] Looks like *husyeȝ* in MS.

VI.

He is little to be praised who loves what he sees.

I halde þat iueler lyttel to prayse.
Þat loueȝ wel þat he seȝ wyth yȝe,
& much to blame & vn-cortoyse,
Þat loueȝ[1] oure lorde wolde make a lyȝe,
Þat lelly hyȝte yo*ur* lyf to rayse,
Þaȝ fortune dyd yo*ur* flesch to dyȝe;
Ȝe setten hys wordeȝ ful westernays
Þat loueȝ[2] no þy*n*k bot ȝe hit syȝe,
& þat is[3] a poy*n*t o sorquydryȝe,
Þat vche god mon may euel byseme
To leue no tale be t*ru*e to tryȝe,
Bot þat hys one skyl may dem[e].

To love nothing but what one sees is great presumption.

Deme now þy-self, if þou con, dayly
As man to god wordeȝ schulde heue.
Þou saytȝ þou schal won i*n* þis bayly;
Me þynk þe burde fyrst aske leue,
& ȝet of grau*n*t þou myȝteȝ fayle;
Þou wylneȝ ou*er* þys water to weue,
Er moste þou ceuer to oþ*er* cou*n*sayl,
Þy corse i*n* clot mot calder keue,
For hit watȝ for-garte, at paradys greue
Oure ȝore fader hit con mysseȝeme;
Þurȝ drwry deth boȝ vch ma dreue,
Er ou*er* þys dam hy*m* dryȝty*n* deme."

To live in this kingdom (*i.e.* heaven) leave must be asked.

This stream must be passed over by death.

"Demeȝ þou me," q*uod* I, "my swete
To dol agayn, þe*n*ne I dowyne;
Now haf I fonte þat I for-lete
Schal I efte for-go hit er eu*er* I fyne?
Why schal I hit boþe mysse & mete?
My p*re*cios perle dotȝ me gret pyne,
What serueȝ tresor, bot gareȝ men grete
When he hit schal efte w*ith* teneȝ tyne?
Now rech I neu*er* forto declyne,
Ne how fer of folde þat man me fleme,

[Fol. 43*b*.]

The father asks his pearl whether she is about to doom him to sorrow again.

[1] Looks at first sight like *lyueȝ*—MS. rubbed, but read *loueȝ*.

[2] Read *loueȝ*.

[3] The MS. reads *īs*.

When I am partleȝ of perleȝ myne.
Bot durande doel what may men deme?"
"Thow demeȝ noȝt bot doel dystresse,"
þenne sayde þat wyȝt "why dotȝ þou so?
For dyne of doel, of lureȝ lesse,
Ofte mony mon for-gos þe mo;
þe oȝte better þy seluen blesse,
& loue ay god &[1] wele & wo,
For anger gayneȝ þe not a cresse.
Who nedeȝ schal þole be not so þro;
For þoȝ þou daunce as any do
Braundysch & bray þy braþeȝ breme,
When þou no fyrre may, to ne fro,
þou moste abyde þat he schal deme.
Deme dryȝtyn, euer hym adyte,
Of þe way a fote ne wyl he wryþe,
þy mendeȝ mounteȝ not a myte,
þaȝ þou for sorȝe be neuer blyþe;
Stynst of þy strot & fyne to flyte,
& sech hys blyþe ful swefte[2] & swyþe,
þy prayer may hys pyte byte,
þat mercy schal hyr crafteȝ kyþe;
Hys comforte may þy langour lyþe,
& þy lureȝ of lyȝtly leme,
For marre oþer madde, morne & myþe,
Al lys in hym to dyȝt & deme."

If he loses his pearl he does not care what happens to him.

The maiden tells her father to suffer patiently.

[1] *in* or *an* (?).

Though he may dance as any doe, yet he must abide God's doom.

He must cease to strive.

[2] MS. *swefte*.

All lies in God's power to make men joyful or sad.

VII.

[Fol. 44a.]

Thenne demed I to þat damyselle,
Ne worþe no wrath þe vnto my lorde,
If rapely raue[1] spornande in spelle.
My herte watȝ al with mysse remorde,
As wallande water gotȝ out of welle;
I do me ay in hys myserecorde.
Rebuke me neuer with wordeȝ felle,
þaȝ I forloyne my dere endorde,

[1] *rane* (?).

The father beseeches the pearl to have pity upon him.

Bot lyþeȝ me kyndely your coumforde,
Pytosly þenkande vpon þysse;
Of care & me ȝe made acorde,
Þat er watȝ grounde of alle my blysse;

He says that she has been both his bale and bliss.

My blysse, my bale ȝe han ben boþe,
Bot much þe bygger ȝet watȝ my mon,
Fro þou watȝ wroken fro vch a woþe.

And when he lost her, he knew not what had become of her.

I wyste neuer quere my perle watȝ gon;
Now I hit se, now leþeȝ my loþe,
& quen we departed we wern at on,
God forbede we be now wroþe,
We meten so selden by stok oþer ston;
Þaȝ cortaysly ȝe carp con,
I am bot mol & mareres mysse,
Bot crystes mersy & mary & Ion,
Þise arn þe grounde of alle my blysse.

And now that he sees her in bliss, she takes little heed of his sorrow.

In blysse I se þe blyþely blent
& I a man al mornyf mate,
Ȝe take þer-on ful lyttel tente,
Þaȝ I hente ofte harmeȝ hate.
Bot now I am here in your presente,
I wolde bysech wythouten debate,
Ȝe wolde me say in sobre asente,

He desires to know what life she leads.

What lyf ȝe lede, erly & late,
For I am ful fayn þat your astate
Is worþen to worschyp & wele Iwysse,
Of alle my Ioy þe hyȝe gate
Hit is in grounde of alle my blysse."

[Fol. 44b.]

"Now blysse burne mot þe bytyde;"

The maiden tells him that he may walk and abide with her, now that he is humble.

Þen sayde þat lufsoum of lyth & lere,
"& welcum here to walk & byde,
For now þy speche is to me dere;
Maysterful mod & hyȝe pryde
I hete þe arn heterly hated here;
My lorde ne loueȝ not forto chyde,
For meke arn alle þat woneȝ hym nere,

& when i*n* hys place þ*ou* schal apere,
Be dep deuote i*n* hol mekenesse;
My lorde þe lamb, loueȝ ay such chere,
Þat is þe grou*n*de of alle my blysse.

All are meek that dwell in the abode of bliss

A blysful lyf þ*ou* says I lede,
Þou woldeȝ knaw þ*er*-of þe stage;
Þow wost wel when þy perle con schede,
I watȝ ful ȝong & tender of age,
Bot my lorde þe lombe, þurȝ hys god-hede,
He toke my self to hys maryage,
Corou*n*de me quene i*n* blysse to brede,
I*n* lenghe of dayeȝ þat eu*er* schal wage,
& sesed i*n* alle hys herytage
Hys lef is, I am holy hysse;
Hys prese, hys prys & hys parage,
Is rote & grou*n*de of alle my blysse."

All lead a blissful life.

She reminds her father that she was very young when she died.

Now she is crowned a queen in heaven.

VIII.

"Blysful," q*uod* I, "may þys be trwe,
Dyspleseȝ not if I speke erro*ur*;
Art þou þe quene of heueneȝ blwe,
Þ*a*t al þys worlde schal do hono*ur*?
We leuen on marye þat grace of grewe,
Þat ber a barne of vyrgyn flo*ur*,
Þe croune fro hyr quo moȝt remwe,
Bot ho hir passed i*n* su*m* fauo*ur*?
Now for synglerty o hyr douso*ur*,
We calle hyr fenyx of arraby,
Þat freles fleȝe of hyr fasor,
Lyk to þe quen of cortaysye."

The father of the maiden does not fully understand her.

Mary, he says, is the queen of heaven.

No one is able to remove the crown from her.

"Cortayse quen" þe*n*ne s[a]yde þat gaye,
Knelande to grou*n*de, folde vp hyr face,
"Makeleȝ moder & myryest may,
Blessed bygy*n*ner[1] of vch a grace!"
Þe*n*ne ros ho vp & con restay,

[Fol. 45a.] The maiden addresses the Virgin.

[1] MS. reads *bÿgyner*.

& spoke me towarde in þat space:

She then explains to her father that each has his place in heaven.

"Sir fele here porchasez & fongez pray
Bot supplantorez none with-inne þys place;
Þat emperise al heuenz hatz,
& vrþe & helle in her bayly;
Of erytage ȝet non wyl ho chace,
For ho is quen of cortaysye.

The court of God has a property in its own being.

The court of þe kyndom of god alyue,
Hatz a property in hyt self beyng;
Alle þat may þer-inne aryue

Each one in it is a king or queen.

Of alle þe reme is quen oþer kyng,
& neuer oþer ȝet schal depryue,
Bot vchon fayn of oþerez hafyng,
& wolde her corounez wern worþe þo fyue,
If possyble were her mendyng.

The mother of Christ holds the chief place.

Bot my lady of quom Iesu con spryng,
Ho haldez þe empyre ouer vus ful hyȝe,
& þat dysplesez non of oure gyng,
For ho is quene of cortaysye.

Of courtaysye, as saytz saynt poule,

We are all members of Christ's body.

Al arn we membrez of ihesu kryst,
As heued & arme & legg & naule,
Temen to hys body ful trwe & t[r]yste;
Ryȝt so is vch a krysten sawle,
A longande lym to þe mayster of myste;

Look that each limb be perfect.

Þenne loke what hate oþer any gawle,
Is tached oþer tyȝed þy lymmez by-twyste,
Þy heued hatz nauþer greme ne gryste,
On arme oþer fynger, þaz þou ber byȝe;
So fare we alle wyth luf & lyste,
To kyng & quene by cortaysye."

The father replies that he can- [Fol. 45b.] not understand how his pearl can be a queen.

"Cortayse," quod I, "I leue
& charyte grete be yow among,
Bot my speche þat yow ne greue,
. . . . . .
Þy self in heuen ouer hyȝ þou heue,

To make þe quen þat watȝ so ȝonge,
What more-hond moȝte he acheue
Þat hade endured in worlde stronge,
& lyued in penaunce hys lyueȝ longe,
With bodyly bale hym blysse to byye?
What more worschyp moȝt ho fonge,
Þen corounde be kyng by cortayse?

He desires to know what greater honour she can have.

IX.

That cortayse is to fre of dede,
ȝyf hyt be soth þat þou coneȝ saye,
Þou lyfed not two ȝer in oure þede,
Þou cowþeȝ neuer god nauþer plese ne pray,
Ne neuer nawþer pater ne crede
& quen mad on þe fyrst day!
I may not traw, so god me spede,
Þat god wolde wryþe so wrange away;
Of countes damysel, par ma fay,
Wer fayr in heuen to halde asstate
Aþer elleȝ a lady of lasse aray,
Bot a quene, hit is to dere a date."

She was only two years old when she died, and could do nothing to please God.

She might be a countess or some great lady but not a queen.

"Þer is no date of hys god-nesse,"
Þen sayde to me þat worþy wyȝte,
"For al is trawþe þat he con dresse,
& he may do no þynk bot ryȝt,
As mathew meleȝ in your messe,
In sothfol gospel of god al-myȝt
In sample he can ful grayþely gesse,
& lykneȝ hit to heuen lyȝte."
"My regne, he saytȝ, is lyk on hyȝt,
To a lorde þat hade a uyne I wate,
Of tyme of ȝere þe terme watȝ tyȝt,
To labor vyne watȝ dere þe date,
[Fol. 46a.] Þat date of ȝere wel knawe þys hyne;

The maiden informs her father that there is no limit to God's power.

The parable of the labourers in the vineyard.

The lord of the vineyard hires workmen for a penny a day.

Þe lorde ful erly vp he ros,
To hyre werkmen to hys vyne,
& fyndeȝ þer summe to hys porpos,
Into acorde þay con de-clyne,
For a pené on a day & forth þay gotȝ,
Wryþen & worchen & don gret pyne,

At noon the lord hires other men standing idle in the market place.

Keruen & caggen & man hit clos;
Aboute vnder, þe lorde to marked totȝ
& ydel men stande he fyndeȝ þer-ate,
"Why stande ȝe ydel" he sayde to þos,
Ne knawe ȝe of þis day no date?

"Er date of daye hider arn we wonne,"
So watȝ al samen her answar soȝt;
"We haf standen her syn ros þe sunne,

He commands them to go into his vineyard, and he will give them what is right.

& no mon byddeȝ vus do, ryȝt noȝt."
"Gos in-to my vyne, dotȝ þat ȝe conne."
So sayde þe lorde & made hit toȝt.
"What resonabele hyre be naȝt be runne,
I yow pray in dede & þoȝte."
Þay wente in to þe vyne & wroȝte,
& al day þe lorde þus ȝede his gate,
& nw men to hys vyne he broȝte;
Wel neȝ wyl day watȝ passed date,

At þe day of date of euen-songe,

At an hour before the sun went down the lord sees other men standing idle.

On oure byfore þe sonne go doun
He seȝ þer ydel men ful stronge
& sa[y]de to hem[1] with sobre soun;
"Wy stonde ȝe ydel þise dayeȝ longe."
Þay sayden her hyre watȝ nawhere boun.

Tells them to go into the vineyard.

"Gotȝ to my vyne ȝemen ȝonge
& wyrkeȝ & dotȝ þat at ȝe moun."
Sone þe worlde by-com wel broun,
Þe sunne watȝ doun &[2] hit wex late;
To take her hyre he mad sumoun;
Þe day watȝ al apassed date.

[1] MS. *hen*.

[2] MS. & &.

X.

Þe date of þe daye þe lorde con knaw,
Called to þe reue "lede pay þe meyny,
Gyf hem þe hyre þat I hem owe,
544 & fyrre, þat non me may repreue,
Set hem alle vpon a rawe,
& gyf vchon i*n*-lyche a peny.
Bygyn at þe laste þat sta*n*deȝ lowe,
548 Tyl to þe fyrste þat þ*ou* atteny;"
& þe*n*ne þe fyrst by-go*n*ne to pleny
& sayden þat þay hade trauayled sore,
Þese bot an [h]oure hem con streny,
552 V*us* þy*n*k v*us* oȝe to take more.
More haf we serued v*us* þy*n*k so,
Þat suffred han þe dayeȝ hete,
Þe*nn* þyse þat wroȝt[e] not houreȝ two,
556 & þ*ou* dotȝ hem v*us* to cou*n*terfete.
Þe*n*ne sayde þe lorde to on of þo,
"Frende no wrang[1] I wyl þe ȝete,
Take þat is þyn owne & go;
560 & I hyred þe for a peny a grete,
Quy bygy*n*neȝ þ*ou* now to þrete;
Watȝ not a pené þy couenau*n*t þore?
Fyrre þe*n* couenau*n*de is noȝt to plete,
564 Wy schalte þ*ou* þe*n*ne ask more?
More weþ*er* louyly is me my gyfte
To do wyth myn quat so me lykeȝ?
Oþ*er* elleȝ þyn yȝe to lyþ*er* is lyfte,
568 For I am goude & no*n* by-swykeȝ."
"Þ*us* schal I," q*uod* kryste, "hit skyfte,
Þe laste schal be þe fyrst þat strykeȝ,
& þe fyrst þe laste, be he neu*er* so swyft,
572 For mony ben calle[d] þaȝ fewe be mykeȝ."
Þ*us* pore men her part ay pykeȝ,
Þaȝ þay com late & lyttel wore,

As soon as the sun was gone down the "reeve" was told to pay the workmen.

To give each a penny.

The first began to complain.

Having borne the heat of the day he thinks that he deserves more.

The lord tells him that he agreed only to give him a penny.

The last shall be first, and the first last.

[1] MS. *wanig*.

The maiden applies the parable to herself.

& þaȝ her sweng wyth lyttel at-slykeȝ,
Þe merci of god is much þe more.

[Fol. 47a.]

"More haf I of ioye & blysse here-inne,
Of ladyschyp gret & lyueȝ blom,
Þen alle þe wyȝeȝ in þe worlde myȝt wynne
By þe way of ryȝt to aske dome.

She came to the vine in eventide, and yet received more than others who had lived longer.

Wheþer wel nygh[t] now I con bygynne,
In euentyde in-to þe vyne I come,
Fyrst of my hyre my lorde con mynne,
I watȝ payed anon of al & sum;
Ȝet oþer þer werne þat toke more tom,
Þat swange & swat for long ȝore,
Þat ȝet of hyre no þynk þay nom,
Paraunter noȝt schal to ȝere more."

The father says that his daughter's tale is unreasonable.

Then more I meled & sayde apert,
"Me þynk þy tale vnresounable,
Goddeȝ ryȝt is redy & euer more rert,[1]
Oþer holy wryt is bot a fable;
In sauter is sayd a verce ouerte
Þat spekeȝ a poynt determynable,
'Þou quyteȝ vchon as hys desserte,
Þou hyȝe kyng ay pretermynable,'[2]
Now he þat stod þe long day stable,
& þou to payment com hym byfore,
Þenne þe lasse in werke to take more able,
& euer þe lenger þe lasse þe more."

XI.

"Of more & lasse in godeȝ ryche,"
Þat gentyl sayde "lys no Ioparde,

In heaven, the maiden says, each man is paid alike.

For þer is vch mon payed inliche,
Wheþer lyttel oþer much be hys rewarde,
For þe gentyl cheuentayn is no chyche,
Queþer-so-euer he dele nesch oþer harde,
He laueȝ hys gyfteȝ[3] as water of dyche,
Oþer goteȝ of golf þat neuer charde;

[1] *ert* (?).

[2] MS. pertermynable.

[3] MS. *gysteȝ*.

Hys fraunchyse is large þat euer dard,
To hym þat matȝ in synne no scoghe[1]
No blysse betȝ fro hem reparde,
612 For þe grace of god is gret I-noghe.
[Fol. 47b.] Bot now þou moteȝ me for to mate
Þat I my pény haf wrang tan here,
Þou sayȝ þat I þat com to late,
616 Am not worþy so gret lere.
Where wysteȝ þou euer any bourne abate
Euer so holy in hys prayere,
Þat he ne forfeted by sumkyn gate,
620 Þe mede sum-tyme of heueneȝ clere;
& ay þe ofter, þe alder þay were,
Þay laften ryȝt & wroȝten woghe
Mercy & grace moste hem þen stere,
624 For þe grace of god is gret in-noȝe.
Bot in-noghe of grace hatȝ innocent,
As sone as þay arn borne by lyne
In þe water of babtem þay dyssente,
628 Þen arne þay boroȝt in-to þe vyne,
Anon þe day with derk endente,
Þe myȝt of deth dotȝ to en-clyne
Þat wroȝt neuer wrang er þenne þay wente;
632 Þe gentyle lorde þenne payeȝ hys hyne,
Þay dyden hys heste, þay wern þere-ine,
Why schulde he not her labour alow,
Ȝy[rd] & pay hem[2] at þe fyrst fyne
636 For þe grace of god is gret in-noghe?
Inoȝe is knawen þat man-kyn grete,
Fyrste watȝ wroȝt to blysse parfyt;
Oure forme-fader hit con forfete,
640 Þurȝ an apple þat he vpon con byte;
Al wer we dampned for þat mete,
To dyȝe in doel out of delyt,
& syþen wende to helle hete,
644 Þer-inne to won with-oute respyt;

God is no niggard.

The grace of God is sufficient for all.

Those who live long on the earth often forfeit heaven by sinning.

Innocents are saved by baptism.

Why should not God allow their labour.

Our first father lost heaven by eating an apple.

And all are damned for the sin of Adam.

[1] In the MS. it looks like *re-scoghe*.

[2] MS. *hym*.

But there came one who paid the penalty of our sins.

Bot þer on com a bote as-tyt.
Ryche blod ran on rode so roghe,
& wynne [&] water, þen at þat plyt
Þe grace of god wex gret in-noghe. 648

[Fol. 48a.]

Innoghe þer wax out[1] of þat welle,
Blod & water of brode wounde;
Þe blod vus boȝt fro bale of helle,
& delyuered vus of þe deth secounde; 652

The water that came from the pierced side of Christ was baptism.

Þe water is baptem þe soþe to telle;
Þat folȝed þe glayue so grymly grounde,
Þat wascheȝ away þe gylteȝ felle,
Þat adam wyth inne deth vus drounde. 656
Now is þer noȝt in þe worlde rounde
Bytwene vus & blysse bot þat he with-droȝ
& þat is restored in sely stounde,
& þe grace of god is gret in-nogh. 660

XII.

Repentance must be sought by prayer with sorrow and affliction.

Grace in-nogh þe mon may haue,
Þat synneȝ þenne new, ȝif hym repente,
Bot with sorȝ & syt he mot hit craue,
& byde þe payne þer-to is bent, 664
Bot resoun of ryȝt þat con not raue,
Saueȝ euer more þe innossent;
Hit is a dom þat neuer god gaue,
Þat euer þe gyltleȝ schulde be schente. 668

The guilty may be saved by contrition.

Þe gyltyf may contryssyoun hente
& be þurȝ mercy to grace þryȝt;
Bot he to gyle þat neuer glente,
At in-oscente is saf & ryȝte. 672

Two sorts of people are saved, the *righteous* and the *innocent*.

Ryȝt þus[2] I knaw wel in þis cas,
Two men to saue is god by skylle;
Þe ryȝt-wys man schal se hys face,[3]
Þe harmleȝ haþel schal com hym tylle, 676

The words of David.

Þe sauter hyt satȝ þus in a pace:
"Lorde quo schal klymbe þy hyȝ hylleȝ

[1] MS. *out out.*

[2] MS. *þus þus.*

[3] MS. *fate.*

Oþer rest *with*-inne þy holy place?"
Hymself to on-sware he is not dylle;
"Hondelynge3 harme þat dyt not ille,
Þat is of hert boþe clene & ly3t,
Þer schal hys step stable stylle,"
Þe innosent is ay saf by ry3t.

The innocent is saved by right.

[Fol. 485.]

The ry3twys man also sertayn
Aproche he schal þat proper pyle,
Þat take3 not her lyf in vayne
Ne glauere3 her nie3bor wyth no gyle;
Of þys ry3t-wys sa3[1] salamon playn,
How kyntly oure con aquyle
By waye3 ful stre3t he con hym strayn,
& scheued hym þe rengne of god a whyle,
As quo says "lo 3on louely yle,
Þou may hit wy*n*ne if þou be wy3te,"
Bot hardyly *with*-oute peryle,
Þe innosent is ay saue by ry3te!

The words of Solomon.

An-ende ry3twys men, 3et sayt3 a gome
Dauid in sauter, if eu*er* 3e se3 hit,
"Lorde þy seruau*n*t dra3 neuer to dome,
For[2] non lyuyande to þe is Iustyfyet."
For-þy to corte quen þou schal com,
Þer alle oure cause3 schal be tryed,
Alegge þe ry3t þou may be in-nome,
By þys ilke spech I haue asspyed;
Bot he on rode þat blody dyed,
Delfully þur3 honde3 þry3t
Gyue þe to passe when þou arte tryed
By innocens & not by ry3te.

David says no man living is justified.

Pray to be saved by innocence and not by right.

Ry3t-wysly quo con rede,
He loke on bok & be awayed
How Ihesuc hym welke in are þede,
& burne3 her barne3 vnto hym brayde,
For happe & hele þat fro hym 3ede,
To touch[3] her chylder þay fayr hym prayed.

When Jesus was on earth, little children were brought unto him.

1 *sat3* (?).

2 MS. *sor*.

3 MS. *touth*.

The disciples rebuked the parents.

Christ said, "Suffer little children to come unto me," etc.

His dessypoleȝ *with* blame let be hy*m* bede,
& wyth her resoune*ȝ* ful fele restayed;
Ihe*su*c þe*n*ne hem swetely sayde,
"Do way, let chylder vnto me tyȝt,
To suche is heuen-ryche arayed,"
Þe i*n*nocent is ay saf by ryȝt.

XIII.

[Fol. 49*a*.]

No one can win heaven except he be meek as a child.

Ihe*su*c con calle to hy*m* hys mylde
& sayde hys ryche no wyȝ myȝt wy*n*ne.
Bot he com þyder ryȝt as a chylde,
Oþ*er* elleȝ neu*er* more com þer-i*n*ne,
Harmleȝ, trwe & vnde-fylde,
W*ith*-outen mote oþ*er* mascle of sulpande sy*n*ne;
Quen such þer cnoken on þe bylde,
Tyt schal hem men þe ȝate vnpy*n*ne,
Þer is þe blys þat con not bly*n*ne,
Þat þe Iueler soȝte þurȝ perre pres
& solde alle hys goud boþe wolen & ly*n*ne,
To bye hy*m* a perle [þat] watȝ mascelleȝ.

The pearl of price is like the kingdom of heaven, pure and clean.

This makelleȝ perle þat boȝt is dere,
Þe Ioueler gef fore alle hys god,
Is lyke þe reme o" heuenesse clere
So sayde þe fader of folde & flode,
For hit is wemleȝ, clene & clere,
& endeleȝ rounde & blyþe of mode,
& co*m*mune to alle þat ryȝtwys[1] were,
Lo! euen i*n* mydde*ȝ* my breste hit stode;
My lorde þe lombe þat schede hys blode,
He pyȝt hit þere i*n* token of pes;
I rede þe forsake þe worlde wode,
& porchace þy perle maskelles."

[1] MS. *ryȝtywys.*

Forsake the mad world and purchase the spotless pearl.

The father of the maiden desires to know who formed her figure and wrought her garments.

"O maskeleȝ perle i*n* perleȝ pure
Þat bereȝ," *quod* I, "þe perle of prys,
Quo formed þe þy fayre fygure?
Þat wroȝt þy wede, he watȝ ful wys;

Her beauty, he says, is not natural.

þy beaute com neu*er* of nature,
Pymalyon paynted neu*er* þy vys,
Ne arystotel nawþ*er* by hys lettrure
Of carpe þe kynde þese p*ro*perteȝ.

Her colour passes the fleur-de-lis.

þy colo*ur* passeȝ þe flo*ur*-de-lys,
þyn angel hauy*n*g so clene corteȝ
Breue me bryȝt, quat-kyn of p*r*iys[1]
Bereȝ þe perle so maskelleȝ."

[Fol. 49*b*.]

The maiden explains to her father that she is a bride of Christ.

"My makeleȝ lambe þat al may bete,"
Q*uod* scho, "my dere destyné
Me ches to hys make al-þaȝ vnmete,
Su*m* tyme semed þ*at* assemblé
When I wente fro yor worlde wete.
He calde me to hys bon*er*té,
'Cu*m* hyder to me my le*m*man swete,

She is without spot or blemish.

For mote ne spot is non i*n* þe:'
He gef me myȝt & als bewté.

Her weeds are washed in the blood of Christ.

I*n* hys blod he wesch my wede on dese,
& coronde clene i*n* v*er*gynté,
& pyȝt me i*n* perleȝ maskelleȝ."
"Why maskelleȝ bryd þat bryȝt con flambe
þat reiateȝ hatȝ so ryche & ryf,

The father asks the nature of the Lamb that has chosen his daughter,

Quat-kyn þy*n*g may be þat lambe,
þat þe wolde wedde vnto hys vyf?
Ou*er* alle oþ*er* so hyȝ þou clambe,
To lede w*ith* hy*m* so ladyly lyf
So mony a cumly on vu*n*der cambe,

and why she is selected as a bride.

For kryst han lyued i*n* much stryf,
& þou con alle þo dere out-dryf,
& fro þat maryag al oþ*er* depres,
Al only þyself so stout & styf,
A makeleȝ may & maskelleȝ."

XIV.

"Maskelles," q*uod* þat myry quene,
"Vnblemyst I am wyth-outen blot,

[1] The MS. has *triys*.

& þat may I with mensk menteene;
Bot makeleȝ quene þenne sade I not,

The Lamb has one hundred and forty thousand brides.

Þe lambes vyueȝ in blysse we bene,
A hondred & forty þowsande flot
As in þe apocalyppeȝ hit is sene;

St John saw them on the hill of Sion in a dream,

Sant Iohan hem syȝ al in a knot,
On þe hyl of syon þat semly clot.
Þe apostel hem segh in gostly drem
Arayed to þe weddyng in þat hyl coppe,

In the new city of Jerusalem.

[Fol. 50a.]

Þe nwe cyte u Ierusalem.
  Of Ierusalem I in speche spelle.
If þou wyl knaw what-kyn he be,

Isaiah speaks of Christ or the Lamb.

My lombe, my lorde, my dere Iuelle,
My ioy, my blys, my lemman fre,
Þe profete ysaye of hym con melle,
Pitously of hys debonerté
Þat gloryous gyltleȝ[1] þat mon con quelle,

He says that He was led as a lamb to the slaughter.

With-outen any sake of felonye,
As a schep to þe slaȝt þer lad watȝ he
& as lombe þat clypper in lande nem,[2]
So closed he hys mouth fro vch query,
Quen Iueȝ hym iugged in Iherusalem.

In Jerusalem was Christ slain.

  In Ierusalem watȝ my lemman slayn
& rent on rode with boyeȝ bolde;
Al oure baleȝ to bere ful bayn,
He toke on hym self oure careȝ colde,

With buffets was His face flayed.

With boffeteȝ watȝ hys face flayn,
Þat watȝ so fayr on to byholde;
For synne he set hym self in vayn,
Þat neuer hade non hym self to wolde,

He endured all patiently as a lamb.

For vus he lette hym flyȝe & folde
& brede vpon a bostwys bem,
As meke as lomb[3] þat no playnt tolde.

For us He died in Jerusalem.

For vus he swalt in Ierusalem:
  Ierusalem, Iordan & galalye,
Þer as baptysed þe goude saynt Ion,

[1] MS reads *gystleȝ*.

[2] MS. *men*.

[3] The MS. reads *lomp*.

His wordeȝ acorded to ysaye ;
820 When Ihesuc con to hym warde gon
He sayde of hym þys professye,
"Lo godeȝ lombe as trwe as ston,
Þat dotȝ away þe synneȝ dryȝe !"
824 Þat alle þys worlde hatȝ wroȝt vpon,
Hym self ne wroȝt neuer ȝet non,
Wheþer on hym self he con al clem,
Hys generacyoun quo recen con,
828 Þat dyȝed for vus in Ierusalem ?

The declaration of St. John, "Behold the Lamb of God," etc.

Who can reckon His generation, that died in Jerusalem?

[Fol. 50b.]
In Ierusalem þus my lemman swatte,
Twyeȝ, for lombe watȝ taken þere,
By trw recorde of ayþer prophete,
832 For mode so meke & al hys fare,
Þe þryde tyme is þer-to ful mete
In apokalypeȝ wryten ful ȝare.
In mydeȝ þe trone þere sayteȝ sete,
836 Þe apostel iohan hym saytȝ as bare,
Lesande þe boke with leueȝ sware,
Þere seuen syngnetteȝ wern sette in-seme
& at þat syȝt vche douth con dare,
840 In helle, in erþe & Ierusalem.

In the New Jerusalem St. John saw the Lamb sitting upon the throne.

XV.

Thys Ierusalem lombe hade neuer pechche
Of oþer huee bot quyt Iolyf
Þat mot ne masklle moȝt on streche
844 For wolle quyte so ronk & ryf,
For-þy vche saule þat hade neuer teche,[1]
Is to þat lombe a worthyly wyf;
And þaȝ vch day a store he feche,
848 Among vus commeȝ non oþer strot ne stryf,
Bot vchon enle[2] we wolde were fyf,
Þe mo þe myryer so god me blesse.
In compayny gret our luf con þryf
852 In honour more & neuer þe lesse.

The Lamb is without blemish.

[1] MS. *tethe.*

Every spotless soul is a worthy bride for the Lamb.

No strife or envy among the brides.

[2] *vch onlepi* (?).

None can have less bliss than another.

Lasse of blysse may non v*us* bry*n*g
Þat beren þys perle vpon oure bereste,
For þay of mote couþe neu*er* my*n*ge,
Of spotleȝ perleȝ þa[y] beren þe creste,
Al-þaȝ oure corses i*n* clotteȝ cly*n*ge,
& ȝe remen for rauþe wyth-outen reste,
We þurȝ-outly hauen cnawy*n*g;

Our death leads us to bliss.

Of [o]n dethe ful oure hope is drest,
Þe lonbe v*us* gladeȝ, oure care is kest;
He myrþeȝ v*us* alle at vch a mes,
Vchoneȝ blysse is breme & beste,
& neu*er* oneȝ hono*ur* ȝet neu*er* þe les.

[Fol. 51a.]

What St. John saw upon the Mount of Sion.

Lest les þou leue my tale[1] farande,
I*n* appocalyppece is wryten i*n* wro
I seghe, says Ioh*an*, þe lou*m*be hy*m* stande,
On þe mou*n*t of syon ful þryuen & þro,
& wyth hym mayde*nn*eȝ an hu*n*dreþe þowsande

About the Lamb he saw one hundred and forty thousand maidens.

& fowre & forty þowsande mo
On alle her forhedeȝ wryten I fande,
Þe lombeȝ nome, hys fadereȝ also.

He heard a voice from heaven, like many floods.

A hue fro heuen I herde þoo,
Lyk flodeȝ fele laden, ru*nn*e*n* on resse,
& as þu*n*der þroweȝ i*n* torreȝ blo,
Þat lote I leue watȝ neu*er* þe les.

Nauþeles þaȝ hit schowted scharpe,
& ledden loude al-þaȝ hit were.

He heard the maiden sing a new song.

A note ful nwe I herde hem warpe,
To lysten þat watȝ ful lufly dere,
As harporeȝ harpen in her harpe,
Þat nwe songe þay so*n*gen ful cler.
In sou*n*ande noteȝ a gentyl carpe,
Ful fayre þe modeȝ þay fonge i*n* fere
Ryȝt byfore godeȝ chayere,

So did the four beasts and the elders "so sad of cheer."

& þe fowre besteȝ þat hy*m* obes,
& þe alder-men so sadde of chere,
Her songe þay songen neu*er* þe les;

[1] MS. *talle*, but *tale* in the catchwords.

Nowþe-lese non watȝ neu*er* so quoy*n*t,
For alle þe crafteȝ þat eu*er* þay knewe.
Þat of þat songe myȝt sy*n*ge a poy*n*t,
Bot þat meyny þe lombe þay swe,
For þay arn boȝt fro þe vrþe aloynte.
As newe fryt to god ful due
& to þe gentyl lombe hit arn amoy*n*t,
As lyk to hym self of lote & hwe,
For neu*er* lesy*n*g ne tale vn-trwe,
Ne towched her tonge for no dysstresse.
Þat moteles meyny may neu*er* remwe,
Fro þat maskeleȝ mayster neu*er* þe les."

This assembly was like the Lamb, spotless and pure.

[Fol. 51*b*.]

"Neuer þe les let be my þonc,"
Q*uod* I, "my perle þaȝ I appose,
I schulde not tempte þy wyt so wlonc,
To krysteȝ chambre þat art Ichose,
I am bot mokke & mul amo*n*g,
& þ*ou* so ryche a reken rose,
& bydeȝ here by þys blysful bone
Þer lyueȝ lyste may neu*er* lose,
Now hynde þat sympelnesse co*n*eȝ enclose,
I wolde þe aske a þy*n*ge expresse,
& þaȝ I be bustwys as a blose
Let my bone vayl neu*er* þe lese.

The father replies to the maiden.

He says he is but dust and ashes.

He wishes to ask one question,

XVI.

Neuer þe lese cler I yow by-calle
If ȝe con se hyt be to done,
As þ*ou* art gloryo*us* w*ith*-outen galle,
W*ith*-nay þ*ou* neu*er* my ruful bone.
Haf ȝe no woneȝ i*n* castel walle,
Ne man*er* þer ȝe may mete & won?
Þou telleȝ me of I*erusal*em þe ryche ryalle,
Þer dauid dere watȝ dyȝt on trone,
Bot by þyse holteȝ hit con not hone
Bot in Iudee hit is þ*at* noble note;

whether the brides have their abode in castle-walls or in manor.

Jerusalem, he says, in Judea.

As ȝe ar maskeleȝ vnder mone,

But the dwelling of the brides should be perfect.

Yo*ur* woneȝ schulde by wyth-outen mote.
Þys moteleȝ meyny þou coneȝ of mele,
Of þousandeȝ þryȝt so gret a route,
A gret cete, for ȝe arn fele,

For such "a comely pack" a great castle would be required.

Yow by-hod haue w*ith*-outen doute;
So cu*m*ly a pakke of Ioly Iuele,
Wer euel don schulde lyȝ þ*er*-oute;
& by þyse bonkeȝ þer I con gele
& I se no bygy*n*g nawhere aboute,
I trowe al-one ȝe lenge & loute,
To loke on þe glory of þys *grac*[i]*ous* gote;
If þou hatȝ oþer lygy*n*geȝ stoute,
Now tech me to þat myry mote.

[Fol. 52*a*.]

The city in Judæa, answers the maiden, is where Christ suffered, and is the Old Jerusalem.

"That mote þou meneȝ in Iudy londe,"
Þat specyal spyce þen to me spakk,
"Þat is þe cyte þat þe lombe con fonde
To soffer i*n*ne sor for maneȝ sake,
Þe olde I*erusalem* to vnder-stonde,
For þere þe olde gulte watȝ don to slake,

The New Jerusalem is where the Lamb has assembled his brides.

Bot þe nwe þat lyȝt of godeȝ sonde,
Þe apostel in apocalyppce i*n* theme con take.
Þe lombe[1] þ*er*, w*ith*-outen spotteȝ blake,
Hatȝ feryed þyder hys fayre flote,
& as hys flok is w*ith*-outen flake,
So is hys mote w*ith*-outen moote.
Of motes two to carpe clene

Jerusalem means the city of God.

& I*erusalem* hyȝt boþe nawþeles,
Þat nys to yow no more to mene,
Bot cete of god oþ*er* syȝt of pes.

In the Old city our peace was made at one.

I*n* þat on oure pes watȝ mad at ene,
W*ith* payne to suffer þe lombe hit chese,

In the New city is eternal peace.

In þat oþ*er* is noȝt bot pes to glene,
Þat ay schal laste w*ith*-outen reles,
Þat is þe borȝ þat we to pres,
Fro þat oure flesch[2] be layd to rote;

[1] The MS. reads *lompe*.

[2] MS. *fresth*.

Þer glory & blysse schal eu*er* encres,
960 To þe meyny þat is wi*th*-outen mote.

XVII.

"Motele3 may so meke & mylde,"
Þen sayde I to þat lufly flor,
"Bry*n*g me to þat bygly bylde,
964 & let me se þy blysful bor."
Þat schene sayde, þat god wyl schylde,
"Þou may not enter wi*th*-i*n*ne hys tor,
Bot of þe lombe I haue þe aquylde
968 For a sy3t þer-of þur3 gret fauor.
Vt-wyth to se þat clene cloystor,
Þou may, bot i*n*wyth not a fote,
To strech in þe strete þou hat3 no vygo*ur*,
972 Bot þou wer clene wi*th*-outen mote.

The father prays his daughter to bring him to the blissful bower.

His daughter tells him that he shall see the outside,

but not a foot may he put in the city.

XVIII.

[Fol. 52*b*.]

If I þis mote þe schal vn-hyde,
Bow vp to-warde þys borne3 heued,
& I an-ende3 þe on þis syde
976 Schal sve, tyl þou to a hil be veued,
Þe*n* wolde [I] no lenger byde,
Bot lurked by lau*n*ce3 so lufly leued,
Tyl on a hyl þat I asspyed
980 & blusched on þe burgh*e*, as I forth dreued,
By-3onde þe brok fro me warde keued,
Þat schyrrer þen su*n*ne wi*th* schafte3 schon;
I*n* þe apokalypce is þe fasou*n* preued,
984 As deuyse3 hit þe apostel Ihon̄.
As Ioh*a*n þe apostel hit sy3 wi*th* sy3t
I sy3e þat cyty of gret renou*n*,
I*erusal*e*m* so nwe & ryally dy3t,
988 As hit wat3 ly3t fro þe heuen adou*n*.
Þe bor3 wat3 al of brende golde bry3t,
As glemande glas burnist brou*n*,

The maiden then tells her father to go along the bank till he comes to a hill.

He reaches the hill, and beholds the heavenly city.

As St. John saw it, so he beheld it.

The city was of burnished gold.

Pitched upon gems,

With gentyl gemmeȝ an-vnder pyȝt;
With banteleȝ twelue on basyng boun,

The foundation composed of twelve stones.

Þe foundementeȝ twelue of riche tenoun;
Vch tabelment watȝ a serlypeȝ ston,
As derely deuyseȝ þis ilk toun,
In apocalyppeȝ þe apostel Iohan.

The names of the precious stones.

As þise stoneȝ in writ con nemme
I knew þe name after his tale;

i. Jasper.

Iasper hyȝt þe fyrst gemme,
Þat I on þe fyrst basse con wale,
He glente grene in þe lowest hemme.

ii. Sapphire.

Saffer helde þe secounde stale,

iii. Chalcedony.

Þe calsydoyne þenne with-outen wemme,
In þe þryd table con purly pale;

iv. Emerald.

Þe emerade þe furþe so grene of scale;

v. Sardonyx.

Þe sardonyse þe fyfþe ston;

vi. Ruby.

Þe sexte þe rybe he con hit wale,
In þe apocalyppce þe apostel Iohan.

[Fol. 53a.]
vii. Chrysolite.

Ȝet Ioyned Iohan þe crysolyt,
Þe seuenþe gemme in fundament;

viii. Beryl.

Þe aȝtþe þe beryl cler & quyt

ix. Topaz.

Þe topasye twynne how þe nente endent;

x. Chrysoprasus.

Þe crysopase þe tenþe is tyȝt;

xi. Jacinth.

Þe Iacyngh[1] þe enleuenþe gent;
Þe twelfþe þe gentyleste in vch a plyt,

xii. Amethyst.

Þe amatyst purpre with ynde blente;
Þe wal abof þe bantels bent,
Masporye as glas þat glysnande schon,
I knew hit by his deuysement,
In þe apocalyppeȝ þe apostel Iohan.

As Iohan deuysed ȝet saȝ I þare.
Þise twelue de-gres wern brode & stayre,

The city was square.

Þe cyte stod abof ful sware,
As longe as brode as hyȝe ful fayre;
Þe streteȝ of golde as glasse al bare,

The wall was of jasper.

Þe wal of Iasper þat glent as glayre;

[1] *Iacynth* (?).

Þe woneȝ wit*h*-in*n*e enurned ware
Wyth alle kyn*n*eȝ perre þat moȝt repayre,
Þen*n*e helde vch sware of þis manayre,
Twelue forlonge space er eu*er* hit fon,
Of heȝt, of brede, of lenþe to cayre,
For meten hit syȝ þe apostel Ioh*a*n.

Twelve thousand furlongs in length and breadth.

XIX.

As Ioh*a*n hy*m* wryteȝ ȝet more I syȝe
Vch pane of þat place had þre ȝateȝ,
So twelue *in* pou*r*sent I con asspye
Þe portaleȝ pyked of rych plateȝ
& vch ȝate of a margyrye,
A parfyt perle þat neu*er* fateȝ;
Vchon *in* scrypture a name con plye,
Of isr*ae*l barneȝ folewande her dateȝ,
Þat is to say as her byrþ whateȝ;
Þe aldest ay fyrst þ*er*-on watȝ done.
Such lyȝt þer lemed *in* alle þe strateȝ
Hem nedde nawþ*er* sun*n*e ne mone.

Each "pane" had three gates.

Each gate adorned with a pearl.

Such light gleamed in all the streets, that there was no need of the sun or moon.

[Fol. 53b.]

Of sun*n*e ne mone had þay no nede
Þe self god watȝ her lompe[1] lyȝt,
Þe lombe her lantyrne wit*h*-outen drede,
Þurȝ hy*m* blysned þe borȝ al bryȝt.
Þurȝ woȝe & won my lokyn*g* ȝede,
For sotyle cler moȝt[2] lette no lyȝt;
Þe hyȝe trone þer moȝt ȝe hede
Wit*h* alle þe apparaylmente vmbe-pyȝte,
As Ioh*a*n þe appostel in termeȝ tyȝte;
Þe hyȝe godeȝ self hit set vpone.
A reu*er* of þe trone þer ran out-ryȝte
Watȝ bryȝter þen boþe þe sun*n*e & mone.

God was the light of those in the city.

The high throne might be seen,

upon which the "high God" sat.

A river ran out of the throne;

Sun*n*e ne mone schon neu*er* so swete;
A! þat foysou*n* flode out of þat flet,
Swyþe hit swange þurȝ vch a strete,
Wit*h*-outen fylþe oþ*er* galle oþ*er* glet.

It flowed through each street.

[1] MS. *lombe*.

[2] MS. *noȝt*.

No church was seen.

Kyrk þer-*in*ne watȝ non ȝete,
Chapel ne temple þat eu*er* watȝ set,

God was the church;

Þe al-myȝty watȝ her mynyster mete,

Christ the sacrifice.

Þe lombe þe saker-fyse þer to reget;
Þe ȝates stoken watȝ neu*er* ȝet,

The gates were ever open.

Bot eu*er* more vpen at vche a lone;
Þer entreȝ non to take reset,
Þat bereȝ any spot an-vnder[1] mone.

The mone may þer-of acroche no myȝte
To spotty, ho is of body to grym,

There is no night in the city.

& al-so þ*er* ne is neu*er* nyȝt.
What schulde þe mone þer compas clym
& to euen wyth þat worþly lyȝt,[2]
Þat schyneȝ vpon þe brokeȝ brym?

The planets, and the sun itself, are dim compared to the divine light.

Þe planeteȝ arn i*n* to pou*er* a plyȝt,
& þe self su*n*ne ful fer to dym.
Aboute þat wat*er* arn tres ful schym,
Þat twelue fryteȝ of lyf con bere ful sone;

Trees there renew their fruit every month.

Twelue syþeȝ on ȝer þay beren ful frym
& re-nowleȝ nwe i*n* vche a mone.

[Fol. 54a.]

An-vnder mone so gret m*er*wayle
No fleschly hert ne myȝt endeure,
As quen I blusched vpon þat baly,
So ferly þ*er*-of watȝ þe falure.

The beholder of this fair city stood still as a "dased quail."

I stod as stylle as dased quayle,
For ferly of þat french[3] fygure,
Þat felde I nawþ*er* reste ne tr*a*uayle,
So watȝ I rauyste wyth gly*m*me pure;
For I dar say, wi*th* conciens sure,
Hade bodyly burne abiden þat bone,
Þaȝ alle clerkeȝ hy*m* hade i*n* cure,
His lyf wer loste an-vnder mone.

XX.

As the moon began to rise he was aware of a procession

Ryȝt as þe maynful mone con rys,
Er þenne þe day-glem dryue al dou*n*,

[1] MS. *an-vndeȝ*.
[2] Or *syȝt*.
[3] *fresch* (?).

So sodanly on a wonder wyse,
1096 I watȝ war of a prosessyou*n*.
Þis noble cite of ryche enpresse
Watȝ sodanly ful w*ith*-outen so*m*mou*n*
Of such v*er*gyneȝ *in* þe same gyse
1100 Þat watȝ my blysful an-vnder crou*n*,
& coronde wern alle of þe same fasou*n*
Depaynt *in* perleȝ & wedeȝ qwyte,
I*n* vchoneȝ breste watȝ bou*n*den bou*n*,
1104 Þe blysful perle w*ith* gret[1] delyt.
With gret delyt þay glod *in* fere,
On golden gateȝ þat glent as glasse;
Hu*n*dreth þowsandeȝ I wot þer were,
1108 & alle in sute her liureȝ wasse,
Tor to knaw þe gladdest chere.
Þe lombe byfore con proudly passe,
Wyth horneȝ seuen of red golde[2] cler,
1112 As praysed perleȝ his wedeȝ wasse;
Towarde þe throne þay trone a tras.
Þaȝ þay wern fele no pres *in* plyt,
Bot mylde as maydeneȝ seme at mas,
1116 So droȝ þay forth w*ith* gret delyt.
[Fol. 54b.] Delyt þ*at* hys come encroched,
To much hit were of for to melle;
Þise alder men quen he aproched,
1120 Grouely*n*g to his fete þay felle;
Legyou*n*es of au*n*gleȝ togeder uoched,
Þer kesten ensens of swete smelle,
Þen glory & gle watȝ nwe abroched.
1124 Al songe to loue þat gay Iuelle,
Þe steuen moȝt stryke þurȝ þe vrþe to helle,
Þat þe v*er*tues of heuen of Ioye endyte,
To loue þe lombe his meyny in melle,
1128 I-wysse I laȝt a gret delyt;
Delit þe lo*m*be forto deuise,
W*ith* much meruayle in mynde went.

of virgins crowned with pearls,

in white robes,

with a pearl in their breast.

As they went along they shone as glass.

The Lamb went before them.

There was no pressing.

The "alder men" fell groveling at the feet of the Lamb.

All sang in praise of the Lamb.

[1] MS. *with outen.*

[2] MS. *glode.*

Best watȝ he, blyþest & moste to pryse,
Þat euer I herde of speche spent,
The Lamb wore white weeds.
So worþly whyt wern wedeȝ hys;
His lokeȝ symple, hym self so gent,
A wide wound was seen near his breast.
Bot a wounde ful wyde & weete con wyse
An-ende hys hert þurȝ hyde to-rente;
Of his quyte syde his blod out-sprent,
A-las! þoȝt I, who did þat spyt?
Ani breste for bale aȝt haf for-brent,
Er he þer-to hade had delyt,
  The lombe delyt non lyste to wene,
Þaȝ he were hurt & wounde hade,
In his sembelaunt watȝ neuer sene,
Joy was in his looks.
So wern his glenteȝ gloryous glade.
I loked among his meyny schene,
How þay wyth lyf wern laste & lade,
The father perceives his little queen.
Þen saȝ I þer my lyttel quene,
Þat I wende had standen by me in sclade;
Lorde! much of mirþe watȝ þat ho made,
Among her fereȝ þat watȝ so quyt!
Þat syȝt me gart to þenk to wade,
For luf longyng in gret delyt.

XXI.

[Fol. 55a.]
Great delight takes possession of his mind.
Delyt me drof in yȝe & ere,
  My maneȝ mynde to maddyng malte;
Quen I seȝ my frely I wolde be þere,
Byȝonde þe water, þaȝ ho were walte,
I þoȝt þat no þyng myȝt me dere
To fech me bur & take me halte;
He attempts to cross the stream.
& to start in þe strem schulde non me stere,
To swymme þe remnaunt, þaȝ I þer swalte,
Bot of þat munt I watȝ bi-talt;
When I schulde start in þe strem astraye,
Out of þat caste I watȝ by-calt;
It was not pleasing to the Lord.
Hit watȝ not at my pryonceȝ paye,

Hit payed hym not þat I so flonc,
Ou*er* meruelou*s* mereȝ so mad arayde,
Of raas þaȝ I were rasch & ronk,
ȝet rapely þer-i*n*ne I watȝ restayed;
For ryȝt as I sparred vn-to þe bonc,
Þat brathe out of my drem me brayde;
Þen wakned I i*n* þat erber wlonk,
My hede vpon þat hylle watȝ layde,
Þer as my perle to grou*n*de strayd;
I raxled & fel i*n* gret affray,
& sykyn*g* to my self I sayd:
"Now al be to þat prynceȝ paye."

The dreamer awakes,

and is in great sorrow.

Me payed ful ille to be out-fleme,
So sodenly of þat fayre regiou*n*,
Fro alle þo syȝteȝ so quykeȝ & queme.
A longeyn*g* heuy me strok i*n* swone,
& rewfully þe*n*ne I con to reme;
"O perle," q*uod* I, "of rych renou*n*,
So watȝ hit me dere þat þou con deme,
I*n* þys v*er*ay avysyou*n*;
If[1] hit be ueray & soth sermou*n*,
Þat þou so stykeȝ i*n* garlande gay,
So wel is me i*n* þys doel dou*n*gou*n*,
Þat þou art to þat prynseȝ paye."

He addresses his pearl;

[1] MS. inf.

laments his rash curiosity.

[FOL. 55*b*.]

To þat pryn*c*eȝ paye hade I ay bente,
& ȝerned no more þen watȝ me geuen,
& halden me þer in trwe entent,
As þe perle me prayed þat watȝ so þryuen,
As helde drawen to goddeȝ p*re*sent,
To mo of his mysterys I hade ben dryuen.
Bot ay wolde man of happe more hente
Þen moȝten by ryȝt vpon hem clyuen;
Þer-fore my ioye watȝ sone to-riuen,
& I kaste of kytheȝ þat lasteȝ aye.
Lorde! mad hit arn þat agayn þe stryuen,
Oþ*er* proferen þe oȝt agayn þy paye;

Men desire more than they have any right to expect.

The good Christian knows how to make peace with God.

To pay þe prince oþer sete saȝte,
Hit is ful eþe to þe god krystyin;
For I haf founden hym boþe day & naȝte,
A god, a lorde, a frende ful fyin. 1204
Ouer þis hyl[1] þis lote I laȝte,
For pyty of my perle enclyin,
& syþen to god I hit by-taȝte,
In krysteȝ dere blessyng & myn, 1208
Þat in þe forme of bred & wyn,
Þe preste vus scheweȝ vch a daye;
He gef vus to be his homly hyne,
Ande precious perleȝ vnto his pay. Amen. Amen. 1212

God give us grace to be his servants!

[1] MS. *hyiil*

CLEANNESS.

I

[Fol. 57a.] Clannesse who-so kyndly cowþe comende,
& rekken vp alle þe resounȝ þat ho by riȝt askeȝ,
Fayre formeȝ myȝt he fynde in forering his speche,
& in þe contraré, kark & combraunce huge;
For wonder wroth is þe wyȝ þat wroȝt alle þinges,
Wyth þe freke þat in fylþe folȝes hym after,
As renkeȝ of relygioun þat reden & syngen,
& aprochen to hys presens, & presteȝ arn called;
Thay teen vnto his temmple & temen to hym seluen,
Reken with reuerence þay r[ec]hen his auter,
Þay hondel þer his aune body & vsen hit boþe.
If þay in clannes be clos þay cleche gret mede,
Bot if þay conterfete crafte, & cortaysye wont,
As be honest vtwyth, & in-with alle fylþeȝ,
Þen ar þay synful hemself & sulped altogeder,
Boþe god & his gere, & hym to greme cachen.
He is so clene in his courte, þe kyng þat al weldeȝ,
& honeste in his hous-holde & hagherlych serued,
With angeleȝ enourled in alle þat is clene,
Boþe with-inne & with-outen, in wedeȝ ful bryȝt.
Nif he nere scoymus & skyg & non scaþe louied,
Hit were a meruayl to much, hit moȝt not falle;
Kryst kydde hit hym self in a carp oneȝ,
Þer as he heuened aȝt happeȝ & hyȝt hem her medeȝ;
Me myneȝ on one amonge oþer, as maþew recordeȝ,
Þat þus of clannesse vn-closeȝ a ful cler speche.

Cleanness discloses fair forms.

God is angry with the unclean worshipper,

and with false priests.

The pure worshipper receives great reward.

The impure will bring upon them the anger of God,

Who is pure and holy.

It would be a marvel if God did not hate evil.

Christ showed us that himself.

St. Matthew records the discourse.

[The clean of heart shall look on our Lord.]

Þe haþel clene of his hert hapeneȝ ful fayre,
For he schal loke on oure lorde with a bone chere,
As so saytȝ, to þat syȝt seche schal he neuer,
Þat any vnclannesse hatȝ on, anwhere[1] abowte:
For he þat flemus vch fylþe fer fro his hert,
May not byde þat burne[2] þat hit his body neȝen;
For-þy hyȝ not to heuen in hatereȝ to-torne,
Ne in þe harloteȝ hod & handeȝ vnwaschen;

[What earthly noble, when seated at table above dukes, [Fol. 57*b*.] would like to see a lad badly attired approach the table with "rent cockers," his coat torn and his toes out? For any one of these he would be turned out with a "big buffet," and be forbidden to re-enter, and thus be ruined through his vile clothes.]

For what vrþly haþel þat hyȝ honour haldeȝ
Wolde lyke, if a ladde com lyþerly attyred,
When he were sette solempnely in a sete ryche,
Abof dukes on dece, with dayntys serued,
Þen þe harlot with haste helded to þe table
With rent cokreȝ at þe kne & his clutte trasches,
& his tabarde to-torne & his toteȝ oute;
Oþer ani on of alle þyse he schulde be halden vtter,
With mony blame ful bygge, a boffet, peraunter,
Hurled to þe halle dore & harde þer-oute schowued,
& be forboden þat borȝe to bowe þider neuer,
On payne of enprysonment & puttyng in stokkeȝ;
& þus schal he be schent for his schrowde feble,
Þaȝ neuer in talle ne in tuch he trespas more.
& if vnwelcum he were to a worþlych prynce
Ȝet hym is þe hyȝe kyng harder in her euen,

[The parable of the "Marriage of the King's Son."]

As maþew meleȝ in his masse of þat man ryche,
Þat made þe mukel mangerye to marie his here dere,
& sende his sonde þen to say þat þay samne schulde,
& in comly quoyntis to com to his feste;

[The king's invitation.]

"For my boles & my boreȝ arn bayted & slayne,
& my fedde fouleȝ fatted with sclaȝt,
My polyle þat is penne-fed & partrykes boþe,
Wyth scheldeȝ of wylde swyn, swaneȝ & croneȝ;
Al is roþeled & rosted ryȝt to þe sete,
Comeȝ cof to my corte, er hit colde worþe."

[Those invited begin to make excuses.]

When þay knewen his cal þat þider com schulde,
Alle ex-cused hem by þe skyly he scape by moȝt:

[1] *aywhere* (?).

[2] Looks like *burre* in MS.

On hade boȝt hym a borȝ he sayde by hys *trawþe*,
Now t[ur]ne I þeder als tyd, þe *toun* to by-holde;
An *oþer* nayed also & nurned þis cawse:
I haf ȝerned & ȝat ȝokkeȝ of oxen,
& for my hyȝeȝ hem boȝt, to bowe haf I *mester*,
To see hem pulle in þe plow aproche me byhoueȝ;
& I haf wedded a wyf, sower[1] *hym* þe þryd,
Excuse me at þe *court*, I may not com þere;
Þus þay droȝ hem adreȝ *with* *daunger* vchone,
Þat non passed to þe place[2] þaȝ he prayed were.
[Fol. 58a.] Thenne þe ludych lorde lyked ful ille
& hade dedayn of þat dede, ful dryȝly he carpeȝ:
He saytȝ "now for her owne sorȝe þay for-saken habbeȝ,
More to wyte is her wrange, þen any wylle gentyl;
Þenne gotȝ forth my gomeȝ to þe grete streeteȝ,
& forsetteȝ on vche a syde þe cete aboute;
Þe wayferande frekeȝ, on fote & on hors,
Boþe burneȝ & burdeȝ, þe *better* & þe wers,
Laþeȝ hem alle luflyly to lenge at my fest,
& bryngeȝ hem blyþly to borȝe as barouneȝ þay were,
So þat my palays plat-ful be pyȝt al aboute,
Þise *oþer* wrecheȝ I-wysse worþy noȝt wern."
Þen þay cayred & com þat þe cost waked,
Broȝten bachlereȝ hem wyth þat þay by bonkeȝ metten,
Swyereȝ þat swyftly swyed on blonkeȝ,
& also fele vpon fote, of fre & of bonde.
When þay com to þe *court*e keppte wern þay fayre,
Styȝtled *with* þe stewarde, stad *in* þe halle,
Ful man*er*ly *with* marchal mad forto sitte,
As he watȝ dere of de-gre dressed his seete.
Þenne segge̡ȝ to þe souerayn sayden þer-*after*,
"Lo! lorde *with* *your* leue at *your* lege heste,
& at þi banne we haf broȝt, as þou beden habbeȝ,
Mony renischche renkeȝ & ȝet is roum more."
Sayde þe lorde to þo ledeȝ, "layteȝ ȝet ferre,
Ferre out *in* þe felde, & fecheȝ mo gesteȝ,

One had bought an estate and must go to see it.

Another had purchased some oxen and wished to see them "pull in the plough."

A third had married a wife and could not come.

The Lord was greatly displeased,

and commanded his servants to invite the wayfaring,

both men and women, the better and the worse,

that his palace might be full.

The servants brought in bachelors and squires.

When they came to the court they were well entertained.

The servants tell their lord that they have done his behest, and there is still room for more guests.

The Lord commands them to go out into the fields,

[1] *swer* (?)

[2] MS. *plate*.

Wayteȝ gorsteȝ & greueȝ, if ani gomeȝ lyggeȝ,
What-kyn folk so þer fare, fecheȝ hem hider,

and bring in the halt, blind, and "one-eyed."

Be þay fers, be þay feble for-loteȝ[1] none,
Be þay hol, be þay halt, be þay onyȝed,
& þaȝ þay ben boþe blynde & balterande cruppeleȝ,

For those who denied shall not taste "one sup" to save them from death.

Þat my hous may holly by halkes by fylled;
For certeȝ þyse ilk renkeȝ þat me renayed habbe
& de-nounced me, noȝt now at þis tyme,
Schul neuer sitte in my sale my soper to fele,
Ne suppe on sope of my seve, þaȝ[2] þay swelt schulde."

[Fol. 58b.] The palace soon became full of "people of all plights."

Thenne þe sergaunteȝ, at þat sawe, swengen þer-oute,
& diden þe dede þat [is] demed, as he deuised hade,
& with peple of alle plyteȝ þe palays þay fyllen;

They were not all one wife's sons, nor had they all one father.

Hit weren not alle on wyueȝ suneȝ, wonen with on fader;
Wheþer þay wern worþy, oþer wers, wel wern þay stowed,

The "brightest attired" had the best place. Below sat those with "poor weeds."

Ay þe best byfore & bryȝtest atyred,
Þe derrest at þe hyȝe dese þat dubbed wer fayrest;
& syþen on lenþe bilooghe ledeȝ inogh,
& ay a segge soerly[3] semed by her wedeȝ;
So with marschal at her mete mensked þay were,
Clene men in compaynye for-knowen wern lyte,

All are well entertained "with meat and minstrelsy."

& ȝet þe symplest in þat sale watȝ serued to þe fulle,
Boþe with menske, & with mete & mynstrasy noble,
& alle þe laykeȝ þat a lorde aȝt in londe schewe.

Each with his "mate" made him at ease.

& þay bigonne to be glad þat god drink haden,
& vch mon with his mach made hym at ese.

II.

The lord of the feast goes among his guests.

Now in-myddeȝ þe mete þe mayster hym biþoȝt,
Þat he wolde se þe semblé þat samned was þere,
& re-hayte rekenly þe riche & þe poueren,[4]
& cherisch hem alle with his cher, & chaufen her Ioye,
Þen he boweȝ fro his bour in to þe brode halle,

Bids them be merry.

& to þe best on þe bench, & bede hym be myry,
Solased hem with semblaunt & syled fyrre;
Tron fro table to table & talkede ay myrþe,

[1] *forleteȝ* (?).
[2] MS. þaȝ þaȝ.
[3] *soberly* (?).
[4] MS. poueuer.

Bot as he ferked ouer þe flor he fande with his y3e,
Hit wat3 not for a haly day honestly arayed,

On the floor he finds one not arrayed for a holyday.

A þral þry3t in þe þrong vnþryuandely cloþed,
Ne no festiual frok, bot fyled with werkke3.
Þe gome wat3 vn-garnyst with god men to dele,
& gremed þer-with þe grete lord & greue hym he þo3t;
"Say me, frende," quod þe freke with a felle chere,
"Hov wan þou into þis won in wede3 so fowle?

Asks him how he obtained entrance,

Þe abyt þat þou hat3 vpon, no haly day hit menske3;
Þou burne for no brydale art busked in wede3!
How wat3 þou hardy þis hous for þyn vnhap [to] ne3e,
In on so ratted a robe & rent at þe syde3?

and how he was so bold as to appear in such rags.

[Fol. 59a.] Þow art a gome vn-goderly in þat goun febele;
Þou praysed me & my place ful pouer & ful [g]nede,
Þat wat3 so prest to aproche my presens here-inne;
Hope3 þou I be a harlot þi erigant to prayse?"

Does he take him to be a harlot?

Þat oþer burne wat3 abayst of his broþe worde3,
& hurkele3 doun with his hede, þe vrþe he bi-holde3;
He wat3 so scoumfit of his scylle, lest he skaþe hent,
Þat he ne wyst on wórde what he warp schulde.

The man becomes discomfited.

He is unable to reply.

Þen þe lorde wonder loude laled & cryed,
& talke3 to his tormenttoure3: "take3 hym," he bidde3,
"Bynde3 byhynde, at his bak, boþe two his hande3,
& felle fettere3 to his fete festene3 bylyue;
Stik hym stifly in stoke3, & steke3 hym þer-after
Depe in my doungoun þer doel euer dwelle3,
Greuing, & gretyng, & gryspyng harde
Of teþe tenfully to-geder, to teche hym be quoynt."

The lord commands him to be bound,

and cast into a deep dungeon.

Thus comparisune3 kryst þe kyndom of heuen,
To þis frelych feste þat fele arn to called,
For alle arn laþed luflyly, þe luþer & þe better,
Þat euer wern ful3ed in font þat fest to haue.

This feast is likened to the kingdom of heaven, to which all are invited.

Bot war þe wel, if þou wylt, þy wede3 ben clene,
& honest for þe haly day, lest þou harme lache,
For aproch þou to þat prynce of parage noble.
He hates helle no more þen hem þat ar sowle.[1]

See that thy weeds are clean.

[1] fowle (?).

Thy weeds are thy works that thou hast wrought.

Wich arn þenne þy wedeȝ þou wrappeȝ þe inne,
Þat schal schewe hem so schene schrowde of þe best?
Hit arn þy werkeȝ wyterly, þat þou wroȝt haueȝ,
& lyued with þe lykyng þat lyȝe in þyn hert,
Þat þo be frely & fresch fonde in þy lyue,
& fetyse of a fayr forme, to fote & to honde,
& syþen alle þyn oþer lymeȝ lapped ful clene,
Þenne may þou se þy sauior & his sete ryche.

For many faults may a man forfeit bliss.

For fele fauteȝ may a freke forfete his blysse,
Þat he þe souerayn ne se þen, for slauþe one,

For sloth and pride he is thrust into the devil's throat.

As for bobaunce & bost & bolnande priyde,
Þroly in-to þe deueleȝ þrote man þryngeȝ bylyue,

[Fol. 59*b*.] He is ruined by covetousness, perjury, murder, theft, and strife.

For couetyse, & colwarde & croked dedeȝ,
For mon-sworne, & men-sclaȝt, & to much drynk,
For þefte, & for þrepyng, vn-þonk may mon haue;

For robbery and ribaldry, for preventing marriages, and supporting the wicked,

For roborrye, & riboudrye & resouneȝ vntrwe,
& dysheriete & depryue dowrie of wydoeȝ,
For marryng of maryageȝ & mayntnaunce of schreweȝ,

for treason, treachery, and tyranny,

For traysoun, & trichcherye, & tyrauntyré boþe,[1]
& for fals famacions & fayned laweȝ;
Man may mysse þe myrþe, þat much is to prayse,

man may lose eternal bliss.

For such vnþeweȝ as þise & þole much payne,
& in þe creatores cort com neuer more,
Ne neuer see hym with syȝt for such sour tourneȝ.

III.

Bot I haue herkned & herde of mony hyȝe clerkeȝ,
& als in resouneȝ of ryȝt red hit my seluen,

The high Prince of all is displeased with those who work wickedly.

Þat þat ilk proper prynce þat paradys weldeȝ
Is displesed at vch a poynt þat plyes to scaþe.
Bot neuer ȝet in no boke breued I herde
Þat euer he wrek so wyþerly on werk þat he made,
Ne venged for no vilté of vice ne synne,
Ne so hastyfly watȝ hot for hatel of his wylle,
Ne neuer so sodenly soȝt vn-soundely to weng,
As for fylþe of þe flesch þat foles han vsed;

[1] *loþe* (?).

For as I fynde þer he forȝet alle his fre þewes,
& wex wod to þe wrache, for wrath at his hert,
For þe fyrste fèlonye þe falce fende wroȝt.
Whyl he watȝ hyȝe in þe heuen houen vpon lofte,
Of alle þyse aþel aungeleȝ attled þe fayrest,
& he vnkyndely as a karle kydde areward,
He seȝ noȝt bot hym self how semly he were,
Bot his souerayn he forsoke & sade þyse wordeȝ:
"I schal telde vp my trone in þe tra mountayne
& by lyke to þat lorde þat þe lyft made.
With þis worde þat he warp, þe wrake on hym lyȝt,
Dryȝtyn with his dere dom hym drof to þe abyme,
In þe mesure of his mode, his metȝ neuer þe lasse,
Bot þer he tynt þe tyþe dool of his tour ryche,
[Fol. 60a.] Þaȝ þe feloun were so fers for his fayre wedeȝ
& his glorious glem þat glent so bryȝt;
As sone as dryȝtyneȝ dome drof to hym seluen,
[Þi]kke þowsandeȝ þro þrwen þer-oute
Fellen fro þe fyrmament, fendeȝ ful blake
Weued[1] at þe fyrst swap as þe snaw þikke,
Hurled in-to helle-hole as þe hyue swarmeȝ;
Fyltyr fenden folk forty dayeȝ lencþe,
Er þat styngande storme stynt ne myȝt;
Bot as smylt mele vnder smal siue smokes for-þikke,
So fro heuen to helle þat hatel schor laste,
On vche syde of þe worlde aywhere ilyche.
Þis[2] hit watȝ a brem brest & a byge wrache,
& ȝet wrathed not þe wyȝ, ne þe wrech saȝtled,
Ne neuer wolde, for wylnesful, his worþy god knawe,
Ne pray hym for no pité, so proud watȝ his wylle,
For-þy þaȝ þe rape were rank, þe rawþe watȝ lyttel;[3]
Þaȝ he be kest into kare he kepes no better.
Bot þat oþer wrake þat wex on wyȝeȝ, hit lyȝt
Þurȝ þe faut of a freke þat fayled in trawþe.
Adam in obedyent[4] ordaynt to blysse,
Þer pryuely in paradys his place watȝ de-vised,

For the first fault the devil committed, he felt God's vengeance.

He, the fairest of all angels, forsook his sovereign,

and boasted that his throne should be as high as God's.

For these words he was cast down to hell.

The fiends fell from heaven, like the thick snow,

for forty days.

From heaven to hell the shower lasted.

The devil would not make peace with God.

Affliction makes him none the better.

For the fault of one, vengeance alighted upon all men.

Adam was ordained to live in bliss.

[1] *wened* (?).

[2] *ȝis* (?).

[3] MS. *lyttlel.*

[4] *obedience* (?).

To lyue þer *in* lykyng þe lenþe of a terme,
& þenne en-herite þat home þat aungeleȝ for-gart,

Through Eve he ate an apple.

Bot þurȝ þe eggyng of eue he ete of an apple
Þat en-poysened alle pepleȝ þat parted fro hem boþe,

Thus all his descendants became poisoned.

For a defonce þat watȝ dyȝt of dryȝtyn seluen,
& a payne þer-on put & pertly halden;
Þe defence watȝ þe fryt þat þe freke towched,
& þe dom is þe deþe þat drepeȝ vus alle.

A maiden brought a remedy for mankind.

Al *in* mesure & meþe watȝ mad þe vengiaunce,
& efte amended *with* a mayden þat make hade neu*er*.

IV.

Bot in þe þryd watȝ forþrast al þat þryue schuld,

Malice was merciless.

Þer watȝ malys mercyles & mawgre much scheued,
Þat watȝ for fylþe vpon folde þat þe folk vsed,

A race of men came into the [Fol. 60*b*.] world, the fairest, the merriest, and the strongest that ever were created.

[Þ]at þen wonyed *in* þe worlde *with*-outen any mayst*er*ȝ;
Hit wern þe fayrest of forme & of face als,
Þe most & þe myriest þat maked wern euer,
Þe styfest, þe stalworþest þat stod eu*er* on feteȝ
& lengest lyf *in* hem lent of ledeȝ alle oþ*er*,
For hit was þe forme-foster þat þe folde bred,

They were sons of Adam.

Þe aþel auncetereȝ suneȝ þat adam watȝ called,
To wham god hade geuen alle þat gayn were,
Alle þe blysse boute blame þat bodi myȝt haue,
& þose lykkest to þe lede þat lyued next aft*er*,
For-þy so semly to see syþe*n* wern none.

No law was laid upon them,

Þer watȝ no law to hem layd bot loke to kynde,
& kepe to hit, & alle hit cors clanly ful-fylle;

Nevertheless they acted unnaturally.

& þenne founden þay fylþe *in* fleschlych dedeȝ
& controeued agayn kynde contraré werkeȝ,
& vsed hem vn-þryftyly vchon on oþ*er*,
& als with oþ*er*, wylsfully, vpon a wrange wyse.

The "*fiends*" beheld how fair were the daughters of these mighty men, and made fellowship with them and begat a race of giants.

So ferly fowled her flesch þat þe fende loked,
How þe deȝt*er* of þe douþe wern dere-lych fayre,
& fallen *in* felaȝschyp *with* hem on folken wyse
& en-gendered on hem ieaunteȝ *with* her Iapeȝ ille.

Þose wern men meþeleȝ & maȝty on vrþe,
Þat for her lodlych laykeȝ alosed þay were.
He watȝ famed[1] for fre þat feȝt loued best,
& ay þe bigest *in* bale þe best watȝ halden;
& þe*n*ne eueleȝ on erþe ernestly grewen
& multyplyed mony-folde *in*-mongeȝ mankynde,
For þat þe maȝty on molde so marre þise oþ*er*.
Þat þe wyȝe þat al wroȝt ful wroþly bygynneȝ.
When he knew vche contre corupte *in* hit seluen,
& vch freke forloyned fro þe ryȝt wayeȝ,
Felle temptande tene towched his hert;
As wyȝe, wo hy*m* with-i*n*ne werp to hy*m* seluen:
"Me for-þy*n*keȝ ful much þat eu*er* I mon made,
Bot I schal delyu*er* & do away þat doten on þis molde,
& fleme out of þe folde al þat flesch wereȝ,
Fro þe burne to þe best, fro bryddeȝ to fyscheȝ;
[Fol. 61a.] Al schal dou*n* & be ded & dryuen out of erþe,
Þat eu*er* I sette saule i*n*ne; & sore hit me rweȝ
Þat eu*er* I made hem my self; bot if I may her-aft*er*,
I schal wayte to be war her wrencheȝ to kepe."
Þe*n*ne *in* worlde watȝ a wyȝe wonyande on lyue,
Ful redy & ful ryȝtwys, & rewled hy*m* fayre;
In þe drede of dryȝtyn his dayeȝ he vseȝ,
& ay glydande wyth his god his *gra*ce watȝ þe more.
Hy*m* watȝ þe nome Noe, as is i*n*nogh*e* knawen,
He had þre þryuen su*n*eȝ & þay þre wyueȝ;
Sem soþly þat on, þat oþ*er* hyȝt cam
& þe Iolef Iapheth watȝ gendered þe þryd.
Now god *in* nwy to Noe co*n* speke,
Wylde wrakful wordeȝ *in* his wylle greued:
"Þe ende of alle-kyneȝ flesch þat on vrþe meueȝ,
Is fallen forþ wyth my face & forþ*er* hit I þenk,
W*ith* her vn-worþelych werk me wlateȝ w*ith*-i*n*ne,
Þe gore þ*er*-of me hatȝ greued & þe glette nwyed;
I schal strenkle my distresse & strye al to-geder,
Boþe ledeȝ & londe & alle þat lyf habbeȝ.

[1] *fained* (?).

The greatest fighter was reckoned the most famous.

The Creator of all becomes exceedingly wroth.

Fell anger touches His heart.

It repents Him that He has made man.

He declares that all flesh shall be destroyed, both man and beast.

There was at this time living on the earth a very righteous man:

Noah was his name.

Three bold sons he had.

God in great anger speaks to Noah.

Declares that He will destroy all "that life has."

Commands him to make "a mansion" with dwellings for wild and tame.

Bot make to þe a manciou*n* & þat is my wylle,
A cofer closed of tres, clanlych planed;
Wyrk wone3 þer*in*ne for wylde & for tame,
& þe*n*ne cleme hit w*it*h clay comly w*it*h-inne,[1]
& alle þe endentur dryuen daube w*it*h-outen.

To let the ark be three hundred cubits in length, and fifty in breadth, and thirty in height,

& þu*s* of lenþe & of large þat lome þou make,
Þre hundred of cupyde3 þou holde to þe lenþe,
Of fyfty fayre ou*er*-þwert forme þe brede;
& loke euen þat þyn ark haue of he3þe þretté,
& a wyndow wyd vpon, wro3t vpon lofte,

and a window in it a cubit square.

In þe compas of a cubit kyndely sware,

Also a good shutting door in the side, together with halls, recesses, bushes, and bowers, and well-formed pens.

A wel dutande dor, don on þe syde;
Haf halle3 þer-i*n*ne & halke3 ful mony,
Boþe boske3 & bou*re*3 & wel bou*n*den pene3;
For I schal waken vp a wat*er* to wasch alle þe worlde,
& quelle alle þat is quik w*it*h quauende flode3.

[Fol. 61*b*.] For all flesh shall be destroyed,

Alle þat glyde3 & got3, & gost of lyf habbe3,
I schal wast with my wrath þat wons vpon vrþe;

except Noah and his family.

Bot my forwarde w*it*h þe I festen on þis wyse,
For þou in reysou*n* hat3 rengned & ry3twys ben eu*er*;
Þou schal ent*er* þis ark w*it*h þyn aþel barne3
& þy wedded wyf; with þe þou take
Þe make3 of þy myry su*ne*3; þis meyny of a3te
I schal saue of mo*n*ne3 saule3, & swelt þose oþ*er*.

Noah is told to take into the ark seven pairs of every clean beast, and one of unclean kind,

Of vche best þat bere3 lyf busk þe a cupple,
Of vche clene comly kynde enclose seuen make3,
Of vche horwed, i*n* ark halde bot a payre,
For to saue me þe sede of alle ser kynde3;
& ay þou meng w*it*h þe male3 þe mete ho-beste3,

and to furnish the ark with proper food.

Vche payre by payre to plese ay þ*er* oþ*er*;
W*it*h alle þe fode þat may be founde frette þy cofer,
For sustnau*n*ce to yow self & also þose oþ*er*."

Noah fills the ark.

Ful grayþely got3 þis god ma*n* & dos gode3 hestes,
In dry3 dred & dau*n*ger, þat durst do non oþer.
Wen hit wat3 fettled & forged & to þe fulle grayþed,
Þe*n*n con dry3ttyn hym dele dry3ly þyse worde3:

[1] MS. *with*-inme.

V.

"Now Noe," q*uod* oure lorde, "art þou al redy?
Hatȝ þou closed þy kyst w*ith* clay alle aboute?"
"ȝe lorde w*ith* þy leue," sayde þe lede þ*enne*,
348 "Al is wroȝt at þi worde, as þou me wyt lanteȝ."
"Enter in þenn," q*uod* he, "& haf þi wyf w*ith* þe,
Þy þre sune*ȝ* w*ith*-outen þrep & her þre wyueȝ;
Besteȝ, as I bedene haue, bosk þ*er*-*inne* als,
352 & when ȝe arn staued, styfly stekeȝ yow þ*erinne*;
Fro seuen dayeȝ ben seyed I sende out by-lyue,
Such a rowtande ryge þat rayne schal swyþe,
Þat schal wasch alle þe worlde of werkeȝ of fylþe;
356 Schal no flesch vpon folde by fonden onlyue;
Out-taken yow aȝt i*n* þis ark staued,
& sed þat I wyl saue of þyse ser besteȝ."
Now Noe neu*er* stysteȝ[1] (þat niyȝ[t] he bygy*n*neȝ),
360 Er al wer stawed & stoken, as þe steuen wolde.
[Fol. 61a.] The*nne* sone com þe seuenþe day, when samned wern alle,
& alle woned i*n* þe whichche þe wylde & þe tame.
Þe*n* bolned þe abyme & bonkeȝ con ryse,
364 Walt*es* out vch walle-heued, i*n* ful wode stremeȝ,
Watȝ no bry*m*me þat abod vnbrosten bylyue,
Þe mukel lauande logh*e* to þe lyfte rered.
Mony clust*er*ed clowde clef alle i*n* clowteȝ,
368 To-rent vch a rayn-ryfte & rusched to þe vrþe;
Fon neu*er* i*n* forty dayeȝ, & þe*n* þe flod ryses,
Ou*er*-walteȝ vche a wod & þe wyde feldeȝ;
For when þe wat*er* of þe welkyn w*ith* þe worlde mette,
372 Alle þat deth moȝt dryȝe drowned þer-i*nne*;
Þer watȝ moon forto make when meschef was cnowen,
Þat noȝt dowed bot þe deth in þe depe stremeȝ.
Wat*er* wylger ay wax, woneȝ þat stryede,
376 Hurled i*n*-to vch hou*s*, hent þat þer dowelled.
Fyrst feng to þe flyȝt alle þat fle myȝt,
Vuche burde w*ith* her barne þe bygy*n*g þay leueȝ,

God asks Noah whether all is ready.

Noah replies that all is fully prepared.

He is commanded to enter the ark,

for God tells him that he will send a rain to destroy all flesh,

Noah stows all safely in the ark.

Seven days are passed.

The deep begins to swell, banks are broken down,

and the clouds burst.

It rains for forty days and the flood rises,

and flows over the woods and fields.

All must drown.

The water enters the houses.

[1] *stynteȝ* (?).

Each woman with her bairns flees to the hills.

& bowed to þe hyȝ bonk þer brentest hit wern,
& heterly to þe hyȝe hylleȝ þay [h]aled on faste;

The rain never ceases.

Bot al watȝ nedleȝ her note, for neuer cowþe stynt
Þe roȝe raynande ryg [&] þe raykande waweȝ,

The valleys are filled.

Er vch boþom watȝ brurd-ful to þe bonkeȝ eggeȝ,
& vche a dale so depe þat demmed at þe brynkeȝ.
Þe moste mountayneȝ on mor þenne watȝ no more dryȝe,

People flock to the mountains.

& þer-on flokked þe folke, for ferde of þe wrake,
Syþen þe wylde of þe wode on þe water flette;

Some swim for their lives.

Summe swymmed þer-on þat saue hemself trawed,
Summe styȝe to a stud & stared to þe heuen,

Others roar for fear.

Rwly wyth a loud rurd rored for drede.

Animals of all kinds run to the hills.

Hareȝ, herteȝ also, to þe hyȝe runnen,
Bukkeȝ, bauseneȝ & buleȝ to þe bonkkeȝ hyȝed,

All pray for mercy.

& alle cryed for care to þe kyng of heuen,
Re-couerer of þe creator, þay cryed vchone,

God's mercy is passed from them.

Þat amounted þe masse, þe mase his mercy watȝ passed,
& alle his pyte departed fro peple þat he hated.

[Fol. 62b.]

Bi þat þe flod to her fete floȝed & waxed,

Each sees that he must sink.

Þen vche a segge seȝ wel þat synk hym byhoued;
Frendeȝ fellen in fere & faþmed togeder
To dryȝ her delful deystyné & dyȝen alle samen;

Friends take leave of one another.

Luf lokeȝ to luf & his leue takeȝ,
For to ende alle at oneȝ & for euer twynne.

Forty days have gone by, and all are destroyed.

By forty dayeȝ wern faren, on folde no flesch styryed,
Þat þe flod nade al freten with feȝtande waȝeȝ,[1]
For hit clam vche a clyffe cubites fyftene,
Ouer þe hyȝest hylle þat hurkled on erþe.

All rot in the mud,

Þenne mourkne in þe mudde most ful nede
Alle þat spyrakle in-spranc,[2] no sprawlyng awayled,

except Noah and his family,

Saue þe haþel vnder hach & his here straunge,
Noe þat ofte neuened þe name of oure lorde,

who are safe in the ark.

Hym aȝt-sum in þat ark as aþel god lyked,
Þer alle ledeȝ in lome lenged druye,

The ark is lifted as high as the clouds,

Þe arc houen watȝ on hyȝe with hurlande goteȝ,
Kest to kytheȝ vncouþe þe clowdeȝ ful nere.

[1] *waweȝ* (?).
[2] *in-sprang* (?).

Hit waltered on þe wylde flod, went as hit lyste,
Drof vpon þe depe dam, in daunger hit semed,
With-outen mast, oþer myke, oþer myry bawelyne,
Kable, oþer capstan to clyppe to her ankreʒ,
Hurrok, oþer hande-helme hasped on roþer,
Oþer any sweande sayl to seche after hauen,
Bot flote forthe with þe flyt of þe felle wyndeʒ;
Wheder-warde so þe water wafte, hit rebounde.
Ofte hit roled on-rounde & rered on ende,
Nyf oure lorde hade ben her lodeʒ-mon hem had lumpen harde.
Of þe lenþe of noe lyf to lay a lel date,
Þe sex hundreth of his age & none odde ʒereʒ,
Of secounde monyth, þe seuenþe day ryʒteʒ,
To-walten alle þyse welle-hedeʒ & þe water flowed,
& þryeʒ fyfty þe flod of folwande dayeʒ,
Vche hille watʒ þer hidde with yreʒ[1] ful graye;
Al watʒ wasted þat þer wonyed þe worlde with-inne,
Þer euer flote, oþer flwe, oþer on fote ʒede,
[Fol. 83a.] That roʒly watʒ þe remnaunt þat þe rac dryueʒ,
Þat alle gendreʒ so ioyst wern ioyned wyth-inne.
Bot quen þe lorde of þe lyfte lyked hymseluen
For to mynne on his mon his meth þat abydeʒ,
Þen he wakened a wynde on wattereʒ to blowe;
Þenne lasned þe llak[2] þat large watʒ are,
Þen he stac vp þe stangeʒ, stoped þe welleʒ,
Bed blynne of þe rayn, hit batede as fast,
Þenne lasned þe loʒ lowkande to-geder.
After harde dayeʒ wern out an hundreth & fyfté,
As þat lyftande lome luged aboute,
Where þe wynde & þe weder warpen hit wolde,
Hit saʒtled on a softe day synkande to grounde.
On a rasse of a rok, hit rest at þe laste,
On þe mounte of mararach of armene hilles,
Þat oþer-wayeʒ on ebrv hit hat þe thanes.
Bot þaʒ þe kyste in þe crageʒ wern closed to byde.

and is driven about,

without mast, bowline, cables, anchors, or sail to guide its course.

At the mercy of the winds.

Oft it rolled around and reared on end.

The age of the patriarch Noah.

Duration of the flood.

The completeness of the destruction.

God remembers those in the ark.

He causes a wind to blow,

and closes the lakes and wells,

and the great deep.

The ark settles on Mount Ararat.

[1] yþeʒ (?).

[2] So in MS.

ȝet fyned not þe flod ne fel to þe boþemeȝ,
Noah beholds the bare earth.
Bot þe hyȝest of þe eggeȝ vnhuled wern a lyttel,
Þat þe burne by*nn*e borde byhelde þe bare erþe;
He opens his window and sends out the raven to seek dry land.
Þe*nn*e wafte he vpon his wyndowe, & wysed þ*er*-oute
A message fro þat meyny hem moldeȝ to seche,
Þat watȝ þe rauen so ronk þat rebel watȝ eu*er*;
He watȝ colored as þe cole, corbyal vn-trwe.
& he fongeȝ to þe flyȝt, & fa*nn*eȝ on þe wyndeȝ,
Houeȝ hyȝe vpon hyȝt to herken tyþy*n*ges.
The raven "croaks for comfort" on finding carrion.
He croukeȝ for comfort when carayne he fyndeȝ;
Kast vp on a clyffe þer costese lay drye,
He hade þe smelle of þe smach & smolt*es* þeder sone,
He fills his belly with the foul flesh.
Falleȝ on þe foule flesch & fylleȝ his wombe,
& sone ȝederly for-ȝete ȝister-day steuen,
How þe cheuetayn hy*m* charged þ*at* þe kyst ȝemed.
Þe rauen raykeȝ hy*m* forth þat reches ful lyttel
How alle fodeȝ þer fare, elleȝ he fynde mete;
Bot þe burne by*nn*e borde[1] þat bod to hys come,
The lord of the ark curses the raven.
Ba*nn*ed hy*m* ful bytterly w*ith* best*es* alle samen,
[Fol. 63b.]
He secheȝ an oþ*er* sondeȝmon & setteȝ on þe doune;[2]
and sends out the dove.
Bry*n*geȝ þat bryȝt vpon borde blessed & sayde,
"Wende worþelych wyȝt v*us* woneȝ to seche,
Dryf ou*er* þis dy*m*me wat*er*; if þou druye fyndeȝ
Bry*n*g bodworde to bot blysse to v*us* alle;
Þaȝ þat fowle be false, fre be þou euer."
The bird wanders about the whole day.
Ho wyrl*e* out on þe weder o*n* wy*n*geȝ ful scharpe,
Dreȝly alle a longe day þat dorst neu*er* lyȝt;
Finding no rest, she returns about eventide to Noah.
& when ho fyndeȝ no folde her fote on to pyche,
Ho vmbe-kesteȝ þe coste & þe kyst secheȝ,
Ho hitteȝ on þe euentyde & on þe ark sitteȝ;
Noe ny*m*mes hir anon & naytly hir staueȝ.
Noah again sends out the dove.
Noe on anoþ*er* day ny*m*meȝ efte þe dovene,
& byddeȝ hir bowe ou*er* þe borne efte bonkeȝ to seche;
& ho skyrmeȝ vnder skwe & skowteȝ aboute,
Tyl hit watȝ nyȝe at þe naȝt & noe þ*en* secheȝ.

[1] MS. *lorde*.
[2] *doune* or *douene* (?).

VI.

The dove returns with an olive branch in her beak.

On ark on an euentyde houeȝ þe downe,
On stamyn ho stod & stylle hym abydeȝ;
What! ho broȝt in hir beke a bronch of olyue,
Gracyously vmbe-grouen al with grene leueȝ;

This was a token of peace and reconciliation.

Þat watȝ þe syngne of sauyté þat sende hem oure lorde,
& þe saȝtlyng of hym-self with þo sely besteȝ.

Joy reigns in the ark.

Þen watȝ þer ioy in þat gyn where Iumpred er dryȝed,
& much comfort in þat cofer þat watȝ clay-daubed.
Myryly on a fayr morn, monyth þe fyrst,

The people therein laugh and look thereout.

Þat falleȝ formast in þe ȝer, & þe fyrst day,
Ledeȝ loȝen in þat lome & loked þer-oute,
How þat wattereȝ wern woned & þe worlde dryed.
Vchon loued oure lorde, bot lenged ay stylle,
Tyl þay had tyþyng fro þe tolke þat tyned hem þer-inne;

God permits Noah and his sons to leave the ark.

Þen godeȝ glam to hem glod þat gladed hem alle,
Bede hem drawe to þe dor, delyuer hem he wolde;
Þen went þay to þe wykket, hit walt vpon sone,
Boþe þe burne & his barneȝ bowed þer-oute;
Her wyueȝ walkeȝ hem wyth & þe wylde after,
Þroly þrublande in þronge, þrowen ful þykke;

Noah offers sacrifice to God.

[Fol. 61a.] Bot Noe of vche honest kynde nem out an odde
& heuened vp an auter & halȝed hit fayre,
& sette a sakerfyse þer-on of vch a ser kynde,
Þat watȝ comly & clene, god kepeȝ non oþer.
When bremly brened þose besteȝ, & þe breþe rysed,

It is pleasing to Him that "all speeds or spoils."

Þe sauour of his sacrafyse soȝt to hym euen
Þat al spedeȝ & spylleȝ; he spekes with þat ilke
In comly comfort ful clos & cortays wordeȝ:

God declares that He will never destroy the world for the sin of man.

"Now noe no more nel I neuer wary,
Alle þe mukel mayny [on] molde for no manneȝ synneȝ,
For I se wel þat hit is sothe, þat alle manneȝ wytteȝ
To vn-þryfte arn alle þrawen with þoȝt of her hertteȝ,
& ay hatȝ ben & wyl be ȝet fro her barnage;
Al is þe mynde of þe man to malyce enclyned,

For-þy schal I neuer schende so schortly at ones,
As dysstrye al for manez synne [in] dayez of þis erþe.
Bot waxez now & wendez forth & worþez to monye,
Multyplyez on þis molde & menske yow by-tyde.
Sesounez schal yow neuer sese of sede ne of heruest,
Ne hete, ne no harde forst, vmbre ne droȝþe,
Ne þe swetnesse of somer, ne þe sadde wynter,
Ne þe nyȝt, ne þe day, ne þe newe ȝerez,
Bot euer renne restlez rengnez ȝe þer-inne."
Þerwyth he blessez vch a best, & bytaȝt hem þis erþe.
Þen watz a skylly skyualde, quen scaped alle þe wylde;
Vche fowle to þe flyȝt þat fyþerez myȝt serue,
Vche fysch to þe flod þat fynne couþe nayte,
Vche beste to þe bent þat[1] bytes on erbez;
Wylde wormez to her won wryþez in þe erþe
Þe fox & þe folmarde to þe fryth wyndez,
Herttes to hyȝe heþe, harez to gorstez,
& lyounez & lebardez to þe lake ryftes,
Hernez & hauekez to þe hyȝe rochez;
Þe hole-foted fowle to þe flod hyȝez,
& vche best at a brayde þer hym best lykez;
Þe fowre frekez of þe folde fongez þe empyre.
Lo! suche a wrakful wo for wlatsum dedez
Parformed þe hyȝe fader on folke þat he made;
Þat he chysly hade cherisched he chastysed ful hardee,
In de-voydynge þe vylanye þat venkquyst his þewez.
For-þy war þe now, wyȝe, þat worschyp desyres,
In his comlych courte þat kyng is of blysse,
In þe fylþe of þe flesch þat þou be founden neuer,
Tyl any water in þe worlde to wasche þe fayly,
For is no segge vnder sunne so seme of his craftez,
If he be sulped in synne, þat [ne] syttez vnclene.
On spec of a spote may spede to mysse
Of þe syȝte of þe souerayn þat syttez so hyȝe,
For þat schewe me schale in þo schyre howsez,
As þe beryl bornyst byhouez be clene,

That summer and winter shall never cease.

Nor night nor day, nor the new years.

God blesses every beast.

Each fowl takes its flight. Each fish goes to the flood. Each beast makes for the plain. Wild worms wriggle to their abodes in the earth. The fox goes to the woods. Harts to the heath, and hares to the gorse. Lions and leopards go to the lakes. Eagles and hawks to the high rocks. The four "frekes" take the empire.

[Fol. 64b.]

Behold what woe God brought on mankind for their hateful deeds!

Beware of the filth of the flesh.

"One speck of a spot" will ruin us in the sight of God.

The beryl is clean

[1] MS. þat þat.

Þat is sounde on vche a syde & no sem habes,
With-outen maskle oþer mote as margerye perle.

and sound,—it has no seam.

VII.

Syþen þe souerayn in sete so sore for-þoȝt
Þat euer he man vpon molde merked to lyuy,
For he in fylþe watȝ fallen, felly he uenged,
Quen fourferde[1] alle þe flesch þat he formed hade,
Hym rwed þat he hem vp-rerde & raȝt hem lyflode,
& efte þat he hem vndyd, hard hit hym þoȝt;
For quen þe swemande sorȝe soȝt to his hert,
He knyt a couenaunde cortaysly with monkynde þere,
In þe mesure of his mode & meþe of his wylle,
Þat he schulde neuer for no syt smyte al at oneȝ,
As to quelle alle quykeȝ for qued þat myȝt falle,
Whyl of þe lenþe of þe londe lasteȝ þe terme.
Þat ilke skyl for no scaþe ascaped hym neuer,
Wheder wonderly he wrak on wykked men after;
Ful felly for þat ilk faute forferde a kyth ryche,
In þe anger of his ire þat arȝed mony;
& al watȝ for þis ilk euel, þat vn-happen glette,
Þe venym & þe vylanye & þe vycios fylþe,
Þat by-sulpeȝ manneȝ saule in vnsounde hert,
Þat he his saueour ne see with syȝt of his yȝen,
[Fol. 65.] Þat alle illeȝ he hates as helle þat stynkkeȝ;
Bot non nuyeȝ hym, on naȝt ne neuer vpon dayeȝ,
As harlottrye vn-honest, heþyng of seluen;
Þat schameȝ for no schrewedschyp schent mot he worþe!
Bot sauyour mon in þy self, þaȝ þou a sotte lyuie,
Þaȝ þou bere þy self babel, by-þenk þe sum-tyme,
Wheþer he þat stykked vche a stare in vche steppe yȝe,
Ȝif hym self[2] be bore blynde hit is a brod wonder;
& he þat fetly in face fettled alle eres
If he[3] hatȝ losed þe lysten hit lyfteȝ meruayle;
Trave þou neuer þat tale, vn-trwe þou hit fyndeȝ,
Þer is no dede so derne þat ditteȝ his yȝen;

When God repented that he had made man, he destroyed all flesh.

But afterwards He was sorry,

and made a covenant with mankind that He would not again destroy all the living.

For the filth of the flesh God destroyed a rich city.

God hates the wicked as "hell that stinks."

Especially harlotry and blasphemy.

Nothing is hidden from God.

[1] *for-ferde* (?).

[2] MS. *sele*.

[3] MS. *he he*.

Þer is no wyȝe in his werk so war ne so stylle
Þat hit ne þraweȝ to hym þre[1] er he hit þoȝt haue;

[1] þer (?).

God is the ground of all deeds.

For he is þe gropande god, þe grounde of alle dedeȝ,
Rypande of vche a ring[2] þe reynyeȝ & hert;

[2] rink or renk (?).

He honours the man that is honest and whole.

& þere he fyndeȝ al fayre a freke wyth-inne
Þat hert honest & hol, þat haþel he honoureȝ,
Sendeȝ hym a sad syȝt to se his auen face,
& harde honyseȝ þise oþer & of his erde flemeȝ.

But for deeds of shame He destroys the mighty ones.

Bot of þe dome of þe douþe for dedeȝ of schame
He is so skoymos of þat skaþe, he scarreȝ bylyue,
He may not dryȝe to draw allyt, bot drepeȝ in hast
& þat watȝ schewed schortly by a scaþe oneȝ.

VIII.

Abraham is sitting before his house-door under a green oak.

Olde Abraham in erde oneȝ he sytteȝ
Euen byfore his hous-dore vnder an oke grene;
Bryȝt blykked þe bem of þe brode heuen,
In þe hyȝe hete þer-of Abraham bideȝ,
He watȝ schunt to þe schadow vnder schyre leueȝ;

He sees three men coming along,

Þenne watȝ he war on þe waye of wlonk wyȝeȝ þrynne.
If þay wer farande & fre & fayre to beholde,
Hit is eþe to leue by þe last ende;
For þe lede þat þer laye þe leueȝ an-vnder,

and goes toward them.

When he hade of hem syȝt he hyȝeȝ bylyue,
& as to god þe good mon gos hem agayneȝ
& haylsed hem in onhede & sayde, "hende lorde

[Fol. 65*b*.] He entreats them to rest awhile,

Ȝif euer þy mon vpon molde merit disserued,
Lenge a lyttel with þy lede I loȝly bi-seche;
Passe neuer fro þi pouere, ȝif I hit pray durst,
Er þou haf biden with þi burne & vnder boȝe rested;

that he may wash their feet.

& I schal wynne yow wyȝt of water a lyttel,
& fast aboute schal I fare your fette wer waschene;
Resteȝ here on þis rote & I schal rachche after

and bring them a morsel of bread.

& brynge a morsel of bred to banne your hertte."
"Fare forthe," quod þe frekeȝ, "& fech as þou seggeȝ;
By bole of þis brode tre we byde þe here."

Þenne orppedly in-to his hous he hyȝed to Saré
Comaunded hir to be cof & quyk at þis oneȝ;
"Þre metteȝ of mele menge & ma kakeȝ,
Vnder askeȝ ful hote happe hem byliue;
Quyl I fete sumquat fat þou þe fyr bete,
Prestly at þis ilke poynte sum polment to make."
He cached to his cobhous[1] & a calf bryngeȝ
Þat watȝ tender & not toȝe; bed tyrne of þe hyde,
& sayde to his seruaunt þat he hit seþe faste
& he deruely at his dome dyȝt hit bylyue.
Þe burne to be bare-heued buskeȝ hym þenne,
Clecheȝ to a clene cloþe & kesteȝ on þe grene,
Þrwe þryftyly þer-on þo þre þerue kakeȝ,
& bryngeȝ butter wyth-al, & by þe bred setteȝ
Mete; messeȝ of mylke he merkkeȝ bytwene,
Syþen potage & polment in plater honest;
As sewer in a god assyse he serued hem fayre,
Wyth sadde semblaunt & swete of such as he hade,
& god as a glad gest mad god chere,
Þat watȝ fayn of his frende & his fest praysed.
Abraham, al hodleȝ with armeȝ vp-folden,
Mynystred mete byfore þo men þat myȝtes al weldeȝ;
Þenne þay sayden, as þay sete samen alle þrynne,
When þe mete watȝ remued & þay of mensk speken,
"I schal efte here away abram," þay sayden,
"Ȝet er þy lyueȝ lyȝt leþe vpon erþe,
[Fol. 66a.] & þenne schal saré consayue & a sun bere,
Þat schal be abrahameȝ ayre, & after hym wynne
With wele & wyth worschyp þe worþely peple
Þat schal halde in heritage, þat I haf men ȝark."
Þenne þe burde byhynde þe dor for busmar laȝed;
& sayde sothly[2] to hir-self saré þe madde:
"May þou traw for tykle þat þou tonne moȝteȝ,
& I so hyȝe out of age & also my lorde,"
For soþely, as says þe wryt, he wern of sadde elde,
Boþe þe wyȝe & his wyf, such werk watȝ hem fayled,

Abraham commands Sarah to make some cakes quickly,

and tells his servant to seethe a tender kid.

Abraham appears bare-headed before his guests.

He casts a clean cloth on the green,

and sets before them cakes, butter, milk, and pottage.

God praises his friend's feast,

and after the meat is removed,

He tells Abraham that Sarah shall bear him a son.

Sarah, who is behind the door, laughs in unbelief.

[1] cov-hous = cow-house (?).

[2] ? softly or sotly = foolishly

Fro mony a brod day by-fore ho barayn ay byene,[1]
Þat selue saré with-outen sede in-to þat same tyme.

God tells Abraham that Sarah laughs at His words.

Þenne sayde oure syre þer he sete "se! so saré laȝes,
Not trawande þe tale þat I þe to schewed;
Hope3 ho o3t may be harde my honde3 to work?
& ȝet I a-vow verayly þe avaunt þat I made,
I schal ȝeply aȝayn & ȝelde þat I hyȝt,
& sothely sende to saré a soñ & an hayre."

Sarah denies that she laughed,

Þenne swenged forth saré & swer by hir trawþe,
Þat for lot þat þay lansed[2] ho laȝed neuer.
"Now innoghe hit is not so" þenne nurned þe dryȝtyn,
"For þou laȝed aloȝ, bot let we hit one."

Abraham's guests set out towards Sodom,

With þat þay ros vp radly as þay rayke schulde,
& setten toward sodamas her syȝt alle at-one3;
For þat Cite þer bysyde wat3 sette in a vale,

two miles from Mamre.

No myle3 fro mambre mo þen tweyne,
Where-so wonyed þis ilke wy3 þat wende3 with oure lorde,
For to tent hym with tale & teche hym þe gate,

The patriarch accompanies them.

Þen glyde3 forth god, þe godmon hym folȝe3.
Abraham helde3 hem wyth, hem to conueye,
In towarde þe Cety of sodamas þat synned had þenne
In þe faute of þis fylþe; þe fader hem þretes,
& sayde þus to þe segg þat sued hym after:

God determines to reveal to Abraham his secret purposes.

"How myȝt I hyde myn hert fro habraham þe trwe,
Þat I ne dyscouered to his corse my counsayl so dere.
Syþen he is chosen to be chef chyldryn fader,

[Fol. 66b.]

Þat so folk schal falle fro, to flete alle þe worlde,
& vche blod in þat burne blessed schal worþe.
Me bos telle to þat folk þe tene of my wylle
& alle myn atlyng to abraham vn-haspe bilyue.

IX.

He informs him of the destruction about to fall upon the cities of the plain,

The grete soun of sodamas synkke3 in myn ere3,
& þe gult of gomorre gare3 me to wrath;
I schal lyȝt in-to þat led & loke my seluen,
If[3] þay haf don as þe dyne dryue3 on-lofte,

[1] ? bycame.
[2] laused (?).
[3] MS. bif.

þay han lerned a lyst þat lykeȝ me ille,
for their great wickedness,
þat þay han founden in her flesch of fauteȝ þe werst,
Vch male matȝ his mach a man as hym seluen,
in abusing the gifts bestowed upon them.
& fylter folyly in fere, on femmaleȝ wyse.
I compast hem a kynde crafte & kende hit hem derne,
& amed hit in myn ordenaunce oddely dere,
The ordinance of marriage had been made for them,
& dyȝt drwry þer-inne, doole alþer-swettest,
& þe play of paramoreȝ I portrayed my seluen;
& made þer-to a maner myriest of oþer,
When two true togeder had tyȝed hem seluen,
By-twene a male & his make such merþe schulde conne;[1]
Wel nyȝe pure paradys moȝt preue no better,
Elleȝ þay moȝt honestly ayþer oþer welde.
At a stylle stollen steuen, vnstered wyth syȝt,
but they foully set it at nought.
Luf lowe hem bytwene lasched so hote,
The flame of love.
þat alle þe meschefeȝ on mold moȝt hit not sleke;
Now haf þay skyfted my skyl & scorned natwre,
& hentteȝ hem in heþyng an vsage vn-clene;
Therefore shall they be destroyed as an example to all men for ever.
Hem to smyte for þat smod smartly I þenk
þat wyȝeȝ schal be by hem war, worlde with-outen ende."
þenne arȝed abraham & alle his mod chaunge[d],
Abraham is full of fear,
For hope of þe harde hate þat hyȝt hatȝ oure lorde;
Al sykande he sayde "sir with yor leue,
and asks God whether the "sinful and the sinless" are to suffer together.
Schal synful & sakleȝ suffer al on payne;
Weþer euer hit lyke my lorde to lyfte such domeȝ,
þat þe wykked & þe worþy schal on wrake suffer,
& weye vpon þe worre half þat wrathed þe neuer?
þat watȝ neuer þy won þat wroȝteȝ vus alle.
[Fol. 67a.] Now fyfty fyn frendeȝ wer founde in ȝonde toune
Whether he will spare the cities provided fifty righteous are found in them?
In þe Cety of Sodamas & also gomorré
þat neuer lakked þy laue, bot loued ay trauþe,
& reȝt-ful wern & resounable & redy þe to serue,
Schal þay falle in þe faute þat oþer frekeȝ wroȝt
& ioyne to her iuggement her iuise to haue?
þat nas neuer þyn note, vnneuened hit worþe,
þat art so gaynly a god & of goste mylde!"

[1] *come* (?).

For the sake of fifty the cities shall be spared.

"Nay for fyfty," quod þe fader, "& þy fayre speche,
&[1] þay be founden in þat folk of her fylþe clene,
I schal for-gyue alle þe gylt þurȝ my grace one,
& let hem smolt al unsmyten smoþely atoneȝ."

[1] An (?).

The patriarch beseeches God to spare the city for the sake of forty-five righteous.

"AA! blessed be þow," quod þe burne, "so boner & þewed,
& al haldeȝ in þy honde, þe heuen & þe erþe,
Bot for I haf þis talke tatȝ to non ille,
ȝif I mele a lyttel more þat mul am & askeȝ;
What if fyue faylen of fyfty þe noumbre,
& þe remnaunt be reken, how restes þy wylle?"

For the lack of five the cities shall not be destroyed.

"And fyue wont of fyfty," quod god, "I schal forȝete alle
& wyth-halde my honde for hortyng on lede."
"& quat if faurty be fre & fauty þyse oþer
Schalt þow schortly al schende & schape non oþer."

For forty the cities shall be spared.

"Nay þaȝ faurty forfete ȝet fryst I a whyle,
& voyde away my vengaunce, þaȝ me vyl þynk."
Þen abraham obeched hym & loȝly him þonkkeȝ,
"Now sayned be þou sauiour, so symple in þy wrath!
I am bot erþe ful euel & vsle so blake,

Abraham entreats God's forbearance for his speech.

Forto mele wyth such a mayster as myȝteȝ hatȝ alle,
Bot I haue by-gonnen wyth my god, & he hit gayn þynkeȝ,
ȝif I for-loyne as a fol þy fraunchyse may serue;
What if þretty þryuande be þrad in ȝon touneȝ,
What schal I leue if my lorde, if he hem leþe wolde?"
Þenne þe godlych god gef hym onsware,

Thirty righteous, found in the cities, shall save them from destruction.

"ȝet for þretty in þrong I schal my þro steke,
& spare spakly of spyt in space of my þeweȝ,
& my rankor refrayne four þy reken wordeȝ."

[Fol. 67b.]

"What for twenty," quod þe tolke, "vntwyneȝ þou hem þenne?"
"Nay, ȝif þou ȝerneȝ hit, ȝet ȝark I hem grace;

For the sake of twenty guiltless ones God will release the rest.

If þat twenty be trwe I tene hem no more,
Bot relece alle þat regioun of her ronk werkkeȝ."
"Now aþel lorde," quod Abraham, "oneȝ a speche
& I schal schape no more þo schalkkeȝ to helpe;

If ten trysty *in* toune be tan *in* þi werkkeȝ
764 Wylt þou mese þy mode & menddy*ng* abyde?"
"I grau*n*t," q*uod* þe grete god, "grau*n*t mercy," þat oþ*er*.
& þe*n*ne arest þe renk & raȝt no fyrre;
& godde glydeȝ his gate by þose grene wayeȝ
768 & he co*n*ueyen hy*m* con w*ith* cast of his yȝe,
& als he loked along þere as oure lorde passed,
ȝet he cryed hy*m* aft*er* w*ith* careful steuen:
"Meke mayst*er* on þy mon to my*n*ne if þe lyked,
772 Loth lengeȝ *in* ȝon leede þat is my lef broþ*er*,
He sytteȝ þer *in* sodomis, þy seruau*n*t so pou*er*e
Among þo mansed men þat han þe much greued;
ȝif þou tyneȝ þat tou*n*, te*m*pre þyn yre
776 As þy mersy may malte þy meke to spare."
Þe*n* he wendeȝ, wendeȝ his way wepande for care
To-warde þe mere of mambre wepande for so[rȝe,][1]
& þere *in* longy*n*g al nyȝt he lengeȝ *in* wones,
780 Whyl þe sou*er*ayn to sodamas sende to spye.

Or if ten only should be found pure.

The patriarch intercedes for Lot.

Beseeches Him to "temper His ire,"

and then departs weeping for sorrow.

[1] *sorewe* is written by a late hand over the original word.

X.

His sondes *in*-to sodamas watȝ sende *in* þat tyme,
I*n* þat ilk euentyde, by au*n*gels tweyne,
Meuand meuande[2] mekely togeder as myry me*n* ȝonge,
784 As loot *in* a loge dor lened hy*m* alone,
I*n* a porche of þat place pyȝt to þe ȝat*es*,
Þat watȝ ryal & ryche, so watȝ þe renk*es* seluen.
As he stared *in*-to þe strete þ*er* stout men played
788 He syȝe þer swey *in* asent swete men tweyne;
Bolde burneȝ wer þay boþe w*ith* berdles chy*n*neȝ,
Royl rollande fax to raw sylk lyke,
Of ble as þe brere flo*ur* where-so þe bare scheweed,
792 Ful clene watȝ þe cou*n*tenau*n*ce of her cler yȝen;
[Fol. 68a.] Wlonk whit watȝ her wede & wel hit hem semed.
Of alle fetureȝ ful fyn & fautleȝ boþe;
Watȝ non autly *in* ouþ*er*, for aungels hit wern,

God's messengers go to Sodom.

[2] So in MS.

Lot is sitting alone at the "door of his lodge."

Staring into the street he sees two men.

Beardless chins they had,

and hair like raw silk.

Beautifully white were their weeds.

& þat þe ȝep vnder-ȝede þat in þe ȝate syttеȝ.

Lot runs to meet them.

He ros vp ful radly & ran hem to mete
& loȝe he louteȝ hem to, loth, to þe grounde,
& syþen soberly [satȝ] "syreȝ I yow by-seche,

Invites them to remain awhile in his house,

Þat ȝe wolde lyȝt at my loge & lenge þer-inne,
Comeȝ to your knaues kote I craue at þis oneȝ;

and in the morning they may take their way.

I schal fette yow a fatte your fette forto wasche;
I norne yow bot for on nyȝt neȝe me to lenge,
& in þe myry mornyng ȝe may your waye take."
& þay nay þat þay nolde neȝ no howseȝ,
Bot stylly þer in þe strete as þay stadde wern,
Þay wolde lenge þe long naȝt & logge þer-oute;
Hit watȝ hous innoȝe to hem þe heuen vpon lofte.

Lot invites them so long that at last they comply.

Loth laþed so longe wyth luflych wordeȝ,
Þat þay hym graunted to go & gruȝt no lenger.
Þe bolde to his byggyng bryngeȝ hem bylyue,

The wife and daughters of Lot welcome their visitors.

Þat ryally [watȝ] arayed, for he watȝ ryche euer.
Þe wyȝeȝ wern welcom as þe wyf couþe,
His two dere doȝtereȝ deuoutly hem haylsed,
Þat wer maydeneȝ ful meke, maryed not ȝet,
& þay wer semly & swete, & swyþe wel arayed.

Lot admonishes his men to prepare the meat,

Loth þenne ful lyȝtly lokeȝ hym aboute,
& his men amonestes mete forto dyȝt,

and to serve no salt with it.

Bot þenkkeȝ on hit be þrefte what þynk[1] so ȝe make,
For wyth no sour[2] ne no salt serueȝ hym neuer.
Bot ȝet I wene þat þe wyf hit wroth[3] to dyspyt,
& sayde softely to hir self "þis vn-sauere[4] hyne
Loueȝ no salt in her sauce ȝet hit no skyl were
Þat oþer burne be boute þaȝ boþe be nyse."

Lot's wife disregards the injunction.

Þenne ho sauereȝ with salt her seueȝ vchone
Agayne þe bone of þe burne þat hit forboden hade,
& als ho scelt hem in scorne þat wel her skyl knewen.
Why watȝ ho wrech so wod, ho wrathed oure lorde!

[Fol. 68b.] The guests are well entertained.

Þenne seten þay at þe soper, wern serued by-lyue,
Þe gestes gay & ful glad, of glam debonere,
Welawynnely wlonk tyl þay waschen hade,

[1] þyng (?).
[2] savour (?).
[3] wroȝt (?).
[4] MS. vn-fauere.

þe trest*es* tylt to þe woȝe & þe table boþe.
Fro þe seggeȝ haden souped & seten bot a whyle,
Er eu*er* þay bosked to bedde þe borȝ watȝ al vp;
Alle þat weppen myȝt welde, þe wakker & þe stronger,
To vmbe-lyȝe lotheȝ hous þe ledeȝ to take,
In grete flokkeȝ of folk, þay fallen to his ȝateȝ,
As a scowte-wach scarred, so þe assery rysed;
Wit*h* kene clobbeȝ of þat clos þay clatȝ on þe woweȝ,
& wyth a schrylle scharp schout þay schewe þyse worde:
"If þ*ou* louyeȝ þy lyf loth i*n* þyse woneȝ
ȝete vu*s* out þose ȝong men þat ȝore-whyle here entred,
þat we may lere hym[1] of lof, as oure lyst biddeȝ,
As is þe asyse of Sodomas to seggeȝ þ*at* passen."
Whatt! þay sputen & speken of so spitou*s* fylþe,
What! þay ȝeȝed & ȝolped of ȝestande sorȝe,
þat ȝet þe wynd, & þe weder, & þe worlde stynk*es*
Of þe brych þat vp-braydeȝ þose broþelych wordeȝ.
þe god man glyfte wit*h* þ*at* glam & gloped for noyse,
So scharpe schame to hy*m* schot, he schrank at þe hert,
For he knew þe costou*m* þat kyþed þose wrecheȝ,
He doted neu*er* for no doel so depe i*n* his my*n*de.
Allas! sayd hy*m* þe*n*ne loth, & lyȝtly he ryseȝ
& boweȝ forth fro þe bench i*n*-to þe brode ȝat*es*.
What! he wonded no woþe of wekked knaueȝ,
þat he ne passed þe port þe p*er*il[2] to abide.
He went forthe at þe wyket & waft hit hy*m* aft*er*,
þat a clyket hit cleȝt clos hy*m* byhynde.
þe*n*ne he meled to þo men mesurable wordeȝ,
For harloteȝ wit*h* his hendelayk he hoped to chast;
"Oo! my frendeȝ so fre, you*r* fare is to strange,
Dotȝ away you*r* derf dyn & dereȝ neu*er* my gest*es*,
Avoy! hit is you*r* vylaynye, ȝe vylen you*r* seluen;
&[3] ȝe ar iolyf gentylmen you*r* iapes ar ille.
[Fol. 69*a*.] Bot I schal ke*n*ne yow by kynde a crafte þat is bett*er*;
I haf a tresor i*n* my telde of tow my fayre deȝt*er*,
þat ar maydeneȝ vnmard for alle men ȝette;

But before they go to rest the city is up in arms.

With "keen clubs" the folk clatter on the walls,

and demand that Lot should deliver up his guests.

The wind yet stinks with their filthy speech.

Lot is in great trouble.

He leaves his guests

and addresses the Sodomites.

He offers to give up to them his two daughters.

[1] *hem* (?).

[2] MS. *p'il*.

[3] *And* = *An* (?).

In sodamas, þaȝ I hit say, non semloker burdes,
Hit arn ronk, hit arn rype & redy to manne;
To samen wyth þo semly þe solace is better,
I schal biteche yow þo two þat tayt arn & quoynt,
& laykeȝ wyth hem as yow lyst & leteȝ my gestes one."

The rebels raise a great noise,

Þenne þe rebaudeȝ so ronk rerd such a noyse,
Þat aȝly hurled in his ereȝ her harloteȝ speche;

and ask who made him a justice to judge their deeds,

"Wost þou not wel þat þou woneȝ here a wyȝe strange,
An out-comlyng, a carle, we kylle of þyn heued.
Who Ioyned þe be iostyse oure iapeȝ to blame,

who was but a boy when he came to Sodom.

Þat com a boy to þis borȝ, þaȝ þou be burne ryche?"
Þus þay þrobled & þrong & þrwe vmbe his ereȝ,
& distresed hym wonder strayt, with strenkþe in þe prece,

The young men bring Lot within doors,

Bot þat þe ȝonge men, so ȝepe, ȝornen þer-oute,
Wapped vpon þe wyket & wonnen hem tylle,
& by þe hondeȝ hym hent & horyed hym with-inne,
& steken þe ȝates ston-harde wyth stalworth barreȝ.

and smite those outside with blindness.

Þay blwe a boffet in blande þat banned peple,
Þat þay blustered as blynde as bayard watȝ euer;

In vain they try to find the door of Lot's house.

Þay lest of loteȝ logging any lysoun to fynde,
Bot nyteled þer alle þe nyȝt for noȝt at þe last;
Þenne vch tolke tyȝt hem þat hade of tayt fayled,
& vchon roþeled to þe rest þat he reche moȝt;
Bot þay wern wakned al wrank[1] þat þer in won lenged,
Of on þe vglokest vnhap þat euer on erd suffred.

[1] *wrang* (?).

XI.

Early in the morning the angels command Lot to depart from Sodom,

Ruddon of þe day-rawe ros vpon vȝten,
When merk of þe mydnyȝt moȝt no more last,
Ful erly þose aungeleȝ þis haþel þay ruþen
& glopnedly on godeȝ halue gart hym vpryse,
Fast þe freke ferkeȝ vp ful ferd at his hert;
Þay comaunded hym cof to cach þat he hade,

with his wife and two daughters,

"Wyth þy wyf & þy wyȝeȝ & þy wlonc deȝtters,
For we laþe þe, sir loth, þat þou þy lyf haue;

[Fol. 63b.]

Cayre tid of þis kythe er combred þou worþe,

With alle þi here vpon haste, tyl þou a hil fynde;
Foundeȝ faste on your fete, bifore your face lokes,
Bot bes neuer so bolde to blusch yow bihynde,
& loke ȝe stemme no stepe, bot strecheȝ on faste,
Til ȝe reche to a reset, rest ȝe neuer;
For we schal tyne þis toun & trayþely disstrye,
Wyth alle þise wyȝeȝ so wykke wyȝtly de-voyde
& alle þe londe with þise ledeȝ we losen at oneȝ,
Sodomas schal ful sodenly synk in-to grounde,
& þe grounde of gomorre gorde in-to helle,
& vche a koste of þis kythe clater vpon hepes.
Þen laled loth, "lorde what is best?
If I me fele vpon fote þat I fle moȝt,
Hov schulde I huyde me fro hem þat hatȝ his hate kynned,
In þe brath of his breth þat brenneȝ alle þinkeȝ,[1]
To crepe fro my creatour & know not wheder,
Ne wheþer his fooschip me folȝeȝ bifore oþer bihynde?"
Þe freke sayde "no foschip oure fader hatȝ þe schewed,
Bot hiȝly heuened þi hele fro hem þat arn combred:
Nov walle þe a wonnyng þat þe warisch myȝt,
& he schal saue hit for þy sake þat hatȝ vus sende hider,
For þou art oddely þyn one out of þis fylþe,
& als Abraham þyn em[2] hit at him self asked."
"Lorde, loued he worþe," quod loth, "vpon erþe!
Þen is a cite herbisyde þat segor hit hatte,
Here vtter on a rounde hil hit houeȝ hit one,
I wolde, if his wylle wore, to þat won scape."
"Þenn fare forth," quod þat fre, "& fyne þou neuer
With þose ilk þat þow wylt þat þrenge þe after,
& ay goande on your gate, wyth-outen agayn-tote,
For alle þis londe schal be lorne, longe er þe sonne rise."
Þe wyȝe wakened his wyf & his wlonk deȝteres,
& oþer two myri men þo maydeneȝ schulde wedde;
& þay token hit as tyt & tented hit lyttel,
Þaȝ fast laþed hem loth, þay leȝen ful stylle.

and to look straight before him,

for Sodom and Gomorrah shall be destroyed.

Lot asks what is best to be done,

that he may escape.

He is told to choose himself a dwelling which shall be saved from destruction.

He chooses Zoar.

The angels command Lot to depart quickly.

He wakes his wife and daughters.

[1] þingeȝ.

[2] broþer is written over in a later hand.

[Fol. 70a.]
All four are hastened on by the angels,

Þe aungeleȝ hasted þise oþer & aȝly hem þratten,
& enforsed alle fawre forth at þe ȝateȝ,
Þo wern loth & his lef, his luflyche deȝter,
Þer soȝt no mo to sauement of cities aþel fyue.

who "preach to them the peril" of delay."

Þise aungeleȝ hade hem by hande out at þe ȝateȝ,
Prechande hem þe perile, & beden hem passe fast.
"Lest ȝe be taken in þe teche of tyraunteȝ here,
Loke ȝe bowe now bi bot, boweȝ fast hence!"

Before daylight Lot comes to a hill.

& þay kayre-ne con & kenely flowen;
Erly, er any heuen glem, þay to a hil comen.

God aloft raises a storm.

Þe grete god in his greme bygynneȝ onlofte;
To wakan wedereȝ so wylde þe wyndeȝ he calleȝ,
& þay wroþely vp-wafte & wrastled togeder,
Fro fawre half of þe folde, flytande loude.
Clowdeȝ clustered bytwene kesten vp torres,
Þat þe þik þunder þrast þirled hem ofte.

A rain falls thick of fire and sulphur.

Þe rayn rueled adoun, ridlande þikke,
Of felle flaunkes of fyr & flakes of soufre,
Al in smolderande smoke smachande ful ille,
Swe[1] aboute sodamas & hit sydeȝ alle,

[1] *Sweyed* (?).

Upon the four cities it comes,

Gorde to gomorra þat þe grounde lansed;
Abdama & syboym, þise ceteis alle faure,
Al birolled wyth þe rayn, rostted & brenned,

and frightens all folks therein.

& ferly flayed þat folk þat in þose fees lenged;
For when þat þe helle herde þe houndeȝ of heuen
He watȝ ferlyly fayn, vnfolded bylyue.

The great bars of the abyss do burst.

Þe grete barreȝ of þe abyme he barst vp at oneȝ,
Þat alle þe regioun to-rof in riftes ful grete,

Cliffs cleave asunder.

& clouen alle in lyttel cloutes þe clyffeȝ aywhere,
As lance leueȝ of þe boke þat lepes in twynne.

The cities sink to hell.

Þe brethe of þe brynston bi þat hit blende were,
Al þo citees & her sydes sunkken to helle.
Rydelles wern þo grete rowtes of renkkes with-inne,
When þay wern war of þe wrake þat no wyȝe achaped,

Such a cry arises that the clouds clatter again.

Such a ȝomerly ȝarm of ȝellyng þer rysed;
Þer-of clatered þe cloudes þat kryst myȝt haf rawþe.

[Fol. 70b.] Þe segge herde þat soun to segor þat ȝede,
& þe wenches hym wyth þat by þe way folȝed;
Ferly ferde watȝ her flesch, þat flowen ay ilyche,
Trynande ay a hyȝe trot þat torne neuer dorsten.

Lot and his companions are frightened,

Loth & þo luly-whit his lefly two deȝter,
Ay folȝed here face, bifore her boþe yȝen;
Bot þe balleful burde, þat neuer bode keped,
Blusched by-hynden her bak, þat bale forto herkken;
Hit watȝ lusty lothes wyf þat ouer he[r] lyfte schulder.
Ones ho bluschet to þe burȝe, bot bod ho no lenger,
Þat ho nas stadde a stiffe ston, a stalworth image
Al so salt as ani se & so ho ȝet standeȝ.

but continue to follow their face.

Lot's wife looks behind her,

and is turned to a stiff stone "as salt as any sea."

Þay slypped bi & syȝe hir not þat wern hir samen feres,
Tyl þay in segor wern sette, & sayned our lorde;
Wyth lyȝt loueȝ vplyfte þay loued hym swyþe,
Þat so his seruauntes wolde see & saue of such woþe.

Her companions do not miss her till they reach Zoar.

Al watȝ dampped & don, & drowned by þenne;
Þe ledeȝ of þat lyttel toun wern lopen out for drede,
In-to þat malscrande mere, marred bylyue,
Þat noȝt saued watȝ bot segor þat sat on a lawe,
Þe þre ledeȝ þer-in, loth & his deȝter;
For his make watȝ myst, þat on þe mount lenged
In a stonen statue þat salt sauor habbes,
For two fautes þat þe fol watȝ founde in mistrauþe;
On, ho serued at þe soper salt bifore dryȝtyn
& syþen, ho blusched hir bihynde, þaȝ hir forboden were;
For on ho standes a ston, & salt for þat oþer,
& alle lyst on hir lik þat arn on launde bestes.

By this time all were drowned.

The people of Zoar, for dread, rush into the sea and are destroyed.

Only Zoar with three therein (Lot and his daughters) are saved.

Lot's wife is an image of salt for two faults:
1. She served salt before the Lord at supper.
2. She looked behind her.

Abraham ful erly watȝ vp on þe morne,
Þat alle naȝt [so] much niye hade no mon in his hert,
Al in longing for loth leyen in a wache,
Þer he lafte hade oure lorde, he is on lofte wonnen;
He sende toward sodomas þe syȝt of his yȝen,
Þat euer hade ben an erde of erþe þe swettest
As aparaunt to paradis þat plantted þe dryȝtyn,

Abraham is up full early on the morn.

He looks towards Sodom,

> now only a pit filled with pitch, [Fol. 71*a*.] from which rise smoke, ashes and cinders, as from a furnace.

Nov is hit plu*n*ged i*n* a pit like of pich fylled.
Suche a roþu*n* of a reche ros fro þe blake,
Aske3 vpe i*n* þe ayre & vselle3 þer flowen,
As a fornes ful of flot þat vpon fyr boyles,
When bry3t bre*n*nande bronde3 ar bet þ*er* an-vnder.
Þis wat3 a uengau*n*ce violent þat voyded þise places,
Þat fou*n*dered hat3 so fayr a folk & þe folde sonkken.

> A sea now occupies the place of the four cities.

Þer faur*e* citees wern set, nov is a see called,
Þat ay is drouy & dym, & ded i*n* hit kynde,
Blo, blubrande, & blak, vnblyþe to ne3e,

> It is a stinking pool,

As a stynkande stanc þat stryed sy*n*ne,
Þat eu*er* of sy*n*ne & of smach, smart is to fele;

> and is called the Dead Sea.

For-þy þe derk dede see hit is demed eu*er* more,
For hit dede3 of deþe duren þere 3et.
For hit is brod & boþe*m*le3, & bitter as þe galle,

> Nothing may live in it.

& no3t may lenge i*n* þat lake þat any lyf bere3,
& alle þe coste3 of kynde hit combre3 vchone;

> Lead floats on its surface.

For lay þ*er*-on a lump of led & hit on loft flete3,

> A feather sinks to the bottom of it.

& folde þ*er*-on a ly3t fyþ*er* & hit to fou*n*s synkke3.
& þ*er* wat*er* may walt*er* to wete any erþe,

> Lands, watered by this sea, never bear grass or weed.

Schal neu*er* grene þ*er*-on growe, gresse ne wod nawþ*er*.
If any schalke to be schent wer schowued þ*er*-i*n*ne,
Þa3 he bode i*n* þat boþe*m* broþely a monyth,

> A man cannot be drowned in it.

He most ay lyue i*n* þat lo3e i*n* losy*n*g eu*er*-more,
& neu*er* dry3e no dethe, to dayes of ende;
& as hit is corsed of kynde & hit cooste3 als,

> The clay clinging to it is corrosive,

Þe clay þat clenges þ*er*-by arn corsyes strong,

> as alum, alkaran, sulphur, etc.,
> [1] *alkatran* (?).
> [2] *augre* = *aigre* (?).
> [3] *spinnande* (?).

As alu*m* & alkaran,[1] þat angré[2] arn boþe,
Soufre sou*r*, & sau*n*dyu*er*, & oþ*er* such mony;
& þer walte3 of þat wat*er* in waxlokes grete,
Þe spuniande[3] aspaltou*n* þat spysere3 sellen;
& suche is alle þe soyle by þat se halues,

> which fret the flesh and fester the bones.
> [4] *festres* (?).

Þat fel fretes þe flesch & festred[4] bones.

> On the shores of this lake grow trees bearing fair fruits,

& þer ar tres by þat terne of trayto*ur*es;
& þay borgoune3 & beres blome3 ful fayre,
& þe fayrest fryt þat may on folde growe,

1044 As orenge & oþer fryt & apple garnade
[Fol. ib.] Also red & so ripe & rychely hwed,
As any dom myȝt deuice of dayntyeȝ oute ;
Bot quen hit is brused oþer broken, oþer byten in twynne,
1048 No worldeȝ goud hit wyth-inne, bot wydowande[1] askes ;
Alle þyse ar teches & tokenes to trow vpon ȝet,
& wittnesse of þat wykked werk & þe wrake after,
Þat oure fader forferde for fylþe of þose ledes.
1052 Þenne vch wyȝe may wel wyt þat he þe wlonk louies,
& if he louyes clene layk þat is oure lorde ryche,
& to be couþe in his courte þou coueytes þenne
To se þat semly in sete & his swete face,
1056 Clerrer counseyl, counsayl con I non, bot þat þou clene worþe.
For clopyngnel in þe compas of his clene rose,
Þer he expouneȝ a speche, to hym þat spede wolde,
Of a lady to be loued, loke to hir sone,
1060 Of wich beryng þat ho be, & wych ho best louyes,
& be ryȝt such in vch a borȝe of body & of dedes,
& folȝ þe fet of þat fere þat þou fre haldes.
& if þou wyrkkes on þis wyse, þaȝ ho wyk were,
1064 Hir schal lyke þat layk þat lyknes hir tylle.
If þou wyl dele drwrye wyth dryȝtyn þenne,
& lelly louy þy lorde & his leef worþe.
Þenne confourme þe to kryst, & þe clene make,
1068 Þat euer is polyced als playn as þe perle seluen.
For loke fro fyrst þat he lyȝt with-inne þe lel mayden !
By how comly a kest he watȝ clos þere,
When venkkyst watȝ no vergynyté, ne vyolence maked,
1072 Bot much clener watȝ hir corse, god kynned þerinne ;
& efte when he borne watȝ in beþelen þe ryche,
In wych puryté þay departed ; þaȝ þay pouer were,
Watȝ neuer so blysful a bour as watȝ abos[2] þenne
1076 Ne no schroude hous so schene as a schepon þare,
Ne non so glad vnder god as ho þat grone schulde ;

which, when broken or bitten, taste like ashes.

All these are tokens of wickedness and vengeance.

God loves the pure in heart.

Strive to be clean.

Jean de Meun tells how a lady is to be loved.

By doing what pleases her best.

Love thy Lord !

Conform to Christ,

who is polished as a pearl.

By how comely a contrivance did he enter the womb of the virgin !

In what purity did he part from her !

No abode was better than his.

[1] MS. wyndowande.

[2] abof (?).

The sorrow of childbirth was turned to joy.

For þer watȝ seknesse al sou*n*de þat sarrest is halden,
& þer watȝ rose reflayr where rote hatȝ ben eu*er*,
& þer watȝ solace & songe wher sorȝ hatȝ ay cryed;

[Fol. 72*a*.] Angels solaced the virgin with organs and pipes.

For au*n*gelles w*ith* i*n*strumentes of organes & pypes,
& rial ry*n*gande rotes & þe reken fyþel,
& alle hende þat honestly moȝt an hert glade,
Aboutte my lady watȝ lent, quen ho delyu*er* were.

The child Christ was so clean that ox and ass worshipped him.

Þe*n*ne watȝ her blyþe barne burnyst so clene,
Þat boþe þe ox & þe asse hym hered at-ones;
Þay knewe hy*m* by his clannes for ky*n*g of nature,
For non so clene of such a clos com neu*er* er þe*n*ne;
& ȝif clanly he þe*n*ne com, ful cortays þ*er*-aft*er*,

He hated wickedness, and would never touch ought that was vile.

Þat alle þat longed to luþ*er* ful lodly he hated;
By nobleye of his norture he nolde neu*er* towche
Oȝt þat watȝ vngoderly oþ*er* ordure watȝ i*n*ne.
Ȝet comen lodly to þat lede, as laȝares monye,

Yet there came to him lazars and lepers, lame and blind. Dry and dropsical folk.

Su*m*me lepre, su*m*me lome, & lom*er*ande blynde,
Poysened & parlatyk & pyned i*n* fyres,
Drye folk & ydropike, & dede at þe laste;
Alle called on þat cortayse & claymed his *gra*ce.

He healed all with kind speech.

He heled hem wyth hynde speche of þat þay ask aft*er*,
For what-so he towched also-tyd tou*r*ned to hele,
Wel cla*n*ner þen any crafte cowþe devyse;
So clene watȝ his hondely*n*g vche ordure hit schonied,

His handling was so good, that he needed no knife to cut or carve with.

& þe gropy*n*g so goud of god & man boþe,
Þat for fetys of his fyngeres fonded he neu*er*
Nauþ*er* to cout[1] ne to kerue, w*ith* knyf ne wyth egge,

The bread he broke more perfectly than could all the tools of Toulouse.

For-þy brek he þe bred blades wyth-outen;
For hit ferde freloker i*n* fete i*n* his fayre honde,
Displayed more pryuyly when he hit part schulde,
Þe*n*ne alle þe toles of tolowse moȝt tyȝt hit to kerue,

How can we approach his court except we be clean?

Þ*us* is he kyryou*s* & clene þat þou his cort askes;
Hov schulde þou com to his kyth bot if þou clene were?
Nov ar we sore & synful & sov[*er*]ly[2] vch one,
How schulde we se, þe*n* may we say, þat syre vpon throne?

[1] *cut* (?).

[2] MS. *sovly*.

ȝis, þat mayster is mercyable; þaȝ þou be man fenny, *God is merciful.*
& al to-marred in myre whyl þou on molde lyuyes,
þou may schyne þurȝ schryfte, þaȝ þou haf schome serued, *Through penance we may shine as a pearl.*
& pure þe with penaunce tyl þou a perle worþe.
[Fol. 72b.] Perle praysed is prys, þer perre is schewed, *Why is the pearl so prized?*
þaȝ hym not derrest be demed to dele for penies,
Quat may þe cause be called, bot for hir clene hwes,
þat wynnes worschyp, abof alle whyte stones?
For ho schynes so schyr þat is of schap rounde,
Wyth-outen faut oþer fylþe ȝif ho fyn were;
& wax euer in þe worlde in weryng so olde, *She becomes none the worse for wear.*
ȝet þe perle payres not whyle ho in pyese lasttes
& if hit cheue þe chaunce vncheryst ho worþe, *If she should become dim, wash her in wine.*
þat ho blyndes of ble in bour þer ho lygges,
No-bot wasch hir wyth wourchyp in wyn as ho askes,
Ho by kynde schal be-com clerer þen are; *She then becomes clearer than before.*
So if folk be defowled by vnfre chaunce,
þat he be sulped in sawle, seche to schryfte *So may the sinner polish him by penance.*
& he may polyce hym at þe prest, by penaunce taken,
Wel bryȝter þen þe beryl oþer browden perles.
Bot war þe wel, if þou be waschen wyth water of schryfte, *Beware of returning to sin.*
& polysed als playn as parchmen schauen,
Sulp no more þenne in synne þy saule þer-after,
For þenne þou dryȝtyn dyspleses with dedes ful sore, *For then God is more displeased than ever.*
& entyses hym to tene more trayþly þen euer
& wel hatter to hate þen hade þou not waschen;
For when a sawele is saȝtled & sakred to dryȝtyn, *The reconciled soul God holds as His own.*
He holly haldes hit his & haue hit he wolde,
þenne efte lastes hit likkes, he loses hit ille,
As hit were rafte wyth vn-ryȝt & robbed wyth þewes.[1] *Ill deeds rob Him of it.*
War þe þenne for þe wrake, his wrath is achaufed,
For þat þat ones watȝ his schulde efte be vn-clene, *God forbids us to defile any vessels used in His service.*
þaȝ hit be bot a bassyn, a bolle, oþer a scole,
A dysche oþer a dobler þat dryȝtyn oneȝ serued,

[1] *þeues.* (?).

To defowle hit euer vpon folde fast he for-bedes,
So is he scoymus of scaþe þat scylful is euer.

In Belshazzar's time, the defiling of God's vessels brought wrath upon the king.

& þat watȝ bared in babyloyn in Baltaȝar tyme,
Hov harde vnhap þer hym hent & hastyly sone,
For he þe vessellees avyled þat vayled in þe temple
In seruyse of þe souerayn sum tyme byfore.

[Fol. 73a.]

ȝif ȝe wolde tyȝt me a tom telle hit I wolde,
Hov charged more watȝ his chaunce þat hem cherych nolde
Þen his fader forloyne þat feched hem wyth strenþe,
& robbed þe relygioun of relykes alle.

XII.

Daniel in his prophecies tells of the destruction of the Jews.

Danyel in his dialokeȝ de-vysed sum tyme,
As ȝet is proued ex-presse in his profecies,
Hov þe gentryse of Iuise & Iherusalem þe ryche
Watȝ disstryed wyth distres, & drawen to þe erþe,

For their unfaithfulness

For þat folke in her fayth watȝ founden vntrwe,
Þat haden hyȝt þe hyȝe god to halde of hym euer;
& he hem halȝed for his & help at her nede
In mukel meschefes mony, þat meruayl [is] to here;

in following other gods,

& þay forloyne her fayth & folȝed oþer goddes,

God allowed the heathen to destroy them,

& þat wakned his wrath & wrast hit so hyȝe,
Þat he fylsened þe faythful in þe falce lawe
To for-fare þe falce in þe faythe trwe;

in the reign of Zedekiah,

Hit watȝ sen in þat syþe þat ȝedechyas[1] rengned,
In Iuda, þat iustised þe iuyne kynges.
He sete on Salamones solie, on solemne wyse,

who practised idolatry.

Bot of leaute he watȝ lat to his lorde hende:
He vsed abominaciones of idolatrye,
& lette lyȝt bi þe lawe þat he watȝ lege tylle;
For-þi oure fader vpon folde a foman hym wakned,

Nebuchadnezzar becomes his foe.

Nabigo-de-noȝar nuyed hym swyþe
He pur-sued in to palastyn with proude men mony,
& þer he wast wyth[2] werre þe wones of þorpes.
He herȝed vp alle israel & hent of þe beste,

He besieges Jerusalem, and

& þe gentylest of Iudee in Ierusalem biseged,

[1] MS. *ȝedethyas*.

[2] MS. *wyth with*.

Vmbe-walt alle þe walles wyth wyȝes ful stronge,
At vche a dor a doȝty duk, & dutte hem wyth-*inne*;
For þe borȝ watȝ so bygge baytayled alofte,
& stoffed wyth-*inne* w*ith* stout men to stalle hem
þ*er*-oute.
þ*enne* watȝ þe sege sette þe Cete aboute,
Skete skarmoch skelt, much skaþe lached;
At vch brugge a berfray on basteles wyse,
þat seuen syþe vch a day asayled þe ȝates,
Trwe tulkkes i*n* tou*res* teueled wyth-*inne*,
In bigge brutage of borde, bulde on þe walles;
þay feȝt & þay fende of, & fylt*er* togeder
Til two ȝer ou*er*-torned, ȝet tok þay hit neu*er*.
At þe laste vpon longe, þo ledes wyth-*inne*,
Faste fayled hem þe fode, enfaminied monie;
þe hote hunger wyth-*inne* hert hem wel sarre,
þen any dunt of þat douthe þat dowelled þ*er*-oute.
þ*enne* wern þo rowtes redles i*n* þo ryche wones,
Fro þat mete watȝ myst, megre þay wexen,
& þay stoken so strayt, þ*at* þay ne stray myȝt
A fote fro þat forselet to forray no goudes.
þ*enne* þe ky*n*g of þe kyth a cou*n*sayl hy*m* takes,
Wyth þe best of his burnes, a blench forto make;
þay stel out on a stylle nyȝt er any steuen rysed,
& harde hurles þurȝ þe oste, er enmies hit wyste,
Bot er þay at-wappe ne moȝt þe wach wyth-oute,
Hiȝe skelt watȝ þe askry þe skewes an-vnder,
Loude alarom vpon lau*n*de lulted watȝ þ*enne*;
Ryche, ruþed of her rest, ran to here wedes,
Hard hattes þay hent & on hors lepes;
Cler claryou*n* crak cryed onlofte.
By þat watȝ alle on a hepe hurlande swyþee,
Folȝande þat oþ*er* flote, & fonde hem bilyue,
Ou*er*-tok hem, as tyd, tult hem of sadeles,
Tyl vche prynce hade his per put to þe grou*n*de;
& þer watȝ þe ky*n*g kaȝt wyth calde pry*n*ces,

surrounds the walls.

The city is stuffed full of men.

Brisk is the skirmish.

[Fol. 73*b*.]

Seven times a day are the gates assailed.

For two years the fight goes on, yet the city is not taken.

The folk within are in want of food.

Meager they become.

For so shut up are they that escape seems impossible.

But on a quiet night they steal out,

and rush through the host.

They are discovered by the enemy.

A loud alarm is given.

They are pursued

and overtaken.

Their king is made prisoner.

& alle hise gentyle for-iusted on ierico playnes,
His chief men are presented as prisoners to Nebuchadnezzar.
& presented wern as presoneres to þe prynce rychest,
Nabigo-de-noȝar noble in his chayer,
& he þe faynest freke þat he his fo hade,
& speke spitously hem to & spylt þerafter.
His sons are slain. His own eyes are put out. He is placed in a dungeon in Babylon. [Fol. 74a.]
Þe kynges sunnes in his syȝt he slow euer vch one,
& holkked out his auen yȝen heterly boþe
& bede þe burne to be broȝt to babyloyn þe ryche,
& þere in dongoun be don to dreȝe þer his wyrdes.
Now se, so þe soueray[n] set hatȝ his wrake;
Nas hit not for nabugo ne his noble nauþer,
Þat oþer depryued watȝ of pryde with paynes stronge,
All for his "bad bearing" against the Lord, who might otherwise have been his friend.
Bot for his beryng so badde agayn his blyþe lorde;
For hade þe fader ben his frende þat hym bifore keped,
Ne neuer trespast to him in teche of mysseleue.
To Colde wer alle Calde & kythes of ynde,
Ȝet take torkye hem wyth her tene hade ben little;
Nebuchadnezzar ceased not until he had destroyed Jerusalem.
Ȝet nolde neuer nabugo þis ilke note leue,
Er he hade tuyred þis toun & torne hit to grounde;
He ioyned vnto Ierusalem a gentyle duc þenne,
Nebuzaradan was "chief of the chivalry."
His name watȝ nabu-ȝardan, to noye þe iues;
He watȝ myster of his men & myȝty him seluen,
Þe chef of his cheualrye his chekkes to make,
He brek þe bareres as bylyue, & þe burȝ after,
& enteres in ful ernestly, in yre of his hert.
What! þe maysterry watȝ mene, þe men wern away,
The best men were taken out of the city.
Þe best boȝed wyth þe burne þat þe borȝ ȝemed;
& þo þat byden wer so[1] biten with þe bale hunger,
Þat on wyf hade ben worþe þe welgest fourre;
Nevertheless Nebuzaradan spared not those left.
Nabiȝardan noȝt for-þy nolde not spare,
Bot bede al to þe bronde vnder bare egge.
Þay slowen of swettest semlych burdes,
Brains of bairns were spilt.
Baþed barnes in blod & her brayn spylled;
Priests pressed to death.
Prestes & prelates þay presed to deþe,
Wives and wenches foully killed.
Wyues & wenches her wombes tocoruen,
Þat her boweles out-borst aboute þe diches,

[1] The MS. reads *fo*.

& al watȝ carfully kylde þat þay cach myȝt,
& alle [þat] swypped vnswolȝed of þe sworde kene,
þay wer cagged & kaȝt on capeles al bare,
Festned fettres to her fete vnder fole wombes,
& broþely broȝt to babyloyn þer bale to suffer,
To sytte in seruage & syte; þat sumtyme wer gentyle,
Now ar chaunged to chorles & charged wyth werkkes,
Boþe to cayre at þe kart & þe kuy mylke,
þat sumtyme sete in her sale syres & burdes.
& ȝet nabuȝardan nyl neuer stynt,
Er he to þe tempple tee wyth his tulkkes alle;
Betes on þe barers, brestes vp þe ȝates,
Slouen alle at a slyp þat serued þer-inne,
Pulden prestes bi þe polle & plat of her hedes,
Diȝten dekenes to deþe, dungen doun clerkkes,
& alle þe maydenes of þe munster maȝtyly hokyllen
Wyth þe swayf of þe sworde þat swolȝed hem alle.
þenne ran þay to þe relykes as robbors wylde,
& pyled alle þe apparement þat pented to þe kyrke,
þe pure pyleres [o]f bras pourtrayd in golde,
& þe chef chaundeler charged with þe lyȝt,
þat ber þe lamp vpon lofte, þat lemed euer more,
Bifore þ[e] sancta *sanctorum* þer selcouth watȝ ofte.
þay caȝt away þat condelstik, & þe crowne als,
þat þe auter hade vpon, of aþel golde ryche;
þe gredirne & þe goblotes garnyst of syluer,
þe bases of þe bryȝt postes & bassynes so schyre;
Dere disches of golde & dubleres fayre,
þe vyoles & þe vesselment of vertuous stones.
Now hatȝ nabuȝardan nomen alle þyse noble þynges,
& pyled þat precious place & pakked þose godes;
þe golde of þe gaȝafylace to swyþe gret noumbre,
Wyth alle þe vrnmentes of þat hous, he hamppred
to-geder.
Alle he spoyled spitously in a sped whyle,
þat salomon so mony a sadde ȝer soȝt to make,

All that escaped the sword were taken to Babylon,

and were made to drag the cart or milk the kine.

[Fol. 74b.]

Nebuzaradan burst open the temple,

and slew those therein.

Priests, pulled by the poll, were slain along with deacons, clerks, and maidens.

The enemy pillages the temple

of its pillars of brass,

and the golden candlestick

from off the altar.

Goblets,

basins,

golden dishes,

all are taken by Nebuzaradan,

and hampered together.

Solomon had made them with much labour.

Wyth alle þe coyntyse þat he cowþe clene to wyrke;
De-uised he þe vesselment, þe vestures clene,
Wyth sly3t of his ciences, his souerayn to loue,
Þe hous & þe anournementes he hy3tled to-gedere.
Now hat3 nabu3ardan numnend[1] hit al samen,

The temple he beats down,

& syþen bet doun þe bur3 & brend hit in askes;
Þenne wyth legiounes of ledes ouer londes he rydes,
Her3e3 of Israel þe hyrne aboute.

and returns to Babylon.

Wyth charged chariotes þe cheftayn he fynde[3],

[Fol. 75a.]

Presents the prisoners to the king,

Bikennes þe catel to þe kyng, þat he ca3t hade,
Presented him þe prisoneres in pray þat þay token,
Moni a worþly wy3e whil her worlde laste,
Moni semly syre sone, & swyþe rych maydenes,
Þe pruddest of þe prouince, & prophetes childer,

among whom were Daniel and his three companions.

As Ananie & a3arie & als Mi3ael,
& dere daniel also, þat wat3 deuine noble,
With moni a modey moder chylde mo þen in-noghe.

Nebuchadnezzar has great joy,

& nabugo-de-no3ar makes much ioye,
Nov he þe kyng hat3 conquest & þe kyth wunnen,
& dreped alle þe do3tyest & derrest in armes,

because his enemies are slain.

& þe lederes of her lawe layd to þe grounde,
& þe pryce of þe profecie prisoners maked;

Great was his wonder when he saw the sacred jewelry.

Bot þe ioy of þe iuelrye so gentyle & ryche,
When hit wat3 schewed hym so schene, scharp wat3 his
  wonder,
Of such vessel auayed þat vayled so huge,
Neuer 3et nas nabugo-de-no3ar er þenne.

He praises the God of Israel.

He sesed hem with solemneté, þe souerayn he praysed,
Þat wat3 aþel ouer alle, israel dry3tyn;

Such vessels never before came to Chaldea.

Such god, such gomes, such gay vesselles
Comen neuer out of kyth, to Caldee reames.

They are thrust into the treasury.

He trussed hem in his tresorye in a tryed place
Rekenly wyth reuerens, as he ry3t hade;
& þer he wro3t as þe wyse, as 3e may wyt here-after,
For hade he let of hem ly3t, hym mo3t haf lumpen worse.
Þat ryche in gret rialté rengned his lyue,

[1] nummen (?).

As *con*querour of vche a cost he cayser watȝ hatte,
Emp*erour* of alle þe erþe & also þe saudan,
& als þe god of þe grou*n*de watȝ grauen his namo
& al þurȝ dome of daniel, fro[1] he deuised hade,
þat alle goudes com of god, & gef hit hy*m* bi samples,
þat he ful clanly bi-cnv[2] his carp bi þe laste,
& ofte hit mekned his my*n*de, his mayst*er*ful werkkes.
Bot al drawes to dyȝe w*it*h doel vp[o]n ende;
Bi[3] a haþel neu*er* so hyȝe he heldes to grou*n*de,
& so nabugo-de-noȝar as he nedes moste;
For alle his empire so hiȝe i*n* erþe is he gr*a*uen.
Bot þe*n*n þe bolde baltaȝar, þat watȝ his barn aldest,
He watȝ stalled i*n* his stud, & stabled þe rengne;
I*n* þe burȝ of babiloyne þe biggest he trawed,
þat nauþ*er* i*n* heuen ne no[4] erþe hade no pere;
For he bigan i*n* alle þe glori þat hym þe gome lafte,
Nabugo-de-Noȝar, þat watȝ his noble fader;
So kene a ky*n*g i*n* Caldee com neu*er* er þe*n*ne.
Bot hono*ur*ed he not hy*m* þat in heuen wonies,
Bot fals fantu*m*mes of fendes, formed with handes
Wyth tool out of harde tre, & telded on lofte,
& of stokkes & stones, he stoute goddes callȝ
When þay ar gilde al with golde & gered wyth sylu*er*,
& þere he kneles & calleȝ, & clepes after help.
&[5] þay reden hi*m* ryȝt rewarde he hem hetes,
& if þay gruchen hi*m* his grace to gremen his hert,
He cleches to a gret klubbe & knokkes hem to peces;
þ*us* in pryde & oliprau*n*ce his Empyre he haldes,
In lust & i*n* lecherye, & loþelych werkkes;
& hade a wyf forto welde, a worþelych quene,
& mony a le*m*man, neu*er* þe lat*er*, þat ladis wer called.
In þe clernes of his *con*cubines & curio*us* wedeȝ,
In notyng of nwe metes & of nice gettes,
Al watȝ þe mynde of þat man, o*n* misschapen þinges,
Til þe lorde of þe lyfte liste hit abate.

Nebuchadnezzar reigns as emperor of all the earth, through the "doom of Daniel," who gave him good counsel.

Nebuchadnezzar dies and is buried.

[Fol. 75*b*.]

Belshazzar succeeds him.

He holds himself the biggest in heaven or on earth.

He honours not God, but worships false phantoms.

He promises them rewards if good fortune befal.

If they vex him he knocks them in pieces.

He has a wife, and many concubines.

The mind of the king was fixed upon new meats and other vain things.

[1] *for* (?).

[2] Looks like *bicuver* in MS.

[3] *be* (?).

[4] *on* (?).

[5] *An* (?).

XIII.

Thenne þis bolde Baltaȝar biþenkkes hym ones,
To vouche on a vayment of his vayne g[l]orie;
Hit is not innoghe to þe nice al noȝty þink[1] vse,
Bot if alle þe worlde wyt his wykked dedes.
Baltaȝar þurȝ babiloyn his banne gart crye,
& þurȝ þe cuntre of caldee his callyng con spryng,
Þat alle þe grete vpon grounde schulde geder hem samen
& assemble at a set day at þe saudans fest.
Such a mangerie to make þe man watȝ auised,
Þat vche a kythyn kyng schuld com þider;
Vche duk wyth his duthe & oþer dere lordes,
Schulde com to his court to kyþe hym for lege,
& to reche hym reuerens & his reuel herkken;
To loke on his lemanes & ladis hem calle,
To rose hym in his rialty rych men soȝtten,
& mony a baroun ful bolde, to babyloyn þe noble.
Þer bowed toward babiloyn burnes so mony,
Kynges, Cayseres ful kene, to þe court wonnen,
Mony ludisch lordes þat ladies broȝten,
Þat to neuen þe noumbre to much nye were.
For þe bourȝ watȝ so brod & so bigge alce,
Stalled in þe fayrest stud þe sterreȝ an-vnder,
Prudly on a plat playn, plek alþer-fayrest,
Vmbe-sweyed on vch a syde with seuen grete wateres,
With a wonder wroȝt walle wruxeled ful hiȝe,
With koynt carneles aboue, coruen ful clene,
Troched toures bitwene twenty spere lenþe,
& þiker þrowen vmbe þour[2]-with ouer-þwert palle.
Þe place, þat plyed þe pursaunt wyth-inne,
Watȝ longe & ful large & euer ilych sware,
& vch a syde vpon soyle helde seuen myle,
& þe saudans sete sette in þe myddes;
Þat watȝ a palayce of pryde passande alle oþer,
Boþe of werk & of wunder & walle al aboute;

Belshazzar, to exhibit his vain-glory, proclaims throughout Babylon, that all the great ones should assemble on a set day, at the Sultan's feast. Kings, dukes, and lords were commanded to attend the court.

[Fol. 76*a*.]

To do the king honour many nobles came to Babylon.

It would take too long to name the number.

The city of Babylon is broad and big.

It is situated on a plain, surrounded by seven streams, a high wall, and towers.

The palace was long and large, each side being seven miles in length.

[1] *þing* (?).

[2] *þore* (?).

Heȝe houses with-inne þe halle to hit med,
So brod bilde in a bay, þat blonkkes myȝt renne.
When þe terme of þe tyde watȝ to vsched of þe feste,
Dere droȝen þer-to & vpon des metten,
& baltaȝar vpon bench was busked to sete,
Stepe stayred stones of his stoute throne.
Þenne watȝ alle þe halle flor hiled with knyȝtes,
& barounes at þe side-bordes bounet ay-where,
For non watȝ dressed vpon dece bot þe dere seluen,
& his clere concubynes in cloþes ful bryȝt.
When alle segges were þer set, þen seruyse bygynnes,
Sturnen trumpen strake steuen in halle,
Aywhere by þe wowes wrasten krakkes,
& brode baneres þer-bi blusnande of gold;
Burnes berande þe[1] bredes vpon brode skeles,
Þat were of sylueren syȝt & seerved[2] þer-wyth,
Lyfte logges þer-ouer & on lofte coruen,
Pared out of paper & poynted of golde,[3]
Broþe baboynes abof, besttes an-vnder,
Foles in foler flakerande bi-twene,
& al in asure & ynde enaumayld ryche,
& al on blonkken bak bere hit on honde.
& ay þe nakeryn noyse, notes of pipes,
Tymbres & tabornes, tulket among,
Symbales & soneteȝ sware þe noyse,
& bougounȝ busch batered so þikke;
So watȝ serued fele syþe. þe sale alle aboute,
With solace at þe sere course, bifore þe self lorde,
Þer þe lede & alle his loue lenged at þe table.
So faste þay weȝed to him wyne, hit warmed his hert
& breyþed vppe in to his brayn & blemyst his mynde,
& al waykned his wyt, & wel neȝe he foles,
For he wayteȝ onwyde, his wenches he byholdes,
& his bolde baronage, aboute bi þe woȝes;
Þenne a dotage ful depe drof to his hert,
& a caytif counsayl he caȝt bi hym seluen.

High houses were within the walls.

The time of the feast has come.

Belshazzar sits upon his throne:

the hall floor is covered with knights.

When all are seated, service begins.

Trumpets sound everywhere.

[Fol. 76b.]

Bread is served upon silver dishes.

All sorts of musical instruments are heard in the hall.

The king, surrounded by his loves, drinks copiously of wine.

It gets into his head and stupifies him.

A cursed thought takes possession of him.

[1] MS. þe þe.
[2] MS. severed.
[3] MS. *glolde* (?).

He commands his marshal to bring him the vessels

Maynly his marschal þe mayst*er* vpon calles,
& comau*n*des hym cofly coferes to lance,
& fech forþe vessel þat his fader broȝt

taken from the temple by Nebuchadnezzar,

Nabugo-de-noȝar, noble i*n* his strenþe,
Conquerd with his knyȝtes & of kyrk rafte
I*n* iude, i*n* *ierusalem* i*n* gentyle wyse:

and to fill them with wine.

"Bryng hem now to my borde, of beu*er*age he*m* fylles,
Let þise ladyes of hem lape, I luf he*m* i*n* hert;
Þat schal I cortaysly kyþe & þay schi*n* knawe sone,

The marshal opens the chests.

Þer is no bou*n*té i*n* burne lyk baltaȝar þewes."

Covers the cupboard with vessels.

Þe*n*ne towched to þe treso*ur* þis tale watȝ sone,
& he w*ith* keyes vn-closes kystes ful mony;
Mony burþen ful bryȝt watȝ broȝt i*n*-to halle,

[Fol. 77*a*.]

& cou*er*ed mony a cupborde with cloþes ful quite.

The Jewels of Jerusalem deck the sides of the hall.

Þe iueles out of *ierusalem*[1] w*ith* ge*m*mes ful bryȝt,
Bi þe syde of þe sale were semely arayed;

The altar and crown,

Þe aþel auter of brasse watȝ hade i*n*-to place;
Þe gay corou*n* of golde gered on lofte,

blessed by bishop's hands, and anointed with the blood of beasts,

Þat hade ben blessed bifore wyth bischopes hondes
& wyth besten blod busily anoynted,
In þe solempne sacrefyce þat goud sauor hade,
Bifore þe lorde of þe lyfte i*n* louy*n*g hy*m* seluen,

are set before the bold Belshazzar.

Now is sette for to serue satanas þe blake,
Bifore þe bolde baltaȝar wyth bost & wyth pryde.

Upon this altar were noble vessels curiously carved,

Houen vpon þis auter watȝ aþel vessel,
Þat wyth so[2] curiou*s* a crafte coruen watȝ wyly;
Salamon sete him s[eue]n ȝere & a syþe more,
W*ith* alle þe syence þat hy*m* sende þe sou*er*ayn lorde,
For to compas & kest to haf hem clene wroȝt;

basins of gold,

For þer wer bassynes ful bryȝt of brende golde clere,
En-aumaylde w*ith* aȝer & eweres of sute;

cups arrayed like castles with battlements,

Cou*er*ed cowpes foul[3] clene, as casteles arayed,
Enbaned vnder batelment w*ith* bantelles quoy*n*t,
& fyled out of fygures of ferlyle[4] schappes.

and towers with lofty pinnacles.

Þe cop*er*ounes of þe canacles þat on þe cuppe reres,
Wer fetysely formed out i*n* fylyoles longe,

[1] MS. *iesuralem*.
[2] MS. *fo*.
[3] *ful* (?).
[4] *ferlyke* (?).

Pinacles pyȝt þer apert þat p*ro*fert bitwene,
& al bolled abof w*ith* braun*ches* & leues,
Pyes & papeiayes purtrayed with-i*nne*,
As þay prudly hade piked of pomgarnades;
For alle þe blomes of þe boȝes wer blyknande perles
& alle þe fruyt i*n* þo formes of flau*m*beande ge*mm*es,
Ande safyres, & sardiners, & semely topace,
Alabau*n*derynes, & amarau*n*ȝ & amaffised stones,
Casydoynes, & crysolytes, & clere rubies,
Penitotes, & pynkardines, ay perles bitwene,
So trayled & tryfled a traue*r*ce wer alle,
Bi vche bekyrande þe bolde, þe brurdes al vmbe;
Þe gobelotes of golde grauen aboute,
& fyoles fretted w*ith* flores & fleeȝ of golde,
Vpon þat avter watȝ al aliche dresset.
Þe candelstik bi a cost watȝ cayred þider sone,
[V]pon þe pyleres apyked þat praysed hit mony,
Vpon hit baseȝ of brasse þat ber vp þe werkes,
Þe boȝes bryȝt þer abof, brayden of golde,
Brau*n*ches bredande þer-on, & bryddes þer seten
Of mony kyndes, of fele-kyn hues,
As þay w*ith* wy*n*ge vpon wynde hade waged her fyþ*er*es,
In-mo*n*g þe leues of þe lampes wer grayþed;
& oþ*er* louelych[1] lyȝt þat lemed ful fayre,
As mony mort*er*es of wax merkked w*ith*-oute,
W*ith* mony a borlych best al of brende golde.
Hit watȝ not wonte i*n* þat wone to wast no serges,
Bot i*n* te*m*ple of þe trauþe trwly to stonde;
Bifore þe *sancta sanctorum* soþefast dryȝtyn,
Expouned his speche sp*irit*ually to special p*ro*phetes.
Loue þou wel þat þe lorde þ*at* þe lyfte ȝemes
Displesed much, at þat play i*n* þat plyt stronge,
Þat his iueles so gent wyth iaueles wer fouled,
Þat p*re*syou*s* i*n* his presens wer proued su*m* whyle.
Soberly i*n* his sacrafyce su*m*me wer anoynted,
Þurȝ þe somones of him selfe þat syttes so hyȝe;

Upon them were pourtrayed branches and leaves,

the flowers of which were white pearls,

and the fruit flaming gems.

[Fol. 77*b*.] The goblets were ornamented with flowers of gold.

The candlestick was brought in,

with its pillars of brass,

and ornamental boughs,

upon which sat birds of various hues.

Lights shone bright from the candlestick,

which once stood before the "Holy of Holies."

The pollution of the sacred vessels is displeasing to God.

[1] Looks like *louflych*.

For "a boaster on bench" drinks from them till he is as "drunken as the devil." God is very angry.

Now a bost*er* on benche bibbes þerof
Tyl he be dronkken as þe deuel, & dotes þ*er* he syttes;
So þe worcher of þis worlde wlates þer-wyth,
Þat in þe poynt of her play he poruayes a mynde;

Before harming the revellers He sends them a warning.

Bot er harme hem he wolde in haste of his yre,
He wayned hem a warny*n*g þat wonder hem þoȝt.
Nov is alle þis guere geten glotoun*es* to serue;
Stad in a ryche stal & stared ful bryȝtȝ,[1]

Belshazzar commands the sacred vessels to be filled with wine.

Baltaȝar in a brayd bede vus þ*er*-of.
"Weȝe wyn in þis won, wassayl!" he cryes.
Swyfte swaynes ful swyþe swepen þ*er*-tylle,

The cups and bowls are soon filled.

Kyppe kowpes in honde kyngeȝ to serue,
In bryȝt bolleȝ, ful bayn birlen þise oþ*er*,
& vche mon for his mayst*er* machches alone.

[Fol. 78*a*.]

Music of all kind is heard in the hall.

Þer watȝ ry*n*ging, on ryȝt, of ryche metalles,
Quen renkkes in þat ryche rok re*n*nen hit to cache,
Clat*er*ing of conacleȝ þat kesten þo burdes,
As sonet out of sau[t]*er*ay songe als myry.
Þen þe dotel on dece drank þat he myȝt,

Dukes, princes, concubines, and knights, all are merry.

& þe*n*ne arn dressed dukeȝ & prynces,
Concubines & knyȝtes, bi cause of þat m*er*the;
As vchon hade hy*m* in helde he haled of þe cuppe,

Drinking of the sweet liquors they ask favours of their gods,

So long likked þise lordes þise lykores swete,
& gloryed on her falce goddes & her *gra*ce calles,
Þat were of stokkes & stones, stille euer more;

who, although dumb,

Neu*er* steuen hem astel, so stoken is[2] hor tonge,
Alle þe goude golden goddes þe gauleȝ ȝet neuenen,
Belfagor & belyal & belssabub als,

are as highly praised "as if heaven were theirs."

Heyred hem as hyȝly as heuen wer þayres,
Bot hy*m* þat alle goudes giues, þat god þay for-ȝeten,
For þer a ferly bifel þat fele folk seȝen;

A marvel befals the feasters. The king first saw it. Upon the plain wall,

Fyrst knew hit þe ky*n*g & alle þe cort aft*er*,
In þe palays pryncipale vpon þe playn wowe,
In contrary of þe candelstik þat clerest hit schyned.

"a palm with pointel in fingers" is seen writing.

Þer apered a paume, wit*h* poyntel in fyngres
Þat watȝ grysly & gret, & grymly he wrytes,

[1] þ *bryȝte.*

[2] MS. Is.

Non o*þer* forme bot a fust faylande þe wryste,
Pared on þe parget, purtrayed lettres.
When þat bolde baltaȝar blusched to þat neue,
Such a dasande drede dusched to his hert,
Þat al falewed his face & fayled þe chere;
Þe stronge strok of þe stonde strayned his ioy*n*tes,
His cnes cachches to close & cluchches his hom*m*es,
& he w*ith* plat-ty*n*g his paumes displayes his lers,[1]
& romyes as a rad ryth þat roreȝ for drede,
Ay biholdand þe honde til hit hade al gr*a*uen,
& rasped on þe roȝ woȝe runisch saueȝ.
When hit þe scrypture hade scraped wyth a scrof[2]
penne,
As a coltour in clay cerues þo forȝes,
Þe*n*ne hit vanist v*er*ayly & voyded of syȝt,
Bot þe lettres bileued ful large vpon plast*er*.
Sone so þe ky*n*ge for his care carpi*n*g myȝt wy*n*ne,
He bede his burnes boȝ to þat wer*e* bok lered,
To wayte þe wryt þat hit wolde & wyt*er* hym to say,
"For al hit frayes my flesche þe fyngres so gry*m*me."
Scoleres skelten þeratte þe skyl forto fynde,
Bot þer watȝ neu*er* on so wyse couþe on worde rede,
Ne what ledisch lore ne langage nau*þer*
What tyþy*n*g ne tale tokened þo draȝtes.
Þe*n*ne þe bolde baltaȝar bred ner wode.
& ede[3] þe Cetë to seche segges þurȝ-out,
Þat wer wyse of wyche-crafte & warlaȝes o*þer*,
Þat con dele wyth dem*er*layk, & deuine lettres:
"Calle hem alle to my cort þo calde clerkkes,
Vn-folde hem alle þis ferly þat is bifallen here,
& calle wyth a hiȝe cry; 'he þat þe ky*n*g wysses,
In expouny*n*g of speche þat spredes *in* þise lettres,
& make þe mat*er* to malt my mynde wyth-i*n*ne,
Þat I may wyt*er*ly wyt what þat wryt menes,
He schal be gered ful gaye *in* gounes of porpre,
& a coler of cler golde clos vmbe[4] his þrote;

The bold Belshazzar becomes frightened.

His knees knock together.

He roars for dread, still beholding the hand, as it wrote on the rough wall.

[Fol. 78*b*.]
The hand vanishes but the letters remain.

The king recovers his speech and sends for the "book-learned;"

but none of the scholars were wise enough to read it.

Belshazzar is nearly mad. Commands the city to be searched throughout for the "wise of witchcraft."

He who expounds the strange letters, shall be clothed in "gowns of purple." A collar of gold shall encircle his throat.

[1] MS. lerns.

[2] MS. *strof*.

[3] *bede* (?).

He shall be the third lord in the realm.

He schal be prymate & prynce of pure clergye,
& of my þreuenest lordeȝ þe þrydde he schal
& of my reme þe rychest to ryde wyth myseluen,
Out-taken bare two & þenne he þe þrydde.' "

As soon as this cry was upcast, to the hall came clerks out of Chaldea,

Þis cry watȝ vp-caste, & þer comen mony
Clerkes out of caldye þat kennest wer knauen,
As þe sage sathrapas þat sorsory couþe;

witches and diviners,

Wycheȝ & walkyries wonnen to þat sale,
Deuinores of demorlaykes þat dremes cowþe rede,

sorcerers and exorcists.

Sorsers & exorsismus & fele such clerkes;

But after looking on the letters they were as ignorant as if they had looked into the leather of the left boot.

& alle þat loked on þat letter as lewed þay were,
As þay had loked in þe leþer of my lyft bote.

The king curses them all and calls them churls.

Þenne cryes þe kyng & kerues his wedes;
What! he corsed his clerkes & calde hem chorles,

[Fol. 79a.]

He orders the harlots to be hanged.

To henge þe harlotes he heȝed ful ofte,
So watȝ þe wyȝe wytles, he wed wel ner.

The queen hears the king chide.

Ho herde hym chyde to þe chambre þat watȝ þe chef quene;

She inquires the cause.

When ho watȝ wytered bi wyȝes what watȝ þe cause,
Suche a chaungande chaunce in þe chef halle,
Þe lady to lauce[1] þat los þat þe lorde hade,

Goes to the king, kneels before him,

Glydes doun by þe grece & gos to þe kyng;
Ho kneles on þe colde erþe & carpes to hym seluen,
Wordes of worchyp wyth a wys speche.
" Kene kyng," quod þe quene, " kayser of vrþe,
Euer laste þy lyf in lenþe of dayes;

and asks why he has rent his robes for grief,

Why hatȝ þou rended þy robe for redles here-inne,
Þaȝ þose ledes ben lewed lettres to rede,
& hatȝ a haþel in þy holde, as I haf herde ofte,

when there is one that has the Spirit of God,

Þat hatȝ þe gostes of god þat gyes alle soþes;
His sawle is ful of syence, saȝes to schawe,
To open vch a hide þyng of aunteres vn-cowþe;

the counsellor of Nebuchadnezzar,

Þat is ho þat ful ofte hatȝ heuened þy fader
Of mony anger ful hote with his holy speche.
When nabugo-de-noȝar watȝ nyed in stoundes,

the interpreter of his dreams,

He de-vysed his dremes to þe dere trawþe,
He keuered hym with his counsayl of caytyf wyrdes;

[1] lance (?).

Alle þat he spured hym *in* space he expowned clene,
Þurȝ þe sped of þe spyryt þat sprad hy*m* *with*-inne,
Of þe godelest goddeȝ þat gaynes ay-where.
For his depe diuinité & his dere sawes,
Þy bolde fader baltaȝar bede by[1] his name,
Þat now is demed danyel of derne coni*n*ges,
Þat caȝt watȝ *in* þe captyuidé *in* cu*n*tre of iues;
Nabuȝardan hy*m* nome & now is he here,
A prophete of þat prouince & pryce of þe worlde.
Sende *in*-to þe cetẽ to seche hy*m* bylyue,
& wy*n*ne hy*m* *with* þe worchyp to wayne þe bote,
& þaȝ þe mat*er* be merk þat merked is ȝender,
He schal de-clar hit also, as hit on clay stande."
Þat gode counseyl at þe quene watȝ cached as[2] swyþe,
Þe burne byfore baltaȝar watȝ broȝt *in* a whyle,
When he com bifore þe ky*n*g & clanly had halsed,
Baltaȝar vmbe-brayde hym & "leue *sir*," he sayde,
"Hit is tolde me bi tulkes, þat þou trwe were
Profete of þat prouynce þat prayed my fader,
Ande þat þou hatȝ *in* þy hert holy co*n*nyn*g*,
Of sapyence þi sawle ful soþes to schawe;
Goddes gost is þe geuen þat gyes alle þy*n*ge*s*,
& þou vnhyles vch hidde þat heuen ky*n*g my*n*tes;
& here is a ferly byfallen, & I fayn wolde
Wyt þe wytte of þe wryt, þat on þe wowe clyues,
For alle calde clerkes han cowwardely fayled;
If þou *with* quay*n*tyse co*n*quere hit, I quyte þe þy mede.
For if þou redes hit by ryȝt & hit to resou*n* bry*n*ges,
Fyrst telle me þe tyxte of þe tede lettres,
& syþen þe mat*er* of þe mode, mene me þ*er*-after,
& I schal halde þe þe hest þat I þe hyȝt haue;
Apyke þe *in* porpre cloþe, palle alþer-fynest,
& þe byȝe of bryȝt golde abowte þy*n* nekke,
& þe þryd þryuenest þat þry*n*ges me aft*er*,
Þou schal be barou*n* vpon benche, bede I þe no lasse."
Derfly þe*n*ne danyel deles þyse wordes:

through the holy Spirit of God.

The name of this man is Daniel,

who was brought a captive from Judæa.

The queen tells the king to send for Daniel.

Her counsel is accepted.

[Fol. 79*b*.]

Daniel comes before Belshazzar.

The king tells him that he has heard of his wisdom,

and his power to discover hidden things,

and that he wants to know the meaning of the writing on the wall.

Promises him, if he can explain the text of the letters and their interpretation,

to clothe him in purple and pall, and put a ring about his neck,

and to make him "a baron upon bench."

Daniel addresses the king,

[1] *be* (?).

[2] MS. *as as*.

"Ryche ky*n*g of þis rengne rede þe oure lorde,
Hit is surely soth, þe sou*er*ayn of heuen
Fylsened eu*er* þy fader & vpon folde cheryched,
Gart hy*m* grattest to be of gou*er*nores alle,
& alle þe worlde i*n* his wylle welde as hy*m* lykes.
Who-so wolde wel do, wel hy*m* bityde,
& quos deth so he deȝyre he dreped als fast;
Who-so hy*m* lyked to lyft, on lofte watȝ he sone,
& quo-so hy*m* lyked to lay, watȝ loȝed bylyue.
So watȝ noted þe note of nabugo-de-noȝar,
Styfly stabled þe rengne bi þe stronge dryȝty*n*,
For of þe hyȝest he hade a hope i*n* his hert,
Þat vche pou*er* past out of [þ]at prynce euen;
& whyle þat watȝ cleȝt clos i*n* his hert,
Þere watȝ no mon vpon molde of myȝt as hy*m* selue*n*,
Til hit bitide on a tyme, towched hy*m* pryde
For his lordeschyp so large, & his lyf ryche;
He hade so huge an insyȝt to his aune dedes,
Þat þe power of þe hyȝe prynce he purely forȝetes.
Þe*n*ne blynnes he not of blasfemyon to blame þe dryȝty*n*,
His myȝt mete to goddes he made w*ith* his wordes:
"I am god of þe grou*n*de, to gye as me lykes,
As he þat hyȝe is i*n* heuen his au*n*geles þat weldes;
If he hatȝ formed þe folde & folk þ*er* vpone,
I haf bigged babiloyne, burȝ alþ*er*-rychest,
Stabled þer-i*n*ne vche a ston i*n* strenkþe of my*n* armes,
Moȝt neu*er* myȝt bot myn make such anoþ*er*."
Watȝ not þis ilke worde wo*n*nen of his mowþe one,
Er þe*n*ne þe sou*er*ayn saȝe souned i*n* his eres,
"Now nabugo-de-noȝar innoȝe hatȝ spoken,
Now is alle þy pryncipalté past at ones,
& þou, remued fro mo*n*nes su*n*es, on mor most abide,
& in wastu*r*ne walk & wyth þe wylde dowelle,
As best, byte on þe bent of braken & erbes,
W*ith* wroþe wolfes to won & wyth wylde asses."
In mydde þe poynt of his pryde de-parted he þere,

and reminds him how that God supported his father,

and gave him power to exalt or abase whomsoever he pleased.

Nebuchadnezzar was established

on account of his faith in God.

So long as he remained true, no man was greater.

[Fol. 80*a*.] But at last pride touches his heart.

He forgets the power of God, and blasphemes His name.

He says that he is "god of the ground,"

and the builder of Babylon.

Hardly had Nebuchadnezzar spoken, when God's voice is heard, saying,

"Thy principality is departed. Thou, removed from men, must abide on the moor, and walk with wild beasts, eat herbs, and dwell with wolves and asses."

Fro þe soly of his solempneté, his solace he leues,
& carfully is out-kast to contré vnknawen,
Fer in-to a fyr fryth þere frekes neuer comen.
His hert heldet vnhole, he hoped non oþer
Bot a best þat he be, a bol oþer an oxe.
He fares forth on alle faure, fogge watȝ his mete,
& ete ay as a horce when erbes were fallen,
Þus he countes hym a kow, þat watȝ a kyng ryche,
Quyle seuen syþeȝ were ouer-seyed someres I trawe.
By þat, mony þik thyȝe þryȝt vmbe his lyre,
Þat alle watȝ dubbed & dyȝt in þe dew of heuen;
Faxe fyltered, & felt flosed hym vmbe,
Þat schad fro his schulderes to his schyre wykes
& twenty-folde twynande hit to his tos raȝt
Þer mony clyuy as clyde hit clyȝt to-geder.
His berde I-brad alle his brest to þe bare vrþe,
[Fol. 80b.] His browes bresed as breres aboute his brode chekes;
Holȝe were his yȝen & vnder campe hores,
& al watȝ gray as þe glede, with ful grymme clawres
Þat were croked & kene as þe kyte paune;[1]
Erne-hwed he watȝ & al ouer-brawden,
Til he wyst ful wel who wroȝt alle myȝtes,
& cowþe vche kyndam tokerue & keuer when hym
lyked;
Þenne he wayned hym his wyt þat hade wo soffered,
Þat he com to knawlach & kenned hym seluen,
Þenne he laued[2] þat lorde & leued in trawþe,
Hit watȝ non oþer þen he þat hade al in honde.
Þenne sone watȝ he sende agayn, his sete restored;
His barounes boȝed hym to, blyþe of his come,
Haȝerly in his aune hwe his heued watȝ couered,
& so ȝeply watȝ ȝarked & ȝolden his state.
Bot þou baltaȝar his barne & his bolde ayre,
Seȝ þese syngnes with syȝt & set hem at lyttel,
Bot ay hatȝ hofen þy hert agaynes þe hyȝe dryȝt[y]n,
With bobaunce & with blasfamye bost at hym kest,

For his pride he becomes an outcast.
He believes himself to be a bull or an ox.
Goes "on all fours,"
like a cow,
for seven summers.
His thighs grew thick.
His hair became matted and thick,
from the shoulders to the toes.
His beard touched the earth.
His brows were like briars.
His eyes were hollow,
and grey as the kite's.
Eagle-hued he was.
At last he recovered his "wit,"
and believed in God.
Then soon was he restored to his seat.
But thou, Belshazzar, hast disregarded these signs,
and hast blasphemed the Lord,

[1] ? panne.
[2] loued (?).

defiled his vessels,

& now his vessayles avyled in vanyté vnclene,
Þat in his hows hym to honour were heuened of fyrst;

filling them with wine for thy wenches,

Bifore þe barounȝ hatȝ hom broȝt, & byrled þerinne
Wale wyne to þy wenches in waryed stoundes;
Bifore þy borde hatȝ þou broȝt beuerage in þede,
Þat blyþely were fyrst blest with bischopes hondes,

and praising thy lifeless gods.

Louande þeron lese goddeȝ, þat lyf haden neuer,
Made of stokkes & stoneȝ þat neuer styry moȝt.

For this sin God has sent thee this strange sight,

& for þat froþande fylþe, þe fader of heuen
Hatȝ sende[1] in-to þis sale þise syȝtes vncowþe,

[1] MS. hatȝ sende hatȝ sende.

the fist with the fingers writing on the wall.

Þe fyste with þe fyngeres þat flayed þi hert,
Þat rasped renyschly þe woȝe with þe roȝ penne.

These are the words:

Þise ar þe wordes here wryten with-oute werk more,
By vch fygure, as I fynde, as oure fader lykes.

"Mene, Tekel, Peres.

" Mane, techal, phares, merked in þrynne,
Þat þretes þe of þyn vnþryfte vpon þre wyse;
Now expowne þe þis speche spedly I þenk.

[Fol. 81a.]
Mene.—God has counted thy kingdom and finished it.

Mane menes als much as, maynful gode
Hatȝ counted þy kyndam bi a clene noumbre,
& ful-fylled hit in fayth to þe fyrre ende.

Tekel.—Thy reign is weighed and is found wanting in deeds of faith.

To teche þe of techal, þat terme þus menes,
Þy wale rengne is walt in weȝtes to heng,
& is funde ful fewe of hit fayth dedes.
& phares folȝes for þose fawtes to frayst þe trawþe,

Peres.—Thy kingdom is divided.

In phares fynde I forsoþe þise felle saȝes;
De-parted is þy pryncipalté, depryued þou worþes,

and given to the Persians.

Þy rengne rafte is þe fro, & raȝt is þe perses,

The Medes shall be masters here."

Þe medes schal be maysteres here, & þou of menske
schowued."

The king commands Daniel to be clothed in a frock of fine cloth.

Þe kyng comaunded anon to cleþe þat wyse,
In frokkes of fyn cloþ, as forward hit asked;

Soon is he arrayed in purple, with a chain about his neck.

Þenne sone watȝ danyel dubbed in ful dere porpor
& a coler[2] of cler golde kest vmbe his swyre.

[2] MS. cloler.

A decree is made, that all should bow to him,

Þen watȝ demed a de-cre bi þe duk seluen,
Bolde baltaȝa[r] bed þat hym bowe schulde
Þe comynes a lo[illegible] calde þat to þe kyng longed,

As to þe prynce pryuyest preued þe þrydde,
Heȝest of alle oþ*er*, saf onelych tweyne,
To boȝ aft*er* baltaȝar i*n* borȝe & i*n* felde.
Þys watȝ cryed & knawen i*n* cort als fast,
& alle þe folk þer-of fayn þat folȝed hy*m* tylle;
Bot how-so danyel watȝ dyȝt, þat day ou*er*-ȝede,
Nyȝt neȝed ryȝt now w*ith* nyes fol mony,
For daȝed neu*er* an oþ*er* day þat ilk derk aft*er*,
Er dalt were þat ilk dome þat danyel deuysed,
Þe solace of þe solempneté i*n* þat sale dured
Of þat farand fest, tyl fayled þe su*n*ne;
Þe*n*ne blykned[1] þe ble of þe bryȝt skwes,
Mourkenes þe mery weder, & þe myst dryues
Þorȝ þe lyst of þe lyfte, bi þe loȝ medoes;
Vche haþel to his home hyȝes ful fast,
Seten at her sop*er* & songen þ*er*-aft*er*,
Þe*n* fou*n*deȝ vch a felaȝschyp fyrre at forþ naȝt*es*.
Baltaȝar to his bedd with blysse watȝ caryed,
[Fol. 81b.] Reche þe rest as hy*m* lyst, he ros neu*er* þer-aft*er*;
For his foes i*n* þe felde i*n* flokkes ful grete
Þat longe hade layted þat lede his londes to strye,
Now ar þay sodenly assembled at þe self tyme,
Of hem wyst no wyȝe þat i*n* þat won dowelled.
Hit watȝ þe dere daryus þe duk of þise medes,
Þe prowde prynce of perce & porros of ynde,
W*ith* mony a legiou*n* ful large, w*ith* ledes of armes,
Þat now hatȝ spyed a space to spoyle caldeeȝ.
Þay þrongen þeder i*n* þe þest*er* on þrawen hepes,
Asscaped ou*er* þe skyre watt*er*es & scaþed þe walles,
Lyfte laddres ful longe & vpon lofte wonen,
Stelen stylly þe tou*n* er any steue*n* rysed,
W*ith*-i*n*ne an oure of þe nyȝt[2] an entré þay hade;
Ȝet afrayed þay no freke, fyrre þay passen
& to þe palays pry*n*cipal þay aproched ful stylle;
Þe*n*ne ran þay i*n* on a res, on rowtes ful grete,
Blastes out of bryȝt brasse brestes so hyȝe.

as the third lord that followed Belshazzar.

The decree was made known, and all were glad.

The day, however, past.

Night came on.

Before another day dawned,

Daniel's words were fulfilled.

The feast lasts till the sun fails.

The skies become dark.

Each noble hies home to his supper.

Belshazzar is carried to bed, but never rises from it,

for his foes are seeking to destroy his land, and are assembled suddenly.

The enemy is Darius, leader of the Medes.

He has legions of armed men.

Under cover of the darkness, they cross the river.

By means of ladders they get upon the walls,

and within an hour enter the city, without disturbing any of the watch.

They run into the palace, and raise a great cry.

[1] *blaykned* (?).

[2] MS. *myȝt*.

Ascry scarred on þe scue þat scomfyted mony.
Men are slain in their beds.
Segges slepande were slayne er þay slyppe myȝt,
Vche hous heyred watȝ, with-inne a honde-whyle;
Belshazzar is beaten to death,
Baltaȝar in his bed watȝ beten to deþe,
Þat boþe his blod & his brayn blende on þe cloþes;
and caught by the heels, is foully cast into a ditch.
The kyng in his cortyn watȝ kaȝt bi þe heles,
Feryed out bi þe fete & fowle dispysed;
Þat watȝ so doȝty þat day & drank of þe vessayl,
Now is a dogge al so dere þat in a dych lygges;
Darius is crowned king,
For þe mayster of þyse medes on þe morne ryses,
Dere daryous þat day dyȝt vpon trone,
and makes peace with the barons.
Þat ceté sescs ful sounde, & saȝtlyng makes
Wyth alle þe barounȝ þer-aboute, þat bowed hym after.
Thus the land was lost for the king's sin.
& þus watȝ þat londe lost for þe lordes synne,
& þe fylþe of þe freke þat defowled hade
Þe orne-mentes of goddeȝ hous þat holy were maked;
He was cursed for his uncleanness,
He watȝ corsed for his vn-clannes, & cached þer-inne,
Done doun of his dyngneté for dedeȝ vnfayre,
and deprived of his honour, as well as of the joys of heaven.
& of þyse worldes worchyp wrast out for euer,
& ȝet of lykynges on lofte letted, I trowe,
Thus in three ways has it been shown,
To loke on oure lofly lorde late bitydes.
Þus vpon þrynne wyses I haf yow þro schewed,
that uncleanness
Þat vn-clannes to-cleues in corage dere
Of þat wynnelych lorde þat wonyes in heuen,
makes God angry.
Entyses hym to be tene, telled[1] vp his wrake;
Cleanness is His comfort.
Ande clannes is his comfort, & coyntyse he louyes,
The seemly shall see his face.
& þose þat seme arn & swete schyn se his face.
God give us grace to serve in His sight!
Þat we gon gay in oure gere þat grace he vus sende,
Þat we may serue in his syȝt, þer solace neuer blynneȝ.
Amen.

[1] *telles* (?).

PATIENCE.

I.

[Fol. 83a.] Pacience is a poynt, þaȝ hit displese ofte,
When heuy herttes ben hurt wyth heþyng oþer elles,
Suffraunce may aswagen[1] hem & þe swelme leþe,
For ho quelles vche a qued, & quenches malyce;
For quo-so suffer cowþe syt, sele wolde folȝe,
& quo for þro may noȝt þole, þe þikker he sufferes;
Þen is better to abyde þe bur vmbe-stoundes,
Þen ay þrow forth my þro, þaȝ me þynk ylle.
I herde on a halyday at a hyȝe masse,
How mathew melede, þat his mayster his meyny con teche,
Aȝt happes he hem hyȝt & vche on a mede,
Sunderlupes for hit dissert vpon a ser wyse:
Thay arn happen þat han in hert pouerté,
For hores is þe heuen-ryche to holde for euer;
Þay ar happen also þat haunte mekenesse,
For þay schal welde þis worlde & alle her wylle haue;
Thay ar happen also þat for her harme wepes,
For þay schal comfort encroche in kythes ful mony;
Þay ar happen also þat hungeres after ryȝt,
For þay schal frely be refete ful of alle gode;
Thay ar happen also þat han in hert rauþe,
For mercy in alle maneres her mede schal worþe;
Þay ar happen also þat arn of hert clene,
For þay her sauyour in sete schal se with her yȝen;

Patience is often displeasing,

[1] MS. *aswagend.*

but it assuages heavy hearts, and quenches malice.

Happiness follows sorrow.

It is better to suffer than to be angry.

Matthew tells us of the promises made by Christ:

Blessed are the poor, for theirs is the kingdom of heaven.

Blessed are the meek, for they shall "wield the world."

Blessed are the mourners, for they shall be comforted.

Blessed are the hungry, for they shall be filled.

Blessed are the merciful, for mercy shall be their reward.

Blessed are the clean of heart, for they shall see the Saviour.

Thay ar happen also þat halden her pese,
For þay þe gracious godes sunes schal godly be called;
Þay ar happen also þat con her hert stere,
For hores is þe heuen-ryche, as I er sayde.
These arn þe happes alle aȝt þat vus bihyȝt weren,
If we þyse ladyes wolde lof in lyknyng of þewes;
Dame pouert, Dame pitce, Dame penaunce þe þrydde,
Dame Mekenesse, Dame mercy & Miry clannesse,
& þenne Dame pes & pacyence put in þer-after.
He were happen þat hade one, alle were þe better,
Bot syn[1] I am put to a poynt þat pouerte hatte,
I schal me poruay pacyence, & play me with boþe;
For in þe tyxte, þere þyse two arn in teme layde,
Hit arn fettled in on forme, þe forme & þe laste,
& by quest of her quoyntyse enquylen on mede,
& als in myn vpynyoun hit arn of on kynde;
For þer as pouert hir proferes ho nyl be put vtter,
Bot lenge where-so-euer hir lyst, lyke oþer greme,
& þere as pouert enpresses, þaȝ mon pyne þynk,
Much maugre his mun,[2] he mot nede suffer,
Thus pouerte & pacyence arn nedes play-feres.
Syþen I am sette with hem samen, suffer me by-houes,
Þenne is me lyȝtloker hit lyke & her lotes prayse,
Þenne wyþer wyth & be wroth & þe wers haue.
Ȝif me be dyȝt a destyné due to haue,
What dowes me þe dedayn, oþer dispit make?
Oþer ȝif my lege lorde lyst on lyue me to bidde,
Oþer to ryde, oþer to renne, to rome in his ernde,
What grayþed me þe grychchyng bot grame more seche?
Much ȝif he me ne made, maugref my chekes,
& þenne þrat moste I þole, & vnþonk to mede,
Þe[t] had bowed to his bode, bongre my hyure.
Did not Ionas in Iude suche Iape sum-whyle,
To sette hym to sewrte, vnsounde he hym feches?
Wyl ȝe tary a lyttel tyme[3] & tent me a whyle,
I schal wysse yow þer-wyth as holy wryt telles.

Blessed are the peace-makers, for they shall be called God's sons. Blessed are they that live aright, for theirs is the kingdom of heaven. These blessings are promised to those who follow poverty, pity, [Fol. 83b.] penance, meekness, mercy, chastity, peace and patience, — Poverty and patience are to be treated together. They are "fettled in one form," and have one meed. Poverty will dwell where she lists, and man must needs suffer. Poverty and patience are play-fellows. What avails impatience, if God send affliction! Patience is best. Did not Jonah incur danger by his folly?

[1] MS. *fyn*.

[2] *mon* (?).

[3] MS. *tyne*.

II.

Hit bi-tydde sum-tyme in þe termes of Iude,
Ionas ioyned watȝ þer-inne ientyle prophete;
Goddes glam to hym glod, þat hym vnglad made,
With a roghlych rurd rowned in his ere;
"Rys radly," he says, "& rayke forth euen,
Nym þe way to nynyue, wyth-outen oþer speche,
& in þat cete my saȝes soghe alle aboute,
þat, in þat place at þe poynt, I put in þi hert;
For Iwysse hit arn so wykke þat in þat won dowelleȝ,
& her malys is so much I may not abide,
Bot venge me on her vilanye & venym bilyue;
Now sweȝe me þider swyftly & say me þis arende."
When þat steuen watȝ stynt, þat stowned his mynde,
Al he wrathed in his wyt & wyþerly he þoȝt,
If I bowe to his bode & bryng hem þis tale,
& I be Nummen in Nuniue, my nyes begynes;
He telles me þose traytoures arn typped schrewes,
I com wyth þose tyþynges, þay ta me bylyue,
Pyneȝ me in a prysoun, put me in stokkes,
Wryþe me in a warlok, wrast out myn yȝen.
þis is a meruayl message a man for to preche,
Amonge enmyes so mony & mansed fendes;
Bot if my gaynlych god such gref to me wolde,
For[1] desert of sum sake þat I slayn were,
At alle peryles, quod þe prophete, I aproche hit no nerre,
I wyl me sum oþer waye, þat he ne wayte after;
I schal tee in-to tarce, & tary þere a whyle,
& lyȝtly, when I am lest, he letes me alone.
þenne he ryses radly, & raykes bilyue
Ionas toward port Iaph, ay Ianglande for tene,
þat he nolde þole, for no-þyng, non of þose pynes,
þaȝ þe fader þat hym formed were fale of his hele.
"Oure syre syttes," he says, "on sege so hyȝe
In his g[l]wande glorye, & gloumbes ful lyttel,

[Fol. 84a.]

Jonah was a prophet of the gentiles.

God's word came to him, saying,

"Rise quickly, take the way to Nineveh.

Say that which I shall put in thine heart.

Wickedness dwells in that city.

Go swiftly and carry my message."

Jonah is full of wrath.

He is afraid that the shrews will put him in the stocks,

or put out his eyes.

He thinks that God desires his death.

He determines not to go near the city,

but fly to Tarshish.

Grumbling, he goes to port Joppa.

He says that God will not be able to protect him.

1 MS. *fos*.

Þaȝ I be nummen in nuniue & naked dispoyled,
On rode rwly to-rent, with rybaudes mony."

Jonah reaches the port, finds a ship ready to sail.

Þus he passes to þat port, his passage to seche,
Fyndes he a fayr schyp to þe fare redy;
Maches hym with þe maryneres, makes her paye,
For to towe hym in-to tarce, as tyd as þay myȝt.

The seamen catch up the cross-sail, fasten the cables, weigh their anchors. [Fol. 84b.]

Then he tron on þo tres & þay her tramme ruchen,
Cachen vp þe crossayl, cables þay fasten,
Wiȝt at þe wyndas weȝen her ankres,
Sprude spak to þe sprete þe spare bawe-lyne,

and spread sail.

Gederen to þe gyde ropes, þe grete cloþ falles;
Þay layden in on ladde-borde & þe lofe wynnes.

A gentle wind wafts the ship along.

Þe blyþe breþe at her bak þe bosum he fyndes,
He swenges me þys swete schip swefte fro þe hauen.

Was never a Jew so joyful as was Jonah then.

Watȝ neuer so Ioyful a Iue, as Ionas watȝ þenne,
Þat þe daunger of dryȝtyn so derfly ascaped;
He wende wel þat þat wyȝ þat al þe world planted,
Hade no maȝt in þat mere no man forto greue.

He has, however, put himself in peril,

Lo! þe wytles wrechche, for he wolde noȝt suffer,
Now hatȝ he put hym in plyt of peril wel more;
Hit watȝ a wenyng vn-war þat welt in his mynde,

in fleeing from God.

Þaȝ he were soȝt fro samarye þat god seȝ no fyrre,
Ȝise he blusched ful brode, þat burde hym by sure,

The words of David.

Þat ofte kyd hym þe carpe þat kyng sayde,
Dyngne dauid on des, þat demed þis speche,
In a psalme þat he set þe sauter with-inne;
O Folcȝ in folk felcȝ oþer whyle,

Does He not hear, who made all ears! He is not blind that formed each eye. Jonah is now in no dread.

& vnderstondes vmbe-stounde, þaȝ he be stape fole,
Hope ȝe þat he heres not þat eres alle made?
Hit may not be þat he is blynde þat bigged vche yȝe.
Bot he dredes no dynt þat dotes for elde,
For he watȝ fer in þe flod foundande to tarce;

He is, however, soon overtaken.

Bot, I trow, ful tyd, ouer-tan þat he were,
So þat schomely to schort he schote of his ame.

The wielder of all things has devices at will.

For þe welder of wyt, þat wot alle þynges,
Þat ay wakes & waytes, at wylle hatȝ he slyȝtes;

He calde on þat ilk crafte he carf *with* his hondes,
Þay wakened wel þe wroþeloker, for wroþely he cleped:
"Ewrus & aquiloun, þat on est sittes,
Blowes boþe at my bode vpon blo watteres."

He commands Eurus and Aquilo to blow.

Þenne watȝ no tom þer bytwene his tale & her dede,
So bayn wer þay boþe two, his bone for to wyrk.

The winds blow obedient to His word.

An-on out of þe norþ est þe noys bigynes,
When boþe breþes con blowe vpon blo watteres;
Roȝ rakkes þer ros *with* rudnyng an-vnder,

Out of the north-east the noise begins.

[Fol. 85*a*.]

Þe see souȝed ful sore, gret selly to here;
Þe wyndes on þe wonne water so wrastel to-geder,
Þat þe wawes ful wode waltered so hiȝe,
& efte busched to þe abyme þat breed fysches;
Durst nowhere for roȝ arest at þe bothem.

Storms arose, winds wrestled together, the waves rolled high,

and never rested.

When þe breth & þe brok & þe bote metten,
Hit watȝ a ioyles gyn þat Ionas watȝ inne,
For hit reled on roun[d] vpon þe roȝe yþes.

Then was Jonah joyless.
The boat reeled around.

Þe bur ber to hit baft þat braste alle her gere,
Þen hurled on a hepe þe helme & þe sterne,
Furst to murte mony rop & þe mast after.

The gear became out of order.

Ropes and mast were broken.

Þe sayl sweyed on þe see, þenne suppe bihoued
Þe coge of þe colde[1] water, & þenne þe cry ryses;
Ȝet coruen þay þe cordes & kest al þer-oute.

A loud cry is raised.

Mony ladde þer forth-lep to laue & to kest,
Scopen out þe scaþel water, þat fayn scape wolde;
For be monnes lode[2] neuer so luþer, þe lyf is ay swete.

Many a lad labours to lighten the ship.

Þer watȝ busy ouer-borde bale to kest
Her bagges, & her feþer beddes, & her bryȝt wedes,
Her kysttes, & her coferes, her caraldes alle,
& al to lyȝten þat lome, ȝif leþe wolde schape;

They throw overboard their bags and feather beds.

Bot euer watȝ ilyche loud þe lot of þe wyndes,
& euer wroþer þe water, & wodder þe stremes.
Þen þo wery for-wroȝt wyst no bote,

But still the wind rages, and the waves become wilder.

Bot vchon glewed on his god þat gayned hym beste;
Summe to vernagu þer vouched a-vowes solemne,
Summe to diana deuout, & derf nepturne,

Each man calls upon his god.

Some called upon Vernagu, Diana, and Neptune,

[1] MS. *clolde*.

[2] *lote* (?).

to the sun and to the moon.

To mahoun & to mergot, þe mone & þe sunne,
& vche lede as he loued & layde had his hert.

Then said one of the sailors: "Some lawless wretch, that has grieved his God, is in the ship.

Þenne bispeke þe spakest dispayred wel nere:
I leue here be sum losynger, sum lawles wrech,
Þat hatȝ greued his god & gotȝ here amonge vus;
Lo al synkes in his synne & for his sake marres!

I advise that we lay lots upon each man.

I lovne þat we lay lotes on ledes vchone,
& who-so lympes þe losse, lay hym þer-oute;

[Fol. 85b.] When the guilty is gone the tempest may cease." This is agreed to.

& quen þe gulty is gon what may gome trawe,
Bot he þat rules þe rak may rwe on þose oþer?
Þis watȝ sette in asent, & sembled þay were,

All are assembled, from all corners of the ship,

Herȝed out of vche hyrne to hent þat falles.
A lodes-mon lyȝtly lep vnder hachches,
For to layte mo ledes & hem to lote bryng,
Bot hym fayled no freke þat he fynde myȝt,

save Jonah the Jew, who had fled into the bottom of the boat.

Saf Ionas þe Iwe þat Iowked in derne.
He watȝ flowen for ferde of þe flode lotes
In-to þe boþem of þe bot, & on a brede lyggede,
On helde by þe hurrok, for þe heuen wrache,

There he falls asleep.

Slypped vpon a sloumbe, selepe, & sloberande he routes.

Soon he is aroused,

Þe freke hym frunt with his fot & bede hym ferk vp,
Þer ragnel in his rakentes hym rere of his dremes;
Bi þe haspede he hentes hym þenne,

and brought on board.

& broȝt hym vp by þe brest & vpon borde sette,

Full roughly is he questioned.

Arayned hym ful runyschly what raysoun he hade
In such slaȝtes of sorȝe to slepe so faste;
Sone haf þay her sortes sette & serelych deled,

The lot falls upon Jonah.

& ay þe[1] lote, vpon laste, lymped on Ionas.

[1] MS. þe þe.

Then quickly they said: "What the devil hast thou done, doted wretch? What seekest thou on the sea?

Þenne ascryed þay hym sckete, & asked ful loude,
"What þe deuel hatȝ þou don, doted wrech?
What seches þou on see, synful schrewe,
With þy lastes so luþer to lose vus vchone?

Hast thou no God to call upon?

Hatȝ þou, gome, no gouernour ne god on to calle,
Þat þou þus slydes on slepe when þou slayn worþes?

Of what land art thou?

Of what londe art þou lent, what laytes þou here
Whyder in worlde þat þou wylt, & what is þyn arnde?

Lo þy dom is þe dyȝt, for þy dedes ille!
Do gyf glory to þy godde, er þou glyde hens."
"I am an Ebru," q*uod* he, "of Israyl borne;
Þat wyȝe I worchyp, Iwysse, þat wroȝt alle þy*n*ges,
Alle þe worlde w*ith* þe welkyn, þe wynde & þe sternes,
& alle þat woneȝ þer w*ith*-i*n*ne, at a worde one.
Alle þis meschef for me is made at þys tyme,
For I haf greued my god & gulty am fou*n*den;
For-þy bereȝ me to þe borde, & baþeþes[1] me þ*er*-oute,
Er gete ȝe no happe, I hope forsoþe."
He ossed hy*m*[2] by vnnyn*g*es þat þay vnder-nomen,
Þat he watȝ flawen fro þe face of frelych dryȝtyn;
Þe*n*ne such a ferde on hem fel & flayed he*m* w*ith*-inne,
Þat þay ruyt hym to rowwe & letten þe ryn*k* one.
Haþeles hyȝed i*n* haste w*ith* ores ful longe,
Sy*n* her sayl watȝ hem aslypped on sydeȝ to rowe;
Hef & hale vpon hyȝt to helpen hym seluen,
Bot al watȝ nedles note, þat nolde not bityde:
In bluber of þe blo flod bursten her ores,
Þe*n*ne hade þay noȝt i*n* her honde þat hem help myȝt;
Þe*n*ne nas no cou*m*fort to keu*er*, ne counsel non oþer,
Bot ionas in-to his Iuis Iugge bylyue.
Fyrst þay prayen to þe prynce þat p*ro*phetes seruen,
Þat he gef hem þe g*ra*ce to greuen hy*m* neu*er*,
Þat þay i*n* baleleȝ blod þer blenden her handeȝ,
Þaȝ þat haþel wer his, þat þay here quelled.
Tyd by top & bi to þay token hy*m* synne,
In-to þat lodlych loȝe þay luche hy*m* sone;
He watȝ no tytter out-tulde[3] þat tempest ne sessed,
Þe se saȝtled þ*er*-w*ith*, as sone as ho moȝt.
Þe*n*ne þaȝ her takel were torne, þat tot*er*ed on yþeȝ,
Styffe stremes & streȝt hem strayned a whyle,
Þat drof hem dryȝlych adou*n* þe depe to serue,[4]
Tyl a swetter ful swyþe he*m* sweȝed to bonk.
Þer watȝ louyn*g* on lofte, when þay þe londe wo*n*nen,
To oure mercyable god, on moyses wyse,

Thou art doomed for thy ill deeds."
Jonah says: "I am a Hebrew, a worshipper of the world's Creator.
All this mischief is caused by me,
[Fol. 86*a*.]
therefore cast me overboard."
He proves to them that he was guilty.
The mariners are exceedingly frightened.
They try to make way with their oars,
but their endeavours are useless.
Jonah must be doomed to death.
They pray to God,
that they may not shed innocent blood.
Jonah is cast overboard.
The tempest ceases and the sea settles.
The stiff streams drive the ship about.
At last they reach a bank.
The seamen thank God.

[1] *baþes* (?).
[2] *hem* (?).
[3] *out-tulte* (?).
[4] *sterue* (?).

and perform solemn vows.

With sacrafyse vp-set, & solempne vowes,
& graunted hym vn-to be god & graythly non oþer;

Jonah is in great dread.

Þaȝ þay be Iolef for Ioye, Ionas ȝet dredes,
Þaȝ he nolde suffer no sore, his seele is on anter;
For what-so worþed of þat wyȝe, fro he in water dipped,
Hit were a wonder to wene, ȝif holy wryt nere.

III.

Jonah is shoved from the ship.

Now is ionas þe Iwe Iugged to[1] drowne;
Of þat schended schyp men schowued hym sone.

[Fol. 86b.] A wild whale swims by the boat.

A wylde walterande whal, as wyrde þen schaped,
Þat watȝ beten fro þe abyme, bi þat bot flotte,
& watȝ war of þat wyȝe þat þe water soȝte,

He opens his swallow,

& swyftely swenged hym to swepe & his swolȝ opened;
Þe folk ȝet haldande his fete þe fysch hym tyd hentes,

and seizes the prophet.

With-outen towche of any tothe he tult in his þrote.
Thenne he swengeȝ & swayues[2] to þe se boþem,
Bi mony rokkeȝ ful roȝe & rydelande strondes,
Wyth þe mon in his mawe, malskred in drede.

It is not to be wondered at that Jonah suffered woe.

As lyttel wonder hit watȝ ȝif he wo dreȝed,
For nade þe hyȝe heuen kyng, þurȝ his honde myȝt,
Warded þis wrech man in warlowes gutteȝ,
What lede moȝt lyue bi lawe of any kynde,
Þat any lyf myȝt be lent so longe hym with-inne?
Bot he watȝ sokored by þat syre þat syttes so hiȝe,

The prophet is without hope.

Þaȝ were wauleȝ[3] of wele, in wombe of þat fissche,
& also dryuen þurȝ þe depe, & in derk waltereȝ.

Cold was his comfort.

Lorde! colde watȝ his cumfort & his care huge,
For he knew vche a cace & kark þat hym lymped;
How fro þe bot in-to þe blober watȝ with a best lachched,
& þrwe[4] in at hit þrote, with-outen þret more,

Jonah was only a mote in the whale's jaws. He entered in by the gills, and by means of one of the intestines of the fish, came into a space as large as a hall.

As mote in at a munster dor, so mukel wern his chawleȝ,
He glydes in by þe giles, þurȝ glaymande glette,
Relande in by a rop, a rode þat hym þoȝt,
Ay hele ouer hed, hourlande aboute,
Til he blunt in a blok as brod as a halle;

[1] MS. to to.
[2] *swaynes* (?).
[3] *wanleȝ* (?).
[4] *þrwen* (?).

& þer he festnes þe fete & fathmeȝ aboute,
& stod vp in his stomak, þat stank as þe deuel;
þer in saym & in sorȝe þat sauoured as helle,
þer watȝ bylded his bour, þat wyl no bale suffer;

The prophet fixes his feet firmly in the belly of the whale.

& þenne he lurkkes & laytes where watȝ le best,
In vche a nok of his nauel, bot nowhere he fyndeȝ
No rest ne recouerer, bot ramelande myre,
In wych gut so euer he gotȝ; bot euer is god swete;

He searches into every nook of its navel.

& þer he lenged at þe last & to þe lede called.
"Now prynce, of þy prophete pité þou haue!
[Fol. 87a.] þaȝ I be fol, & fykel, & falce of my hert,
De-woyde now þy vengaunce, þurȝ vertu of rauthe;
Thaȝ I be gulty of gyle as gaule of prophetes,
þou art god, & alle gowdeȝ ar grayþely þyn owen;
Haf now mercy of þy man & his mys-dedes,
& preue þe lyȝtly a lorde, in londe & in water."

The prophet calls upon God.

He cries for mercy.

With þat he hitte to a hyrne & helde hym þer-inne,
þer no de-foule of no fylþe watȝ fest hym abute;
þer he sete also sounde, saf for merk one,
As in þe bulk of þe bote, þer he by-fore sleped.
So in a bouel of þat best he bideȝ on lyue,
þre dayes & þ[r]e nyȝt ay þenkande on dryȝtyn,
His myȝt & his merci, his mesure þenne;
Now he knaweȝ hym in care þat couþe not in sele.

He sits safely in a recess,

in a bowel of the beast, for three days and three nights.

Ande euer walteres þis whal bi wyldren depe,
þurȝ mony a regioun ful roȝe, þurȝ ronk of his wylle,
For þat mote in his mawe mad hym, I trowe,
þaȝ hit lyttel were, hym wyth to wamel at his hert,
Ande assayled þe segge; ay sykerly he herde
þe bygge borne on his bak & bete on his sydes;
þen a prayer ful prest þe prophete þer maked
On þis wyse, as I wene, his wordeȝ were mony:

The whale passes through many a rough region.

Jonah makes the whale feel sick.

The prophet prays to God in this wise:

IV.

"Lorde to þe haf I cleped, in careȝ ful stronge,
Out of þe hole þou me herde, of hellen wombe

"Lord! to thee have I cried out of hell's womb.

I calde, & þou knew myn vncler steuen;
Thou dippedst me in the sea.
Þou diptez me of þe dep̄e se, in-to þe dymme hert,
Thy great floods passed over me.
Þe grete flem of þy flod folded me vmbe;
Alle þe gotez of þy guferes, & groundelez powlez,
The streams drive over me.
& þy stryuande stremez of stryndez so mony,
In on daschande dam, dryuez me ouer;
I am cast out from thy sight.
& zet I say, as I seet in þe se boþem,
'Care-ful am I kest out fro þy cler yzen
& deseuered fro þy syzt; zet surely I hope,
Efte to trede on þy temple & teme to þy seluen.'
I am wrapped in water to my wo stoundez,
The abyss binds me.
Þe abyme byndes þe body þat I byde inne;
[Fol. 87b.] *The rushing waves play on my head.*
Þe pure poplande hourle playes on my heued,
To laste mere of vche a mount man am I fallen;
Þe barrez of vche a bonk ful bigly me haldes,
Thou possessest my life.
Þat I may lachche no lont[1] & þou my lyf weldes;
Þou schal releue me renk, whil þy ryzt slepez,
Þurz myzt of þy mercy þat mukel is to tryste.
In my anguish I remembered my God,
For when þacces of anguych watz hid in my sawle,
Þenne I remembred me ryzt of my rych lorde,
and besought His pity.
Prayande him for peté his prophete to here,
Þat in-to his holy hous myn orisoun mozt entre.
I haf meled with þy maystres mony longe day,
Bot now I wot wyterly, þat þose vnwyse ledes
Þat affyen hym[2] in vanyté & in vayne þynges,
For þink[3] þat mountes to nozt, her mercy forsaken;
When I am delivered from this danger,
Bot I dewoutly awowe þat verray betz halden,
Soberly to do þe sacrafyse when I schal saue worþe,
I will obey thy commands."
& offer þe for my hele a ful hol gyfte,
& halde goud þat þou me hetes; haf here my trauthe."
God speaks fiercely to the whale,
Thenne oure fader to þe fysch ferslych biddez,
Þat he hym sput spakly vpon spare drye;
and he vomits out the prophet on a dry space.
Þe whal wendez at his wylle & a warþe fyndez,
& þer he brakez vp þe buyrne, as bede hym oure lorde.
Jonah has need to wash his clothes.
Þenne he swepe to þe sonde in sluchched cloþes,
Hit may wel be þat mester were his mantyle to wasche;

[1] *lond* (?).
[2] *hem* (?).
[3] *þing* (?).

Þe bonk þat he blosched to & bode hym bisyde,
Wern of þe regiounes ryȝt þat he renayed hade;
Þenne a wynde of goddeȝ worde efte þe wyȝe bruxleȝ,
"Nylt þou neuer to niniue bi no-kynneȝ wayeȝ?"
"Ȝisse lorde," quod þe lede, "lene me þy grace
For to go at þi gre, me gayneȝ non[1] oþer."
"Ris, aproche þen to prech, lo þe place here!
Lo! my lore is in þe loke,[2] lance hit þer-inne."
Þenne þe renk radly ros as he myȝt,
& to niniue þat naȝt he neȝed ful euen;
Hit watȝ a ceté ful syde & selly of brede,
On to þrenge þer-þurȝe watȝ þre dayes dede.
[Fol. 88a.] Þat on Iournay ful Ioynt Ionas hym ȝede,
Er euer he warpped any worde to wyȝe þat he mette,
& þenne he cryed so cler, þat kenne myȝt alle;
Þe trwe tenor of his teme he tolde on þis wyse:
"Ȝet schal forty dayeȝ fully fare to an ende,
& þenne schal Niniue be nomen & to noȝt worþe;
Truly þis ilk toun schal tylte to grounde,
Vp-so-doun schal ȝe dumpe depe to þe abyme,
To be swolȝed swyftly wyth þe swart erþe,
& alle þat lyuyes here-inne lose þe swete."
Þis speche sprang in þat space & spradde alle aboute,
To borges & to bachcleres, þat in þat burȝ lenged;
Such a hidor hem hent & a hatel drede,
Þat al chaunged her chere & chylled at þe hert.
Þe segge sesed not ȝet, bot sayde euer ilyche
"Þe verray vengaunce of god schal voyde þis place."
Þenne þe peple pitosly pleyned ful stylle,
& for þe drede of dryȝtyn doured in hert;
Heter hayreȝ þay hent þat asperly bited,
& þose þay bounden to her bak & to her bare sydeȝ,
Dropped dust on her hede & dymly bisoȝten,
Þat þat penaunce plesed him þat playneȝ on her wronge.
& ay he cryes in þat kyth tyl þe kyng herde;
& he radly vp-ros & ran fro his chayer,

God's word comes to the prophet.

He is told to preach in Nineveh.

By night Jonah reaches the city.

Nineveh was a very great city.

Jonah delivers his message;

"Yet forty days and Nineveh shall come to an end.

It shall be turned upside down,

and swallowed quickly by the black earth."

This speech spreads throughout the city.

Great fear seizes all.

The people mourn secretly,

clothe themselves in sackcloth,

and cast ashes upon their heads.

The message reaches the ears of the king.

[1] MS. mon.

[2] loken (?).

He rends his robes,

His ryche robe he to-rof of his rigge naked,
& of a hep of askes he hitte in þe myddeȝ;

clothes himself in sackloth,

He aske3 heterly a hayre & hasped hym vmbe,
Sewed a sekke þer abof, & syked ful colde;

and mourns in the dust.

Þer he dased in þat duste, with droppande teres,
Wepande ful wonderly alle his wrange dedes.

He issues a decree,

Þenne sayde he to his seriauntes, "samnes yow bilyue,
Do dryue out a decre demed of my seluen,

that all in the city, men, beasts, women and children, prince, priest, and prelates, should fast for their sins.

Þat alle þe bodyes þat ben with-inne þis borȝ quyk,
Boþe burnes & bestes, burdeȝ & childer,
Vch prynce, vche prest & prelates alle,
Alle faste frely for her falce werkes;

Children are to be weaned from the breast.

Seseȝ childer of her sok, soghe hem so neuer,
Ne best bite on no brom, ne no bent nauþer,
Passe to no pasture, ne pike non erbes,

The ox is to have no hay, nor the horse any water.

Ne non oxe to no hay, ne no horse to water;
Al schal crye for-clemmed, with alle oure clere strenþe,
Þe rurd schal ryse to hym þat rawþe schal haue;

Who can tell if God will have mercy?

What wote oþer wyte may ȝif þe wyȝe lykes,
Þat is hende in þe hyȝt of his gentryse?

Though He is mighty, He is merciful,

I wot his myȝt is so much, þaȝ he be mysse-payed,
Þat in his mylde amesyng he mercy may fynde;
& if we leuen þe layk of oure layth synnes,
& stylle steppen in þe styȝe he styȝtleȝ hym seluen,
He wyl wende of his wodschip, & his wrath leue,

and may forgive us our guilt.

& for-gif vus þis gult ȝif we hym god leuen."

All believed and repented.

Þenne al leued on his lawe & laften her synnes,
Par-formed alle þe penaunce þat þe prynce radde;

God forgave them through his goodness.

& god þurȝ his godnesse forgef as he sayde,
Þaȝ he oþer bihyȝt, [&] with-helde his vengaunce.

V.

Much sorrow settles upon Jonah.

Muche sorȝe þenne satteled vpon segge Ionas,
He wex as wroth as þe wynde towarde oure lorde,

He becomes very angry. He prays to God and says:

So hatȝ anger onhit his hert; he calleȝ
A prayer to þe hyȝe prynce, for pyne, on þys wyse:

"I biseche þe syre now þou self iugge,
Watȝ not þis ilk my worde þat worþen is nouþe,
"Was not this my saying,
Þat I kest in my cuntre, when þou þy carp sendeȝ,
when Thy message reached me in my own country?
Þat I schulde tee to þys toun, þi talent to preche?
Wel knew I þi cortaysye, þy quoynt soffraunce.
I knew Thy great goodness,
Þy bounté of debonerté & þy bene grace,
Þy longe abydyng wyth lur, þy late vengaunce,
Thy long-suffering,
& ay þy mercy is mete, be mysse neuer so huge.
and Thy mercy.
I wyst wel when I hade worded quatsoeuer I cowþe,
To manace alle þise mody men þat in þis mote dowelleȝ,
I knew these men might make their peace with Thee,
Wyth a prayer & a pyne þay myȝt her pese gete,
& þer-fore I wolde haf flowen fer in-to tarce.
therefore I fled unto Tarshish.
Now lorde lach out my lyf, hit lastes to longe,
Bed me bilyue my bale stour, & bryng me on ende,
Take my life from me, O Lord!
[Fol. 89a.] For me were swetter to swelt, as swyþe as me þynk,
Þen lede lenger þi lore, þat þus me les makeȝ."
It is better for me to die than live."
Þe soun of oure souerayn þen swey in his ere,
Þat vpbraydes þis burne vpon a breme wyse:
God upbraids Jonah, saying:
"Herk renk! is þis ryȝt so ronkly to wrath,
"Is this right to be so wroth?"
For any dede þat I haf don oþer demed þe ȝet?"
Ionas al Ioyles & Ianglande vp-ryses
Jonah, jangling, uprises,
& haldeȝ out on est half of þe hyȝe place,
& farandely on a felde he fetteleȝ hym to bide,
For to wayte on þat won what schulde worþe after.
Þer he busked hym a bour, þe best þat he myȝt,
and makes himself a bower,
Of hay & of euer-ferne & erbeȝ a fewe,
of hay and ever-fern,
For hit watȝ playn in þat place for plyande greueȝ,
For to schylde fro þe schene, oþer any schade keste.
to shield him from the sun.
He bowed vnder his lyttel boþe, his bak to þe sunne,
& þer he swowed & slept sadly al nyȝt,
He slept heavily all night.
Þe whyle god of his grace ded growe of þat soyle,
Þe fayrest bynde hym abof þat euer burne wyste.
God prepared a woodbine.
When þe dawande day dryȝtyn con sende,
Þenne wakened þe wyȝ vnder wodbynde,
Jonah awakes, and is exceedingly glad of the bower.
Loked alofte on þe lef þat lylled grene;
Such a lefsel of lof neuer lede hade,

For hit watȝ brod at þe boþem, boȝted onlofte,
Happed vpon ayþer half a hous as hit were,
A nos on þe norþ syde & nowhere non elleȝ,
Bot al schet in a schaȝe þat schaded ful cole.

The prophet, under its gracious leaves,

Þe gome glyȝt on þe grene graciouse leues,
Þat euer wayued a wynde so wyþe & so cole;
Þe schyre sunne hit vmbe-schon, þaȝ no schafte myȝt

is protected from the sun's rays.

Þe mountaunce of a lyttel mote, vpon þat man schyne,
Þenne watȝ þe gome so glad of his gay logge,
Lys loltrande þer-inne, lokande to toune,
So blyþe of his wodbynde he balteres þer vnde[r],
Þat of no diete þat day þe[1] deuel haf, he roȝt;

Jonah wishes he had such a lodge in his own country.

[Fol. 89b.]

& euer he laȝed as he loked þe loge alle aboute,
& wysched hit were in his kyth, þer he wony schulde,
On heȝe vpon Effraym oþer ermonnes hilleȝ,
"I-wysse a worþloker won to welde I neuer keped."
& quen hit neȝed to naȝt nappe hym bihoued;
He slydeȝ on a sloumbe, slep sloghe vnder leues,

God prepared a worm, that made the woodbine wither.

Whil god wayned a worme þat wrot vpe þe rote,
& wyddered watȝ þe wodbynde bi þat þe wyȝe wakned;
& syþen he warneȝ þe west to waken ful softe,
& sayeȝ vnte[2] ȝeferus þat he syfle warme,
Þat þer quikken no cloude bi-fore þe cler sunne,
& ho schal busch vp ful brode & brenne as a candel.

Jonah awakes and finds his woodbine destroyed. The leaves were all faded.

Þen wakened þe wyȝe of his wyl dremes,
& blusched to his wodbynde þat broþely watȝ marred,
Al welwed & wasted þo worþelych leues;
Þe schyre sunne hade hem schent, er euer þe schalk wyst,

The sun beat upon the head of Jonah.

& þen hef vp þe hete & heterly brenned;
Þe warm wynde of þe weste wertes he swyþeȝ.
Þe man marred on þe molde þat moȝt hym not hyde,
His wodbynde watȝ away, he weped for sorȝe,

He is exceedingly angry,

With hatel anger & hot, heterly he calleȝ:
A! þou maker of man, what maystery þe þynkeȝ
Þus þy freke to forfare forbi alle oþer,

[1] *de* altered to þe.

[2] *vnto*(?).

With alle meschef þat þou may, neuer þou me spareȝ?
I keuered me a cumfort þat now is caȝt fro me,
My wod-bynde so wlonk þat wered my heued,
Bot now I se þou art sette my solace to reue;
Why ne dyȝteȝ þou me to diȝe; I dure to longe?"
ȝet oure lorde to þe lede lansed a speche:
"Is þis ryȝt-wys þou renk, alle þy ronk noyse,
So wroth for a wodbynde to wax so sone,
Why art þou so waymot wyȝe for so lyttel?"
"Hit is not lyttel," quod þe lede, "bot lykker to ryȝt,
I wolde I were of þis worlde wrapped in moldeȝ."
"þenne byþenk þe mon, if þe for-þynk sore,
If I wolde help my honde werk, haf þou no wonder;
þou art waxen so wroth for þy wod-bynde,
& trauayledeȝ neuer to tent hit þe tyme of an howre,
[Fol. 89a.] Bot at a wap hit here wax & away at an oþer,
& ȝet lykeȝ þe so luþer, þi lyf woldeȝ þou tyne;
þenne wyte not me for þe werk þat I hit wolde help,
& rwe on þo redles þat remen for synne.
Fyrst I made hem myself of materes myn one,
& syþen I loked hem ful longe & hem on lode hade;
& if I my trauayl schulde tyne of termes so longe,
& type doun ȝonder toun when hit turned were,
þe sor of such a swete place burde synk to my hert,
So mony malicious mon as mourneȝ þer-inne;
& of þat soumme ȝet arn summe such sotteȝ for madde,
As lyttel barneȝ on barme þat neuer bale wroȝt,
& wymmen vnwytté þat wale ne couþe
þat on hande fro þat oþer, for[1] alle þis hyȝe worlde,
Bitwene þe stele & þe stayre disserne noȝt cunen,
What rule renes in roun bitwene þe ryȝt hande
& his lyfte, þaȝ his lyf schulde lost be þer-for;
& als þer ben doumbe besteȝ in þe burȝ mony,
þat may not synne in no syt hem seluen to greue,
Why schulde I wrath wyth hem, syþen wyȝeȝ wyl torne,
& cum[2] & cnawe me for kyng, & my carpe leue?

and prays God that he may die. God rebukes the prophet.

"Dost thou well," He says, "to be angry for the gourd?"

Jonah replies "I would I were dead."

God asks if it is to be wondered at that He should help His handy work.

Is not Jonah angry that his woodbine is destroyed, which cost him no labour?

God is not to be blamed for taking pity upon people that He made.

Should He destroy Nineveh the sorrow of such a sweet place would sink to His heart.

In the city there are little bairns who have done no wrong.

And there are others who cannot discern between their right hand and their left hand.

There are also dumb beasts in the city incapable of sinning.

[1] MS. *fol.*

[2] *Or* cun.

Wer I as hastif a[s] þou, heere were harme lu*m*pen,
Couþe I not þole bot as þou þer þryued ful fewe;
I may not be so mal[i]ciou*s* & mylde be halden,

Judgment must be tempered with mercy.

For malyse is noȝ[t] to may*n*tyne boute mercy w*ith*i*n*ne;
Be noȝt so gryndel god man, bot go forth þy wayes."

He that is too hasty to rend his clothes must afterwards sit with worse ones to sew them together.

Be preue & be pacient, i*n* payne & i*n* Ioye,
For he þat is to rakel to renden his cloþeȝ,
Mot efte sitte w*ith* more vn-sou*n*de to sewe he*m* togeder.

Poverty and pain must be endured.

For-þy when pou*er*té me enpreceȝ & payneȝ i*n*-noȝe,
Ful softly w*ith* suffrau*n*ce saȝttel me bihoueȝ,

Patience is a noble point, though it displeases oft.

For þe penau*n*ce & payne to preue hit i*n* syȝt,
Þat pacience is a nobel poy*n*t, þaȝ hit displese ofte. Amen.

NOTES.

Page 1. l. 2, *to*, very. 8 *sengeley in synglure*, ever in singleness (uniqueness).

Now is Susan in sale *sengeliche* arayed.

Pistel of Susan, Vernon MS., fol. 317.

11 *dewyne*, pine ; *for-dolked*, for-wounded (severely hurt). 16 *heuen my happe*, increase my happiness. 17 *þrych my hert þrange*, through my heart pierce. 20 *stylle stounde*, a secret sorrow.

23 *O moul þou marreȝ a myry mele*,

O mould (earth) thou spoilest a merry discourse.

P. 2. l. 27 *Blomeȝ blayke & blwe & rede*,

Flowers yellow, blue, and red.

49 *spenned*, wrung.

51, 52 A secret grief in my heart dinned (resounded),

Though reason set myself at peace.

53 *spenned*, allured, enticed away.

54 *Wyth fyrte skylleȝ þat faste faȝt*,

With trembling doubts that fast fought (struggled).

P. 3. l. 76 bolleȝ=*boleȝ*, trunks of trees. 78 *on vcha tynde*, on each branch. 92 *reken myrþe*, pleasant, joyous mirth.

P. 4. l. 99 *Þe derþe þer-of*, the value (preciousness) thereof. 101 *in wely wyse*, in joyful mood. 102 *dereȝ*, injuries, harms. 103 *fyrre*, farther. 105 *raweȝ & randeȝ*, borders and paths. 107 *I wan to*, I reached. *Winne* in O.E. was used much in the same way as we now employ the word *get*.

112 *Wyth a rownande rourde raykande aryȝt*,

With a murmuring (whispering) sound flowing aright.

113 *founce*, bottom ; *stepe*, bright. 114 *glente*, shone ; *glyȝt*, glistened. 115 *A[s] stremande sterneȝ*, as glittering stars ; *stroþe*, stout, brave. 119 *loȝe*, deep. 125 *dryȝly haleȝ*, strongly (*or* deeply) flows. 126 *bred ful bred-ful*=*bretful* (?), full to the brim.

P. 5. l. 131 *wayneȝ*, grants. 132 *hitteȝ*, seeks. 138 *gayn*, opposite.

142 *I hopede þat mote merked wore*,

I supposed that building was devised.

149 *stote & stare*, stand (loiter) and gape.

150–1 *To fynde a forþe, faste con I fonde,*
Bot woþeȝ mo I-wysse þer ware,
To find a way fast did I go,
But paths more indeed there were.

153 *wonde*, cease, abstain (from fear). 155 *nwe note*, a new matter. 163 *blymande whyt*, glistening white. See 197.

P. 6. l. 165 *schere*, purify, refine.

169 *Þe more I frayste hyr fayre face.*
The more I examined her fair face.

frayst (fraist) usually signifies to try, tempt.

170 *fonte*, tried, examined, *found*.

176 *Such a burre myȝt make myn herte blunt,*
Such a blow might make mine heart faint.

179 *Þat stonge myn hert ful stray atount,*

Should we not read—Þat stonge myn hert ful stray a stount (?), "full stray a stount" = a blow full stray.

187 *chos*, was following, was seeking.

188 *Er I at steuen hir moȝt stalle,*
Before I could place her within reach of discourse.

190 *seme* = *semely*, seemly.

P. 7. l. 208 *flurted*, figured. Cf. *flurt*-silk, figured-silk.

210 *Her here heke al hyr vmbe-gon,*
Her hair eke (also) all her about gone.

212 *Her ble more blaȝt*, her complexion whiter. 213 *schorne golde schyr* refined gold pure. 216 *porfyl*, hem of a dress, or rather an embroidered hem. 217 *poyned*, ornamented, trimmed.

223–4 *A manneȝ dom myȝt dryȝly demme.*
Er mynde moȝt malte in hit mesure,
A man's judgment might greatly dim,
Before (his) mind could discourse of it in sufficient terms of praise.

226 *No* = *ne* (nor) would be a better reading. 230 *wyþer half*, opposite side.

P. 8. l. 243 *myn one*, myself. 244 *layned*, kept secret, hidden. 251 *Fro*, from the time that. *towen & twayned*, made two and separated.

P. 9. l. 272 *is put in pref*, has been proved. 275 *bote of þy meschef*, the remedy of thy misfortune (misery).

290 *Wy borde ȝe men so madde ȝe be?*
Why should you talk, so foolish you are?

P. 10. l. 307 *westernays*, wrongly, in vain? It may be another form of westernways, from the A. Sax. *wéste*, barren, empty; *wéstern*, a desert place. Or is it connected with A. Sax. *winstre*, the left hand?

320 *Þy corse in clot mot calder keue,*
Thy body in earth (clods) must colder plunge.

321 *for-garte* forfeited. 322 *ȝore fader* for *form-fader*, first-father. 323 *drwry* = *drery*, dreary (?). *boȝ* (= *bos* = *bus*?) *vch ma* (*man*?) *dreue*, behoves each man to drive (go). See B. l. 687.

327–8 *Now haf I fonte þat I for-lete*
Schal I efte forgo hit er euer I fyne?
Now I have found what I have lost.
Shall I again forego it ere ever I die?

P. 11. l. 336 *durande doel*, lasting grief.

343 *For anger gaynez þe not a cresse,*
For anger avails the not a cress,

(*i.e.* not a mite). Cf. the following passage from "Piers' Ploughman," p. 174, l. 5629: "Wisdom and wit now
Is noght worth a *kerse*."

353 *Stynst (stynt?) of þy strot & fyne to flyte,*
Leave off thy complaining and cease to chide.

354 *blyþe* is here used as a substantive in the sense of bliss, joy. *swefte* = swift. 356 *hyr craftez kyþe*, manifest her powers.

359–60 *For marre oþer madde, morne & myþe,*
Al lys in him to dyȝt & deme.
For to ruin, or make foolish, grieve or to soothe,
All lies in him to order and doom.

363 *If rapely raue*, etc. = *If rapely I raue*, etc. (?) 368 Though I go astray, my dear, adored one.

P. 12. l. 369 *lyþez*, grant.

374 *Bot much þe bygger ȝet watz my mon,*
Fro þou watz wroken fro vch a woþe.
But much the greater yet was my moan (sorrow),
From (the time) thou wast banished from every path.

377 *now leþez my loþe*, now my sorrow ceases (is softened). 382 *marerez* = *marez* (?). 386 *mate*, dejected. 402 *I hete þe*, I promise the.

P. 14. l. 446 *in hyt self beyng*, in its very being. 455 *gyng*, company. 460 *Temen*, are united, joined. *tryste*, trusty, faithful, firm.

P. 16. l. 511 *wryþen*, toil, literally to turn, twist. 512 *keruen*, dig. *caggen*, draw. *man* = *maken*, make. Cf. *ma* = make, *ta* = take, *tan* = taken. 522 *toȝt*, binding, firm. 524 *pray* (so in MS.), read *pay*. 535 *at ȝe moun*, that ye are able.

P. 17. l. 560 *a grete*, in the gross, a head. 563 *plete*, plead, ask for.
572 *be* = *he* (?).

P. 18. l. 575 *Þaȝ her sweng wyth lyttel at-slykez,*
Though their labour (blow) with little falls off (fails to accomplish much).
605 *chyche*, niggard. 608 *gotez*, streams; *charde*, past tense of *charre*, to turn, deviate.

P. 19. l. 617 *bourne abate* = *burne abade*, man continued. 626 *by lyne*, by lineage descent.

P. 20. l. 645 *Bot þer on com a bote as-tyt,*
But there came one as a remedy at once.
659 *in sely stounde*, in a happy moment. 671 *glente*, fell, slided.

P. 21. l. 680 *dylle*, slow, sluggish. 681 *dyt* = *dyde*, did (?), or *dotz*, does (?). 690 *oure*, prayer.

P. 22. l. 726 *sulpande synne*, defiling, polluting, sin. 727 *bylde*, building. 735 *reme*, realm.

P. 23. l. 752 *Of carpe*, discourse of. 754 *hauyng*, condition, behaviour. 757 *bete*, save, ransom. 759 *make*, wife. 775 *ender cambe* = *under-cam*, came under, took an inferior position (?).

P. 24. l. 802 *& as a lombe þat clypper in lande nem,*
And as a lamb that a *shearer* has taken, etc.

813–4 For us he let himself be scourged and buffetted, and stretched upon a rough tree (*i.e.* nailed to the cross).

P. 25. l. 836 *as bare*, (?) *al bare*, openly. See 1025.

837 *Lesande þe boke with leueȝ sware*,
Opening the book with leaves square.

839 *& at þat syȝt vche douth con dare*,
And at that sight each doughty (one) did tremble (with fear).

849 enle=*eneli*=onely or *onlepi* (?)=singly, alone.

P. 26. l. 864 *talle farande*=*tale farande*, pleasing story.

873 *hue*, cry, voice. 876 *lote*, sound.

P. 27. l. 896 *lote*, features. 909 *hynde*=*hende*, gentle, courteous (one). 911 *bustwys as a blose*, boisterous (wild) as a blaze (flame).

916 *With nay þou neuer my ruful bone*,
Do thou never refuse my mournful request.

P. 28. l. 948 *So is hys mote with-outen moote*,
So is his building without mote (blemish).

P. 29. ll. 975–6 *& I an-endeȝ þe on þis syde*
Schal sue, tyl þou to a hil be veued,
And I opposite thee on this side
Shall go, till thou to a hill be passed.

980–81 *& bluschede on þe burghe, as I forth dreued*,
Byȝonde þe brok fro me warde keued,
And looked on the city, as I forth drove (urged),
Beyond the brook that cut me off from (the object of my desire).

P. 30. l. 1018 *Masporye*=*was pure* (?). 1022 *brode & stayre*, broad and steep (high).
1025 *þat glent as glayre*, that shone as amber.

P. 31. l. 1030 *fon*, ceased, the preterite of *fine*. 1038 *fateȝ*=*fadeȝ*, fades. 1041 *whateȝ*=*watȝ*, was.

P. 32. ll. 1065–66 *Þe ȝates stoken watȝ neuer ȝet*,
Bot euer more open at vche a lone.
The gates shut were never yet,
But ever more open at every lane.

1073 *to euen with*, to equal with, to match with. 1084 *falure*=*fasure*, form (?).

P. 33. l. 1124 *to loue*, to praise. 1127 *in melle*=*in-melle*=*i-melle*, among. Cf. *in-lyche* and *i-lyche*, etc.

P. 34. l. 1141 *Þe lombe delyt non lyste to wene*,
The lamb's delight none desired to doubt.

1146 *laste and lade*, followed and preceded (?).

1161 *Bot of þat munt I watȝ bi-talt*,
But from that purpose I was aroused (shaken).

1163 *bi-calt*=*bi-called* (?), called away.

P. 35. l. 1165 *flone*=*flong* (?), flung. 1193 *helde*, willingly (inclined).

P. 37. l. 3 *forering*=*for-bering* (?). 10 *reken*, reverently, solemnly. 12 *cleche gret mede*, take great reward. 16 *& hym to greme cachen*, and him to wrath drive. 18 *hagherlych*, fitly, decently. 21 *scoymous & skyg*, scrupulous and particular; *skyg* implies dread, fear, shyness. 23 *in a carp*, in a discourse. 24 *heuened aȝt happeȝ*, exhibited eight blessings. 25 *me myneȝ*, I remember.

P. 38. l. 27 *hapeneȝ*, is happy, blessed. 29 *as so saytȝ*, as one says.

32 *May not byde þat burne* (? *burre*) *þat hit his body neȝen*,

Maynot abide (suffer) that man (? blow), that it (? he) should approach his body.

39 *helded*, approached. 41 *toteȝ* = *totȝ* = toes. 49 *worþlych*, worshipful (? *worldlych*, worldly). 50 *in her* (? *herin*). 52 *here dere*, beloved heir. 54 *comly quoyntis*, comely attire. 56 *with sclaȝt*, against (for) slaughter. 59 *roþeled*, ready prepared, literally hastened. 62 *skyly*, device, excuse.

P. 39. l. 65 *nayed*, refused; *nurned*, uttered. 71 *a-dreȝ*, aback, aside.

76 *More to wyte is her wrange, þen any wylle gentyl*,

More to blame is their fault, than any forlorn gentile.

Wylle has the significations of wandering, astray; as "*wyl dremes*," wandering dreams, "*wylle of wone*," astray from human habitations, having lost one's way; and hence *wylle* is often used to denote uncertainty, bewilderment. 81 *laþeȝ*, invite. 90 *styȝtled*, established, placed. 91 *þe marchal*, i.e. the marshal of the hall, whose duty it was, at public festivals, to place every person according to his rank and station. 95 *at þi banne*, at thy command. 96 *renischche renkeȝ*, strange men. 97 *layteȝ ȝet ferre*, search yet farther.

P. 40. l. 99 *wayteȝ*, watch. 103 *balterande cruppeleȝ*, limping cripples. *Balter* signifies to jump, skip, hop, etc. 110 *demed*, decreed.

112 *Hit weren not alle on wyueȝ suneȝ, wonen with on fader*,

They were not all one wife's sons, begotten with one father.

127 *& rehayte rekenly þe riche & þe poueren*,

And cheer, prince-like (nobly), the rich and the poor.

Rehete is the most common form of the word:

"Him would I comforte and *rehete*."—Rom. Rose, l. 6509.

131 *syled fyrre*, proceeded farther. 132 *Tron fro table to table*, went from table to table. *Tron* is the pret. of the verb *tryne*, to go, walk.

P. 41. l. 134 *Hit watȝ not*, there was one (who) was not. 135 *þryȝt*, thrust; *unþryuandely*, badly. 144 *ratted*, rent, torn. 145 *goun febele*. Cf. *feble wede*, bad or poor clothing.—Havelok the Dane, l. 418. 149 *broþe wordeȝ*, angry (fierce) words. 150 *Hurkele*, cower, hang. *Hurkele* signifies, literally, to squat, nestle, rest. 153 *laled*, spoke (quickly). 164 *fulȝed*, baptised. 166 *harme lache*, take hurt.

P. 42. l. 179 *As*, also; *bolnande priyde*, swelling pride.

180 *Þroly in-to þe deueleȝ þrote man þryngeȝ bylyue*,

Roughly into the devil's throat man is thrust soon.

181 *colwarde*, deceitful, treacherous. I have not been able to meet with the word *colle* used as noun or verb in any writer of the 14th or 15th century. *Col* occurs, however, as a prefix, in *Col-prophet* (false prophet), *Col-fox* (crafty fox), used by Chaucer; *Col-knyfe* (treacherous knife), which occurs in the "Townley Mysteries." 200 *hatel of his wylle*, anger of his will.

P. 43. l. 207 *attled*, endowed. 215 *metȝ* = *mess* (?), pity. 216 *tynt þe tyþe dool*, lost the tenth part. 222 *weued*, cut off. *swap*, blow. 230 *þe wrech saȝtled*, appeased the vengeance. 231 *wylnesful*, wilfulness.

233 *For-þy þaȝ þe rape were rank, þe rawþe watȝ lyttel*,

Wherefore, though the blow were smart, the sorrow was little.

237 *in obedyent* = *in-obedyent* (?), disobedient.

P. 44. l. 246 *drepe*, destroy (slay). 257 *forme-foster* should be *forme-fosterez*, being in apposition with *aunceterez*. 261 For *lede* read *ledez* (?). 270 *dezter of þe douþe*, the daughters of the mighty (doughty) ones. 271 *on folken wyse*, after the manner of men.

P. 45. l. 273 *meþelez*, immoderate, intemperate. 274 *alosed*, (? noted). 298 *þryuen*, grown up, adult. 306 *nuyed*=annoyed, *i.e.* displeased.

P. 46. l. 320 *dutande*, shutting. 321 *halkez*, recesses. 331 *þis meyny of azte*, this company (household) of eight. 335 *horwed*, unclean.

P. 47. l. 350 *with-outen þrep*, without contradiction, gainsaying. 354 *a rowtande ryge*, a rattling shower. 359 *stystez*=*styntez*, stops, ceases. 362 *& alle woned in þe whichche*, and all abode in the ark. *Whichche* is another (and genuine) form of *hutch*.

365 *Waltes out vch walle-heued, in ful wode stremez*,

Bursts out each well-head (spring, fountain) in full wild streams.

365 *brymme*, stream. 366 *þe mukel lauande loghe*, the great flowing deep. 369 *fon*, ceased. 373 *moon*, moan, sorrow. 374 *dowed*, availed. 375 *wylger*, wilder, fiercer. 376 *dowelled*=*dwelled*. 377 *feng to þe flyzt*, took to flight. 378 *Vuche burde with her barne*, each woman with her child (bairn).

P. 48. l. 379 *bowed*, hastened; *brentest*, highest, steepest. 380 *heterly*, quickly, (hotly); *haled*, rushed. 381 *Bot al watz nedlez her note*, but their device was altogether in vain. 382 *þe roze raynande ryg*, the rough raining shower; *raykande wawez*, flowing waves. 383 *boþom*, a *bottom* or valley. 384 *demmed*, collected, accumulated. 391 *þe hyze*, the heights, high grounds. 392 *bausenez*, badgers. 394 *re-coverer*, succour, refuge. 395 *Þat amounted*, etc., read *Þat amounted þe mase*, etc., that the astonishment increased. (Professor Child). 397 *Bi þat*, by that time. This phrase is still preserved in the North of England.

399 *Frendez, fellen in fere, faþmed to-geder*.

Friends, fallen in company, *embraced* (fathomed) together.

The verb *faþme* in Early English also signifies to *grope*. 400 *dryz*, suffer; *delful*, doleful. 404 *freten*, devoured; *wazez*, waves. 406 *hurkled*, rested. This word is still preserved in the local dialects of the North of England, with the sense of "to cower," "squat." 407 *mourkne*, rotten. 409 *here*, company. 411 *azt-sum*, in care, sorrowful. 413 *hurlande gotez*, rushing streams. 414 *kythez*, *vncouþe*, unknown regions.

P. 49. l. 421 *flyt*, current, flitting. 424 *lumpen*, the passive participle of *lympen*, to befal, happen. 430 *yrez* is evidently an error for *yþez*, waves. 433 *Rac*, moving clouds, mists. Still in provincial use. 436 *meth*, pity, mercy. 438 *lasned*, lessened, became smaller. 439 *stac vp þe stangez*, closed up the pools. *Stang*=*stanc*, *stank*, a word still used in the North of England. 441 *loz*=*logh*, deep. 443 *lome*=*loom*, i.e., the ark. 446 *rasse*=the provincial *raise*, a mound. 448 *wern*=*were* (?). 449 *kyste*= chest (ark).

P. 50. l. 451 *eggez*, *edges*, banks, hills; *vnhuled*, uncovered. 452 *bynne*, within. Cf. *boute*, without. 461 *smach smack, scent; smoltes* (? *smolte*, i.e. smelt). 463 *zederly*, quickly, soon; *steuen*, command, literally voice. 466 *fodez*, persons; *allez*, provided that. 469 *doune*=*dovene*, a female dove (see line 481).

476 *dreȝly*, drearily, sorrowfully. 480 *naytly*, dexterously (neatly). 482 *borne*=*burne*, stream. 483 *skwe*, sky, cloud; *skowteȝ*, looks.

P. 51. l. 485 *downe*=*dovene* (see ll. 469, 481). 487 *What!* lo! 490 *saȝtlyng*, reconciliation. 496 *woned*=*waned*, decreased, gone down. 498 *tyned*, enclosed. 499 *godeȝ glam*, God's message (word); *glod*, came, literally glided. 501 *walt wafte* (?) (see B. l. 857). 504 *þroly þrublande in þronge*, quickly pressing in throng (crowd), *i.e.*, huddling together. 509 *breþe*, steam, savour. 511 *spedeȝ & spylleȝ*, prospers (speeds) and spoils. 517 *barnage*, childhood.

P. 52. l. 525 *sadde*, sharp, bitter. 529 *þen watȝ a skylly skyvalde*, then was a design (purpose) manifested (ordered). 531 *nayte*, use, employ. 533 *wryþeȝ*, crawl, creep. 534 *folmarde*, polecat. 536 *lake ryftes*, fissures of the lake. 537 *Herneȝ*=*erneȝ*, eagles. 539 *at a brayde*, in a moment.

P. 53, l. 558 *merked*, ordained. 561 *raȝt*, extended to, gave. 566 *syt*, fault. 567 *quykeȝ*, living (things); *qued*, wickedness. 573 *vnhappen glette*, unfortunate filth, unhappy sin. 579 *heþyng of seluen*, contempt of [God's] self. 583 *steppe yȝe*, bright eye; *steppe*=*stepe* is often explained by steep, deep set; but we often meet with such phrases as "*stepe* stones," bright stones, "*stepe* starres," bright stars. 586 *losed þe listen*, lost the hearing; *lysten*, in O.E. has frequently the meaning of *to hear*. 587 *trave*=*trawe*, trow, believe.

588 *þer is no dede so derne þat ditteȝ his yȝen.*

There is no deed so secret that closes His eyes (*i.e.* that He does not see).

P. 54. l. 591 *gropande*, searching, examining.

592 *Rypande of vche a ring þe reynyeȝ & hert*

Trying (probing) the reins and heart of every man.

Rype is still used in the North of England in the sense of to plunder. Cf. our modern use of the word *ransack* with its earlier meanings of to try, probe, search. 596 *honyseȝ*, disgraces, ruins, destroys. 598 *scarreȝ*, literally *scares*, is frightened, startled. 599 *to drawe allyt*=*to draw a lyte*=to draw back a little. 603 *blykked*, shone, glared. 605 *schunt*, aside, from *schunt*, to slip away, retreat.

P. 55. l. 623 *orppedly*, quickly, hastily. 626 *happe*, cover, still in use in the north provincial dialects. 627 *som quat fat*, some sort of a vessel; *þe fyr bete*, make up the fire; *bete* signifies, literally, to mend. 632 *deruely*=*derfely*, quickly. 635 *þerue kakeȝ*=*therfe* or *tharfe* cakes, *i.e.*, cakes made without leaven. 646 *mensk*, thanks. 648 *leþe*, cease. 652 *ȝark*, select, chosen. 653 *for busmar*, in scorn.

655 *May þou traw for tykel þat þou tonne moȝteȝ*,

Mayst thou trow (believe) for the uncertainty (of such a thing) that thou mightest conceive; *for tykel*, on account of the uncertainty. 655 *sothly*= truly (? *sotly*, foolishly or *softly*).

P. 56. l. 659 *byene*=*ben*, been or *bycame*. The sense would require *hade* before *byene*, if *byene*=*ben*.

668 *Þat for lot þat þay lansed ho laȝed neuer*,

That for (any) sound that they uttered, she never laughed;

lot=late, in the sense of *sound*, is not very common in Old English authors. 670 *a-loȝ*=lowly, softly. 686 *blod*, child. 687 *bos*, behoves. 688 *atlyng*, intention, purpose; *vn-haspe*, disclose.

P. 57. l. 696 *fylter*, join. 698 *amed*, placed; *oddely dere*, singularly dear. *Oddely* occurs in some northern works with the sense of illustriously, nobly. 699 *drwry*, love; *doole alþer-swettest*, the sweetest of all gifts; gift the sweetest of all. 703 *conne* is probably an error for *come*, but it may signify, be kindled, produced, begotten. 706 *stollen*, stealthy, secret. 711 *smod*= the Scotch *smot*, *smad*, stain, filth. 719 *þe worre half*, the weaker portion, literally, the worse half. 723 *laue*, law.

P. 53. l. 732 *smolt*, be at peace. 740 *for hortyng*, for hurting=for fear of hurting. This sense of *for* is very common in writers of the 16th and 17th centuries. 743 *fryst*, delay, put off. 747 *vsle*, ashes, cinders. 752 *leþe*, destroy. 754 *I schal my þro steke*, I shall moderate (literally, shut up) my anger. 756 *reken*, wise.

P. 59. l. 764 *mese þy mode*, temper thy wrath. 778 *mere*, boundary, *meer*. 784 *lened*=leaned, reclined; but we may read *leued*=*beleued*, remained.

P. 60. l. 796 *vnder-ȝede*=*vnder-ȝete*, understood. 801 *knaueȝ kote*, servant's house. It looks at first sight like *kuchieȝ kote*. 802 *fatte*=*vat*, vessel. 803 *norne*=*nurne*, request. 810 *gruȝt*, gruched=begrudged. 813 *couþe*, knew. 814 *haylsed*, saluted. 824 *boute*, without. 830 *of glam debonere*, of pleasant, courteous conversation. 831 *wela-wynnely*, very joyfully.

P. 61. l. 832 *woȝe*=*wowe*, wall. 835 *wakker* comp. of *wayk*, weak. 836 *vmbe-lyȝe*, surround. 838 *scowte-wach*, sentinel; *asscry*, cry, shout, noise. 846 *ȝeȝed* =chattered, gaggled; *ȝestande sorȝe*, afflicting (or frothing) sorrow. 848 *brych*=what is low, vile, filthy (? *bryth*, breath); *vpbraydeȝ*, raises. 849 *glyfte with þat glam*, was frightened at that speech. 855 *wonded no woþe*. avoided no danger (hurt). 859 *meled*, spoke. 860 *hendelayk*, courtesy, civility.

P. 62. l. 871 *tayt*=lively. 874 *aȝly*=*awly*, fearfully. 876 *out-comlyng*, a stranger. In this form it is still known in the North of England. *Comlyng* is the more usual form of the word in our early literature; *carle*=*churl*. 881 *ȝornen*, ran. 882 *wapped*, beat. 885 *in blande*=together (?); *banned*, cursed. 888 *nyteled*, laboured, toiled. 889 *of tayt*, from fear. *Teyt*, fear, alarm, occurs in the northern romance of Alexander. 890 *roþeled*, hastened. 892 *vglokest vnhap*, the most dreadful misfortune.

893 *Ruddon of þe day-rawe ros vpon vȝten*.
The light of the day-break rose on the morn.

894 *merk*, darkness. 895 *ruþen*, rouse. 901. *cayre tid of þis kythe*, depart quickly from this land.

P. 63. l. 905 *stemme no stepe*, stop (keep back), no step. Cf. our modern phrase "*stem* the tide." 909 *losen*, destroy. 911 *gorde*, rush. 912 *clater*, shatter. 915 *kynned*, kindled. 916 *þe brath of his breth*, the fierceness of his wrath. 918 *foo-schip*, enmity. 921 *walle*=*wale*, choose; *wonnyng*, dwelling, abode. 927 *vtter*, without. 928 *wore*=*ware*=were. Cf. *thore*=*thare*=there. 931 *agayn-tote*, looking back; *tote* (toot) occurs frequently with the sense of "to peep," "look," in Early English.

P. 64. l. 944 *Loke ȝe bowe now bi bot*, Look ye go now by (according to) command. 947 *greme*, wrath. 948 *wakan*, arouse, stir up. 950 *flytande*, chiding, murmuring. 955 *smachande*, savouring, smelling. 964 *ryftes*, fissures.

965 *cloutes*, pieces. 969 *Rydelles*=*redeless*=without counsel, helpless; *rowles*, companies.

971 *Such a ȝomerly ȝarm of ȝellyng þer rysed,*
Such a mournful (pitiful) outcry of yelling there rose.

P. 65. l. 976 *Trynande ay a hyȝe trot*, going ever (at) a great pace. 987 *loueȝ*, not *loaves*, but=the provincial *looves*=hands. 989 *dampped*=*dumped*, beaten down. 991 *malscrande mere*, accursed lake. 992 *on a lawe*, on a hill.

1000 *& alle lyste on hir lik* (i.e. *lick*) *þat arn on launde bestes.*

"Als so sco loked hir behind,
A stan sco standes bi þat way
And sua sal do to domesday;
In a salt stan men seis hir stand
þat best likes o þat land;
þat anes o þe wok day,
þan is sco liked al away
And þan þai find hir on þe morn,
Hale als sco was ar beforn."
(Cott. MS. Vesp. A. iii. fol. 17*b*.)

1002 *niye*, anguish.

P. 66. l. 1009 *a roþun of a reche*, a rush of smoke, a mass of vapour; *blake*, the black (pit). 1011 *flot*, fat, grease. 1016 *drouy*, turbid, from *droue*, to trouble. 1024 *costeȝ of kynde*=natural properties. 1030 *boþem broþely*, filthy pit. 1031 *losyng*, perdition. 1033 *coosteȝ*=properties. 1035 *alkaran*, Mandeville employs the term *alkatran*; *angré*=poisonous or grievous, or *augre*=*aigre*, sharp. 1036 *saundyuer*=*sandiver*, glass-gall. 1037 *waxlokes*, waves. 1038 *spuniande*, cleaving, sticky. 1039 *se halues*, sea coasts. 1041 *terne*=*tarne*, lake. 1044 *apple garnade*=pomegranate.

P. 67. l. 1072 *kynned*, conceived. 1076 *a schepon*=a stable.

P. 68. l. 1079 *reflayr*, smell, odour; *rote*, decay. 1082 *þe reken fyþel*, the merry fiddle. 1094 *lomerande blynde*, the hesitating (slow, creeping), blind. The primitive meaning of *lomerande* seems to be that of *slow*, sluggish. 1108 *tyȝt*, endeavour.

P. 69. l. 1113 *fenny*, dirty, filthy, and hence sinful. 1118 *to dele*, to exchange. 1123 For "*& wax euer*," etc., the sense seems to require that we should read "*& wax ho euer*," etc. 1124 *in pyese*=whole. 1126 *blyndes of ble*, becomes dull of hue, loses its colour. 1127 *No-bot*, only. 1141 *lastes*, vices. 1142 *þewes*=*þeues* (?), thieves, or *unþewes*, vices (?)

P. 70. l. 1153 *tyȝt me a tom*=give me an opportunity; *tom* has the sense of *leisure* and not of *time*. 1167 *fylsened*, helped, aided. 1172 *lat*, late, slow. 1178 *þorpes*, cities.

P. 71. l. 1186 *skete skarmoch*, *skelt*, brisk skirmish, hastened (came on quickly). 1190 *brutage*=*bretage*, parapets of a wall. 1202 *blench*, stratagem. 1205 *at-wappe*, escape. 1206 *skelt*, spread. 1208 *ruþed*, roused. 1209 *hard hattes*, (?) hats made of tow; *herd*, *hard* (*harden*, *hards*), in O. English signify cloth made of tow.

P. 72. l. 1219 *faynest*, gladdest. 1224 *dreȝe þer his wyrdes*, endure there his destiny. 1246 *to þe bronde*, to the sword.

P. 73. l. 1254 *on capeles*, on horses. 1255 *fole wombes*, bellies of foals. 1259 *to cayre at þe kart & þe kuy mylke*, to drag at the cart and milk the cows. 1265 *plat of*, strike off. 1284 *hamppred*=*hampered*, packed up for removal.

P. 74. l. 1290 *hyȝtled*, ornamented. 1303 *modey*=*moody*, proud. 1313 *sesed*, took possession of.

P. 75. l. 1327 *bi-cnv*=*bicneu*, acknowledged. 1330 *heldes*, descends. 1332 *grauen*, buried. 1334 *stalled in his stud*, placed in his stead (position). 1342 *tre*, wood; *telded*, raised. 1344 *gered*, covered, decked. 1346 *reden*, advise. 1354 *notyng*, devising, contriving; *gettes*, devices.

P. 76. l. 1358 *avayment*, exhibition. 1361 *banne*, proclamation. 1362 *callyng*, decree. 1366 *vche a kythyn kyng*, every king of countries. 1375 *ludisch lordes*, lords of nations. 1379 *plek*, spot (plot of ground).

P. 77. l. 1396 *Stepe stayred* [*þe*] *stones of his stoute throne*,
Bright shone the stones of his firm throne.
1397 *hiled*=covered. 1398 *bounet*, went about. 1402 *strake steuen*= struck up sound. 1403 *wrasten krakkes*, sounds (notes) are raised. 1410 *foles*, fowls, birds. *flakerande*, flickering, fluttering. 1412 *on blonkken bak*, on the back of horses. In lines 1407–1412 we have evidently an allusion to the "table subtilties" of the fourteenth century. 1420 *seruyd*, served. 1425 *dotage*, folly.

P. 78. l. 1435 *schin*, shall. 1446 *besten blod*, blood of beasts; *busily*, laboriously. 1462 *fylyoles*, round towers.

P. 79. l. 1472 Penitotes. So in MS., but read *Peritotes*. 1478 *cost*, contrivance. 1495 *iaueles*=worthless wretches, used by Hall and Spenser.

P. 80. l. 1501 *wlates*, is disgusted. 1504 *wayned*, granted. 1505 *glotoun*, a general term of reproach. 1507 *vus*=*use*, drink. 1510 *kyppe*, take, seize, catch up. 1511 *birlen*, pour out. 1517 *dotel*, fool. 1520 as each one was disposed so tossed he off the cup.

P. 81. l. 1537 *neue*, fist. 1542 *lers*, features, but (?) *fers*, fears. 1543 *as a rad ryth*, as a frightened hound (literally mastiff). 1545 *runisch saueȝ*, strange words. 1554 *skelten*, hasten. 1557 *þo draȝtes*, the characters. 1559 *ede*=went, but *bede*, bade, commanded. 1560 *warlaȝes*, wizards. 1566 *malt*, to soothe. 1568 *gered*, clothed.

P. 82. l. 1585 *he wed wel ner*, he became nearly mad. 1603 *in stoundes*, at times.

P. 83. l. 1606 *spured*, asked, enquired of. 1634 *tede*=*tene*, ten (?) 1637 *apyke*, adorn, clothe.

P. 84. l. 1650 *loȝed*, made low. 1654 *pouer*, power. 1674 *wasterne*, wilderness; *dowelle*, dwelle. 1675 *braken*, fern.

P. 85. l. 1678 *soly*, seat. 1684 *ay* (?)=hay. 1686 *ouer-seyed*, passed over. 1690 *wykes*, members. 1692 *clyde*, plaister (?). 1694 *bresed*, rough, bristly; Sir F. Madden interprets it *broken*. 1695 *campe hores*, shaggy hairs. 1697 *glede*, kite. 1701 *wayned*, recovered. 1707 *haȝerly*, properly.

P. 86 l. 1713 *auyled*, defiled. 1716 *wale wyne*, choice wine; *in waryed stoundes*, in accursed moments.

P. 87. l. 1755 *daȝed*, dawned. 1759 *blykned*=*blaykned*, became dark, blackened. 1760 *Mourkenes*, becomes murky. 1761 *lyst*, path. 1768 *layted*, sought. 1773 *ledes of armes*, men of arms. 1775 *þester*, darkness.

P. 88. l. 1785 *slyppe*, escape. 1786 *honde-whyle*, a moment. 1788 *blende*, mingled. 1792 *now is a dogge also dere*, now is as valuable as a dog. 1808 *telled* = raised (?) *telles* = raises. 1811 *gere*, clothing.

P. 89. l. 3 *þe swelme leþe*, lessen the heat. 4 *qued*, evil. 5 *syt*, sorrow; *sele*, happiness. 6 *þro*, anger.

7 *þen is better to abyde þe bur umbe-stoundes*,
Then is it better to abide the blow sometimes.

10 *melede*, related. 11 *aȝt*, eight. 12 *sunder-lupes*, severally. 13 *happen*, blessed.

P. 90. l. 30 *lyknyng*, likeness; *þewes*, virtues. 42 *lyke oþer greme*, pleasing or displeasing. 47 *lyȝtloker*, more easily; *lotes*, forms. 50 *what dowes me þe dedayn*, what avails me anger. 53 *grayþed*, availed. 56 *þe(t) had bowed*, etc., That should have been obedient.

P. 91. l. 63 *Goddes glam to hym glod*, God's message came to him. 66 *wythouten oþer speche*, without contradiction, without more words. 67 *my saȝes soghe*, etc., my saws (words) sow, etc. 77 *typped schrewes*, great sinners; literally, extreme, tip-top, schrews. 78 *ta me*, take me, seize me. 82 *mansed*, cursed. 94 *glwande*, glowing, bright; *gloumbes*, sees (indistinctly).

P. 92. l. 98 *to the fare*, to the voyage. 101 *tramme*, gear.

104 *Sprude spak to þe sprete þe spare bawlyne*,
Spread quickly to the sprit the spar bowline (?).

106 *ladde-borde*, larboard. 107 *blyþe breþe*, gentle wind; *bosum*, tide. 108 *He* refers to *breþe*. 112 *maȝt*, might; *mere*, sea. 115 *wenyng*, supposition. 117 *burde*, behoved. 119 *demed*, uttered. 122 *stapefole* = *stapeful* = high (?).

P. 93. l. 131 *crafte*, power. 135 *tom*, interval. 140 *souȝed*, sobbed, moaned; *selly*, marvel. 141 *wonne*, pale. 143 *busched* = *busked*, went. 144 *for roȝ* = for roughness. 148 *bur* = wave. 150 *to murte*, (?) *to-marte*, crushed, broken in pieces. 152 *coge*, boat. 155 *scaþel*, hurtful, dangerous. 156 *lode* = *lote*, lot. 160 *leþe*, calm, quiet. 161 *lot*, noise, roar.

P. 94. l. 173 *I lovne*, I offer (this advice), propose. 183 *flode lotes*, the noises of the flood. 184 *brede*, board. 185 *hurrok*, oar. 191 *runyschly*, fiercely. 192 *slaȝte*, strokes. 198 *lastes*, crimes.

P. 95. l. 208 *at a worde one*, at a word alone. 213 *ossed*, showed, proved; *onnynges*, signs. 216 *ruyt*, rush, hasten. 227 *baleleȝ*, innocent. 229 *synne*, after.

P. 96. l. 247 *as wyrde þen schaped*, as fate then devised. 255 *malskred*, entranced, bewildered. 258 *warlowes*, monster's. 259 *lyue* = *leue*, believe. 262 *wauleȝ* = shelterless, destitute, but *wanleȝ* = *wonleȝ* = hopeless, is perhaps a better reading. 268 *chawleȝ*, jaws. 269 *glaymande glette*, slimy mud. 270 *rop*, gut, intestine.

P. 97. l. 273 *faþmeȝ*, gropes. 275 *saym*, fat, grease. 277 *le*, shelter. 291 *merk*, darkness. 292 *bulk*, stern. 302 *borne* = *burne*, man.

P. 98. l. 309 *flem* = *flum*, stream. 316 *to my wo stoundeȝ* = ? until my woe overpowers (confounds) me. 320 *to laste* ? to the last; *mere*, boundary. 325 *þacces*, blows. 329 *meled*, conversed. 338 *spare drye* dry *spar* (rafter) but ? *spare* = *space*. 339 *a warthe*, a ford. 341 *sluchched* = *sluched*, dirty, muddy. 342 *mester*, need.

P. 99. l. 345 *bruxle}*, reproaches, upbraids. 350 *loke*=*loken*, fastened. 362 *dumpe*. be thrust. 364 *swete*, life; *to lose þe swete*=to lose the (sweet) life. 372 *doured*, mourned, grieved. Cf. Sc. *dour*. 373 *Heter hayre} þay hent*, etc., rough hair shirts they took, etc.

P. 100. l. 395 *for-clemmed*, very hungry, starved. 396 *rurd*, cry. 400 *amesyng*=*mesyng*=*mese*, pity, mercy. 403 *wodschip*, wrath. 411 *on-hit*, struck or inflamed (?); *calle}*, addresses.

P. 101. l. 418 *bene*, bountiful, kind. 419 *lur*, loss. 426 *bale-stour*, death-pang; *bale* in the sense of death is not very common. 447 *lylled*, flourished. 448 *lefsel*=*leaf-bower*. See Glossary.

P. 102. l. 449 *bo}ted*, curved. 450 *happed*, covered. 451 *a nos*=a projection, opening (?) or is it a clerical error for *aboƒ*=*above*. 452 *scha}e*=wood, shaw. 453 *gly}t*, glanced. 460 *þe deuel* ? *ded euel*, did evil. 470 *syfle*, blow. 473 *wyl*, wandering. 478 *wertes he swyþe}*, herbs he scorches.

P. 103. l. 486 *wered*, protected. 489 *lansed*, uttered. 492 *waymot* = angry, passionate. 502 *remen*, mourn, lament. 509 *soumme*, company.

P. 104. l. 524 *gryndel*, angry. 526 *rakel*, hasty.

GLOSSARIAL INDEX.

Abate, lessen, put an end to. A. 123; B. 1356.

Abate, abode, A. 617.

Abayst, downcast, abashed, B. 149, pret. of *abaisse* or *abash*, Fr. *esbahir*.

Able, A. 599.

Abof, above, A. 1023.

Abominacione, B. 1173.

Abroched, commenced, A. 1123.

Abyde, (*a*) await, B. 436, 486; (*b*) endure, C. 7. A.S. *abidan*.

Abydyng, *sb.* C. 419.

Abyme, abyss, B. 363; C. 143.

Abyt, habit, dress, B. 141.

Accorde, Acorde, } agreement, A. 509, Fr. *accorder*, to agree with.

Achaped, escaped, B. 970.

Achaufe, kindle, B. 1143.

Acheue, accomplish, A. 475.

Acroche, encroach, A. 1069, Fr. *accrocher*, to hook on; from *croc*, a hook.

Adaunt = daunt, A. 157.

Adoun, down, A. 988; B. 953.

Adreȝ, aside, aback, B. 71. The word is used by Gower under the form *adrigh*. *O-dreghe*, *one-dreghe*, are other forms of the word. Sc. *on-dreich*.

"The tother withdrewe, *one-dreghe*
And durste do none other."
(Morte Arthure, p. 352.)

"The tother droȝhe him *o-dreghe* for
drede of the knyȝte."
(Anturs of Arther, xliv. 3.)

"He with drogh hym *a draght* & a dyn
made." (T. B. 1224.)

Adubbement, Adubmente, } adornment, A. 84, 85, O.Fr. *adoubement*; *dober*, *douber*, garnish, deck; Fr. *douber*, to rig or trim a ship; Prov. Fr. *adobar*, to arrange, prepare.

Adyte, A. 349.

Affraye, *sb.* fear, A. 1174; *vb.* frighten, B. 1780; Fr. *effrayer*, to scare, affright; *effroi*, terror. Cf. *fray*, to scare birds.

Affyen, trust, C. 331.

Agayn, Agayne, Agaynes, } against, B. 266, 826, 1711.

Agayneȝ, towards, B. 611.

Agayn-tote, *sb.* a looking back, B. 931. *Tote*, look, peep, as a verb or a noun, is common in Old English writers.

"She went up wightly by a wall syde,
To the toppe of a tower, & *tot* ouer the water." (T. B. 862.)

Age, A. 412, B. 426.
Aglyȝte, slipped from, A. 245. *Glyȝt*, as a verb, signifies not only to slip but to *glance*, look. Cf. *leme* = gleam, glance, slip.
Alabaunderynes, B. 1470.
Alarom, alarm, B. 1207.
Al-bare, clearly, A. 1025.
Alce = als, also, B. 1377.
Alder = elder, A. 621, *Aldest*, A. 1042, B. 1333.
Alder-men, elders, A. 887.
Alegge, alledge, A. 703.
Aliche, alike, B. 1477.
Alkaran = alkatran, B. 1035.
Alle-kynneȝ, all kinds of, A. 1028.
Allyt = a lyt = ? a little, B. 599.
Almyȝt, almighty, A. 498.
Alofte, on high, B. 1183.
Al-one, A. 933.
Al-only, except, A. 779.
Alosed, destroyed, B. 274. See *lose*.
Alow, approve, praise, reward, A. 634. O. Fr. *louer*. Lat. *laudare*.
Aloynte, removed, far from (from O.E. *aloigne*, *alogne*, to remove, carry off. O. Fr. *aloigner*).
Aloȝ, alow, softly, B. 670.
Als, also, B. 253, 827, C. 516.
Also, as, B. 984, 1045, 1792.
Also-tyd, Als-tyd, As-tyd, } at once, immediately, B. 64. See *tyd*.
Al-þaȝ, although, A. 759.
Alþer-fayrest, fairest of all, B. 1379.
Alþer-fynest, finest of all, B. 1637.
Alþer-rychest, richest of all, B. 1666.
Alþer-swettest, sweetest of all, B. 699.
Alum, B. 1035.
Amaffised, B. 1470.
Amaraunȝ, B. 1470.
Amatyst, amethyst, A. 1016.
Ame, (1) *vb.* place, B. 698; (2) *sb.* purpose, C. 128. Germ. *ahmen*. Bavarian, *amen*, *hämen*, to guage a cask, fathom, measure.
Amended, B. 248.
Amesyng, *sb.* moderation, C. 400. See *mese*.
Amoneste, admonish, B. 818.
Amounted, B. 395.
Amoynt, company, A. 895.
And = an, if, B. 864.
An-ende (on-ende), lastly, finally, A. 186.
An-ende = anente, opposite, A. 1136; respecting, A. 697.
An-endeȝ = anentes, opposite, A. 975. Sc. *anens*.
Anger, A. 343, B. 572.
Angré, bitter, B. 1035.
Anguych, anguish, C. 325.
Ankreȝ, anchors, B. 418, C. 103.
Anon, at once (= anane, onane, in one moment), A. 584.
Anournement, ornament, B. 1290.
Anoynted, B. 1446.
Answar, answer, A. 518.
Anter, peril, C. 242. To *aunter*, put a thyng in daunger, or adventure, *adventurer* (Palsgrave).

An-vnder, under, A. 1081. Sc. *anonder*. Cf. *down* and *adown*, *low* and *alow*.
Aparaunt, B. 1007.
Apassed, past, A. 540.
Apert, openly, A. 589.
Apparaylmente, ornaments, A. 1052.
Apparement, ornaments, B. 1270. Fr. *appareiller*, to fit, suit.
Appose, *vb.* question, A. 902. Fr. *apposer*, to lay or set on, or near to.
Aproche, A. 686, B. 8, 167. Fr. *approcher*, draw near. Lat. *prope*, near.
Apyke, adorn, B. 1479, 1637.
Aquyle, demand, ask, obtain, A. 690, 966. O.Fr. *aquillir*, to gather.
Aray, } A. 719, 1166; B. 816,
Araye, } 1442. O.Fr. *arroyer*, *arréer*, dispose, set in order.
Arayned, arraigned, C. 191. O.Fr. *arraisonner*, *arraigner*.
Are, before, previously, B. 438, 1128.
Arende, errand, message, C. 72, A.S. *aerend*, *aerende*.
Arest, *sb.* abode, resting place, B. 906.
Areset, *vb.* stop, cease, B. 766, remain, C. 144. Fr. *arrester*. Lat. *arestare*.
Arewarde, apostate, B. 208. Sc. *areird*, backward.
Arn, } are, A. 458, 628, B. 8,
Arne, } 1810.
Aryue, A. 447.
Aryȝt, aright, A. 112.
Arȝe, terrify, frighten, fear, B. 572, 713. Provincial *arfe*, *arghe*, afraid. Cf. "*Arwe* or ferefulle (*arwhe*, K. arowe or ferdfulle P.). Timidus, pavidus, formidolus." (Prompt. Parv.) The original notion is that of laziness, inertness, and hence timidity, fear, etc. A.S. *earg*, inert, timid, weak. Ger. *arg*, bad. Du. *erg*. Icel. *argr*, lazy, cowardly. Sc. *argh*, *arch*, to hesitate, be reluctant.

"Antenor *arghet* with austerne wordes."
(T. B. 1977.)

"Antenor, *arghly* auntrid of ship."
(T. B. 1831.)

"A! Anec. quoth the qwene
me *arȝes* of my selfe,
I am all in aunter, sa
akis me the wame."
(K. Alex. p. 29.)

"Sir Alexander and his ost was *arȝed* unfaire."
(*Ibid.* p. 132.)

Ar, are, B. 1725.
Are? ane, one, A. 711.
As, also, B. 179.
As-bare, ? *al bare*, clearly, openly, A. 836.
Asayl, B. 1188.
Ascape, escape, B. 569.
Ascry, *sb.* cry, outcry, B. 1784. *vb.* C. 195. Swed. *anskri*, outcry, scream. O.N. *skri*, cry.
Asent, } A. 391, "in *asent*," B.
Asente, } 788.
Askeȝ, ashes, B. 626.
Askry, shout, cry, B. 1206. See *ascry*.
Aslypped, escaped, lost, C. 218.
Aspaltoun, asphalt, B. 1038.
Asperly, sharply, C. 373.

Assayl, C. 301.
Asscaped, escaped, B. 1776.
Asscry, cry, shout. See *ascry*.
Assemble, B. 1364, 1769.
Assemblé, A. 760.
Asspye, espy, see, A. 704, 1035.
Assyse, } form, fashion, A. 97, B.
Asyse, } 844, service, B. 639.
Astate, state, A. 393.
Astraye, A. 1162.
Astel, stole from, B. 1524.
As-tyt, immediately, at once, A. 645, B. 935.
Asure, B. 1411.
Aswage, C. 3.
At, that, A. 672.
Atlyng, purpose, B. 688. Sc. *ettle*, to endeavour. N. Prov. E. *ettle*, *attle*, intend. Icel. *aetla*.

"Armur & all thing *atlet* before." (T. B., 855).

Aþel, noble, B. 258, 411, 940, gracious, B. 761, fine, B. 1276, A.S. aeþele, noble, excellent.
Atount, so much (?), A. 179.
At-slyke, slip away, A. 575.
Atteny, attain, reach, A. 548.
Attled, endeavoured. See *atlyng*.
Attled, endowed, B. 207. It sometimes occurs under the form *aghteld*. N. Prov. E. *ettle*, to deal out, distribute. A.S. *aeht*, possession.

"She was eldist & heire *etlit* to his londes." (T. B., 394.)

At-wappe, escape, B. 1205. See *Wap*.
Atyre, B. 114.
Augoste, august, A. 39.
Auncetereȝ, auncestors, B. 258.
Aven, } own, B. 11, 1222.
Aune, }
Aunte, A. 233.
Aunter, adventure, marvel, B. 1600. See T. B., 1899.
Auter, altar, B. 10.
Autly, noble, B. 795. A.S. *áhtlice*, courageously, manfully.
Avaunt, *sb.* promise, B. 664.
Avayment, show, B. 1358. F. *avoier*.
Auaye, show, B. 1311.
Auenture, adventure, A. 64. O.Fr. *aventure*.
Auise, advise, B. 1365.
Avow, B. 664.
Avoy, away! B. 863.
Avyle, defile, B. 1151, 1713.
Avysyoun, vision, A. 1184.
Awayed, shown, A. 710.
Awayle, avail, B. 408.
Awowe, avow, C. 333.
Ay, always, ever, A. 33, 720. A.S. *áva*, *a*, all, ever. O.Fris. *a*. Germ. *je*, ever.
Ayre, heir, B. 650, 1709.
Ayþer, each, A. 831.
Aywhere, everywhere, B. 228.
Aȝer = asure, B. 1457.
Aȝly = awly, fearfully, B. 874, 937. Dan. *ave*, fear. Eng. *awe*. O. Eng. *agh*. Cf. A.S. *agláe*, misery, grief.
Aȝt, } ought, *pret.* of *aȝe*, *agh*,
Aȝte, } or *awe*, B. 122.
Aȝt, eight, B. 357, C. 11, 29.
Aȝt-sum, sorrowful, B. 411.
Aȝtþe, eighth, A. 1011.

Baboyne, baboon, B. 1409.
Babtem, A. 627. See Baptem.

Bachlereȝ, batchelors, young men not yet raised to the order of knighthood, B. 86.

Baft, abaft, C. 148. A.S. *baefta*, the hinder part.

Bagge, baggage. C. 158,

Bale, bales, C. 157. Sw. *bal.* Fr. *balle*, *bal*, a ball or pack.

Bale, sorrow, woe; also misery, calamity, A. 18, 373; B. 1243, 1256; *baleȝ*, A. 123, 807. O. Fris. *bale.* A.S. *bealu*, torment, destruction. Icel. *böl.* Phrases: "bodyly *bale*" (pain), A. 478; "*bale* (torment) of helle," A. 651, "*bale*-stour," death pang, C. 426.

Baleleȝ = baleless, innocent, C. 227.

Balke, ridge of land, balk, A. 62. Icel. *balkr*, the division between the stalls in a cow-house. Sw. *balka*, to partition off.

> "To my shepe wylle I stalk, and herkyn anone,
> Ther abyde on a *balk*, or sytt on a stone."—(Town. Myst. p. 99.)

Balleful = baleful, wretched, wicked, B. 979.

Balter, hop, jump, skip, C. 459.

Balterande, halting, limping, B. 103. Sc. *balter*, to dance.

> "He baltyrde, he bleryde."
> (Morte Arthure, p. 66.)

Etymologically it is connected with *palter* and *falter*, and is applicable either to the unsteady gait of the lame or faltering steps of the blind.

Baly = bayly, authority, jurisdiction, dominion, A. 1083.

Baneres, B. 1404.

Banne, proclamation, decree, B. 95, 1361.

Banne, curse, B. 468, 885. Sw. *bann*, excommunication; *banna*, to reprove, chide, curse.

> "*Bannet* worthe the bale tyme þat ho borne was." T.B. 1388.

Banne, comfort, strengthen, B. 620. O.Sc. *bawne.*

Bantel, A. 991, 1017; B. 1459, posts, pillars.

Baptem, baptism, A. 627, 653.

Baptysed, A. 818.

Barayn, barren, B. 659.

Bare, *adj.* naked, B. 452; *sb.* 791.

Bare, only, B. 1573. Sw. *bara.*

Bared, disclosed, B. 1149.

Bare-heued, bare-headed, B. 633.

Bareres, Barreȝ, } bars, barriers, B. 963, 1239; C. 321. W. *bar*, rail, shaft. Fr. *barre*; *barrière*, a barrier. Cf. Sw. *s-parre.* Eng. *s-par.*

Barme, bosom, C. 510. A.S. *bearm.* "*Barme* gremium." (Prompt. Parv.)

> "He fond Horn in arme
> On Rymenhilde *barme.*"
> (K. Horn, p. 294.)

Barnage, childhood, B. 517.

Barne, child, son, A. 426; *barneȝ*, A. 1040; B. 1085. Sc. *bairn.* A.S. *bearn.*

Baronage, nobility, B. 1424. See T. B., 211.

Barouneȝ, barons, B. 82, 1398.

Barreȝ, Barers, } bars, B. 884, 1263.

Barst, burst, B. 963.

Base, Basse, base, foundation, A. 1000, B. 1278. See T.B. 1652.

Bassyn, basin, B. 1145, 1278.

Bastele, B. 1187. "*Bastyle* of a castelle or cytye. Fascennia." (Prompt. Parv.)

Basyng, base, A. 992.

Bated, abated, B. 440.

Bater, B. 1416.

Batelment, B. 1459.

Baþe, dip, plunge, B. 1248.

Bausen, badger, B. 392. "*Bawstone* or *bawsone*, or a gray, Taxus, melota." (Prompt Parv.)

Bawelyne, bow-line, B. 417.

Bay, recess, B. 1392. The original meaning seems to be *opening* of any kind. Cf. *bay*, space in a building between two main beams (Forby).

Bayly, dominion, A. 315, 442.

Bayn, *adv.* readily, willingly, A. 807, B. 1511; ready, C. 136. N. Prov. E. *bane*, near, convenient. "*Beyn* or plyaunte. Flexibilis." (Prompt. Parv.) *Bainly*, readily, T. B. 135.

Baysment, abasement, A. 174.

Bayte, B. 55. O.N. *beita*.

Baytayled, fortified, B. 1183.

Beauté, A. 749.

Bed, Bede, bid, command, invite; *p.p.* *beden*, A. 715, B. 95, 440. See T. B. 389.

Beke, beak, B. 487.

Bekyrande, *sb.* bikering, fighting, B. 1474. "*Bekyryn* or fyghtyn (*bikkeringe*), Pugno, dimico." (Prompt. Parv.)

"Bolde men to batell and *biker* with hond." T. B. 2944.

Bele, *vb.* boil, A. 18. N. Prov. E. *bele*.

Bem, beam, ray, "*bem* of þe brode heuen," B. 603.

Bem, tree, A. 814.

Ben, Bene, are, *3rd pers. pl.* A 572.

Bench, seat, B. 130, 854.

Bene, fair, A. 198.

Bene, *adj.* kind, merciful, C. 418.

Bent, field, plain, B. 532, 1675. See T. B. 1192.

Ber, bore, *pret.* of *bere*, to bear, A. 426, B. 1480.

Berdles, beardless, B. 789.

Bereste, breast, A. 854.

Berfray, watch tower, B. 1187. O.F. *berfroi*, *beffroit*. Fr. *beffroir*. M. Lat. *belfredum*. The modern English *belfry* is a corruption of *berfray*.

Beryl, A. 110, 1011.

Beryng, condition, state, behaviour, B. 1060, 1228.

Best, beast, B 288, 351.

Beste, *sb.* best (one), A. 279.

Besten, of beasts, B. 1446.

Bete, (the fire) mend, repair, kindle, B. 627, *p.p.* *bet*, B. 1012. Prov. E. *beat*, to mend, repair. A.S. *bétan*, (1) to improve, repair; (2) joined with *fyr* to mend a fire, to light or make a fire, to kindle.

Bete, save, A. 757. A.S. *bétan*, to remedy. Du. *boeten*, mend, fine, expiate.

Betȝ = bes, shall be, A. 611. Present tense with future signification.

Beuerage, drink, liquor, B. 1433,

1717. Fr. *beuvrage*, from Lat. *bibere*.

Bewar, beware, B. 292.

Bewté, A. 765.

Beyng, *sb.* being, existence, A. 446.

Bibbe, sip, drink, B. 1499. Prov. E. *beb*. Du. *biberen*, to drink much.

> "Bacus he was brayne-wode
> for *bebbing* of wynes."
> (K. Alex. p. 154.)

Bicalt, becalled, called from, A. 1163.

> "The kyng was full curteus, *calt* on a maiden. (T. B. 388.)

Bi-cnv, acknowledged, B. 1327.

Bidde, bide, abide. C. 51.

Biden, *p.p.* of *bide=abide*, B. 616.

Bifalle, Byfalle, } befal, A. 186.

Bifore, before, A. 49.

Bigge, Bygge, } great, B. 43, *bygger*, A. 374.

Bigge, build, B. 1666. A. Sax. *byggan*. Icel. *byggia*. O.Sw. *bygga*, build, also inhabit.

Bigly, strongly, C. 321. See T. B. 904.

Bigonne, began, B. 123.

Bihynde, behind, B. 918.

Biholde, behold, B. 150.

Bihyȝt, promised, C. 29.

Bikenne, give, hand over, B. 1296.

Bilde, built, B. 1392.

Bileue, remain, B. 1549.

Bilooghe, below, B. 116.

Birle, pour out, B. 1511. Prov. E. *burl*. A.S. *byrelian*, to give to drink.

> "And seruanz war at this bridale
> That *birled* win in cupp and schal."
> (Met. Hom. p. 120.)

Birolled, berolled, B. 959.

Biseche, beseech, B. 614.

Bisoȝten, besought, C. 375.

Bispeke, speak, C. 169.

Bisyde, beside, B. 926.

Bi-talt, aroused, A. 1161. A.S. *tealtian*, *tealtrian*; (1) to *tilt*, shake; (2) to be in danger. William of Shoreham uses one form of this word:

> "For ȝef that water his kende lest
> That cristninge stant *to-tealte*."
> (Poems, p. 9.)
>
> "For if that water its kind loseth,
> That christening standeth tottery, insecure" (*i.e.* not binding).

Bitechе, give up to, entrust to, B. 871; pret. *bitaȝt*.

Bited, bit, C. 373.

Biþenkke, Biþenke, } bethink, B. 1357.

Biþoȝt, bethought, B. 125.

Bityde, betide; *pret.* bitydde, C. 61

Bityde, befall, B. 1804.

Blade, B. 1105.

Blake, black, A. 945; B. 747, 1449.

Blame, *vb.* A. 275; B. 877, 1661; *sb.* B. 43.

Blande, "in blonde," together, B. 885. See *blende*.

Blasfamye, Blasfemyon, } B. 1661, 1712.

Blayke, yellow, A. 27. Brockett has *blayke* with the sense of yellow, of a golden colour. "*Bleyke* of coloure." Pallidus, subalbus. (Prompt. Parv.)

> "Ther (in paradyse) were floures bothe blew and *blake*,
> Of alle frutes thei myth ther take."
> (Cov. Myst. p. 2.)

Blaȝt, white, A. 212, *p.p.* of *bleach*, just as *raȝt* is of *reach*. Sc. *blaucht*.

> "As *blaȝt* ere thaire wedis
> As any snyppand snawe."
> (K. Alex. p. 54.)

Ble, colour, complexion, A. 76, 212; B. 791, 1759. Prov. E. *ble*, *bly*. A.S. *bleo*.

Bleaunt, a robe of fine linen, A. 163. O. Eng. *bliant*, fine linen, W. *llian*, linen. The *bl* is merely an imitation of the Celtic *ll*.

> "A blewe *bleaunt* obofe brade him al ovir."
> (K. Alex. p. 167.)

Blench, stratagem, device, B. 1202. O.N. *blekkia*.

Blemyst, blemished, B. 1421. O.Fr. *blesmir*.

Blende, } Blente, } blended, mingled, mixt. A. 385, 1016; B. 967, 1788. A.S. *blendian*. Icel. *blanda*, to mix.

Blo = bla, blue, livid, pale. B. 1017; C. 134. O.H.G. *blao*, N. Fris. *bla*. O. Sc. *bla*.

Blober, } Bluber, } = blubber, waves, C. 221, 266. Prov. E. *blubber*, bubble; *blob*, *bleb*, a bubble. "*Blobure* (blobyre, P.) Burbulium." (Prompt. Parv.) "*Blober* upon water (or bubble) bouteillis." (Palsg.) "The water *blubbers* up." (Baker, Northamptonshire Glossary.)

Blod, a child, B. 686. Supposing the *bl* to represent *ll* we might refer it to the W. *llawd*, a youth, *lad*. O.Sw. *g-lott*. Cf. *bliant*, *bleant*, from W. *llian*.

> "Þis Abel was a blissid *blod*,
> Bot Caim was the findes (devil's) fode (offspring)."
> (Cott. MS. Vesp. A. iii. fol. 7*b*.)

Blod, blood, A. 650.

Blok, space, C. 272.

Blom, } Blome, } flower, bloom, A. 578, B. 1467. Sw. *bloma*, a flower. Du. *bloeme*. Ger. *blume*. "*Blome* flowre. Flos." (Prompt. Parv.)

Blomeȝ, blooms, flowers, A. 27.

Blonk, horse, *pl.* *blonkeȝ*, B. 87, 1392. See T. B. 2371.

Blonkken, *gen. pl.* of horses, B. 1412.

Blosched, looked, C. 343. See *Blusch*.

Blose = blese, blaze, flame. A. 911. Icel. *blossi*, a flame. A.S. *bluese*, a torch. Dan. *blus*.

Blot, spot, blemish, defilement, A. 782.

> "Ye ben worthy, he saide, to be *blottede* and *spottede*, foulede and defoulede with fenne (mire) and with drit of water (*luto inquinari*), and of blode, that in tyme of werre ne were nat be bespreynt, ne be wette with ennemyes blode." (Quoted by Way, from Roy. MS. 18, A. xii. B. iii. c. 10.)

Blubrande = blubbering, bubbling, foaming, B. 1017. See *blobber*.

Blunt, rushed, C. 272.

Blunt, faint, A. 176. Icel. *blunda* to sleep. Sw. *blunda*, to close the eyes. Dan. *blende*, to dazzle. Cf. "Blunt of wytte. Hebes." (Prompt. Parv.)

Blusch, } look, glance, A. 980,
Blusche, } 1083, B. 904, 998, 1537. N. Prov. E. *blush*, resemblance. Cf. "At the first *blush*," at the first appearance, at first sight. Dan. *blusse*, to blaze, flame, glow. There seems to be an etymological connection with words signifying to look, glow, blaze, shine, etc.

> "The kyng *blyschit* on the beryne (man) with his brode eghne."
> (Morte Arthure, p. 10.)
> "He *blusshed* ouer backeward to þe brodesee." (See T. B. 1316.)

Blusnande, } shining, B. 1404.
Blysnande, } Icel. *blys*. Dan. *blus*, a torch. Du. *blos*, redness. Dan. *blusse*, to glow. Icel. *lysa*, to shine. Pl. D. *bleistern*, to glisten.

Bluster, B. 886, to wander or stray about.

> "Ac there was wight noon so wys
> The wey thider kouthe,
> But *blustreden* forth as beestes
> Over bankes and hilles."
> (Piers Ploughman, p. 108.)

Blwe, blue, A. 423.

Blwe, blew, B. 885.

Blykked, shone, B. 603. A.S. *blican*, glitter, dazzle. Ger. *blicken*, shine, glance, look. Du. *blicken*, glitter; *blick*, a flash.

> "Hire bleo *blyketh* so bryht
> So feyr heo is ant fyn."
> (Lyric Poems, p. 52.)

Blyknande, shining, B. 1467.

Blykned=blaykned, became black, B. 1759.

Blynde, to become faded, dull, B. 1126.

Blynne, cease, A. 729, B. 440, 1661, 1812. A.S. *blinnan* (for *be-linnan*).

Blysfol, } blissful, A. 279, 409.
Blysful, }

Blysnande, shining, A. 163. See *blusnande*.

Blysned, shone, A. 1048.

Blyþe, joy, A. 354. Blythe is still used as a noun in the North of England.

Blyþely, joyfully, A. 385.

Bobaunce, boasting, Fr. *bobance*, B. 179, 1712.

Bod, } command, B. 979; C. 56.
Bode, } A.S. *bod*, *gebod*, command, precept, message. "*Bode* or massage (*boode*, H.) nuncium." (Prompt. Parv.)

Bod=abode, *pret.* of *bide*=abide, A. 62; B. 982; wait for, B. 467.

Bodworde, message, B. 473. See T. B. 6262.

Bodyly, A. 478.

Boffet, blast, B. 885.

Boffetez, buffets, blows, A. 809; *boffet*, B. 43.

Bok-lered, book-learned, B. 1551.

Bold, bad, A. 806. A.S. *báld*, audacious. Sw. *båld*, proud, haughty, warlike. In early English writers the term was applied indifferently to men and women of bad character.

> "Þou do me bote again þis *bald* (bad one)
> For al þe soth I haf þe tald."
> (Cott. MS. Vesp. A. iii. fol. 48*b*.)

Bol, bull, B. 1682; *pl. bolez*, B. 55.

Bole, the round stem of a tree, B. 622. It enters also into composition in the word *throte*-bolle. *Pl. bollez*, A. 76. Icel. *bolr*. Dan. *bul*. Sw. *bål*, trunk of a man's body. See T. B. 4960.

Bolle, bowl, B. 1145, 1511. A.S. *bolla*. Icel. *bolli*.

Bolled, embossed, B. 1464.

Bolnande, swelling, B. 179.

Bolne, swell, A. 18; B. 363. Icel. *bolgna*. Sw. *bulna*, to swell. In some early English works we find *bollen* (ibolȝe) the *p.p.* of a verb *bolȝe*=bulge, swell. "Bolnyn, Tumeo, turgeo, tumesco." (Prompt. Parv.)

Bonc, bank, A. 907.

Bone, prayer, petition, command (=boon). A. 912, 916; B. 826. A.S. *bēn*. S. Sax. *bone*. O.N. *bón* rogatio. "*Bone* or graunte of prayer (*boone* P.) Precarium, peticio." (Prompt. Parv.)

Bone, good, B. 28.

Boner, } good, B. 733.
Bonere, }

Bonerté, goodness, A. 762.

Bongre, willingly, agreeably to, C. 56. See *Gre*.

Bonk, bank, hill, A. 931, B. 379. Ger. *bank*, bench, bank of a river, etc.

Bor, bower, chamber, dwelling, A. 964. A.S. *bur*, a chamber. Icel. *bur*. N. Prov. E. *boor*, a parlour.

Bore, born, A. 239, B. 584.

Borde, table, B. 1433, 1717.

Borde, board of a vessel, B. 470; C. 211.

Borez, boars, B. 55.

Borges, burgess; sometimes written *burgeise*, C. 366. O. Fr. *bourgeois*, from Lat. *burgensis*.

Borgoun, to burgeon, bud forth, B. 1042. Fr. *bourgeon*, *bourjon*, young bud or sprig. Prov. Fr. *boure*, bud. Fr. *abourioner*, to bud or sprout forth. See T. B. 4964.

Borlych, burly, B. 1488.

Borne=burne, stream, water, B. 482; *bornez heued*, head of the stream, source, A. 974. A.S. *burne*. Goth. *brunna*. Icel. *brunnr*. G. *born*, *brunnen*, well, spring.

Bornyst, burnished, A. 77, 220, B. 554. Fr. *brunir*, to polish.

Boroȝt=broȝt, brought, A. 628.

Borȝ, } city, town, A. 957, 989, B.
Borȝe, } 45, 834, 1750. A.S. *burg*, *burh*. Goth. *baurgs*. Icel. *borg*.

Bos=bus=behoves, B. 687.

Bosk, take, B. 351; *boske* to, go to, B. 834. See *Busk*.

Boskez, bushes, B. 322. Icel. *buskr*.

Bosum, bay, C. 107. Cf. N. Prov. E. *bosom*, the eddy.

"Eneas and his feris on the strand
Wery and forwrocht, sped thame to the nerrest land,
And at the cost of Lyby arryvit he.
Ane havyn place with a lang hals or entre
Thar is, with an ile enveronyt on ather part,
To brek the wallis and storm of every art,
Within, the water in a *bosum* gays."
(G. Doug. vol. i. p. 33.)

Bost, boast, arrogance. B. 179, 1450.

Boster, boaster, B. 1499.

Bostwys = busteous, boisterous, rough, fierce, A. 814. Pl. Du. *büster*, wild, fearful, savage. Cf. "*Boystowe*, rudis." (Prompt. Parv.) *Bustus*, rudis, rigidus, to be *bustus*, rudere. (Cath. Angl.) The form *bostwys* would seem to point to *bost*, boast, as the probable root.

Bot, "to bot," to boot, B. 473.

Bot, command, B. 944. A.S. *beot*, threat, promise.

Bot, only, A. 18, 382, except, A. 972; *bot-if*, unless, B. 1110.

Bote, saviour, A. 275, 645; remedy, safety, C. 163. A.S. *bót*, amends, atonement; *gebétan*, to make amends. Du. *boet*, remedy; *boeten*, to mend.

Boþe, booth, tent, C. 441.

Boþem, Boþom, } valley, dale, B. 383, 450; pit, sea, B. 1030. *Bottom*, a valley, is still used in many of our provincial dialects, and is a frequent element in local names. A.S. *botm*, lowest point, depth, abyss. Du. *bodem*. Germ. *boden*. Icel. *botn*.

Bothem, bottom, C. 144.

Boþemleȝ, bottomless, B. 1022.

Bouel, Bowel, } bowel, gut, B. 1251; C. 293.

Bougoun (?) B. 1416.

Boun, (1) ready; (2) finished, A. 534, 992, 1103. See T. B. 827. N. Prov. E. *boun*. Icel. *bua*, to prepare, p.p. *buinn*, prepared, ready.

Bounden, fastened, B. 322; bound (*p.p.* of *binde*), A. 1103.

Bounet, went, *pret.* of *boun* or *bown*, to go, B. 1398. See *boun*. See T. B. 827, 5230.

> "And (he) *bownnes* over a brode mede
> With breth (anger) at his herte."
> (M. Arthure, p. 290.)

Bounté, goodness, B. 1436.

Boureȝ (bowers), chambers. B. 322. See *Bor*.

Bourne = burne, man, A. 617.

Bourȝ = borȝ, city, B. 1377. See *Borȝ*.

Boute, without, B. 260, 824; C. 523.

Bow, Bowe, } to go, walk, literally, to bend (one's steps). A. 126, 974; B. 45, 379, 482.

> "Forth heo gunnen *bugen*
> In to Bruttaine."
> (Laȝ. 2, 410.)
>
> "The burd *bowet* from þe bede."
> (T. B. 775.)

A.S. *búgan*, to *bow*, *bend*, avoid, flee.

Bowe, obey (bend to), C. 56, 75.

Boy, a boy, youth, B. 878.

Boyeȝ, boys, men of low position, servants; generally used in a bad sense, "*boyeȝ bolde*," A. 806.

> "—— bot a *boys* one (alone)
> Hoves by hym on a blonke (horse) and his spere holdes."
> (Morte Arthure, p. 211.)
>
> "I wende no Bretones walde bee basschede for so lyttille
> And fore bare-legyde *boyes* that one the bente houys."
> (*Ibid.* p. 178.)

Boȝ = bow, go, A. 196; B. 1242, 1551. See *Bow*.

Boȝe, bough, B. 616, 1467.

Boȝt, bought, A. 651.

Boȝted, curved, C. 449. A.S. *bugan*, to bend. Dan. *bugt*, bend, turn. Sc. *bought*, to fold, bend.

Brade, broad, A. 138.

Brake vp=break up, throw up, spew, C. 340. Ger. *sich brechen*. Du. *braeken*, to vomit. "*Brakyn*, or castyn or spewe. Vomo." (Prompt. Parv.)

Braken (*brake*, *bracken*), fern, B. 1675, Sw. *bräken*, Dan. *bregne*, Icel. *brok*, sedge. "A *brakane* filix, a *brakun*, *buske* filicarium." (Cath. Angl.)

Braste, burst, C. 148.

Brathe = breþe, anger, ire, also fierceness. A. 1170; B. 916. O.N. *braedi*, anger. It sometimes signifies angry.

> "Bade hom blyn of hor *brathe*."
> (T. B. 5075.)

> "For this word was Saul wrath,
> For oft-sith was he bremli brath."
> (Cott. MS. Vesp. A. iii. fol. 42*b*.)

Braþeȝ, *pl.* of braþe, A. 346.

Braunches, B. 1464.

Braundysch, display, A. 346.

Bray, utter (aloud), roar, A. 346. Sw. *bräka*.

Brayde, brought, A. 712; aroused, awakened, A. 1170; "at a *brayde*," at a start (Icel. at *bragdi*), at once, B. 539; "in a *brayd*," in a moment, B. 1507. O.N. *bregtha*, weave, move, brandish, seize, awake, to leap, start. *Bragth*, quick motion.

> "Þe Philistienes wituten les
> Ran on Sampson in a res,
> Bot Sampson þat selcuth smert,
> Ute o þair handes son he stert
> And gave a *braid* sa fers and fast,
> Þat alle þe bandes of him brast."
> (Cott. MS. Vesp. A. iii. fol. 40*b*.)

Brayden, ornamented, *p.p.* of *braid*, B. 1481.

Bred, bread, B. 636.

Brede, Bred, } =breed, become, B. 1558; replenish, A. 415, 814; B. 257.

Brede, board, C. 184. "*Brede* or lytylle borde. Mensula, tabula, tabella, asserulus." (Prompt. Parv.) A.S. *bred*, plank, board, etc.

Brede, breadth, A. 1030.

Brede, stretch out, A. 814.

Breed, bred, C. 143.

Bref, short, brief, A. 268.

Brek, broke, B. 1105, 1239.

Breme, full, complete, A. 863. A.S. *breme*, famous, glorious.

Breme, fierce, A. 346; B. 229; C. 430. Du. *bremen*, to burn with desire. Fris. *brimme*, to rage.

> "A *brem* lowe." (T. B. 860.)

Bremly, vigorously, B. 509.

Brend, Brende, } =brente, burnt, bright, A. 989; B. 1292.

Brennande, burning, B. 1012.

Brenne, burn, B. 509, 916.

Brent, burnt, bright, A. 106.

Brent, steep; *superl.* *brentest*, highest, B. 379. N. Prov. E. *brant*, steep. Sw. *brant*, steep, a precipice.

"A man may syt on a *brante* hyll syde."
(Ascham's Toxoph. p. 58, ed. Arber.)
"Apon the bald Bucifelon *brant* up he sittes."
(K. Alex. p. 124.)
"Thane come thai blesnande till a barme of a *brent* lawe (hill)."
(*Ibid.* p. 164.)

Brere, briar, B. 791, 1694. N. Prov. E. *brere, breer.* A.S. *brér.*

Bresed, rough, like bristles, shaggy (?), B. 1694. Cf. Sc. *birs, birse,* bristle.

Brest, attack, outburst, B. 229. N. Prov. E. *birst,* attack (Brockett). O.E. *burst*=injury, A.S. *byrst.*

Breste, to burst, B. 1783.

Breth, } Brethe, } wind, C. 107, 138; smell, vapour, B. 509, 967. Cf. "*brethe* of smoke." (Hampole's Pricke of Conscience, l. 4727.) Sc. *broth.* Ger. *brodem, broden,* steam, vapour. A.S. *bræth,* an odour, scent, breath.
"*Brethe* at his wille."
(T. B. 1945.)

Breth, wrath, B. 916. See *Brath.*

Breue, tell, A. 755.
"*Breve* us thi name." (K. Alex. p. 78.)

Breued, related, written, B. 197. O.N. *brefa.*

Breyþed, rushed, B. 1421. See *Braid.*

Brod, great; "*brod* wonder," B. 584.

Brode, broad, A. 650.

Brok, } Broke, } brook, river, stream, A. 981; *pl. brokeȝ.* A. 1074, sea; C. 145. A.S. *broca.*

Brom (broom), heath, C. 392. A.S. *bróm.*

Bronch, branch, B. 487.

Bronde, sword, B. 1246. O.N. *brandr.*

Brond, brand, B. 1012.

Broþe, angry, fierce, rough, B. 149, 1409. The original form in O.E. is *brathe.* It is connected with *brethe, brathe,* anger, wrath.
"Wreth it es a *brath* on-fall (outburst)
Menging o mode that cums o galle."
(The Deadly Sins, in Cott. MS. Vesp. A. iii.)

Broþely, } Broþelych, } fierce, rough, and hence vile, bad, B. 848, 1030; vilely, B. 1256; C. 474. The original form is *braþly,* fiercely, vigorously.
"Thoner o-loft fal sal he (Antichrist) gar,
And tres *brathli* blomes bere;
Brathli to do the see be reth (stormy)
And *brathli* to do it be smeth."
(Cott. MS. Vesp. A. iii. fol. 124*a*.)

Broun, brown, A. 537, 990.

Browden, clustered, B. 1132.

Broȝt, brought, A. 286.

Brugge=brigge, bridge, B. 1187 A.S. *bricge.*

Brunt, blow, A. 174.
"All þat was bitten of the best (beast) was at a brunt dede."
(K. Alex. p. 134.)

Brurd, border, edge, B. 1474. Sc. *breard.* A.S. *brerd, breard, briord, breord,* brim, margin, rim, shore, brink.

Brurd-ful, brimful, full up to the brim, B. 383. Chaucer uses *bret-ful* in the same sense.

Brutage = bretage, parapets of a wall, ramparts, B. 1190. Fr. *breteche*.

Bruxle, upbraid, reprove, C. 345. O.N. *brixla*, to reprove, reproach.

Brych, filth, uncleanness, B. 848, The meaning here assigned to *brych* is conjectural. Cf. Du. *brack*, refuse, damaged. Gr. *brechen*, to vomit, *Bryche* as an adjective occurs in Robt. Brunne's "Handlyng Synne," p. 182, where it is glossed low (loghe) *i.e.* vile.

> "Now ys Pers bycome *bryche*
> That er was bothe stoute and ryche."

In the Romance of Alexander, ed. Stevenson, we find the form *bicchid* = *briched* (?). Cf. *shille* and *shrille*, etc.

> "And on the aȝtent day, eftire the prime
> A basilisk in a browe, breis (annoys) thaim unfaire,
> A straȝtill and a stithe worme *stinkande* of elde,
> And es so bitter, and so breme, and *bicchid* (foul) in himselfe,
> That with the *stinke* and the strenth he stroyes noȝt allane,
> Bot quat he settes on his siȝt, he slaes in a stonde."
>
> (p. 165.)

Bryd, lady, A. 769. A.S. *bryd*, a bride, a wife, woman.

Brydde, bird, B. 288, 1482.

Brydale, wedding, marriage, B. 142.

Brym, } bank, shore, A. 232,
Brymme, } 1074. Dan. *bremme*.

Brymme, stream, water, B. 365. A.S. *brym*, the sea. In this sense *brymme* seems to have been unknown to the Southern dialect.

> "O þis water þat sua stane
> Wa was þam þat it nedings drane,
> Þat toþer oncom þat him felle,
> Was frosse þat na tung moght telle,
> Þat ute o *brim* and brokes bred,
> And siþen over al Egypte spred."
>
> (Cott. MS. Vesp. A. iii. fol. 32*b*.)

Brynkeȝ, brinks, banks, B. 384.

Brynston, brimstone, B. 967.

Bryȝt, *adj.* bright, A. 110; *sb.* bright one, A. 755.

Bukkeȝ, bucks, B. 392.

Bulde, built, B. 1190.

Buleȝ, bulls, B. 392.

Bulk, stern of a ship. A.S. *bolca*, O.H.G. *pl. balkun*. Agiavia, loca per quæ ad remiges acceditur. (Graff. iii. p. 108.)

Bur, } blow, assault, A. 176;
Burre, } C. 7. O.Sc. *byr*, a blow. N. Prov. *birre*, *burr*. W. *bur*, violence, rage. See Wicliffe, St. Luke, viii. 33.

> "—— no buerne might ffor the *birre* it abide."
>
> (T. B. 170. Cf. T. B. 571, 1902.)

Bur, wave, C. 148. Prov. E. *bore*. Icel. *bara*. O.Ger. *bare*. Du. *baar*, wave, billow. In Laȝamon, vol. iii. p. 121, *þe beares* occurs in the latter version for *þa yðen* of the older copy.

Burde, behoved, A. 316; C. 117, 507. O.N. *byrjar*. Dan. *bör*.

Burde, a woman, lady. B. 80, 653. See *Bryd*. See T. B. 3384.

Burghe, Burȝ, Burȝe, city, town, A. 980; B. 982; C. 366.

Burne, man, A. 397, 712; B. 1202; "*burneȝ & burdeȝ*," men and women, B. 80. A.S. *beorn*, warrior, hero.

Burnist, Burnyst, burnished, B. 1085.

Burre, blow, A. 176. See *bur*.

Burþen, burden, B. 1439.

Butter, B. 636.

Burȝ, city, town, B. 1666. See *burghe*.

Busch, Busche, =buske, to go, B. 1416; C. 143, 472.

> "& he (she) wist it as wel or bet as ȝif it were hire owne,
> Til hit big was & bold to *buschen*, on felde."
> (William and the Werwolf. p. 7.)

Busily, laboriously, B. 1446.

Busk, prepare, made ready, dress, to direct one's steps towards a place, to go, hasten. B. 142, 333, 351, 633, 1395; C. 437. Icel. *at buast* (for *at buasc*)=*at bua sig*, to bend one's steps, to prepare, etc. See T. B. 1186.

Busmar, scorn, mockery, B. 653. A.S. *bismer*, reproach, blasphemy.

Bustwys, impetuous, fiery, A. 911. See *bostwys*.

Busyeȝ=busies, troubles, A. 268.

Buyrne=burne, man, C. 340. See *Burne*.

Bycalle, call, A. 913.

Bycalt, aroused, called, A. 1163.

Bycom, became, A. 537.

Byde, abide, A. 399; suffer, A. 664; B. 32; remain, B. 449, 622,

Bydene, quickly, A. 196.

Bye, buy, A. 732.

Byfallen, befallen, B. 1629.

Byfore, before, A. 530.

Bigge, Byge, great, B. 229.

Byggyng, Bygyng, building, A. 932; dwelling, B. 378. A.S. *byggan*, to build, Icel. *byggia*. See T. B. 1379.

Bygly, great, strong; "*bygly bylde*," great building, A. 963. See T. B. 5216.

Bygonne, Bygonnen, begun, *p.p.* of *byginne*, A. 33; B. 749; began, A. 549.

Bygyn, begin, A. 547.

Bygynner, beginner, A. 436.

Byhelde, beheld, B. 452.

Byhod, behoved, A. 928. Cf. *bud*, behoved; *bus*, behoves.

Byholde, behold, A. 810; B. 64.

Byhynde, Byhynden, behind, B. 653, 980.

Byld, Bylded, built. See *Bulde*.

Bylde, building, A. 727, 963.

Bylyue, immediately, at once, quickly, B. 353, 610.

Bynde, bine, woodbine, C. 444. Sw. *binda*. Ger. *winde*. Eng. *bind*-weed.

Bynne, within, B. 452, 467.

Byrled, poured out, B. 1715. See *Birle*.

Bysech, Byseche, beseech, A. 390.

Byseme, beseem, A. 310.

Bysulpe, defile, B. 575. See *Sulpe.*

Byswyke, defraud, A. 568. A.S. *swícan*, deceive.

Bysyde, beside, B. 673,

Bytaȝt, } =betaught, entrusted,
Bytaȝte, } confided; *pret.* of *biteche*, A. 1207; B. 528.

Byte, fierce, A. 355.

Byþenk, repent, B. 582.

Bytterly, *adv.* B. 468.

Bytwene, between, A. 140, 658.

Bytwyste, betwixt, A. 464.

Bytyde, betide, happen, A. 397; B. 522.

Byye, buy, A. 478.

Byȝe, crown, A. 466; ring, collar, B. 1638. A.S. *beáh, beág*, ring, collar, diadem.

Byȝonde, beyond, A. 141, 146, 158, 981.

Cable, C. 102.

Cace, case, chance, C. 265.

Cache, } =catch, drive away,
Cachche, } take away. (1) "*cache* to," run to, B. 629; (2) take, B. 898, 1252. *Cachche*, to knock together, B. 1541. *Cached*, caught, B. 1800. Prov. Fr. *cacher*. Fr. *chasser*. It. *cacciare*.

Cachen (3*d pers. pl.* of *cache*), B. 16.

Cagged, drawn along (?), B. 1254.

Caggen (3*d pers. pl. pres.* of *cagge*), draw (?), A. 512.

"Cables were *caget* togedur."
(T. B. 3703.)

"He plyes ovir the pavement
with pallene webis.
Mas on hiȝt ovir his hede
for hete of the sone,
Sylours of sendale to sele
ovire the gatis,
And sammes thaim on aither side
with silken rapis,
And then he *caggis* up one
Cordis, as curteyns it ware."
(K. Alex. p. 52.)

Cal, *sb.* call, invitation, B. 61.

Calder, colder, A. 320.

Calleȝ, addresses, C. 411.

Callyng, *sb.* proclamation, B. 1362. N. Prov. E. calling, notice. "*Callynge*, or clepyng to mete: Invitacio." (Prompt. Parv.)

Calsydoyne, chalcedony, A. 1003.

Cambe, came, A. 775.

Canacle, B. 1461. M. Lat. *canicellus*, a little box, chest.

Candel, C. 472.

Candelstik, B. 1478.

Capeles, horses, B. 1254. *Capul* or *caple*, horse. Caballus. (Prompt. Parv.)

Capstan, B. 418.

Captyuidé, captivity, B. 1612.

Caraldes, C. 159.

Carayne, carrion, B. 459.

Care, sorrow, A. 50, 371; B. 777. A.S. *cáru*. Goth. *kara*.

Careful, sorrowful, B. 770.

Carf, carved, formed, C. 131.

Carfully, sorrowfully, B. 1252.

Carle, a low fellow, a churl, B. 876. A.S. *ceorl*, a man, countryman. Du. *kaerle*. Ger. *kerl*.

Carneles, battlements, embrasures, B. 1382.

Carpe, *sb.* discourse, A. 883;

parable, B. 23; speech, B. 1327.

Carpe, *vb.* to discourse, talk, speak, A. 381; B. 74; of carpe, discourse of, A. 752. "*Carpyn* or talkyn, fabulor, confabulor, garrulo." (Prompt. Parv.) Port. *carpire*, cry.

Carping, discourse, speech, B. 1550.

Cas, case, A. 673.

Cast, Caste, Kest, } condition, A. 1163.

Cast, look, B. 768.

Casydoyne, B. 1471. See *Calsydoyne*.

Catel, wealth, B. 1296.

Cawse, reason, B. 65.

Cause, A. 702.

Cayre, to turn one's steps to a place, to go, A. 1031; B. 85, 901, 1259. "Kaire to þi londe," T. B. 836. A.S. *cérran*. Ger. *kehren*. Du. *keeren*, to turn.

Cayser, emperor, B. 1322.

Caytif, wretched, B. 1426.

Caȝt, Caȝte, } caught, A. 50; caȝte of, took off, A. 237; caȝt away, B. 1275; C. 485. See *Cache*.

Certeȝ, truly, B. 105.

Cerue, cut, dig, B. 1547.

Cetê, city, A. 927.

Ceuer, recover, reach, A. 319.

Chace, drive, A. 443.

Chambre, A. 904; B. 1586.

Chapel, A. 1062.

Charde, turned, A. 608. A.S. *cérran*, to turn, avert. Cf. *ajar*, older form a-*char*, on-*char*.

Charged, commanded, B. 464.

Charged, loaded, B. 1154, 1295.

Chariote, B. 1295.

Charytê, A. 470.

Chast, chasten, B. 860.

Chastyse, B. 543.

Chaufen, heat, increase, B. 128.

Chaunce, chance, B. 1125.

Chaundeler, candlestick, B. 1272.

Chaunge, change, B. 1588.

Chawleȝ, jaws, C. 268. N. Prov. E. *chavel*. A.S. *ceafl*. S. Sax. *cheuele*. Cp. the vulgar phrase "cheek by *jowl*."

Chayer, Chayere, } chair, seat, A. 885; B. 1218.

Chef, chief, B. 684, 1238.

Cheftayn, chieftain, B. 1295.

Chekke, B. 1238.

Chere, cheer, A. 407; countenance, A. 887. Prov. Sp. *cara*, O.Fr. *chiere*, countenance, favour, look.

Cheryche, Cherisch, } cherish, B. 128, 543, 1154, 1644.

Ches, chose (*pret.* of *chese*), A. 759.

Cheualrye, chivalry, B. 1238.

Cheue, achieve, accomplish, B. 1125. Fr. *achever*, to bring to a head, accomplish. Fr. *chévir*, to compass.

Cheuetayn, Cheuentayn, } chieftain, A. 605; B. 464. O.Fr. *chevetaine*,

Childer, Chylder, } children, A. 718: B. 1300.

Chorles, churl, B. 1258. See *Carle*.

Chos, went. See "chosen," T.B. 490.

Chyche, niggard, A. 605. Fr.

chice, avarice. *Chynche* and *kynche* are other forms of the same word.

Chyde, A. 403.

Chyldryn, (*gen. pl.*) of children, B. 684.

Chylled=chilled, shivered, became cold, C. 368.

Chysly=choysly, aptly, well, B. 543.

Ciences, sciences, knowledge, B. 1289.

Clam (*pret.*), climbed, B. 405.

Clambe (2 *sing. pret.*), climbedst, A. 773.

Clanner, cleaner, B. 1100.

Clanly, } cleanly, purely, A. 2;
Clanlych, } B. 264, 1089, 1327; neatly, B. 310. T. B. 53.

Clannes, clannesse, cleanness, purity, B. 1, 12, 1809.

Claryoun, clarion, B. 1210.

Çlater, } shatter, B. 912.
Clatter, }

> "So hard was she beseged soth for to telle,
> And so harde sautes to the cite were ȝeuen,
> That the komli kerneles were to-*clatered* with engines."
>
> (William and the Werwolf, p. 103.)

Clatering, clattering, B. 1515. Du. *klateren*, to rattle.

Clatȝ, clash, clatter, B. 839. Ger. *klatschen*, to clap; *klatsch*, slap, clash.

Clawres, claws, B. 1696. *Clawres* is perhaps an error for *clawes*. It may, however, be another form of O.E. *clever*, *claver*, a claw. Du. *klaveren*, *kleveren*. N. Prov. E. *claiver*, to claw oneself up, to scramble.

Clay, B. 312. *Clay*-daubed, B. 492.

Clayme, call for, cry for, B. 1096.

Cleche, receive, take, B. 12. "*Cleches* to," takes, lays hold of, B. 634. Sc. *cleik*, *clek*, *cluke*, claw, hook; *cleke*, *cleik*, catch, snatch. O.Sw. *klaencka*, to snatch, seize.

Clef, cleft, split (*pret.* of *cleve*), B. 367.

Clem, claim, A. 826.

Cleme, daub, plaster with clay, B. 312. N. Prov. E. *cleam*. *Clam*, to daub, glue. S. Prov. E. *cloam*, earthenware; *clomer*, a potter. A.S. *clem*, *clám*, clay; *clæmian*, to *clam*, smear.

> "I stoppe thys ouyn wythowtyn dowte.
> With clay I *clome* yt uppe ryght fast,
> That non heat cum [ther] owte."
>
> (The Play of the Sacrament, p. 132.)

Clene, perfect, whole, B. 1731.

Clenge, cling, stick, B. 1034. Dan. *klynge*, to cluster, crowd. S. Prov. E. *clunge*, to crowd, squeeze; *clungy*, sticky.

Clente, clenched, fastened, A. 259. Cf. *queynte*=quenched, *dreynte* =drenched.

Clepe, to call, B. 1345. A.S. *clypian*.

Cler, } clear, A. 2, 207; bright,
Clere, } A. 620, 735; plain, B. 26.

Clergye, learning, B. 1570.

Clerkeȝ, clerks, scholars, B. 193.

Clernes, clearness, beauty, B. 1353.

Cleþe, clothe, B. 1741.

Cleȝt, } = clutched, fastened,
Clyȝt, } (*p.p.* of *cleche*), B. 858; fixed, B. 1655.

Clobbeȝ, clubs, B. 839.

Clos, enclosure, house, B. 839.

Clos, closed, A. 183; B. 12.

Closed, enclosed, B. 310.

Clot, mount, hill, A. 789. In the "Owl and Nightingale," 999, we find *clude*, a hill. A.S. *clúd*. Low Ger. *kloot*, a hill.

Clot, soil, earth, A. 22, 320. Du. *klot*, *klotte*, clod, clot.

Clotteȝ, clods, A. 857.

Cloþ, sail, C. 105.

Cloutes, } pieces, B. 367, 965.
Clowteȝ, }

Cloystor, cloister, A. 969.

Cluchche, clutch, B. 1541.

Clustered, B. 367, 951. See T. B. 1647.

Clutte, clouted, patched (?), B. 40. A.S. *clút*, a clout.

Clyde, plaister (?), B. 1692. A.S. *clitha*. Cf. "*Clyte*, *clete*, or vegge (*clete* or wegge, K.) cuneus." (Prompt. Parv.)

Clyffe, cliff, A. 159; B. 405, 965.

Clyket, clicket, latch, B. 858. Prov. Fr. *cliche*, a latch, bolt. *Clyket* of a dore, *clicquette*. (Palsgrave.)

Clynge, wither, decay, A. 857. A.S. *clingan*.

Clyppe, fasten, B. 418. A.S. *clyppan*, to embrace.

"I wold yonder worthy weddit me hade,
So comly, so cleane to *clippe* uppon nightes." (T. B. 474.)

Clypper, shearer, A. 802.

Clyue, } cleave, cling to, B. 1630,
Clyuy, } 1692. Du. *kleeven*, *klijven*, to fasten. A.S. *clifan*.

Clyuen, cleave, A. 1196.

Clyȝt, clutched, stuck, B. 1692.

Cnawe, know, acknowledge, C. 519.

Cnawyng, *sb.* knowledge, A. 859.

Cnoken, knock, A. 727.

Cob-hous = cov (cow)-house (?), B. 629. *Cob* may be another form of Prov. Ger. *colb*, a heifer.

Cof, quickly, B. 60, 898; quick, B. 624. A.S. *cáf*, quick, expert.

Cofer, } coffer, chest, coffin, A.
Cofere, } 259; ship, ark, B. 310, 339; jewel box, 1428. Fr. *coffre*.

Cofly, quickly, B. 1428.

Coge, boat, C. 152. *Cogges* with cablis cachyn to londe, T. B. 1077.

Cokreȝ, cockers, a kind of rustic high shoes or half boots fastened with laces or buttons, B. 40. "*Cocur* boote. Ocrea. coturnus." (Prompt. Parv.) The term is still used in the north of England = gaiters, leggings.

Cole, coal, B. 456.

Cole, cool, C. 452.

Colde, great, severe, A. 50; "*careȝ* colde," great sorrow, A. 808.

Coler, collar, B. 1569, 1744.

Colored, B. 456.

Colour, A. 753.

Coltour = coulter, (of a plough), B. 1547. Fr. *coultre*. Lat. *culter*.

Colwarde, deceitful, B. 181. See note on this word. Cf. *kolsipe* (col-ship), deceit.
Comaunde, B. 1428.
Combre, to trouble, destroy, B. 901, 1024. Du. *kommer, kombre*, loss, adversity, care, grief.
Combraunce, trouble, B. 4. See T. B. 726.
Come, *sb.* coming, arrival, A. 1116; B. 467

"Of his *come* fayne." (T. B. 975.)

Comende, B. 1.
Comfort, } *sb.* A. 55, 857.
Comforte, }
Comly, } comely, A 259; B.
Comlych, } 546.
Commune, common, A. 739.
Comparisune, *vb.* compare, B. 161.
Compas, A. 1072, B. 319, 1455.
Compast, B. 697.
Compaynye, company, B. 119.
Comyne, B. . See T. B. 12863.
Con=can, did (used as an auxiliary of the past tense), A. 453; B. 1561; *conez*, didst, A. 482.
Conacle=canacle, cup, B. 1515.
Conciens, conscience, A. 1089.
Concubine, B. 1353.
Condelstik, candlestick, B. 1275.
Confourme, conform, B. 1067.
Coninge, } wisdom, science, B.
Connyng, } 1611, 1625.
Conquere, B 1431, 1632.
Conquerour, B. 1322.
Conquest, conquered, B. 1305.
Consayue, conceive, B. 649.
Conterfete, counterfeit, feign, B. 13.
Contraré, contrary, B. 4, 266; in *contrary*, opposite, B. 1532.
Controeued, contrived, B. 266.
Contryssyoun, contrition, A. 669.
Conueye, guide, B. 678, 768.
Coostez, properties, B. 1033.
Coperounes, tops, B. 1461. "*Coporne* or *coporoun* of a thyng (*coperone*, K.H. *coperun*, P.), capitellum." (Prompt. Parv.) "The Catholicon explains *capitellum* as signifying merely the capital of a column, but in the Medulla it is rendered '*summa pars capitis*.'" (A. Way, in Prompt. Parv.)
Coppe, top; "hyl *coppe*," A. 791. A.S. *copp*, head, top, apex.

"Now bowis furth this baratour and bidis na langir,
Up at a martene mountane, he myns with his ost,
And viii daies bedene the drize was and mare,
Or he mizt covir to the *copp*, fra the cave undire."
(K. Alex. p. 163.)

Corage, heart, B. 1806.
Corbyal, raven, B. 456.
Cordes, C. 153.
Coroun, *sb.* A. 237; *vb.* A. 415, 767.
Cors, course, B. 264.
Corse, corpse, A. 320.
Corse, to curse, B. 1032, 1583.
Corsye, corrosive, B. 1034.
Cortays, } courteous, A. 433; B.
Cortayse, } 512; pure, B. 1089,
Cortaysye, courtesy, A. 468, 480; good conduct, B. 13.
Cortaysly, courteously, A. 381; kindly, B. 564, 1435.
Corte, court, A. 701.

Cortel, kirtle, A. 203. A.S. *cyrtel.* Dan. *kjortel*, a garment either for a man or woman.
Corteȝ, courteous, A. 754.
Corupte, B. 281.
Coruen (*p.p.* of *kerue*), cut, reaped. A. 40; B. 1407.
Cost, contrivance, B. 1478. A.S. *costian.* O. Sw. *kosta.* Du. *koste*, to try, attempt. This word is sometimes written *cast.* See "William and the Werwolf," p. 167.
Cost, coost, property, B. 1024, 1033.
Cost, coast, border, side, B. 85.
Costoum, custom, B. 851.
Coumforde, comfort, A. 369.
Counseyl, } counsel, A. 319; B.
Counsayl, } 683, 1201.
Counte, B. 1685, 1731.
Countenaunce, appearance, B. 792.
Counterfete, defraud, A. 556.
Countes, countess, A. 489.
Courtaysye, courtesy, A. 457.
Cout, cut, B. 1104.
Couthe, knew, known, B. 813, 1054.
Coueyte, covet, desire, B. 1054.
Couenaunde, } covenant, A. 562,
Couenaunt, } 563.
Couetyse, covetousness, B. 181.
Cowpe, cup, B. 1458.
Cowþe, could; cowþeȝ, couldst, A. 484.
Cowwardely, cowardly, B. 1631.
Coyntyse, skill, craft, B. 1287. *Coint*, skilful, occurs in T. B. 125. "hir *coint* artys." Cf. *Coyntly*, T. B. 164.
Crafte, power, wisdom; *pl.* crafteȝ, A. 356; contrivance, A. 890; power, C. 131.
Crageȝ, crags, B. 449.
Crak, sound, B. 1210.
Craue, ask, pray for, A. 663; beg, B. 801.
Crede, creed, A. 485.
Cresse, cress, A. 343.
Creste, A. 856.
Croked, bad, B. 181.
Crokeȝ, reapinghooks, sickles, A. 40.
Croneȝ, cranes, B. 58.
Crossayl, cross-sail, C. 102.
Croukeȝ, croaks, B. 459.
Cruppeleȝ, cripples, B. 103.
Cry, proclamation, B. 1574.
Crysolite, } chrysolite, A. 1009.
Crysolyt, }
Crysopase, chrysoprasus, A. 1013.
Crystal, A. 159.
Cumly, A. 929. See *Comly.*
Cupborde, B. 1440.
Cupyde, } B. 315, 319, 405.
Cubit, }
Cumfort, C. 485.
Cupple, pair, B. 333.
Cure, care, A. 1091.
Curious, B. 1353.
Cyté, } city, A. 927, 939.
Ceté, }

Dale, B. 384 (phrase: "doun and *daleȝ*," hill and dale), A. 121.
Dalt, dealt, fulfilled, B. 1756.
Dam, stream, A. 324; the deep, B. 416. Icel. *dammr.* Dan. *dam*, a fish pond.
Dampned, damned, condemned, A. 641.
Dampped, quelled, B. 989. Ger.

dampfen, to suffocate, choke. Du. *dempen*. Sw. *dåmpa*, to extinguish, repress, damp.
Damysel, damsel, A. 489.
Dare, to tremble, be afraid, A. 839. Sw. *darra*, to tremble, shake.
Dard=dured, endured, A. 609.
Daschande, dashing, C. 312.
Dasande, stupefying, B. 1538.
Dase, lie hid, cower, C. 383. Cf. *dare*, to lie hid, cower. For the interchange of *r* and *s* compare O.E. *gaure*, to gaze.
Dased, stupid, frightened, A. 1085. Sc. *dozen*, *dosen*, to stupefy, benumb. Du. *daesen*, to lose one's wits; *daes*, *dwaes*, foolish, mad. (Kil.) Prov. Ger. *dasen*, to be still.

> "For he was *dased* of the dint and half dede him semyd."
> (K. Alex. p. 136.)

Date, A. 492; limit, A. 493; time, A. 504, 516; age, A. 1040.
Daube, daub, plaister, B. 313, 492. Prov. E. *daub*, clay. "*Dawber* or cleyman; *dawbyn*, lino, muro." (Prompt. Parv.)
Daunce, dance, A. 345.
Daunger, power, A. 11; insolence, B. 71.
Dawande, dawning, C. 445. A.S. *dagian*, to become day. Icel. *dagan*, dawn.
Daweȝ, days; "don out of *daweȝ*," deprived of life, dead, A. 282.
Dayly, A. 313.
Daynty, B. 38, 1046.
Day-rawe, daybreak, B. 893; *rawe* or *rewe* signifies a *streak*. Cf. *day-rim*, in "Owl and Nightingale," l. 328.

> "Qwen the *day-rawe* rase,
> he rysis belyfe."
> (K. Alex. p. 14.)

Daȝed, dawned, became day, B. 1755. See *Dawande*.
Debate, strife, contest, A. 390.
Debonere, gracious, courteous, kind, A. 162; B. 830.
Debonerté, goodness, A. 798; C. 418.
Dece=dese, seat of honour, B. 38, 1399. See *Dese*.
Declar, explain, B. 1618.
Declyne, A. 333.
Decre, decree, B. 1745; C. 386.
Dedayn, disdain, displeasure, B. 74; C. 50.
Defence, prohibition, B. 243, 245.
Defoule, defilement, C. 290.
Defowle, to defile, B. 1129, 1147.
Degre, degree, condition, B. 92.
Degres, steps, A. 1022.
Dekenes, deacons, B. 1266.
Dele, deal, distribute, give, A. 606; exchange, B. 1118.
Dele, utter, B. 344.
Dele (dole), sorrow, A. 51.
Deled, dealt, C. 193.
Delful, doleful, sorrowful, B. 400.
Delfully, dolefully, sorrowfully, A. 706.
Delyt, delight, A. 642, 1116.
Delyuer, delivered, B. 1084.
Delyuer, deliver, A. 652; B. 500.
Deme, deem, judge, A. 312, 313; B. 1118; utter, decree, B. 1745; C. 119; call, name, B. 1020, 1611. A.S. *déman*.

Demerlayk, } magic, glamour, B. Demorlayk, } 1561, 1578. S. Sax. *dweomer-lake*, magic. A.S. *dweomere*, a juggler.

"And all this *demerlayke* he did bot be the devylle craftes." (K. Alex. p. 15.)

Demme, *vb.* become faded, lost, A. 223. A.S. *dem*, damage, hurt, loss.

Demmed=dammed, collected (?), B. 384. A.S. *demman*, to dam, stop water. Carr gives *demin*, a term applied to clouds when collected in masses. Sw. *dämma*. O. Fris. *demma*, to stop, obstruct.

Dene, vale, dale, A. 295. A.S. *dene*, *denu*.

Denely, loud, A. 51.

Denned, resounded. If it does not signify *dinned*, it must mean settled, took up its abode. A. 51.

Denounce, renounce, forsake, B. 106.

Departe, separate, part, A. 378; B. 396, 1677.

Depaynt, painted, adorned, A. 1102.

Dep, } profound, A. 406; B. Depe, } 1609.

Depres, depress, A. 778.

Depryue, A. 449; take away, B. 185.

Dere, *vb.* to harm, injure, A. 1157; B. 862. See T. B. 1260. A.S. *derian*, to hurt, damage, injure.

Dere, precious, A. 400; valuable, B. 1792. A.S. *deóre*, dear, precious.

Dere, dear ones, A. 777.

Derelych, } =dearly, beautifully, Derely, } excellently, A. 995; very, B. 270.

Dereȝ, *sb.* harms, injuries, A. 102. See T. B. 920. A.S. *dar*, *daru*, hurt, harm.

"Thai dreȝe him up to the drye (land), and he na *dere* sufird." (K. Alex. p. 189)

Derf, great, bold, B. 862. O.N. *diafr*. Sw. *djerf*, strong, bold. "A *derfe* dragon," T. B. 166. "Dang him *derffly* don in a ded hate." *Ib.* 1339.

Derfly, quickly, B. 1641; C. 110.

Derk, dark, B. 1020; C. 263; night, B. 1755. A.S. *deorc*.

Derne, *adj.* secret, hidden, B. 588, 1611; *adv.* secretly, B. 697. See T. B. 1962. A.S. *dearn*, dark, secret, hidden.

Derrest, dearest, B. 115, 1306.

Derþe=dearth, preciousness, value, worth, A. 99. See *Dere*.

Deruely=derfely, quickly, B. 632.

Derworth, precious, beautiful, A. 109. See *Dere*.

Des, } dais, seat of honour, A. Dese, } 766; B. 115, 1394.

Desert, C. 84.

Desserte, desert, A. 595.

Deseuered, severed, C. 315.

Dessypele, disciple, A. 715.

Destyné, A. 758; C. 49.

Desyre, B. 545.

Determynable, A. 594.

Deuine, *sb.* divine, B. 1302; *vb.* B. 1561.

Deuinores, diviner, B. 1578.

Deuote, devout, A. 406.

Deuoutly, B. 814.
Deuoydc, do away with, destroy, A. 15; B. 908.
Deuyce, Deuyse, Deuice, } devise, imagine, B. 1046, 1100; describe, A. 99, 984; order, B. 110, 238.
Deuyse, *sb.* device, A. 139.
Deuysement, description, A. 1019.
Devoydynge, putting away, *sb.* B. 544.
Dewoutly, devoutly, C. 333.
Dewoyde=devoyde, C. 284.
Dewyne=dwine, pine, A. 11.
Deystyné, destiny, B. 400.
Deȝter, Deȝteres, Deȝtters, } daughters, B. 270, 866, 899, 933, 939. See T. B. 1489.
Dialoke, discourse, B. 1157.
Dispayred, in despair, C. 169.
Display, B. 1107.
Displese, C. 1.
Dispit, spite, C. 50.
Dispoyled, stripped, C. 95.
Disserued, B. 613.
Disstrye, destroy, B. 907, 1160.
Disserne, discern, C. 513.
Dissert, desert, C. 12.
Distres, B. 880, 1160.
Diuinité, B. 1609.
Ditteȝ, stops up, closes, B. 588. N. Prov. E. *ditt*, to stop up. A.S. *dyttan*.
Diȝe, die, C. 488.
Diȝte, order, arrange, B. 1266. A.S. *dihtan*, to set in order, dispose, arrange, direct, etc.
Do, doe, "*daunce as any do*," A. 345.
Dobler, dish, B. 1146. O.Fr. *doublier*.
Doc, duke, A. 211.
Doel, Dol, } sorrow, A. 326, 339, 642; B. 852.
Dole, part, A. 136.
Dom, Dome, } doom, judgment, purpose, A. 157, 580, 667; B. 597; command, B. 632; doom, C. 203.
Dongoun, dungeon, B. 1224.
Dool, part, B. 216.
Dool (dole), sorrow. See *Doel*.
Doole, gift, B. 699.
Dor, door, B. 320.
Dotage, folly, B. 1425.
Dote, act foolishly, B. 286, 1500; C. 125; be astonished, frightened, B. 852. Sc. *doit*. Icel. *dotta*, to slumber. Du. *doten*, *dutten*, delirare, desipere. (Kilian.) "Maddyn, or *dotyn*, desipio." (Prompt. Parv.)
Doted, foolish, wicked, C. 196. N. Prov. E. *doited*, stupid.
Dotel, a fool, B. 1517.
Doun, down, A. 230.
Doun, down, hill, A. 121.
Doungoun, dungeon, A. 1187.
Doured, grieved, mourned, C. 372. Sc. *dour*.
Dousour, sweetness, A. 429.
Doute, doubt, A. 928.
Douth, Douþe, } brave, noble, A. 839, B. 270, 597, A.S. *duguth*, the nobility, senate, etc. *Dugeth*, good, virtuous. *Dugan*, to profit, avail, be good, etc.
Doune, Dovene, } a female dove, B. 469, 481. Cf. O.E. *wulvene*, a female wolf, and E. *vixen*, a female fox.
Dowe, avail, profit, B. 374; C.

50. See T. B. 5001. See *Douth*.

Dowelle, dwell, B. 376, 1770; C. 69.

Downe, dove, B. 485.

Downeȝ, downs, hills, A. 73, 85.

Dowyne, dwine, pine, A. 326.

Dowrie, B. 185.

Doȝter, daughter, B. 814.

Doȝty, doughty, valiant, B. 1182, 1791. See *Douthe*.

Doȝtyest, bravest, B. 1306.

Draȝ, draw, A. 699.

Draȝt = draught, character, B. 1557.

Drede, doubt, A. 1047.

Drepe, to kill, slay, B. 246; destroy, B. 599, 1306.

> "This stone with his stremys stroyed all the venym,
> And *drepit* the dragon to the dethe negh." (T. B. 929.)

A.S. *drepan*. O.N. *drepa*.

Dresse, order, direct, prepare, A. 495, 860; B. 92; *pret. dressed, drest*.

Dreue, drive, A. 323.

Dreued, drove, went, A. 980.

Dreȝe = dreghe, suffer, endure, B. 1224. Sc. *dree*. A.S. *dreógan*, to bear, suffer, endure. Cf. "dyntes full *dregh*." T. B. 935.

Dreȝly, sorrowfully, B. 476. See T. B. 2379.

Drof, drove, A. 30, 1153.

Drouy, turbid, B. 1016. A.S. *dréfe*, muddy, foul; *dréfan*, to trouble, make turbid. O.E. *drove*, to trouble. Goth. *drobjan*, to trouble. Du. *droeven*. "*Drovy* turbidus, turbulentus." (Cath. Ang.)

> "He (the fool-large) is like to an hors that seketh rather to drynke *drovy* watir and trouble, than for to drinke water of the welle that is cleer."
> (The Persones Tale: *Remedium contra avariciam*.)

Drowned, was drowned, B. 372.

Droȝ, drew, A. 1116; B. 71; *pl. droȝen*, B. 1394.

Droȝthe = drouthe, drought. A.S. *druguth*. Du. *drooghte*. Sc. *drouth*, from A.S. *dryg*. Du. *droogh*, dry.

Druye, dry, B. 412; dry land, B. 472.

Drwry, dreary (?), A. 323.

Drwry = drury, love, B. 699, 1065. O.Fr. *druerie, drurie*.

Dryȝ, Dryȝe, } dry, B. 385.

Dryȝ, Dryȝe, } heavy, sorrowful, A. 823; B. 342.

Dryȝe, suffer, B. 372, 400, 1032. See *Dreȝe*.

Dryȝly, Dryȝlych, } strongly, rapidly, A. 125; wrathfully, angrily, B. 74, 344; C. 235.

Dryȝtyn, Lord, A. 349; B. 1065. A.S. *drihten*.

Dubbed, Dubbet, } decked, A. 73, 97, 202; adorned, B. 115. See T. B. 1683.

Dubbement, adornment, A. 121.

Dublere, a dish, B. 1279. See *Dobler*.

Due, A. 894; C. 49.

Duk, duke, B. 38, 1182; leader, B. 1771.

Dumpe, be dashed, fall, C. 362.

"*Dumpe* in þe depe."—(T. B. 1996.)
"Þan sal þe rainbow descend,
In hu o galle it sal be kend;
Wit þe wind sal it melle,
And drive þam dun alle until helle;
And *dump* the devels þider in,
In þair bale alle for to brin."
(*Signa Ante Judicium*, in Cott. MS. Vesp. A. iii.)

Dungen, 3*d pers. pl. pret.* of *ding*, to beat, B. 1266. Sw. *dänga*.

"So *dang* he þat dog with dynt of his wappon." (T. B. 302.)

Dunne, dun, A. 30. See T. B. 925.

Dunt, blow. See *Dynt*.

Durande, lasting, during, A. 336.

Dure, last, B. 1021; C. 488.

Dusched, struck, B. 1538. Sc. *dusche*, to smite; *dusch*, a blow.

"All *dusshet* into the diche." (T. B. 4776.)

Dan. *daske*, to slap. Icel. *dust*, a blow.

Dutande, shutting, closing (from *dutte*, to shut), B. 320. See *Ditteȝ*.

Dutte, fasten, close, B. 1182. Prov. E. *dyt*, stop up. O.N. *ditta*.

Dych, ditch, A. 607; B. 1792.

Dyd, caused, A. 306.

Dylle = dull, slow, sluggish, foolish, A. 680. N. Prov. E. *dull*, hard of hearing. O.N. *dilla*, lallare.

Dym, black, B. 1016.

Dymly, secretly, C. 375.

Dymme, dark, B. 472.

Dyn, noise, B. 862.

"All *dynnet* the *dyn* the dales aboute." (T. B. 1197.)

Dyngne, worthy, C. 119.

Dyngneté, dignity, B. 1801.

Dynt, blow, C. 125.

Dyscreuen, describe, A. 68.

Dyscouere, reveal, make known, B. 683.

Dysheriete, disinherit, B. 185.

Dysplese, to be displeased, A. 422; to displease, A. 455; B. 1136.

Dyspyt, spite, B. 821.

Dyssente, descend, A. 627.

Dysstrye, destroy, B. 520.

Dystresse, distress, A. 280, 337.

Dystryed, destroyed, A. 124.

Dyt, doeth, A. 681.

Dyȝe, die, A. 306.

Dyȝt, decked, A. 202, 987; ordered, prepared, B. 243, 632; ordained, C. 49; placed, seated, A. 920; B. 1794.

Dyȝtteȝ, causest, C. 488.

Efte, again, A. 328; afterwards, A. 332; B. 562.

Egge = *edge*, hill, B. 451.

Egge, edge (of a knife), B. 1104; of a hill, B. 383. A.S. *ecge*. O.N. *egg*, edge. Du. *egghe*, an angle, corner, angle. Ger. *ecke*, a corner.

Eggyng, instigation, B. 241. Prov. E. "egg on." O.N. *egg*, an edge; *eggia*, to sharpen, and hence instigate.

Elde, age, B. 657; C. 125. A.S. *eld*, *yld*, age.

Elleȝ, else, otherwise, A. 32; 724; so that, B. 466.

Emerad, Emerade, } emerald, A. 118, 1005.

Emperise, empress, A. 441.

Empire, Empyre, } A. 454; B. 540, 1332.

Enaumayld, Enaumaylde, } enamelled, B. 1411, 1457.
Enbaned, supported (?), B. 1459. Sir F. Madden renders it *ornamented.*
Enclose, B. 334.
Enclynande, inclining, bowing, A. 236.
Enclyned, prone, B. 518.
Enclyin, Enclyne, } incline, A. 630, 1206.
Encres, increase, A. 959.
Encroche, approach, A. 1117; receive, C. 18.
Ende, die, B. 402; *on ende*, to death, C. 426. Cf. *ender-day*, and *ending* day = the day of one's death.
Endeleȝ, endless, A. 738.
Endente, A. 639, 1012.
Endentur, crevices, holes, B. 313. O.Fr. *endenter*, to notch, jag.
Endorde, adored, A. 368.
Endure, Eudeure, } A. 476, 1082.
Endyte, indite, A. 1126.
Ene, once; *at ene*, at once, A. 291; *at ene*, at one, A. 953. A.S. *æne*, once.
Enfaminied, famished, B. 1194.
Enforsed, forced, B. 938.
Engendered, begat, B. 272.
Enherite, inherit, B. 240.
Enle = enely (? *onlepi*), alone, singly, A. 849.
Enleuenþe, eleventh, A. 1014.
Enmie, Enmye, } enemy, B. 1204.
Enourled, encircled, surrounded, B. 18. Fr. *ourler*, to hem. *Orle* in Heraldry = border. Ital. Orlo = hem, edge. Spanish and Portug. Orla = selvedge, border.
Enprece, Enpresse, } press, C. 43, 528.
Enpresse, impress, A. 1097.
Enpoysened, poisoned, B. 242.
Enprysonment, imprisonment, B. 46.
Enquylen, obtain, C. 39. See *Aquyle.*.
Ensens, incense, A. 1122.
Entent, intent, A. 1191.
Entre, enter, A. 38, 1067.
Entré, entrance, B. 1779.
Entyse, to provoke, B. 1137, 1808.
Enurned, adorned, decked, A. 1027.
Er, ere, before, A. 324, 328; B. 648.
Erber, Erbere, } arbour, A. 9, 38, 1171.
Erbes, herbs, B. 1684.
Erde, land, abode, A. 248; B. 596, 601, 1006. A.S. *eard*, native soil, country, region; *eardian*, to dwell, inhabit.

> "Eson afterward *erdand* on lyffe,
> Endured his dayes drowpyaite
> (? *drowpande*) on age."
> (T. B. 121.)

Erigant, arrogance, B. 148.
Erly, early, A. 392.
Ernde, errand, message, C. 52. See *Arende.*
Erne, eagle, B. 1698. A.S. *earn*, eagle.
Ernestly, quickly, rapidly, B. 277, 1240. A.S. *eornostlice.*
Errour, A. 422.

Erytage, heritage, A. 443.
Eþe, easy, A. 1202; B. 608. A.S. *eáth.*
Euen (wyth), *vb.* to be equal to, A. 1073.
Euen-songe, vespers, A. 529.
Euentyde, A. 582; B. 479.
Euer-ferne, ever-fern, C. 438. A.S. *eforfearn*, polypodium vulgare. See Gloss. to Saxon Leechdoms, ii. 381.
Ewere, ewer, B. 1457.
Excuse, A. 281.
Expoun, Expoune, Expowne, } expound, A. 37; B. 1058, 1729.
Expounyng, *sb.* expounding, B. 1565.
Expresse, A. 910; B. 1158.

Fable, A. 592.
Face, B. 1539.
Fader, father, A. 872.
Falce, False, } B. 205, 474.
Falewed, became pale, faded, B. 1539. Ger. *falb*, pale, faded. A.S. *fealo*, pale, reddish or yellowish; *fealwian*, to grow yellow.
Fale, good, C. 92. A.S. *fæl*, clean, good, true.
Falleȝ, falls, happens, B. 494.
Falure, A. 1084.
Famacion, defamation, B. 188.
Famed, celebrated, B. 275.
Fande, found, A. 871.
Fanneȝ, fans, flaps, B. 457.
Fantumme, phantom, B. 1341.
Farande, pleasing, A. 865; handsome, B. 607; joyous, B. 1758. N. Prov. E. *farant*, decent, pleasant, nice. Gael. *farranta*, stout, brave.
Farandely, pleasantly, C. 435. N. Prov. E. *farantly.*
Fare, *vb.* go, A. 129, 147; B. 100, 621, 929; fare, B. 466. A.S. *faran.* O.N. *fara.*
Fare, *sb.* voyage, course, C. 98. A.S. *faru*, *fær.*

"Þe caf he cast o corn sum quile,
In þe flum þat hatt þe Nile;
For-qui þat flum þat rennes þar,
Til Joseph hus it has þe *fare.*"
(Cott. MS. Vesp. A. iii. fol. 27*b.*)

Fare, conduct, A. 832; B. 861.
Faren, gone, passed, B. 403.
Fasor, form, A. 431. See T. B. 3956.
Fasoun, fashion, A. 983, 1101.
Fat, B. 627.
Fateȝ, fades, A. 1038.
Fathme, (*a*) embrace, B. 399; (*b*) grope, C. 273.

(*a*) "Als I sat upon that lawe,
I bigan Denemark for to awe,
The borwes, and the castles stronge,
And mine armes weren so longe,
That I *fadmede*, al at ones,
Denemark with mine longe bones."
(Havelok the Dane, l. 1291.)

O.N. *fadma.* Dan. *fadme.* A.S. *fæthmian*, to embrace.
Fatte, vessel, B. 802. A.S. *fæt.*
Fatted, fattened, B. 56.
Faunt, child, maiden, A. 161.
Faure, four, B. 958.
Faurty, forty, B. 741, 743.
Faut, Faute, } fault, B. 177, 236, 571.
Fautleȝ, faultless, B. 794.
Fauty, faulty, sinful, B. 741.

Fauor, Fauour, A. 428; "gret fauor," A. 968.

Fawre, four, B. 938.

Fawte, fault, B. 1736.

Fax, Faxe, hair, B. 790, 1689. A.S. *feax.*

Fay, *in faye*, in faith, indeed, A. 263; *par ma fay*, by my faith, A. 489.

Faylande, failing, lacking, B. 1535.

Fayle, be wanting, B. 737. Set (of the sun), B. 1758.

Fayly, fail, A. 34; B. 548.

Fayn, glad, A. 393; *fayn of*, B. 642; *fayneet*, B. 1219.

Fayned, false, B. 188.

Fayth, "in *fayth*" indeed, B. 1732; gen. sing, B. 1735.

Faȝte, fought, A. 54.

Febele, Feble, poor, bad, B. 47, 101, 145.

Fech, Feche, fetch, A. 847, 1158; B. 621.

Fede, A. 29.

Fees, cities, B. 960. Fr. *fief.* Prov. Fr. *feu, fieu.* M. Lat. *feudum.* Eng. *fee.* The origin of this term is to be found in Goth. *faihu*, possessions. O.H.G. *fihu, fehu*, cattle. O.N. *fe.* A.S. *feoh*, cattle, money.

Fel, bitterly, B. 1040. A.S. *fell*, cruel, severe.

Felaȝschyp, fellowship, B. 271.

Felde, field, B. 1750.

Fele, (?) hide, B. 914.

Fele, many, A. 21, 927. A.S. *féla.*

Fele (feel), taste, B. 107.

Fele-kyn, many kinds of, B. 1483.

Felle, cruel, severe; *felle chere*, stern countenance. B. 139; sharp, A. 367; B. 156, 1737; boisterous, rough, B. 421; bitter, B. 954.

Felly, fiercely, bitterly, B. 559, 571.

Felonye, crime, sin, A. 800; B. 205.

Feloun, sinner, criminal, B. 217.

Felt, hair, B. 1689. A.S. *felt.* Du. *velt*, felt, cloth. Cf. W. *gwallt.* Gael. *falt*, hair of the head.

Femmale, female, B. 696.

Fende, fiend, devil, B. 205, 1341.

Fende, fend, B. 1191. Fr. *defendre.*

Fenden, of fiends, B. 224.

Feng, took (*pret.* of fonge), B. 377.

Fenny, dirty, vile, B. 1113. Cf. S. Prov. E. *venny*, mouldy. A.S. *fenn*, mud, dirt. Goth. *fani.*

Fenyx, phenix, A. 430.

Fer, far, A. 334.

Ferd, Ferde, frightened, B. 897, 975.

Ferde, fear, B. 386; C. 215. A.S. *forhtian*, to fear; *forht*, fear.

Ferde, went, *pret.* of *fare*, B. 1106.

Fere, a companion; *in fere*, in company, together, A. 89, 884; B. 985, 1062. A.S. *fera, gefera*, a companion.

Fereȝ, carries, A. 98. A.S. *férian.*

Fereȝ, companions, A. 1150. See *fere.*

Ferke up, get up, B. 897; ferke over, go, walk over, B. 133.

> "The freike upon faire
> wise *ferke* out of lyne."
> (T. B. 145.)

"He salle *ferkke* before
And I salle come aftyre."
(Morte Arthure, p. 347.)
"Now *ferkes* to the fyrthe,
thees fresche mene of armes."
(*Ibid.* p. 209.)
"The kyng *ferkes* furthe
on a faire stede."
(*Ibid.* p. 202.)

In T. B. 185, it is used transitively. The verb *to ferk* seems to be related to the Eng. *firk*, a quick movement, jerk, etc. A.S. *frician*, to dance.

Ferly, *adj.* wondrous, A. 1084; *adv.* wonderfully, B. 269, 960; *sb.* wonder, astonishment, A. 1086; marvel, B. 1529. A.S. *fær*, *færlice*, sudden.

Ferlyly, exceedingly, B. 962.

Ferre, farther, *comp.* of *fer*, B. 97, 98.

Fers, fierce, B. 101.

Ferslych, fiercely, C. 337.

Feryed, ferried, A. 946. O.N. *feria* (from *fara*, to go), to transport; set over.

Fest, fast, C. 290.

Fest, Feste, feast, A. 283; B. 642, 1758..

Festen, fasten, establish, B. 156, 327, 1255; C. 273.

Fester, B. 1040.

Festiual, festive, B. 136.

Fete, *in fete*, indeed, B. 1106. O.Fr. *faict*. Fr. *fait*, a deed, feat.

Feþer-beddes, C. 158.

Fetly = featly, aptly, fitly, B. 585. See *fete*.

Fette, fetch, B. 802.

Fettle, set in order, provide, make, B. 343, 585; C. 38, 435. Prov. E. *fettle*, set in order, etc. O. Fris. *fitia*, to adorn. Goth. *fetjan*. Norse, *fitla*, to labour at a thing in order to get it right. Pl. D. *fisseln*, to bustle about.

Fettre, fetter, B. 1255.

Feture, feature, B. 794. .

Fetys, } neat, well made, B.
Fetyse, } 174; dexterity, B. 1103. O.Fr. *faictis*. Lat. *factitius*, well made, neat, handsome.

Fetysely, handsomely, beautifully, B. 1462.

Feȝt, fight, B. 275, 1191. A.S. *feoht*. Ger. *fecht*, fight. See T. B. 1751.

Feȝtande, fighting, struggling, B. 404.

Filed, defiled. See *Fyled*

Flake, flake; *flake of soufre*, B. 954. O.N. *flak*, plank, slice.

Flake = fleck, spot, blemish, A. 947. O.N. *fleckr*. Ger. *fleck*, spot, blot, stain.

Flakerande, flickering, fluttering, B. 1410. Ger. *flackern*, to flare, blaze, flutter.

Flambe, flame, A. 769.

Flaumbande, flaming, A. 90; shining, B. 1468.

Flaunke, spark, B. 954. Prov. E. *flanker*, a flying spark. Pl. D. *flunkern*, to flicker, sparkle. Ger. *flunke*, spark.

Flauore, flavour, A. 87.

Flawen, fled, C. 214.

Flay, terrify, B. 960, 1723; C. 215. See T. B. 4593. N. Prov. E. *flay*, *flee*.

Flayn, flayed, A. 809.
Flaȝt, plot of ground, a flat, A. 57.
Fleeȝ, fleece (of golde), B. 1476.
Flem, Fleme, } banish, A. 334; B. 31, 596. A.S. *flyman*.
Flem, stream, C. 309. Cf. Prov. E. *flume, flem, fleme*, a mill-stream. Norse, *flom, flaum*, flood, overflow of water; *flauma*, to overflow.
Fleschlych, Fleschly, } fleshly, carnal, B. 265; A. 1082.
Flet, *pret.* of flete, to flow, A. 1058.
Flete, Flet, } flow, B. 1025; to people, B. 685. See T. B. 278, 4715. A.S. *fleotan*. Sw. *flyta*, flow, float. O.N. *fliota*. Prov. E. *fleet*.
Flette, floated, *pret.* of *flete*, to float, B. 387.

"Childer," he said, "yee list and lete,
I sagh caf on þe water *flete*."
(Cott. MS. Vesp. A. iii. fol. 27*b*.)

Fleȝe, flew, A. 431.
Flod, Flode, } flood, A. 874, 1058; B. 369.
Flokke, flock, company, B. 386, 1767.
Flonc=flong=flung, A. 1165.
Flor, flower, A. 29, 962; *pl.* *flores*.
Flor, floor, B. 133.
Flosed, flossed, B. 1689. Cf. *floss*-silk. Ital. *floscio flosso*, drooping, flaccid.
Flot, grease, fat, B. 1011. A.S. *flótan*, to float; *flót-smere*, scum of a pot, floating fat. O.N. *flót*, the act of floating, the grease swimming on the surface of broth. Prov. E. *fleet*.
Flot, Flote, } company, A. 786, 946; army, B. 1212. O.Fr. *flote*, a crowd.
Flot, Flote, Flotte, } flowed, floated, A. 46; B. 421, 432; C. 248.
Floty (? *flotery*), waving, A. 127.
Flour-de-lys, lily, A. 753.
Floury, flowery, A. 57.
Flowen, flew, fled, A. 89; B. 945.
Flowred, flowered, A. 270.
Floȝed, flowed, B. 397.
Flurted, flowered, figured, A. 208.
Flyt, force, literally chiding, B. 421. O.S. *flit*, contention.
Flyte, to quarrel, strive, A. 353. Prov. E. *flite*, scold. A.S. *flitan*,
Flytande, chiding, B. 950.
Flyȝe, flay (?), A. 813.
Flyȝt, flight, B. 377.
Fo, enemy, B. 1219.
Fode, person, people, B. 466; *fode*, a child (King Horn, 1384); *fodder*, producer, mother (King Alys. 645); A.S. *fedan, afedan*, to bring forth, give birth to, rear. O.N. *fæda*. Dan *föde*.
Fogge, dry grass, B. 1683. W. *ffwg*.
Fol, full, B. 1754.
Fol, fool, B. 750, 996.
Fol, foolish, C. 283.
Folde, folded, A. 434.
Folde, earth, A. 334; B. 403, 950.
Folde, to beat, buffet, A. 813.
Fole, fowl, B. 1410.
Fole, fool, B. 202.
Fole, foal, B. 1255.
Foler, B. 1410.

Foles, acts foolishly, B. 1422.

Folewande, } following, A. 1040,
Folwande, } B. 429, 1212.

Folk, } people, B. 100, 542, 960.
Folke, }

Folken, of people, B. 271.

Folmarde. Properly the beech-martin, but commonly applied to the pole-cat. O.Fr. *foine*, *faine* (Lat. *fagina*), beechmast.

Folyly, foolishly, B. 696. See T. B. 575.

Folȝe, follow, A. 127; B. 6, 677, 918, 1752. A.S. *folgian*.

Folȝed, baptized, A. 654. A.S. *fullian*, *fulwian*, to baptize.

Foman, enemy, B. 1175.

Fon, ceased, *pret.* of *fyne*, A. 1030; B. 369. The northern form is *fan*.

> "Bot ai þe quils he ne *fan*
> To behald þe leve maidan."
> (Cott. MS. Vesp. A. iii, fol. 20*a*.)

Fonde, to found, establish, A. 939; B. 173.

Fonde, to go, proceed, A. 150.

Fonde, try, B. 1103. A.S. *fandian*.

Fonden, found, B. 356.

Fonge, take, receive, A. 439, 479; B. 540; *fongeȝ to the flyȝt*, takes to flight, B. 457. A.S. *fon*. Ger. *fangen*, take, seize. Goth. *fahan*.

Font, B. 164.

Fonte=*fond*, examined, A. 170, 327.

Fooschyp } enmity, B. 918, 919.
Foschip, }

For, from, B. 740; because, B. 323.

Forbede, forbid, A. 379; B. 1147.

Forbi, beyond, C. 483.

Forboden, forbidden, B. 826, 998.

Forbrent, burnt, A. 1139.

For-clemmed, starved, C. 395. Prov. E. *clem*, to starve, pinch with hunger. Du. *klemmen*, to pinch, compress.

For-didden, did away with, A. 124.

For-dolked, severely wounded, A. 11. A.S. *dolc*, *dolh*, *dolg*, a wound; *dilgian*, to destroy.

Forering, B. 3. See Note.

Forfare, destroy; also to perish, B. 1168; C. 483; *forferde*, (*pret.*), B. 571, 1051.

Forfete, A. 619, 639; B. 743.

Forfyne, lastly.

Forgart, } =for-did, lost, *pret.*
Forgarte, } of for-gar, ruin, destroy, lose, A. 321; B. 240. See *Gar*.

Forged, made, B. 343.

Forhede, forehead, A. 871.

Foriusted, overthrown, defeated, B. 1216. Fr. *jouster*, to tilt.

> "So mony groundes he *for-justede* & of joy broght."
> (T. B. 296.)

Forlete, lost, A. 327.

For long, very long, A. 586.

Forlonge, furlong, A. 1030.

Forloteȝ=forleteȝ, forsake, B. 101.

> "Þe laghes bath he (Adam) þan *forlete*
> Bath naturel and positif."
> (Cott. MS. Vesp. A. iii. fol. 52*b*.)

Forloyne, forsake, depart, go astray, err, A. 368; B. 282, 750, 1155, 1165. Fr. *loin*, far.

For-madde, very mad (foolish), C. 509.

Formast, first, foremost, B. 494.

Forme, first, C. 38.

Forme-fader, } first-father, pro-
Forme-foster, } genitor, A. 639; B. 257.

Fornes, furnace, B. 1011.

For-payned, severely troubled, A. 246.

Forray, forage, B. 1200. Fr. *fourrager*, to fodder, forrage, prey. O.Fr. *fourrer*. Mid. Lat. *foderare*, *forrare*, from A.S. *foder*. Ger. *futter*, food, victuals.

Forsclet, a fortified place, B. 1200. "*Forcelet*, stronge place (*forslet*, H.P.) Fortalicium." (Prompt. Parv.) O.Fr. *forcier*. It. *forciere*. Mid. Lat. *forsarius*, a strong box, safe, coffer.

Forser = forcer, forcet, A. 263. See preceding word.

Forsette, compass, B. 78.

Forsothe, forsooth, indeed, C. 212.

Forst, frost, B. 524. A.S. *forst*.

Forþe, way, passage, A. 150. See T. B. 4094, 4166. Welsh, *ffordd*, a way.

> "The kyng fraystez [seeks] a *furth*
> over the fresche strandez,
> One a strenghe by a streme in thas
> straytt landez."
> (Morte Arthure, p. 103.)

Forth-lep, forth-leapt, C. 154.

Forþoȝt, repented, B. 557.

Forþrast, for-thrust, B. 249.

Forþy, therefore, wherefore, A. 234; B. 545, 1020.

Forþynke, repent, B. 285.

Fortune, A. 306.

Forwarde = forward, covenant, promise, B. 327, 1742. A.S. *fore-weard*. "*Forwarde*, or cuuinawnt, convencio, pactum." (Prompt. Parv.)

Forwroȝt, over-worked, weary, C. 163.

Forȝes, furrows, B. 1547. A.S. *furh*. Ger. *furche*, a furrow.

Forȝete, forgat, B. 203.

Fote, foot, A. 970.

Foted, footed, B. 538.

Founce, bottom, A. 113. See Founs.

Foundande, going, C. 126.

Founde, to go, B. 903.

> "Quen we suppose in our sele
> to sit alther heist,
> Than *fondis* furth dame fortoun
> to the flode ȝates,
> Draȝes up the damme borde
> and drenchis us evir."
> (K. Alex p. 64.)

> "Fflorent and Floridas with fyve
> score knyghttez,
> ffollowede in the foreste, and on the
> way *foundys*,
> Fflyngande a faste trott,
> and on the folke dryffes."
> (Morte Arthure, p. 231.)

Foundemente, foundation, A. 993.

Foundcn, found, B. 547.

Foundered, destroyed, perished, B. 1014.

Founs, } bottom, B. 1026.
Founce, }

> "Onone as thai on Alexander
> and on his ost waites,
> Thai flee as fast into flode,
> and to the *founce* plungid."
> (K. Alex p. 141.)

Fourferde, perished, *pret.* of *forfare*, B. 560.

Fowle, foully, B. 1790.

Fowled, became defiled, foul. B. 269.

Fowre, four, A. 886.

Foysoun, abundant, A. 1058. Fr. *foison*. O.Fr. *fuson*, from Lat. *fusio*, pouring out.

Fraunchyse, liberality, A. 609; B. 750.

Fray, terrify, B. 1553. See *Afray*.

Frayneȝ, demands, asks, desires, A. 129. A.S. *fregnan*, to ask. Goth. *fraihnan*.

Frayste (*a*), sought, A. 169; (*b*) literally, to try, prove, B. 1736. O.N. *fresta*.

(*a*) "Bot wete thou wele this iwis, within a wale time,
Fra that I *fraist* have that faire (faice?) of my faire lady,
I sall the seke with a sowme of seggis enarmed."
(K. Alex. p. 69.)

Frek, Freke, } man, B. 6, 79, 540. This word is used by Skelton. A.S. *freca*, a daring warrior, from *frec*, *freca*, bold, daring, eager. The adjective *freke* (*frek*, *frike*), was not unknown to O.E. writers of the 14th century.

"Israel wit þis uplepp,
Þat moght noght forwit strid a step,
Witouten asking help of sun;
Þat quak wit ilk lim was won,
Þat first for eild moght noght spek,
To bidd hast now es nan sa frek."
(Cott. MS. Vesp. A. iii. fol. 29*b*.)

Frelcs, blameless, A. 431. O.N. *fryja*, to blame. *Frie*, to blame, occurs in the romance of *Havelok the Dane*, 1998.

Freloker, more freely, B. 1106.

Frely, lordly, B. 162; beautiful, B. 173; freely, C. 20.

Frelych, lordly, B. 162; bountiful, C. 214.

French, an error for *frech* (*fresh*) or *frelich*, A. 1086.

Frete, gnaw, eat, devour, B. 1040. A.S. *fretan*.

Freten, devoured, B. 404.

Frette, furnish, B. 339; ornament, B. 1476. A.S. *frætu*, ornament; *frætewian*, *frætwian*, trim, deck, adorn.

Fro, from, A. 427; B. 396. This is another form of the Northumbrian *fra*. O.N. *frá*; "*to ne fro*," A. 347.

Frok, Frokke, } dress, garment, frock, B. 136, 1742.

Froþande, frothing, frothy, filthy, B. 1721.

Frunt, kicked, C. 187. See T. B. 5968.

Frym, beautiful, fresh, vigorous, A. 1079. Prov. E. *frim*; *frum*, tender, fresh. A.S. *freme*, advantageous, good. Drayton uses the phrase "*frim* pastures," *i.e.* luxuriant pastures.

Fryst, delay, put off, B. 743. A.S. *fyrstan*, to give respite; *fyrst*, a space of time, interval. Icel. *frest*, delay; "*to frist*, to trust for a time" (Ray); to delay (Jam.).

Fryt, Fryte, } fruit, A. 29; B. 1044.

Fryth, wood, A. 89; B. 534, 1680. Gael. *frith*, a heath, deer park, forest.

Ful, foul, B. 231.
Fulfille, accomplish, B. 264, 1732.
Fulȝed, baptized, B. 164. See *Folȝed*.
Fundament, foundation, A. 1010.
Funde, found, B. 1735.
Fust, fist, B. 1535.
Fyf, five, A. 849.
Fygure, A. 170, 747.
Fykel, treacherous, deceitful, C. 283.
Fyldor, gold thread, A. 106. Fr. *fil d'or*.
Fyled, defiled, dirty, B. 136.
Fyled, formed, B. 1460.
Fylsened, strengthened, aided, supported, B. 1167, 1644. A.S. *fylst*, help, assistance; *fylstan*, to help, aid.
Fylter, huddle together, B. 224; join, B. 696; meet together in battle, B. 1191; become ragged, entangled. Prov. E. *felter*, entangle, clot. Fairfax uses the phrase "*feltred* locks." Cf. the phrase "a *filtered* fole," a shaggy foal. Baker says that the term *felt* is applied to a matted growth of grass.

> "His fax and his foretoppe
> was *filterede* togeder."
> (Morte Arthure, p. 91.)

Fylyoles (=*fyells*, *phiolls*), round towers, B. 1462. Cf. *Fala*, a tour of tre. Med. Gram.
Fyne, *vb.* end, die, A. 328; cease, A. 353; B. 450; delay, B. 929.
Fyne, *sb.* cessation, A. 635.
Fynne, fin, B. 531.
Fyole, B. 1476.
Fyrmament, B. 221.
Fyrre, *adv.* farther, comp. of *fer*, A. 103, 127; B. 766; C. 116; *adj.* distant, A. 148. A.S. *fyrre*.
Fyrte, fearful, trembling, A. 54. A.S. *fyrhto*; *fyrhtu*, fear, fright, trembling; *forht*, fearful, timid.
Fyþel, fiddle, B. 1082.
Fyþere, feather, B. 530, 1026.

Galle, gall, stain, filth, A. 1060; B. 1022. Cf. to *gall*, fret. Fr. *galler*. W. *gwall*. O.N. *galli*, fault, imperfection. Dan. *gal*, wrong, ill.
Gain, against, A. 138.
Gardyn, A. 260.
Gare, cause, make, drive, A. 331; B. 690. N. Prov. E. *gar*. O.N. *göra*, *gera*.
Garlande, A. 1186.
Garnyst, garnished, ornamented, B. 1277.
Gart, forced, made, A. 1151. See *gare*; *garten*, *3d pers. pl.* A. 86.
Gate, way, A. 395, 526; B. 676, 931. See T. B. 6292. O.N. *gata*.
Gaule, Gawle, } A. 463; C. 285. See *galle*.
Gay, Gaye, } A. 260; B. 830, 1315.
Gayn, *vb.* avail, A. 343; C. 164; prevail, B. 1608. Sc. *gane*; *gain*, to be fit or suitable.
Gayn, Gayne, } useful, available, good, B. 259, 749.
Gaynly, Gaynlych, } gainly, gracious, B. 728; C. 83. Cf. ungainly=awkward. O.N. *gegn*,

convenient, suitable; *gegna*, to meet.
Gaȝafylace, royal treasury, B. 1283.
Geder, gather, C. 105.
Gef, gave, A. 174.
Gele, spy, see, A. 931.
Gemme, A. 253.
Gendered, engendered, B. 300.
Gendreȝ, genders, kinds, B. 434.
Generacyoun, A. 827.
Gent, Gente, } gentle, noble, gracious, A. 118, 253, 265; B. 1495.
Gentryse, nobleness, B. 1159, 1216.
Gentyl, noble, A. 278; *gentyleste*, A. 1015; B. 1180.
Gentylmen, B. 864.
Gere, gear, B. 16; C. 148.
Gere, clothing, attire, B. 1811.
Gered, covered, clothed, ornamented, B. 1344, 1568. O.N. *gerfi*. A.S. *gearwa*, habiliments. O.H.G. *garawi*, ornament, dress. A.S. *gearwan*; *gearwian*, make ready, prepare, supply.
Gesse, tell, A. 499. Norse, *gissa*.
Geste, tale, saying, A. 277.
Geste, Gest, } guest, B. 98, 640.
Gettes, devices, B. 1354. O.N. *geta*, to conceive. A.S. "and-*gitan*," get, know, understand.
Geuen, given, A. 1190.
Gilde, gilt, B. 1344.
Giles, gills, C. 269.
Gilofre, gilly flower, A. 43. Fr. *giroflée*. Lat. *caryophyllus*, a clove.
Glace=glance, A. 171. Fr. *glacer*, *glacier*, slide, slip. Cf. O.E. *glace*, to polish, glance as an arrow turned aside.
Glade, *vb.* to gladden, A. 861.
Glam, word, message, B. 499; C. 63; talk, speech, B. 830; noise, B. 849. Obsolete Swedish, *glamm*, talk, chatter; *glamma*, to talk, chatter. Gael. *glam*, outcry. O.N. *glam*, clash; *glamra*, to rattle. Sc. *glamer*, noise, clatter.

> "Alle thire he closis in that cliffe,
> and cairis on forthire,
> To the occyann at the erthes ende,
> and, ther in an ilee, he heres
> A grete *glaver* and a *glaam* of grekin
> tongis."
> (K. Alex. p. 188.)

Glas, Glasse, } A. 990, 1025.
Glauere, to deceive, A. 688. Cf. N. Prov. E. *glaver*, *glaiver*, to talk foolishly; *glaver*, flattery. W. *glafr*. Irish *glafaire*, a babbler.

> "Sir," sais syr Gawayne,
> "So me gode helpe,
> Siche *glaverande* gomes
> greves me bot lyttille."
> (Morte Arthure, p. 212.)

See extract under word *glam*.
Glaymande, slimy, C. 269. Cf. "gleyme or rewme, reuma;" "gleymyn or *yngleymyn*, visco, invisco." (Prompt. Parv.)
Glayre, glare, amber, A. 1026. A.S. *glære*, amber. O.N. *gler*. Dan. *glar*, glass.
Glayue, a sword, A. 654. Fr. *glaive*. Lat. *gladius*.
Gle, joy, glee, A. 95, 1123.
Glede, kite, B. 1696. A.S. *glida*.

Glem, } gleam, light, A. 79;
Gleme, } brightness, B. 218; *day-glem*, daylight, A. 1094; *heven-glem*, heaven light, B. 946.

Glemande, gleaming, shining, A. 70, 990.

Glene, glean, gather, A. 955.

Glent, } shone, A. 70, 114, 1026;
Glente, } B. 218. Sc. *glent*, *glint*, to gleam. Dan. *glindse*, to glisten; *glindre*, to glitter.

> "The schaftes of the schire sone schirkind the cloudis,
> And gods glorious gleme *glent* tham emannge."
> (K. Alex. p. 164.)

Glent, } slipped, fell, A. 671. Sc.
Glente, } *glint*, *glent*, not only signifies to gleam, shine, but also to glide, slide. W. *ysglentio*, to slide.

> "Glissonand as the glemes þat *glenttes* of þe snaw." (T. B. 3067.)

Glenteȝ, *sb.* looks, A. 1144.

Glet, } dirt, mud, slime, and
Glette, } hence filth, sin, A. 1060; B. 306, 573; C. 269. Pl. D. *glett*, slippery. Sc. *glit*, pus. O.N. *glæta*, wet.

Glewed, called, prayed, C. 164. Fr. *glay*, cry.

Glodeȝ, glades, A. 79.

Gloped, was terrified, frightened, amazed, B. 849. O.N. *glapa*, stare, gaze, gape. O.Fris. *glupa*, to look, peep. Dan. *glippe*, to wink. N. Prov. E. *glop*, *gloppen*, to be amazed, to frighten.

> "Bees not *aglopened* madame ne greved at my fadire."
> (K. Alex. p. 30.)

> "Thane *glopned* the glotone and glorede unfaire."
> (Morte Arthure, p. 90.)

> "O, my hart is rysand in a *glope*!
> For this nobylle tythand thou shalle have a droppe."
> (Town. Myst. p. 146.)

Glopnedly, fearfully, B. 896.

Glory, A. 934; B. 1522.

Gloryous, }
Glorious, } A. 799, 915.
Gloryus, }

Glotoun, a wicked wretch, a loose fellow, a ribald, B. 1505.

Gloumb, look, observe, C. 94. Chaucer uses *glombe* in the sense of looking gloomy, sullen, frowning. It seems to be connected with O.N. *glampa*, to glitter, shine. Cf. O.E. *glent*, to shine, and *glent*, to look. So also *stare* signifies not only to look steadfastly at, but to shine, glitter.

Glowed, shone, A. 114. O.N. *glod*, to glow, burn, shine.

Glwande, glowing, shining, bright, C. 94.

Glydande, going, walking, B. 296.

Glyde, to go, walk, slip along, B. 325, 677, 1590. Pl. D. *gliden*, *glien*, slip, glide.

Glyfte, became frightened, B. 849. Originally to stare, look astonished.

> "Þys munke stode ande lokede þarto,
> And hade þerof so moche drede,
> Þat he wende have go to wede:
> As he stode so sore *aglyfte*
> Hys ryȝt hande up he lyfte,
> Ande blessede hym self stedfastly."
> (Handlyng Synne, l. 3590.)

Gliffe, in O.E. signifies also to

look, shine, glow. Sc. *glevin*, to glow; *gliff*, a glimpse; *gliffin*, to wink. Dan. *glippe*, to wink.

Glymme, brightness, A. 1088. O. Sw. *glimma*, to shine.

Glysnande, shining, glistening. A. 1018. A.S. *glisnian*. O.N. *glyssa*, to sparkle, glitter.

Glyȝt, shone, A. 114; looked, C. 453. Du. *glicken*, to shine. Icel. *glugga*, to peep. *A-glyȝte*, slipped from, in line 245, is evidently another form of *glyȝt*. Cf. N. Prov. E. *glea*, *aglea*, crooked, aside; *gledge*, to look asquint. Sc. *gley*, *gly*, to squint, all of which originally signified simply to look, shine. See T. B. 3943.

Gnede, niggardly, beggarly, B. 146. The MS. reads nede, but *gnede* is the correct form. Dan. *gnide*, to rub. A.S. *gnidan*. Cf. O.E. *nithing*, a miser. A.S. *gnethen*, moderate, sparing.

> "Sua lang has thir tua boght þair sede,
> Þat þair moné wex al *gnede*."
> (Cott. MS. Vesp. A. iii. fol. 81*a*.)

> "Bot fra þair store bigan to sprede
> The pastur þam bigan to *knede*."
> (*Ibid.* fol. 15*a*.)

> "Bot al he tok in godds nam,
> And thold luveli al þat scam;
> For al to *gnede* him thoght þe gram
> Þat he moght thol on his licam"
> (*Ibid.* fol. 51*a*.)

Goande, going, B. 931.

Goblote, goblet, B. 1277.

God, Gode, } good, wealth. See *Goud*.

Godhede, godhead, A. 413.

Godlych, good, B. 753.

Golf, deep, abyss, A. 608.

Gome, man, A. 231; B. 1315.

Gorde=*girde*, rush, go headlong, B. 911, 957. See T. B. 169.

Gore, filth, B. 306. A.S. *gor*, wet, filth, mud. N. *gor*.

Gorste, gorse, B. 99, 534. W. *gores*, *gorest*, waste, open.

Gost, Goste, } spirit, A. 86; B. 325, 1598.

Gostly, spiritual, ghostly, A. 790.

Gote, stream, A. 934; B. 413; C. 310; *pl.* goteȝ, A. 608. Prov. E. *gote*, *goit*, *gowt*, ditch, sluice, mill-stream. Du. *gote*, kennel, conduit. A.S. *geotan*, to pour.

> "As *gotes* out of *guttars* in golanand, (glomand?) wedors,
> So voidis doun the venom be vermyns schaftes."
> (K. Alex. p. 163.)

Goud, Goude, God, } *adj.* good, A. 33, 568; *sb.* wealth, riches, A. 731, 734; B. 1326.

Goun, Goune, } gown, dress, B. 145, 1568.

Governor, B. 1645; C. 199.

Gowdeȝ, goods, C. 286.

Grace, A. 436.

Gracios, Gracious, } A. 95, 260, 934; C. 26.

Gracyously, B. 488.

Grame, wrath, vengeance, C. 53. A.S. *grama*. Ger. *gram*, anger, displeasure.

Graunt, *sb.* leave, permission, A. 317; *vb.* grant, B. 765; C. 240.

Grauayl, gravel, pebbles, A. 81.

Grauen, graven, B. 1324.

Grauen, buried, B. 1332.

Grayne3, grains, A. 31.

Grayþed, prepared, B. 343, placed, B. 1485; availed, C. 53. See T. B. 229. O.N. *greitha*, to make ready. N. Prov. E. *graid*.

Grayþely, quickly, readily, B. 341; truly, A. 499; C. 240. N. Prov. E. *gradely*. See T. B. 54.

> "On Gydo, a gome þat *graidly* had soght,
> And wist all þe werks by weghes he hade."
> (T. B. 229.)

Cf. *Graiþe*=ready.

Gre, will, desire, C. 348; hence *bongre, malgre*, etc. O. Fr. *gret*. Fr. *gré*, will, pleasure. Lat. *gratus*, pleasing.

Grece, step, B. 1590.

Gredirne, gridiron, B. 1277.

Greffe, grief, A. 86.

Greme, *adj*. displeasing, C. 42; wrath, B. 16, 947; *vb*. to make angry, displease, B. 138, 1347. A.S. *gremian*, to displease.

Greme, spot, blemish, A. 465. Norse *grima*, a spot.

Gresse, grass, A. 10, 245; B. 1028.

Grete, the whole, A. 637, ? altogether A. 851; a *grete*, in the gross—a head, A. 560.

Grete, weep, A. 331. A.S. *grætan*, Prov. E. *greet*.

Gretyng, *sb*. weeping, B. 159.

Greue, grieve, A. 471; B. 138, 302, 306.

Greue, grove, A. 321; B. 99.

Greuing, *sb*. sorrowing, grief, B. 159.

Gromylyoun, the herb *gromwell*, grey millet, (Lithospermum officinale), A. 43. "*Gromaly* herbe. Milium solis." (Prompt. Parv.)

Grone, groan, B. 1077.

Gropande, searching, trying, B. 591. A.S. *grápian*, to touch, feel, seize, grope. O.N. *greipa*.

Gropyng, *sb*. handling, B. 1102.

Grounde, ground, sharpened, A. 654.

Groundele3, bottomless, C. 310.

Grouelyng, on the face, A. 1120. O.N. *grufa*; *grufa nidr*, to stoop down. *Liggia á grufu*, to lie face downwards, to lie groveling.

Gruche, begrudge, B. 1347.

Gru3t, *pret*. of *gruche*, B. 810.

Grychchyng, *sb*. murmuring, repining, C. 53.

Grym, black, A. 1070.

Grymly, sharply, A. 654; roughly, B. 1534.

Grymme, horrible, B. 1553; sharp, B. 1696. A.S. *grim*; *grimm*, fury, rage,; sharp, bitter; "a *grym* toole," T. B. 938.

Grynde, A. 81.

Gryndel, angry, C. 524. Norse *grina*, wry the mouth; *grinall*, sour looking. Du. *grinnen*, *grinden*, to grin, snarl.

Grysly, horrible, B. 1534. A.S. *grislic*, horrible; *a-grisan*, to dread, fear greatly.

Gryspyng, *sb*. gnashing of the teeth. A.S. *grist-bitung*.

Gryste, dirt (?), A. 465.

Gucre, gear, B. 1505.

Guferes, evidently an error for *guteres*, C. 310. See T. B. 3072. See extract under word *gote*.

Gult, } guilt, A. 942; B. 690.
Gulte, }

Gulty, guilty, C. 210, 285.

Gut, C. 280.

Gyde-ropes, C. 105.

Gye, govern, B. 1598. Fr. *guider*; *guier*, direct, guide.

Gyle, guile, A. 671, 688; C. 285.

Gylt, guilt, B. 731.

Gylteȝ, A. 655.

Gyltleȝ, guiltless, A. 668.

Gyltyf, guilty, A. 669.

Gyn, machine; applied to the ark, B. 491; to a boat, C. 146.

Gyng, company, A. 455. A.S. *genge*. See T. B. 1225.

"Þan was Jacob busked yare,
Wit al þe *gynge* þat wit him ware."
(Cott. MS. Vesp. A. iii. fol. 30*a*.)

Gyngure, ginger, A. 43.

Gyse, guise, A. 1099.

Gyternere, A. 91. Fr. *guiterre*; *guiterne*, a gittern. (Cot.) Lat. *cithara*, a harp.

Habbe, have, B. 75; *habes*, *habbes*, has, B. 555, 995.

Hach, } hatch (of a ship), B. 409; C. 179.
Hachche, }

Hafyng. See *Hauyng*.

Hagherlych, fitly, B. 18. See *Haȝerly*.

Haldande, holding, C. 251.

Halde, hold, A. 454, 490; B. 652.

Halden, held, A. 1191; B. 42.

Hale, flow, A. 125. The original meaning is to drag along. Ger. *holen*. O.N. *hala*. Fr. *haler*. Cf. T. B. 1782.

Hale, toss, B. 1520; C. 219.

Half, side, quarter, B. 950. O.N. *halfa*.

Halke, recess, B. 104, 321. A.S. *hylca*, hooks, turnings. "*Halke* or hyrne. Angulus, latibulum." (Prompt. Parv.) See Canterbury Tales, 11433.

Halse, salute, wish one health, B. 1621. O.N. *heilsa*. Sw. *halsa*, to salute. O.N. *heilsa*, health. See T. B. 367.

Halt, lame, B. 102. O.N. *halltr*, lame; *haltra*, *halta*, to limp.

Halue, behalf, B. 896.

Halue, side, border, B. 1039.

Halyday, holy day, B. 134; C. 9.

Halȝed, hallowed, sanctified, B. 506, 1163.

Hampre, to pack up for removal, B. 1284.

Han (3*d pers. pl. pres.*), have, A. 776.

Hande-helme, B. 419.

Hapeneȝ, is blessed, B. 27.

Happe, joy, A. 16, 1195; *happeȝ*, blessings, B. 24; C. 11. O.N. *happ*.

Happe, cover, B. 626; C. 450. Prov. E. *hap*, to cover; *happing*, covering.

"Lord, what (lo) these weders ar cold, and I am ylle *happyd*."
(Town. Myst. p. 98.)

"*Happyn* or *whappyn'* yn cloþys." "*Lappyn'*, or *whappyn'* yn cloþys (*happyn* togedyr, S.; *wrap* to-geder in clothes, P.) Involvo." (Prompt. Parv.)

Happen, *adj.* happy, blessed, C. 13, 17, 19, 21.

Hard, coarse cloth made of tow, "*hard* hattes," B. 1209. A.S. *heordan*, *heordas*, hards, refuse of tow.

> "Sum araies thaim in ringes, and sum in row breuys,
> With *hard hattes* on thaire hedis hied to thaire horsis."
> (K. Alex. p. 102.)

Hardy, bold, B. 143.

Hardyly, boldly, A. 3.

Hare, B. 391.

Harlot, underling, B. 39; servant, profane jester, B. 860, 1584; *harlote*ȝ, harlot's, B. 34; harlots, B. 860. This term was not originally confined to females, nor even to persons of bad character. W. *herlawd*, *herlod*, a youth; *herlodes*, a damsel. Cf. "*harlotte* scurrus." "Gerro a tryfelour or a harlott." Med. MS. Cant. "An *harlott*, balator, rusticus, gerror, mima, joculator, nugatur, scurrulus, manducus. An *harlottry*, lecacitas, inurbanitas," etc. To do *harlottry*, scurrari." Cath. Ang. in Prompt. Parv.

> "Ffore *harlottez* and *hauss-mene* (house-men) salle helpe bott littille."
> (Morte Arthure, p. 229.)

Harlottrye, profane speaking, B. 579.

Harme, *sb.* wrong, sin, C. 17; *pl.* *harme*ȝ, harms, A. 388.

Harmleȝ, guiltless, A. 676, 725.

Harpe, A. 881.

Harpen (*3d pers. pl. pres.*), play on the harp, A. 881.

Harporeȝ, harpers, A. 881.

Haspe, fasten, B. 419; clothe, cover; C. 381. O.N. *hespa*, a clasp, buckle. Cf. "*haspyng* in armys. T. B. 367.

Haspede, hook, C. 189. Cf. Dan. *haspe*, windlass, reel; *haspevinde* capstan of a ship.

Hastif, }
Hastyf, } hasty, C. 520.

Hastyfly, } hastily, quickly, B.
Hastyly, } 200, 1150.

Hat, call, B. 448. A.S. *hátan*, to call.

Hatel, } anger, B. 200; fierce,
Hattel, } B. 227; keen, sharp, C. 367, 481. S. Saxon, *hatel*, *hetel*, keen, sharp, bitter. A.S. *hétel*, fierce. O. Sax. *hatol*. A.S. *atol*, dire, cruel.

Hatere, clothing, garments, B. 33. A.S. *hætern*, *hæter*, clothing, apparel.

Haþel, man, literally noble, A. 676; B. 27, 409, 1597. A S. *æthele*, noble; *ætheling*, a ruler, man.

> "Homer was holden *haithill* of dedis."
> (T. B. 38.)

Hatte, is called, B. 926; C. 35.

Haunte, practise, C. 15. Fr. *hanter*, frequent, haunt, literally, to follow a certain course.

Haueke, hawk, B. 537.

Hauen, haven, port, B. 420.

Hauyng, condition, behaviour, A. 450, 754.

Haylsed, saluted, A. 238; B. 612, 814. See *Halse*. See T. B. 1792.

Hayre, heir, B. 666.

Hayreȝ, shirts of horse-hair, hair-cloth, sack-cloth, C. 373. A.S. *héra.*

Haȝerly, fitly, properly, B. 18. This word occurs in the Ormulum under *haȝherrlike.* O.N. *hægr*, dexter, facilis. Dan. *haage*, to please ; *haagelig*, agreeable, acceptable.

Hede, notice, A. 1051.

Hef, heaved, raised, C. 219.

Heke=eke, also, A. 210.

Helde, bend to, come to, B. 1330. A.S. *healdan* ; *hyldan*, incline, lean to. Dan. *helde.*

Helde, *adv.* willingly, A. 1193 ; *in helde*, in mind, in purpose, disposed, B. 1520.

Helded, approached, B. 39.

Heldeȝ, goes, walks, B. 678.

> "Þir brether *helid* ai forth þair wai
> Þat to þair fader ful suith com þai."
> (Cott. MS. Vesp. A. iii. fol. 29*b*.)

Hele, safety, C. 335 ; health, B. 1099 ; pleasure, A. 16. A.S. *hél.*

Helle-hole, B. 223.

Hellen, of hell, C. 306.

Helme, C. 149.

Hem, them, C. 180.

Hemme, border, A. 1001.

Hende, gracious, B. 612 ; C. 398 ; pleasant, B. 1083. Norse *hendt*, adapted ; *hendug*. Dan. *hændig*, handy, dextrous. Cf. *hendly*, T. B. 1792.

Hendelayk, mildness, civility, B. 860. Hard-*laike* occurs in T. B. 2213.

Heng, } Henge, } hang, B. 1584, 1734.

Hens, hence, C. 204.

Hent, } Hente, } take, seize, receive, A. 388, 669 ; B. 151, 376 883, 1150. O.N. *henda.* A.S. *hentan.*

Hepe, heap, company. B. 1775.

Her, their, A. 888.

Here, heir, B. 52.

> "Bede his doughter come downe and his *dere heire*." (T. B. 389.)

Here, hair, A. 210.

Here, company, B. 409, 902. T.B. 6253. A.S. *here*, an army, host, etc.

Hered, honoured, B. 1086. A.S. *hérian*, to praise, commend.

Herken, } Herkne, } hearken, B. 193, 458.

Herneȝ, brains, A. 58. O.N. *hjarni*. Sw. *hjerna.*

Herneȝ=erneȝ, eagles, B. 537.

Hert, heart, B. 1723.

Hertte, hart, B. 391, 535.

Heruest, harvest, B. 523.

Hery, honour, praise, B. 1527. See *hered.*

Herytage, } Heritage, } A. 417 ; B. 652.

Herȝe, harry, B. 1179, 1294 ; drag out, C. 178. Sc. *herry* ; *harry*, rob, spoil, pillage. A.S. *hergian*, *herian*, to plunder, afflict, vex. Fr. *harrier*, provoke, molest. O.N. *heria*, to make an inroad on.

Hest, } Heste, } command, A. 633 ; B. 94, 341 ; promise, B. 1636.

Hete, promise, vow, A. 402 ; B. 1346 ; C. 336. O.N. *haeta*, to threaten. T. B. 240.

Heter, rough, C. 373. See T. B.

5254. N. Prov. *hetter, hitter,* eager, earnest.
Heterly, quickly, greatly, fiercely, A. 402; B. 380, 1222; C. 381, 477. See T. B. 3499.
Heþe, heath, B. 535.
Heþen, hence, A. 231. O.N. *hëthan.* See T. B. 5115.
Heþyng, scorn, contempt, B. 579, 710; C. 2. O.N. *háthung.* See T. B. 1753, 1818.
Heue, heave, raise, A. 314, 473. O.N. *hefia.*
Heued, head, A. 459, 465.
Heuen, raise, exalt, A. 16; B. 24, 506; increase, "*heuen þi hele,*" B. 920. We also meet with the phrase to "*heuen harm.*"

> "Qua folus lang wit uten torn,
> Oft his fote sal find a spurn;
> Reu his res þan sal ho sare,
> Or *heuen* his harme with foli mare.
> (Cott. MS. Vesp. A. iii. fol. 25*a*.)

Heuen-ryche, the kingdom of heaven, A. 719; C. 14.
Heuy, sorrowful, A. 1180; C. 2.
Heyred, harried, dragged, pulled, B. 1786. See *Herȝe.* "*Harryn'* or *drawyn'* trahicio, pertraho" (Prompt. Parv.)
Heyred = heryed, honoured, B. 1527. See *Hered.*
Heȝe, high, lofty, B. 1391, 1749.
Heȝe, hasten, B. 1584. See *Hyȝe.*
Heȝt, Heȝþe, } height, A. 1031; B. 317.
Hide, Hidde, } hid, hidden, B. 1600, 1628.
Hidor, fear, C. 367. O.Fr. *hisdour; hidour,* dread.
Hiled, covered, B. 1397. A.S. *hélan, hélian.* Prov. E. *hele, hill, hile,* to cover. O.N. *hylia,* to hide.
Hitte, to make for, C. 289; come, B. 479; C. 380. O.N. *hitta,* to light on, find.

> "Þai turne into Tessaile withouten tale more,
> *Hit* up into a havyn all the hepe samyn."
> (T. B. 991.)

Hiȝe = high, loud, B. 1564.
Hiȝly, greatly, B 920.
Ho, she, A. 232, 233; B. 659. A.S. *heo.* Prov. E. *hoo.*
Ho-besteȝ, she-beasts, B. 337.
Hod, hood, B. 34.
Hodleȝ, hoodless, B. 643.
Hofen, (*p. p.* of *heve*), exalted, raised, B. 1711.
Hokyllen, beat, B. 1267. Is this an error for *hollkyen?* See *Holkke.*
Hol, whole, B. 102, 594.
Hole-foted, B. 538.
Holde, dominion, B. 1597.
Holkke, thrust out, B. 1222. The original meaning seems to be "to make hollow, dig out, pierce." A S. *holian,* to hollow; *hol, holh,* a hole. Cf. O.Sc. and O.E. *holket,* hollow; *holk,* dig out. Prov. E. *hulk,* to take out entrails of rabbits and hares (Baker). Sw. *holka, hulka,* to hollow.
Holly, wholly, B. 104, 1140.
Holteȝ, woods, A. 921. A.S. *holt,* wood, grove; "*holte woddes,*" T. B. 1351.

Holȝe, hollow, B. 1695. A.S. *holh.*

Homly, familiar, domestic, A. 1211.

Hommes, hams, thighs, B. 1541. O.N. *höm*, the back of the thigh.

Honde, hand, A. 49, 706; B. 174.

Hondel, handle, B. 11.

Hondelyng, *sb.* handling, B. 1101.

Hondelynge, *adv.* with hands, A. 681.

Honde-werk, handwork, C. 496.

Honde-whyle, a moment, B. 1786. A.S. *hand-hwil*; "in a *hond-while*," T. B. 406.

Hone, to delay, abide, A. 921. See Met. Hom., p. 129.

Honest, B. 14, 18.

Honestly, B. 134, 705.

Honour, A. 852; B. 594.

Honyseȝ, destroys, ruins, B. 596. O.Fr. *honeison*, shame; *honnir*, to shame, blame, borrowed from Goth. *haunjan*. Ger. *höhnen*.

"And Alexander alle that quile as-perly rydis
To the grete flode of Granton, and it one a glance fyndes,
Or he was soȝt to the side ȝit sondird the qwerynes,
His hors it *hunyschist* for evir, and he with hard schapid."
(K. Alex. p. 102.)

Hope, expect, think, suppose, A. 142; B. 663.

Hores, theirs, C. 14.

Hores (?), B. 1695.

Hortyng, *sb.* hurting, harm, B. 740.

Horwed, unclean, B. 335. A.S. *horwa*, *hóru*, dirt; *hyrwian*, to defile.

Horyed, hurried, B. 883.

Hot, Hote, } angry, B. 200.

Hourlande, rolling, rushing, hurling, C. 271.

Hourle, wave, C. 319.

Household, B. 18.

Houe, abide, B. 927. W. *hofian*; *hofio*, to fluctuate, hover, suspend.

Houeȝ, hovers, B. 458, 485.

Houen, exalted, raised, B. 206, 413, 1451.

Hue, cry, voice, A. 873.

Hue, Huee, } hue, complexion, A. 842; B. 1483.

Huge, great, B. 4, 1659.

Hunger, *vb.* C. 19.

Hurkele, hang, B. 150; rest, 406. The original meaning is to nestle, crouch, squat. N.Prov.E *hurkle*, to squat, crouch, nestle. Du. *hurken*, to squat. O.N. *hruka*.

"Then come ther in a litill brid into his arme fleȝe,
And ther *hurkils* and hydis as sche were hande tame,
Fast scho flekirs about his fete, and fleȝtirs aboute."
(K. Alex. p. 18.)

Hurlande, hurling, rushing, B. 413, 1211.

Hurle, rush, B. 44, 223, 376, 874, 1204; "*hurlet* out of houses," T. B. 1365.

Hurrok, oar, B. 419; C. 185. Prov. E. *orruck*. "*Orruck*-holes, oar-drawing holes, as distinct from thole-pins, which are less used in our boats: *rykke*, to draw (Dan.). Compare English *rullocks*." Norfolk

Words: Miss A. Gurney in Transactions of Philological Society for 1855, p. 34.
Huyde, hide, B. 915.
Huyle, while, A. 41.
Hwe, hue, A. 896; *hwes*, B. 1119.
Hwed, coloured, B. 1045.
Hyde, skin, A. 1136.
Hyl-coppe, hill-top, A. 791. See *Coppe*.
Hynde=hende, courteous, A. 909; B. 1098.
Hyne, servants; *hinds*, A. 505, 632, 1211. A.S. *hina*, *hine* (for *higna*, *higne*), a domestic. O.N. *hion*, family.
Hyre, *sb.* hire, wages., A. 534, 539.
Hyre, *vb.* A. 507, 560.
Hyrne, corner, B. 1294; C. 178. A.S. *hyrne*. "Hyd hom in houles and *hyrnys* aboute," T. B. 1362.
Hytteȝ, strives, seeks, A. 132.
Hyue, hive, B. 223.
Hyure, hire, C. 56.
Hyȝe, high grounds, heights, B. 391.
Hyȝe, Hyȝ, } high, A. 39, 395; B. 380; "on *hyȝe*," B. 413; "*hyȝe* trot," quick pace, B. 976.
Hyȝe, hie, hasten, B. 33, 392, 538; C. 217. A.S. *higan*, *higian*.
Hyȝe, labourer, servant, B. 67. A.S. *higo*, a servant. See *Hine*.
Hyȝly, greatly, B. 1527.
Hyȝt, named, called, promised, A. 305, 950; B. 24, 665, 1162.
Hyȝt, height, B. 458; C. 398.
Hyȝtled, ornamented, decorated, B. 1290.

"He had a hatt on his hede *hiȝtild* o floures." (K. Alex. p. 156.)

I-brad, extended, reached, B. 1693. See *Brayde*.
Ichose, chosen, A. 904.
Idolatrye, B. 1173.
Ilk, same, B. 1755.
Ille, bad, evil, B. 577.
Ilyche=alike, B. 228, 975; C. 161. A.S. *gelic*.
Image, B. 983.
In-blande, together, B. 885. Dan. *iblandt*. See *Bland*.
Inflokke, flock in, B. 1767.
Inlyche, alike, A. 546, 603.
In-melle, among, A. 1127. This word is usually written *i-melle*. Icel. *á-milli*.
In-monge, In-mongeȝ, } among, amidst, B. 278, 1485.
In-mydde, In-myddeȝ, } amidst, B. 125, 1677.
Innocens, innocence, A. 708.
Innoghe, Innoȝe, } enough, sufficiently, A. 612, 625, 637; abundant, C. 528.
In-nome, taken in, A. 703.
Innossent, Inoscente, } innocent, A. 666, 672, 684.
Inobedyent, disobedient, B. 237. Fr. *inobedient*.
In-seme, together, A. 838. A.S. *gesome*. O.E. *ysome*.
In-stoundes, at times, B. 1603.
Instrumente, B. 1081.
Insyȝt, opinion, B. 1659.
Ire, wrath, B. 572.

Iwysse, truly, indeed, B. 84. A.S. *gewis.*
In-wyth, within, A. 970.

Jacynth, A. 1014.
Janglande, muttering, C. 90. O.Fr. *jangler*, to chatter.
Jape, device, sin, B. 272, 864; C. 57. Fr. *japper*, to yelp, chatter. The original meaning of *jape* is in O.E. to deceive, to lie.
Jasper, A. 999.
Jauele, a wicked wretch, a base fellow, B. 1495. "*Javel*, Joppus, gerro." (Prompt. Parv.)

"The Lieutenant of the Tower advising Sir Thomas Moor to put on worse cloaths at his execution, gives this reason, because he that is to have them is but a *javel*; to which Sir Thomas replied, shall I count him a *javel* who is to doe me so great a benefit."—MS. Lansd. 1033, in Hall.)

Jeaunte, giant, B. 272.
Jolef, Jolyf, Joly, } handsome, happy, true, A. 842, 929; B. 300, 864; C. 241.
Joparde, jeopardy, A. 602.
Jostyse, justice, judge, B. 877.
Journay, C. 355.
Jowked, slept, C. 182.
Joy, Joye, } A. 266.
Joyfol, A. 288.
Joyleȝ, joyless, sorrowful, A. 252; C. 146.
Joyne, B. 726.
Joyned, A. 1009; B. 434.
Joyned, enjoined, B. 877; C. 62, 355.
Joynte, B. 1540.
Joyst, B. 434.
Juel, Juele, } jewel, A. 249, 253, 278.
Jueler, Juelere, } jeweller, A. 252, 264.
Juelrye, jewelry, B. 1309.
Jugge, judge, A. 7, 804; C. 224.
Juggement, judgment, B. 726.
Juis, Juise, } judgment, doom, B. 726; C. 224.
Jumpred (? *Jumpre* from A.S. *geomer*, miserable, sad), trouble, B. 491.
Justyfyet, justified, A. 700.

Kable, B. 418.
Kake, B. 625, 635.
Kark, sorrow, C. 265. W. and Gael. *care*, care.
Karle, churl, B. 208. See *Chorle.*
Kart, B. 1259.
Kayrene, to go, B. 945. See *Cayre.*
Kayser, emperor, B. 1593.
Kaȝt, caught, B. 1215.
Kene, great, noble, B. 839, 1593; sharp, B. 1697.
Kenely, quickly, B. 945.
Kenne, to know, make known, show, A. 55; B. 865, 1707; C. 357. O.N. *kenna.* Norse *kjenna*, to perceive by sense, recognise, observe.
Kennest, keenest, B. 1575.
Kepe, care for, regard, B. 508.
Kerve, dig, A. 512; cut, B. 1104; rend, B. 1582.
Kest, Keste, } contrive, B. 1070, 1455; cast, A. 66; B. 414.
Keue, depart, A. 320.
Keued, separated, A. 981.
Keuer, recover, restore, B. 1605, 1700.

Keye, key, B. 1438.
Klubbe, club, B. 1348.
Klyffeȝ, cliffs, A. 66, 74.
Knaue, knave, B. 855; servant, B. 801.
Knaue, Knaw, Knawe, } know; *knawen*, known, A. 637; B. 1435, 1575.
Knawlach, knowledge, B. 1702; See T. B. 1083.
Knot, crowd, company, A. 788.
Knyt, knit, unite, establish, B. 564.
Kost, coast, border, B. 912.
Kote, house, B. 801.
Koynt=quaint, curious, crafty, B. 1382.
Krakke, sound, B. 1403.
Kuy, kine, cows, B. 1259.
Kyd, Kydde, } showed, proved, (*pret.* of *kythe*, B. 23, 208. *Kyde*, as an *adj.*=renowned.

"This kyde realme." (T. B. 213.)

Kylle, to strike, B. 876. See T. B. 1211, 1213.
Kyndam, kingdom, B. 1700.
Kynde, nature, species, B. 266, 505, 507.
Kyndely, Kyndly, } naturally, properly, B. 1, 319.
Kynne, conceive, B. 1072. A.S. *cennan*, to conceive, beget.
Kynned, kindled, B. 915. O.N. *kynda*.
Kynneȝ, "alle kynneȝ=of every kind," A. 1028.
Kyntly=kyndly, naturally, A. 690.
Kyppe, take up, seize, B. 1510. Prov. E. *kep*. O.N. *kippa*. A.S. *cépan*. See Robt. of Glouc. 125. Havelok the Dane, 2407. "*Kyppyn*' idem quod *Hynton*;" "*Kyppynge* or *hyntynge* (*hentynge*, K.P.), Raptus." (Prompt. Parv.)
Kyrk, Kyrke, } church, temple, A. 1061; B. 1270.
Kyryous=curious, careful, particular, B. 1109.
Kyst, Kyste, } chest, ark, B. 449, 1438; C. 159.
Kyþe, show, exhibit, A. 356; B. 851, acknowledge, B. 1368. A.S. *cithan*, to make known.

"Ye *kyþe* me suche kyndnes," (T. B. 557.)

Kyþ, Kyþe, } city, land, region, A. 1198; B. 414, 571, 901, 912; C. 18. A.S. *cyth*, a region, home, native place.

"Ther was a kyng in þat coste þat þe *kithe* ought." (T. B., 103.)

Kyþyn (*gen. pl.* of *kyþe*), of cities, B. 1366.

Labour, *sb.* A. 634; *vb.* A. 504.
Lache, Lachche, } =latch, take, receive, B. 166; *lached*, received, B. 1186; taken, C. 266; reach, C. 322; "*lach* out," take away, C. 425. A.S. *læccan*.
Lad, led, A. 801.
Ladde=lad, man (of inferior station), B. 36; C. 154. O.H.G. *laz*, libertinus. Ger. *lasse*. Du. *laete*, a peasant.
Ladde-borde, larboard, C. 106.
Laddres, ladders, B. 1777.
Lade, led, A. 1146.

Ladyly, A. 774.

Ladyschyp, A. 578.

Lafte, left, B. 1004.

Laften, (3d *pers. pl. pret.*) left, A. 622; C. 405.

Lake, Llak, } lake, deep, B. 438, 536.

Lakke, sin against, abuse, B. 723. Dan. and Sw. *lak*, fault, vice. Dan. *lakke*, decay, decline.

Lalled, Laled, } spoke, B. 153, 913. Dan. *lalle*, to prattle. Bavarian *lallen*, to speak thick, talk. Gr. *λαλειν*, to talk.

Lance, take, C. 350.

Langage, language, B. 1556.

Langour, sorrow, A. 357.

Lansed (? *laused*), uttered, B. 668; C. 489. *Launch*, in the dialect of Worcestershire, signifies to cry out, groan.

Lansed, ? quaked, B. 957.

Lanteȝ (? *lanceȝ*), lentest, gavest, B. 348.

Lantyrne, A. 1047.

Lape, lap, taste, B. 1434. *Lape*, lape, taste (Baker's Northampton Glossary).

Lappe, *sb.* A. 201. A.S. *læppa*, border, hem. "*Lappe*, skyrte (*lappe*, barme, K.). Gremium." (Prompt. Parv.).

"The word *lap*, according to many ancient writers, signified the skirt of a garment. Thus G. de Bibelsworth says,

'Car par deuant avez eskours (*lappes*),
Et d'en costé sont vos girouns (sidgoren).'

It denoted, likewise, the hinder skirt." (Way in Prompt. Parv.)

Lapped, folded, clothed, B. 175. See T. B. 236.

Lasched, B. 707. ? became hot, lascivious.

Lasned = lessened, made smaller, B. 438, 441.

Lasse, less, A. 599, 600; B. 1640.

Laste, follow, A. 1146; C. 320. A.S. *last*, footstep. Goth. *laistjan*, to follow after.

Laste, fault, crime, C. 198.

Lastes, becomes faulty, B. 1141. Dan. *last*, vice, fault. O.N. *löstr*. S. Sax. *last*, calumny, blame. Icel. *last*. Ger. *lästerung*, slander.

Lat, slow, late, B. 1172. A.S. *læt*, slow, late. Cf. "*lat*-a foot, slow in moving." (Wilbraham's Cheshire Glossary.)

Laþe, to invite, B. 81. A.S. *lathian*. O. Sax. *lathian*,. O. N. *lada*. Prov. E. *lathe*, to invite. A.S. *lathu*, invitation. N. Prov. E. *lathing*, invitation.

Lauce, loosen, do away with (?) B. 1589.

Laue, law, B. 723.

Lauande, pouring, flowing, B. 366.

Laue, pour out, A. 607; C. 154. A.S. *lafian*.

Launceȝ, branches (of trees), A. 978.

Launde, an open space between woods, a park; *lawn*, B. 1000, 1207. "*Saltus* a lawnd." (Nominale MS.) Welsh *llan*. "*Lawnde* of a wode. Saltus." (Prompt. Parv.) "*Indago*, a parke, a huntynge place, or a *launde*." (Ortus.) "*Lande*, a *land* or *launde*, a wild untilled shrubbie or bushy plaine." (Cotg.) O.Fr. *lande*, saltus.

> "Sythyne [he] wente into Wales wyth his wyes alle;
> Sweys into Swaldye with his snelle houndes,
> For to hunt at the hartes in thas hye *laundes*."
> (Morte Arthure, p. 6.)

Lawe, hill, B. 992. Sc. *law*. A.S. *hlæw*, mound, mount. Goth. *hlaiw*.

Lawles, C. 170.

Lay, put down, B. 1650.

Layke, *sb.* sport, play, amusement, B. 122, 1053.

Layke, *vb.* to play, B. 872. A.S. *lác*, play; *lácan*, to play.

Layke, device, B. 274; C. 401.

Layned, kept secret, A. 244. N. Prov. E. *lane*, to hide. O.N. *leyna*.

Layth, vile, evil, C. 401. A.S. *láth*, evil, harm; *láth*, hateful, evil; "*laithe* hurtes," T. B. 1351.

Layte, seek, search, B. 97, 1768. N. Prov. E. *late*. Icel. *leita*. Sw. *leta*, to look for; "*laytyng* aboute," T. B. 2348.

Laȝares, lepers, B. 1093.

Laȝe, laugh, B. 653, 661.

Laȝte, } =laught, took, A. 1128,
Laȝt, } 1205. See *Lache*.

Le, shelter, C. 277. A.S. *hleo*, shade, shelter. Cf. T. B. 2806. O.N. *hlja*, to protect. Cf. *Leeside* =the sheltered side of a ship.

> "——— thar I the tell
> Is the richt place and sted for ȝour cite,
> And of ȝour travell ferm hald to rest in *le*." (G. Doug. vol. i. p. 152.)
>
> "Þe wicked alsua þe gode sal se,
> Wit-in þair gamen stad and gle,
> Þat þai þe sorfuller sal be,
> Þat losen folili has þat *le*" (*i.e.* heaven).
> ("De Penis," quoted in "Hampole's Pricke of Conscience," l. 4, p. xii.)

Leauty, loyalty, B. 1172.

Lebarde, leopard, B. 536.

Lecherye, B. 1350.

Led, } man, person, A. 542; B.
Lede, } 412. A.S. *leód*, man.

Led, } people, nation, B. 691,
Leede, } 772, 909. A.S. *leóde*, people, folk.

Ledden=leden, sound, A. 878. Chaucer uses the word *leden* in the sense of *speech*, *language*. A.S. *hlyd*. O.N. *hliod*, a sound.

Ledisch, national, pertaining to a people or country, B. 1556. S. Sax. *leodisce*. See *Lede*.

Leef, } *adj.* dear, precious; *sb.*
Lef, } dear one, wife, A. 266, 418; B. 772, 939, 1066. A.S. *leóf*.

Lefly, dear, beloved, B. 977. A.S. *leóflic*.

Lefsel, bower, house formed of leaves, C. 448.

> "By a lauryel ho (Dame Gaynour) lay, vndur a *lefe-sale*,
> Of box and of barberè, byggyt ful bene."
> (The Anturs of Arther in Robson's Met. Rom. p. 3, vi. 5.)
>
> "With *lefsales* uppon lofte lustie and faire." (T. B. 337.)

A.S. *leaf*, a leaf, and *sel*, dwelling, hall. Sw. *löfsal*, a hut built of green boughs. *Levesel* (another form of *lefsel*) is used by Chaucer (Reve's Tale, 4059), but is left unexplained in the glossary to Wright's edition. Tyrwhitt's derivation of this term from A.S. *lefe*, folium, and *setl*, sedes, is certainly very near the mark. Cf. "*levecel* beforne a wyndowe, or other place. Umbraculum." (Prompt. Parv.)

Lege, liege, subject, B. 94, 1174.

Legioune, A. 1121, B. 1293.

Lel, true, B. 425. "Leve this for *lell*." T. B. 239.

Lelly, truly, faithfully, A. 305; B. 1066. See T. B. 420.

Leme, glide away, A. 358.

Leme, shine, gleam, A. 119, 1043; B. 1273. A.S. *leóma*, a ray of light; *leóman*, to shine. See T. B. 699.

Lemman = leof-man, beloved one, mistress, A. 763, 796, 805; B. 1352. A.S. *leóf*, dear, and *man*. O.E. *leofmon*, a lover.

Lene, grant, C. 347. A.S. *lænian*.

Lenge, dwell, abide, A. 261, 933; B. 81, 412, 497, 994; C. 42. See T. B. 1937.

Lenger, longer, A. 600, 977; B. 810; *lengest*, B. 256.

Lenghe, length, A. 416.

Lent (*pret.* of *lend*), abode, dwelt, B. 256; *watȝ lent*, had dwelt, B. 1084.

Lent, arrived, C. 201. A.S. *gelandian*, to land, arrive.

> "Langour *lent* is in land, all lychtnes is lost."
>
> (G. Douglas, vol. i. p. 447.)

Lenþe, length, A. 1031; B. 425, 1594.

Lep, leaped, C. 179.

Lere, to teach, B. 843. A.S. *læran*.

Lere, reward, ? *here*, A. 616.

Ler, Lere, } countenance, A. 398; *pl.* *lers*, features, B. 1542. A.S. *hleor*. See T. B. 480.

Lese, false, A. 865. See *Lese*.

Lesande, loosening, opening, A. 837. O.E. *lese*, *les*, to loose. Goth. *lausjan*.

Lese, false, B. 1719. A.S. *leas*.

Lest, Leste, } lost, A. 9; B. 887.

Lesyng, *sb.* lie, A. 897. A.S. *leasung*.

Leþe, assuage, lessen, cease, bate, cool. A. 377; B. 648; C. 3. A.S. *leothian*, to release, slacken. See Met. Hom. p. 135.

Leþe, *sb.* calm, C. 160. N. Prov. E. *leath*, rest, quiet. Stratmann compares O. Du. *lede*, ease, *leath*.

Lether, leather, B. 1581.

Lette, hinder, prevent, A. 1050; B. 1803.

Letter, B. 1580.

Lettrure, letters, learning, A. 751.

Leue, "*aske leue*," A. 316; "*take leue*," B. 401.

Leue, forsake, C. 401.

Leue, believe, A. 69, 865, 876; B. 1493.

Leued, leaved, A. 978.

Lewed, ignorant, B. 1580. A.S. *leóde*, *leúd*, the people.

Lik, to lick, B. 1000.

Likke, sip, drink, B. 1521.

Liureȝ, dresses, garments, A. 1108. O.Fr. *livree*.

Lode, lot, C. 156.

Lode, course, conduct, guidance, C. 504. A.S. *lád*, *ládu*, way. O.N. *leid*, course. Cf. *lode*, a way for water.

Lodesmon, conductor, pilot, B. 424; C. 179. A.S. *ládman*, a leader.

Lodly, } loathsome, hateful, vile,
Lodlych, } B. 274, 1090, 1093. N. Prov. E. *laidly*, ugly, foul. A.S. *láthlíc*, odious, detestable.

"He laid on þat *loodly*, lettyd he noght." (T. B. 934.)

Lofly, dear, lovely, B. 1804.

Lofte, "*upon lofte*," on high, B. 206, 318, 808. O.N. *lopt*, sky, air.

Loge, } tent, lodge, B. 784, 807,
Logge, } 1407; C. 457. Fr. *loge*, a hut. See T. B. 1140, 1369.

Logging, lodging, B. 887.

Loghe, } =low, lau, pit, deep,
Loȝ, } abyss, B. 366. O.N. *lagr*. Sw. *låg*, low.

Lokande, looking, C. 458.

Loke=loken, enclosed, C. 350.

Loke, guard, watch over, C. 504.

Lokyng, *sb.* sight, looking, A. 1049.

Loltrande, ? *loitrande*, lolling, loitering, C. 458. Du. *loteren*, to loiter. O.N. *lotra*, to go lazily.

Lombe, lamb, A. 841, 1047.

Lome, lame, B. 1094.

Lome, vessel, instrument of any kind; (1) ark; (2) boat, B. 314, 412, 443; C. 160. A.S. *gelóma*, *lóma*.

Lomerande, hesitating, creeping, B. 1094. This term seems to be connected with *lumber*. O.E. *lumer*, *lomer*, to move heavily. O.Du. *lammer*, *lemmer*, impedimentum, molestia. (Kil.) Dan. *belemre*. Du. *belemmern*, to encumber, impede.

Lompe, lamp, A. 1046.

Londe, land, A. 148, 937.

Lone, path, lane, A. 1066. N. Prov. E. *lone*, *lannin*. Fris. *lona*, *lana*, a narrow way between gardens and houses. Is it connected with O.N. *leyna*, to hide, conceal?

Longande, belonging, A. 462.

Longed, belonged, B. 1090, 1747.

Lont, land, C. 322.

Lopen (*p. p.* of *lepe*, to leap), leapt, B. 990.

Lore, wisdom, learning, B. 1556. A.S. *lár*.

Lore, mode, wise, A. 236.

Lorn, lost, destroyed, B. 932.

Los, loss, B. 1589.

Lose, destroy, B. 909; C. 198; depart, be lost, A. 908.

Losed, lost, B. 586.

Losyng, perdition, B. 1031.

Losynger, *sb.* liar, deceiver. O. Fr. *losengier*.

Lot, } sound, noise, roar, A. 876;
Lote, } C. 161, 183; word, B. 668. Sw. *låta*, to sound; *låt*, sound; *låte*, cry, voice. A.S. *hleóthor*, a sound, noise. O.E. *lud*, voice. The original form of the word is *late*.

"Than have we liking to lithe (listen to) the *lates* of the foules." (K. Alex. p. 149.)

"(He) *late* so lathely a *late* and sa loude cried
That all the fest was aferd and othire folke bathe."
(K. Alex. p. 17.)

"He gaped, he groned faste, with grucchande *lates*."
(Morte Arthure, p. 90.)

Lote=late, countenance, feature, form, manner, A. 899; C. 47. This word occurs in Laȝamon under the form *late*, looks, glances. Glossarial remarks to Laȝamon, p. 449. *Lete*, countenance, is found in the Owl and Nightingale, 35, 403. A.S. *wlite*. O.N. *læti*.

Lote, lot, A. 1205; C. 173.

Lote=lout, bow, A. 238. A.S. *lútan*, to bend, bow, stoop. Sw. *luta*. See T. B., 1900.

Loþe, *sb.* sorrow, A. 377. A.S. *láth*, evil, harm.

Loþelych, wicked, bad, B. 1350.

Loute, abide, sit, A. 933.

Loute, bow, make obeisance. B. 798. See *Lote*.

Louande, praising, B. 1719.

Loue, praise, A. 285, 1124, 1127; B. 497, 987. A.S. *lofian*.

Loueȝ, hands, B. 987. N. Prov. E. *leuf*, palm of the hand, and hence used for the hand itself. *Palm* is used for the hand in early English authors. O.N. *lofi*. Sc. *loof*.

"(He) held the letter in his *love*."
(K. Alex. p. 71.)

"——— he takis
The licor in his awen (one) *loove*, the letter in the tothire."
(*Ibid.* l. 2569.)

Loueloker, more lovely, A. 148.

Lovne, offer (advice), propose, C. 173. N. Prov. E. *loave*, *loff*, to offer. O.N. *lofa*, promise, praise. Du. *looven*. Flem. *loven*, estimate. Cf. "*Lovon* and bedyn as chapmen, Licitor." (Prompt. Parv.)

Louy, love, B. 841, 1053.

Louely, Louyely, Louyly, Louelych, } lovely, A. 565, 693; B. 1486.

Lowe, flame; "*luf lowe*," flame of love, B. 707. O.E. *logh* (see T. B. 168) "the *lowe hot*," T. B. 494.

Lowkande, locking, shutting, B. 441.

Loȝ, Loȝe, } the deep, pit, sea, A. 119; B. 441, 1031; C. 230. See *Loghe*.

Loȝ, Loȝe, low, B. 798, 1761.

Loȝed, made low, abased, B. 1650.

Loȝen, laughed (*3rd pers. pl. pret.* of *laȝe*), B. 495.

Loȝly, humbly, B. 614, 745.

Luche, pitch, throw, C. 230. N. Prov. E. *lutch*, to pulsate strongly. W. *lluchio*, to fling, throw violently. Stratmann suggests A.S. *lyccan*, pull, lutch.

Ludych, Ludisch, } national, B. 73, 1375. See *Ledisch*.

Luf, *gen. sing.*, of love, B. 707.

Lufly, Luflych, Luflyly, } lovely, A. 880; B. 81; 939; C. 419.

Lufsoum, *sb.* lovesome, beloved one, A. 398.

Luged, was pulled, B. 443. O.N. *lugga*.

Lulted, sounded, B. 1207. O.N. *lulla*, to lull, sing to sleep. Cf. "*lullit* on slepe," T. B. 648. Ger. *lallen*, to sing without words, only repeating the syllable *la*. N. Prov. E. *lilt*, to sing with a loud voice; *lilt*, a song.

Luly-whit, lilly-white, B. 977.

Lumpen, befallen, B. 424, 1320. See *Lympe*.

Lur, loss, C. 419.

> "What *lure* is of my lyfe & I lyffe here." (T. B. 582.)

Lureȝ, losses, A. 339, 358. A.S. *lyre*, *lor*.

Lurke, Lurkke, A. 978; C. 277. See T. B. 1140.

Lusty, B. 981.

Luther, bad, wicked, B. 163, 1090; C. 156. A.S. *lyther*.

Luuy, love. See *Louy*.

Lyf, life, B. 1719.

Lyflode, sustenance in life, B. 561. A.S. *lif-láde*, from *lád*, a way.

Lyft, Lyfte, heavens, firmament, sky, B. 212, 366, 1356, 1448. A.S. *lyft*.

Lyftande, lifting, rising, B. 443.

Lyfte, raised, A. 567.

Lyfte, left, B. 981, 1581.

Lygge, lie, B. 1126, 1792. A.S. *licgan*.

Lyke, *vb. impers.* please, A. 566; B. 36, 411, 693, 1646.

Lyke, *adj.* pleasing, C. 42.

Lykker, more like, C. 493.

Lykneȝ, likens, compares, A. 500; is like, B. 1064.

Lyknyng, *sb.* likeness, C. 30.

Lykoreȝ, liquors, drinks, B. 1521.

Lykyng, *sb.* pleasure, A. 247; B. 172, 1803. See T. B. 2912.

Lylled, flourished, shone, C. 447. N. Prov. E. *lilli-lo*, a bright flame. Cf. Mod. Gr. λουλούδι, a blossom; λουλουδιαζω, to flourish, bloom. Is *lylle*, to flourish, connected with the word *lilly*?

Lympe, befall, happen, C. 174, 194. See T. B. 36. A.S. *limpan*, to happen, concern.

Lyne, lineage, A. 626.

Lynne, linen, A. 731.

Lyre, flesh, B. 1687. A.S. *lira*.

Lysoun, trace, B. 887.

Lyst, Lyste, *sb.* pleasure, A. 467, 908; B. 843; lust, B. 693; *vb.* desire, please, A. 146; B. 415, 1766.

Lyst, path, border, B. 1761. Du. *lijst*, edge, border.

Lysten, to hear, A. 880.

Lysten, hearing, B. 586. A.S. *hlist*, hearing; *hlistan*, to hear, listen. O.N. *hlust*, an ear.

Lyte, little, B. 119.

Lyth, limb, A. 398. A.S. *lith*.

Lyþe, assuage, lessen, A. 357. See *Leþe*.

Lyþe, grant, A. 369.

Lyþer, evil, wickedly, A. 567. See *Luþer*.

Lyþerly, badly, negligently, B. 36.

Lyuie, Lyuy, live, B. 558, 581; C. 364.

Lyuyande, living, A. 700.

Lyȝe, lie, A. 304.

Lyȝt, light, A. 69, 1043; bright, A. 500; innocent, guiltless, pure, A. 682; B. 987; *lette ly͡ʒt*, esteem, treat lightly, B. 1174, 1320.

Lyʒt, } *vb.* to light, fall upon, A.
Lyʒte, } 247, 943, 988; B. 213, 1069.

Lyʒten, to lighten, C. 160.

Lyʒtly, easily, A. 358; soon, quickly, B. 817, 853; C. 88. Comp. *lyʒtloker*, C. 47.

Ma, make, A. 283; B. 625.

Ma, man (?), A. 323.

Mach, } =make, fellow, com-
Machche, } panion, B. 124, 695, 1512. See *Make*.

Mache, to make familiar with, C. 99.

Mad, } foolish, A. 267, 290,
Madde, } 1166; B. 654. Prov. Ger. *maden*, to tattle; *madeln*, to mutter.

> "Thi momlyng and thi *mad* wordes."
> (See T. B. 1864.)

Madde, *vb.* to render foolish, A. 359.

Maddyng, folly, A. 1154.

> "*Madding* marrid has thi mode, and thi mynd changid."
> (K. Alex. p. 121.)

Mak, } = mach, match, equal,
Make, } fellow, wife, A. 759; B. 248, 331, 994. A.S. *maca*, a mate; *mace*, a wife.

> "Þe king him (Joseph) did a wiif to tak,
> Hight Assener, a doghti *mak*."
> (Cott. MS. Vesp. A. iii. fol. 27*a*.)

Makeleʒ, matchless, A. 435, 733, 757, 780.

Male, B. 337, 695.

Malicious, C. 508.

Malscrande, accursed, B. 991.

Malskred, bewildered, C. 255. Bosworth quotes "*malscra*, a bewitching," upon the authority of Somner.

Malt, } ease, assuage, soothe, B.
Malte, } 776, 1566. O.N. *melta*, to dissolve.

Malte, discourse, speak, A. 224, 1154. A.S. *mælan*, to speak, converse; *mathelian*, *mæthlan*, to discourse.

Malyce, } B. 250, 518; C. 4.
Malys, }

Man=maken (*3d pers. pl. pres.*), make, A. 512.

Manace, threaten, C. 422.

Manayre, manor, A. 1029.

Mancioun, mansion, B. 309.

Maner, manner, B. 701.

Maner, manor, A. 918.

Manerly, properly, decently, B. 91.

Mangerie, feast, B. 52, 1365. Fr. *manger*, to eat, from Lat. *manducare*.

Mankyn, mankind, A. 637.

Mansed, cursed, B. 774; C. 82. A.S. *a-mánsumian*, to excommunicate.

Mantyle, mantle, C. 342.

Marchal, marshal, B. 91, 118.

Mare, more, A. 145.

Margary, } pearl, A. 199, 1037;
Margyrye, } B. 556.

Marie, marry, B. 52.

Marked, market, A. 513.

Marre, corrupt, spoil, destroy, perish, A. 23; B. 279, 991; C. 172, 474. O.H.G. *marrjan*, to hinder, make void. A.S. *merran*,

myrran, to hinder. Du. *merren*, to obstruct.
Marereȝ = marreȝ (?). A. 382.
Maryag, Maryage, } A. 414, 778; B. 186.
Maryed, married, B. 815.
Marryng, *sb.* spoiling, preventing, B. 186.
Marschal, B. 1427.
Maryners, C. 99.
Mas, mass, A. 1115.
Mascelleȝ, spotless, A. 732.
Mascle, spot, A. 726. Du. *maese*, *masche*, *maeschel*, a spot, stain; *maschelen*, to stain.
Mase (masse), astonishment, alarm, B. 395.
Maskeleȝ, Maskelles, Maskelleȝ, } spotless, A. 744, 745, 756, 768.
Maskle, spot, stain, B. 556. See *Mascle*.
Masporye (?), A. 1018.
Mate, dejected, downcast, subdued, A. 386. Fr. *mat*.
Mate, to overcome, A. 613. Fr. *mater*. O.Fr. *amater*. Cf. Du. *mat*, exhausted, overcome. Ger. *matt*, feeble, faint.
Mater, subject, B. 1617.
Matere, matter, C. 503.
Maugre, Maugref, Mawgre, } C. 44, 54. Fr. *malgré*, in spite of, against the will of; *mal*, ill; *gré*, will, pleasure. In B. 250 *mawgre* is used as a *sb.*=displeasure.
Mawe, stomach, C. 255. Ger. *magen*. Du. *maag*.
May, maid. A. 435, 780. A.S. *mæg*.
Maynful, great, powerful, A. 1093; B. 1730. A.S. *mægen*, power, force, strength. O.N. *megin*, strength; *mega*, to be able.
Maynly, loudly, B. 1427.
Mayntnaunce, maintenance, B. 186.
Mayntyne, maintain, C. 523.
Mayster, master, lord, A. 462, 900; B. 1793.
Maysterful, powerful, A. 401; B. 1328.
Maystery, mastery, C. 482.
Maȝt, power, C. 112. Goth. *mahts*. Ger. *macht*, might, power.
Maȝty, mighty, B. 273, 279.
Maȝtyly, mightily, B. 1267.
Mede=meed, reward, B. 1632.
Medoes, meadows, B. 1761.
Megre, meagre, lean, B. 1198. Fr. *maigre*. Lat. *macer*, lean.
Mekne, make meek, B. 1328.
Mele, meal, B. 625.
Mele, *sb.* discourse, A. 23.
Mele, *vb.* to talk, relate, say, A. 497, 589; B. 736; C. 10.
"To *mele* of this mater." (T. B. 209.)
Melle, speak, A. 797. See *Malte*.
Membreȝ, members, A. 458.
Mendes, amends, A. 351.
Mendyng, *sb.* improvement, repentance, A. 452; B. 764.
Mene, general, common, B. 1241. A.S. *gemæne*. Ger. *gemein*.
Mene, mean, A. 293.
Mene, tell, explain, B. 1635. A.S. *mænan*, to tell.
Meng, Menge, } mix, join, B. 337, 625. A.S. *mengan*.
Mensk, Menske, } *sb.* honour, A. 162, 783; B. 121, 522; thanks, B. 646; *vb.* to honour,

B. 141, 1740. A.S. *mennisc*, human. N. Prov. E. *mense*, to grace, deck; *mense*, decency, good manners.
Mensked, honoured, B. 118.
Menteene, maintain, A. 783.
Mercy, A. 576, 623.
Mercyable, merciful, B. 1113; C. 238.
Mercyles, B. 250.
Mere=meer, boundary, B. 778; C. 320. Du. *meere*. O.N. *mæri*, boundary.
Mere, sea, lake, stream, A. 140, 158, 1166; B. 991; C. 112. A.S. *mere*. O. Sax. *meri*. O.N. *mar*.
Merit, B. 613.
Merk, *adj*. dark, obscure, B. 1617.
Merk, *sb*. darkness, B. 894; C. 291. A.S. *myrc*, dark. O.N. *myrkr*, darkness; *myrka*, to darken, grow dark.
Merke, make, devise, order, place, B. 558, 637, 1487, 1617. A.S. *mearcian*. O.N. *merkia*, to mark, perceive, signify.
Mersy, A. 383; B. 776.
Meruayle, Merwayle, } *adj*. marvellous, C. 81; *sb*. a marvel, A. 1081, 1130; B. 586.
Meruelous, A. 1166.
Mery, pleasant, B. 1760.
Mes, A. 862. See *Messe*.
Message, B. 454; C. 81.
Meschef, evil, misfortune, A. 275; B. 373, 1164.
Mese, moderate, temper, assuage, B. 764. See *Methe*.

"Sir Pylate mese you now no more,
But *mese* youre hart, and mend youre mode." (Town. Myst. p. 175.)

"Kyng Eolus set hie apon his chare,
With ceptoure in hand, thar muyd (mood) to *meys* and stille."
(G. Douglas, vol. i. p. 27.)
"The blastis *mesit*."
(*Ibid*. p. 130.)
"A *mes* you of malice,
but a mene qwile."
(T. B. 12842.)

Messe, mass, service, A. 497.
Messeȝ, messes (of meat), B. 637.
Mester, need, B. 67; C. 342.
Mesure, measure, moderation, A. 224; B. 215, 247, 565; C. 295.
Mesurable, mild, temperate, B. 859.
Metalles, B. 1513.
Mete, meat, food, applied to an apple, A. 641.
Meten, to measure, A. 1032.
Meth, Meþe, } moderation, mildness, pity, B. 247, 436, 565.

"And Mari ledd hir life with *methe*
In a toun that hiht Nazarethe."
(Met. Hom. p. 107.)

A.S. *mæthian*, to measure, estimate, use gently; *mæth*, measure, degree; *mæthlic*, kind, courteous. N. Prov. E. *meedless*, without measure, immoderate.
Meþeleȝ, immoderate, B. 273.
Mette, measure, B. 625.
Metȝ=mese (?), pity, B. 215.
Meuande, moving, B. 783.
Meue, move, A. 156; B. 303.
Meuen (3rd *pers. pl. pres.*), move, A. 64. See T. B. 384.
Meyny, labourers, servants, A. 542; household, B. 331; company, A. 892, 899, 925; B. 454; C. 10.
Miry, pleasant, C. 32.
Misschapen (monstrous), wicked, B. 1355.

Mistrauthe, unbelief, B. 996.

Mo, more, A. 870, 1194; B. 674.

Mod, } =mood, pride, A. 401,
Mode, } 738; B. 565, 764.

Moder, mother, A. 435.

Modey, } =proud, haughty, B.
Mody, } 1303; C. 422.

Mokke, muck, dirt, A. 905.

Mol=mul, dust, A. 382. Flem. *mul, gemul,* dust. Du. *mullen,* to crumble. Pl. D. *mull,* loose earth, dust. Cf. "peat-*mull,*" the dust and fragments of peat. (Brockett.)

Molde, earth, B. 279; *moldeȝ,* lands, B. 454; "*on molde,*" on earth, B. 514, 1114; "*in moldeȝ,*" in earth, C. 494. A.S. *molde,* mould, earth. Goth. *mulda.* O.H.G. *molta.* Dan. *muld.*

> "Loo! here the duchez dere to daye was cho takyne,
> Depe dolvene and dede, dyked *in moldeȝ.*"
> (Morte Arthure, p. 82.)

Mon, man, A. 310.

Mon, moan, sorrow, A. 374.

Mone, moon, A. 923.

Monkynd, mankind, B. 564.

Mon-sworne, perjury, B. 182. Other forms of this word are *main-sworn, man-sworn.* O.H. Ger. *meinsweridi,* perjury, from *main, mein,* spot, stain, injury, impure, bad. O.N. *mein,* sore, crime.

Mony, many, A. 572; B. 1164.

Monyth, month, B. 493, 1030.

Moon, moan, sorrow, B. 373.

Moote=mote, spot, blemish, A. 948.

Mor, moor, B. 385, 1673. A.S. *mór,* a moor, heath.

Morehond, more, A. 475. Cf. *nerehande,* near; *betuixande,* betwixt.

Morn, } morning, B. 493; mor-
Morne, } row, B. 1001.

Mornyf, mournful, A. 386.

Mornyng, *sb.* mourning, A. 262.

Morteres, mortars, B. 1487.

Most, } greatest, B. 254, 385.
Moste, }

Mot, must, may, A. 397, 663.

Mot, } spot, blemish, sin, A. 764,
Mote, } 843, 855. Du. *mot,* dust.

Mote, *vb.* speak to, A. 613. A.S. *mótian,* to moot, debate. Then Medea with mowthe *motys* thus agayne. T. B. 610.

Mote, building, dwelling, abode, A. 142, 936, 937, 948, 949; city, C. 422. *Mote* signifies a hill, mound, moat, and hence a city on a hill (?). Mid. Lat. *mota,* hill or mound. O.Fr. *mote.*

> "Þe bryght ceté of heven is large and brade,
> Of whilk may na comparyson be made
> Tille na cetè þat on erth may stand,
> Ffor it was never made with mans hand.
> Bot yhit, als I ymagyn in my thoght,
> I lyken it tylle a cetè þat war wroght
> Of gold, of precyouse stones sere,
> Opon a *mote,* sett of berylle clere,
> With walles, and wardes, and turrettes,
> And entré, and yhates, and garrettes."
> (Hampole's Pricke of Conscience, p. 239, l. 8896.)

MS. Lansd. 348, reads *mount* for *mote.*

Moteles, Moteleȝ, spotless, A. 899.

Moul = mould, earth, A. 23.

Moun (*3rd pers. pl.* of *mowe*, to be able), are able, A. 536.

Mount, A. 868; B. 447.

Mountaunce, amount, C. 456.

Mountayne, B. 385.

Mountes, Mounteȝ, = amounts, avails, A. 351; C. 332.

Mourkenes, *mirkens*, becomes dark, B. 1760. O.N. *myrka*, to darken, Dan. *mörkne*.

Mourkne, to rot, become rotten, B. 407. From this verb is derived the O.E. *morkin*, a dead beast, carrion, a scarecrow. O.N. *morkinn*, rotten; *morkna*, to rot.

Mourne, to mourn, C. 508.

Moȝt, might, could, B. 1108, 1668.

Mudde, B. 407.

Mukel, great, B. 52, 366, 1164. O.N. *mikill*.

Mul, dust, dirt, A. 905; B. 736. See *Mol*.

Multyplyed, B. 278.

Mun, C. 44. This may be another form of *mon* = moan. But the phrase "*maugre his mun*," leads us to reject this interpretation. *Maugre* is generally used with some part of the body, as "*mawgre his tethe*," "*maugre his chekes*," etc. *Mun* may therefore signify the mouth. (Sw. *mun*, a mouth.) The term is still retained in the north of England. Halliwell quotes the following:

"A common cry at Coventry on Good Friday is—
'One a penny, two a penny, hot cross buns,
Butter them and sugar them and put them in your *muns*.'"

Munster = minster, church, cathedral, temple, B. 1267; C. 268.

Munt, purpose, A. 1161. N. Prov. E. *munt*, a hint. See *Mynt*.

Murte, break, crush, C. 150. Pl. D. *murten*, to crush. See *tomurte*. In T. B. 4312 we have *myrte* = to crush. Bothe mawhownus & maumettes *myrtild* in peces.

Myddeȝ, midst, A. 740. See *Inmyddeȝ*.

Mydnyȝt, midnight, B. 894.

Myke, *sb.* B. 417. Cf. Du. *mik*. The crutches of a boat, which sustain the main boom or mast and sail when they are lowered for the convenience of rowing.

Mykeȝ, free labourers (?), A. 572. A.S. *mecg*, a man. In the *Cursor Mundi*, Cott. MS. Vesp. A. iii. fol. 17, the angels are represented as speaking to Lot as follows:

"'Has þou her,' þai said, 'ani man,
Sun or dogłter, *mik* or mau,
To þe laugand, or hei or lau
Þou lede þam suith out o þis tun
Ar þat hit be sunkeu dou.'"

But ? *he mykeȝ* = he *mykeȝ*, he chooses.

Myneȝ, "*me myneȝ*," I remember, B. 25. A.S. *mynan*, to remember. O.N. *minna*.

Mynge, record, mention, A. 855. A.S. *myngian*, to remind.

Mynne, recollect, remember, A. 583; B. 436, 771. See T. B. 1434. See *Myneȝ*.
Mynte, devise, purpose, B. 1628. A.S. *myntan*, *myntian* to dispose, settle, appoint. "*Myntyn'* or *amyn'* towarde for to assayen. Attempto." (Prompt. Parv.)
Mynstralsy, B. 121.
Mynyster, minster, temple, A. 1063.
Mynystre, *vb.* B. 644.
Myre, B. 1114.
Myrþeȝ, joys, A. 140.
Myrþeȝ, gladdens, A. 862.
Myri, } =merry, pleasant, A. 23,
Myry, } 158; B. 417, 804; *myryer*, A. 850; *myryest*, A. 435.
Myryly, pleasantly, joyously, B. 493.
Mys, } wrong, sin, A. 262; C.
Mysse, } 420.
Myserecorde, mercy, A. 366.
Myse-tente, misunderstood, A. 257.
Mysse, to lose, A. 329; B. 189. O.N. *missa*, to lose. Du. *missen*, to fail, miss.
Mysse, loss, grief, A. 364.
Mysseleue, unbelief, B. 1230.
Mysse-payed, displeased, C. 399.
Mysse-ȝeme, mis-use, A. 322.
Myst, B. 1760.
Myste, mysteries, secrets, (?), A. 462.
Mysterys, A. 1194.
Myþe, to trouble, weary (?), A. 359. A.S. *méthe*, wearied; *méth*, feeble.
Myȝt, might, A. 630.
Myȝtes=mights, powers, B. 644, 1699.

Nadde=ne hadde, had not, B. 404.
Nakeryne (*gen. pl.* of *naker*), B. 1413; *naker*, *nacaire*, seems to signify a kettle-drum.
Nas=ne was, was not, B. 727, 983.
Nature, A. 749.
Nauel, C. 278.
Naule, nail, A. 459.
Nauþeleȝ, } nevertheless, A. 877,
Nawþeles, } 950.
Nauþer, } neither, A. 1087; B.
Nawþer } 1226.
Nawhere, nowhere, A. 534.
Nay, refuse, deny, B. 805.
Nayed, refused, B. 65.
Nayt, use, employ, B. 531. See T. B. 1038. A.S. *neotan*. O.N. *nyta*.
Naytly, neatly, dexterously, B. 480. See T. B. 2427. Nestor, a noble man, *naitest* in werre. T. B. 1038. N. Prov. E. *nately*, neatly.
Naȝte, night, A. 1203; B. 484, 807, 1002.
Ne, nor, B. 1226.
Nece, niece, A. 233.
Nedde, needed, A. 1044; hem nedde=they needed.
Nede, } of necessity, A. 344.
Nedeȝ, }
Nedleȝ, needless, useless, B. 381; C. 220.
Nee=ne, nor, A. 262.
Nel, ne wille, will not, B. 513.
Nem, took (*pret.* of *nimme*), A. 802; B. 505.
Nemme, name, A. 997. See T. B. 152.

Nente, ninth, A. 1012.

Nere, *ne were*, were not, B. 21.

Nere, Ner, near, nigh, A. 286, 404; *wel ner*, nearly, B. 1585.

Nerre, nearer, A. 233; C. 85.

Nesch, gently, A. 606. A.S. *hnesc*, soft, tender.

Neue, fist, hand, B. 1537. N. Prov. E. *neve*, *neif*, a fist. O.N. *hnefi*.

Neuen, name, B. 410, 1376, 1525. O.N. *nafn*, a name; *nefna*, to name.

Neȝ, Neȝe, nigh, near, A. 528; B. 803.

Neȝ, Neȝe, Neȝen, approach, B. 32, 143, 805 1017, 1754,

Nice, *adj.* foolish, B. 1354; *sb.* B. 1359. Fr. *nice*, foolish, simple.

Nif, ne-if, if not, B. 30.

Niye, trouble, B. 1002.

Noble, A. 1097.

Nobley, nobleness, B. 1091.

No-bot, only, B. 1127. N. Prov. E. *no-bot*.

Nok, nook, C. 278.

Nolde, ne wolde, would not, B. 805, 1091.

Nom, Nome, took, A. 587; B. 1613; *pret.* of *nimme*, to take.

Nome, name, A. 872.

Nomen, seized, taken; *p.p.* of *nimme*, B. 1281; C. 360.

Norne, entreat, ask, B. 803. A.S. *gnornian*, to complain, murmur.

Norture, nurture, B. 1091.

Note, city, A. 922; B. 1233.

Note, devise, ordain, B. 1651; C. 220.

Note, device, purpose, A. 155; B. 381, 727. A.S. *nota*, use, duty, employment; *notian*, to employ, use.

"The Bibel telles us openlye
Of Nembrot and his maistri,
Hou the folc that was wit him
Bigan to mak a tour that tim,
That suld reche to the lifte;
Bot Godd that skilfulli kan skift.
Mad them alle serely spekand,
That nan moht other understand,
And gert them lef thair wilgern werk,
Bot of thair *not* yet standes merk,
In Babilony the tour ȝet standes,
That that folk mad wit thair handes."
(Met. Hom. p. 61.)

"Mony noble for þe nonest to þe *note* gode." (T. B. 284.)

Note, A. 879, 883.

Notyng, device, devising, B. 1354. See *Note*.

Noumbre, number, B. 1283, 1376.

Nouþe, now, C. 414.

Nowþelese, nevertheless, A. 889.

Noye, trouble, annoy, B. 1236.

Noys, Noyse, B. 849; C. 490.

Noȝt, naught, nothing, A. 520; B. 888; not, B. 106.

Noȝty, bad, B. 1359.

Nummen (*p.p. nimme*), taken, B. 1291; C. 76.

Nurne, speak, say, B. 669.

Nuye, displease, B. 578.

Nuyed, troubled, B. 1176.

Nw, Nwe, new, A. 527; anew, A. 1079.

Nwy, wrath, B. 301.

Nwyed, displeased, B. 306.

Nye, trouble, B. 1376; *nyes*, troubles, B. 1754; C. 76.

Nyed, troubled, B. 1603.

Nyf=ne if, if not, B. 424.

Nyl, ne wyl, will not, B. 1261; C. 41.

Nylt, ne wylt, wilt not, C. 346.

Nym, } take, B. 481. A.S.
Nymme, } *niman*.

Nys, ne ys, is not, A. 951.

Nyse, nice, dainty, B. 824.

Nyteled, laboured, toiled, B. 888. Prov. E. *nattle*, to endeavour, to be busy about trifles. O.E. *nyte*, to use, employ, enjoy. O.N. *nyta*.

Nyȝe, nigh, B. 484; *wel nyȝe*, B. 704.

Nyȝt, } night, A. 243; B. 526.
Nyȝte, }

Obeche, reverence, B. 745. Prov. Fr. *obesir*.

Obes, obey, A. 886.

Odde, (1) not even, B. 426; (2) spotless, faultless, B. 505. See T. B. 4401, 6157, 6172, 6179, 6189, 6194, 6198.

Oddely, (*a*) alone, B. 923; (*b*) nobly, B. 698.

(*b*) "I Alexandre the aire and eldest childe hattene,
Of kyng Philip the fers, that fest am in Grece,
And of the quene Olimpades, the *oddest* under heven,
To all ȝow of Athenes, thus I etill my saȝes."
(K. Alex. p. 79.)

"For thai the mesure and the mett of alle the mulde couthe,
The sise of alle the grete see and of the gryme wawys,
Of the ordere of that *odde* home [heaven] that overe the aire hingis."
(*Ibid.* p. 2.)

Oke, oak, B. 602.

Olipraunce, vanity, fondness for gay apparel, B. 1349. Prov. E. *olypraunce*, a merry making.

"Of tournamentys y preue thereynne
Seven poyntes of dedly synne;
Fyrst ys pryde, as þou wel wost
Avauntement, bobaunce and bost;
Of rych atyre ys here avaunce,
Prykyng here hors wyth *olypraunce*."
(Robt. of Brunne's Handlyng Synne, p. 145.)

On, an, A. 9.

One, alone, self, B. 872, 923, 1669.

Onelych, only, B. 1749.

Oneȝ, once, B. 801.

Onhede, unity, concord, B. 612.

On-hit, struck, inflamed with anger (?), C. 411. A.S. *onhætan*, to inflame, heat.

On-lofte, aloft, on high, B. 692; 947.

On-ryȝt, aright, B. 1513.

On-sydeȝ, aside, C. 219.

On-wyde, about, B. 1423.

On-yȝed, one-eyed, B. 102.

Ordaynt, ordained, B. 237.

Ordenaunce, ordinance, B. 698.

Ordure, filth, B. 1092.

Ore, oar, C. 218.

Orenge, orange, B. 1044.

Organe, B. 1081.

Orisoun, prayer, C. 328.

Ornemente, ornament, B. 1709.

Orppedly, quickly, B. 623. N. Prov. E. *orput*, quick (at learning). Orped is generally derived from O.N. *verpa*, to throw; *p.p. orpinn*. But this etymology is very doubtful. Cf. "*Orpud*, audax, bellipotens." (Prompt. Parv.)

Ossed, showed, C. 213. N. Prov.

E. *awse*, *oss*, to attempt, offer. W. *osi*.

"Quat and has thou *ossed* to Alexander this *ayndain* (angry) wirdes."
(K. Alex., p. 70.)

Oste, host, army, B. 1204.

Oþer, or, A. 141.

Ouer-borde, C. 157.

Ouer-brawden, covered over, B. 1698.

Ouer-seyed, passed over, gone, B. 1686.

Ouer-tan, overtaken, C. 127.

Ouer-þwert, across, B. 316, 1384.

Ouer-tok, B. 1213.

Ouer-torne, past, B. 1192.

Ouer-walte, overflowed, B. 370.

Ouer-ȝede, past, went, B. 1753.

Ouerte, open, clear, A. 593.

Ouerture, opening, A. 218.

Oure, prayer, A. 690.

Out-borst, *vb.* outburst, B. 1251.

Out-comlyng, a stranger, B. 876. N. Prov. E. *out-cumling*, a foreigner, stranger. The more usual form in early English is *comling*.

Out-dryf, drive out, A. 777.

Out-fleme, banished, A. 1177. See *Fleme*.

Out-kast, B. 1679.

Out-sprent, outburst, A. 1137.

Out-taken, excepted, B. 1573.

Out-tulde, thrown out, C. 231.

Oȝe=owe, ought, A. 552.

Oȝt, Oȝte, } *vb.* ought, A. 341.

Oȝt, Oȝte, } *pr.* aught, A. 274; B. 663.

Pace, passage, A. 677.

Pacience, Pacyence, } C. 1, 36.

Pakke, pack, B. 1282.

Pakke, company, A. 929.

Palayce, Palays, } B. 83, 1389, 1531.

Pale, A. 1004.

Palle=pall, fine cloth, B. 1384, 1637.

Pane, a side, division of a building, A. 1034. Lat. *pagina*, a leaf, any flat expanse. "A *pane*, piece or pannel of a wall, of wainscot, of a glasse window." (Cotg.) "*Pane* of a wall, *pan de mur*." (Palsg.)

Panne, head, but we may read *paune*, paws, claws, B. 1697.

Papeiay=a popinjay, a parrot, B. 1465. It. *papagallo*. O.Fr. *papegau*, *papegay*. Sp. *papagayo*, parrot.

Parage, kindred, rank, nobleness, A. 419; B. 167. O.Fr. *parage*.

Paramoreȝ, paramours, lovers, B. 700. Fr. *par amour*, by way of love.

Paraunter, peradventure, A. 588

Parchmen, parchment, B. 1134.

Pare, cut, B. 1408, 1536.

Parform, perform, B. 542; C. 406.

Parfyt, perfect, A. 638.

Parget, plaister of a wall, B. 1536. "*Pariette* for walles, blanchissure." (Palsg.)

Parlatyk, paralytic, B. 1095.

Partleȝ, partless, portionless, A. 335.

Partrykes, partridges, B. 57.

Pass, surpass, A. 428.

Passage, journey, C. 97.

Passande, passing, B. 1389.
Pasture, C. 393.
Pater, paternoster, A. 485.
Paume, palm, hand, B. 1533, 1542.
Pay, } pleasure, A. 1, 1164, 1176;
Paye, } C. 99.
Pay, please, A. 1165, 1177.
Payment, A. 598.
Paynt, A. 750.
Payre, pair, B. 335.
Payre=appayre, become worse, fade, B. 1124. Lat. *pejor*, worse. "To *appayre* to waxe worse." (Palsg.)
Payred, impaired, A. 246.
Pechche, sin, fault, A. 841. Fr. *péché*.
Penance, } A. 477.
Penaunce, }
Peneȝ, pens, folds (for cattle), B. 322.
Penitotes, (? *Peritotes*), a kind of stone (the *peritot* or *peridot* Marsh), B. 1472.
Penne, B. 1724.
Penne-fed, B. 57.
Pensyf, pensive, A. 246.
Pented, appertained, belonged to, B. 1270.
Peraunter, peradventure, B. 43.
Pere, } equal, peer, A. 4; B. 1214,
Per, } 1336.
Pereȝ, pears, A. 104.
Perile, B. 856, 942.
Perré, precious stones, jewelry, A. 730; B. 1117.
Pertly=apertly, openly, B. 244. See T. B. 1130. Cf. "*pert* wordes," T. B. 977.
Peryle, A. 695; C. 85.

Pes, peace, A. 952.
Pich, pitch, B. 1008.
Pike=pick, pluck, B. 1464.
Pinnacle, B. 1463.
Pité, pity, B. 232.
Pitously, } A. 370, 798.
Pytosly, }
Planed, B. 310.
Planete, A. 1075.
Plaster, B. 1549.
Plat, flat, B. 1379.
Plat, struck (*pret.* of *plette*, to strike), B. 1265. A.S. *plættian*.

"Hwan he hauede him so schamed,
His hand (he) of *plat*, and yvele lamed."
(Havelok the Dane, 2755.)

Plater, plate, platter, B. 638.
Plateȝ, A. 1036.
Plat-ful, brimful, B. 83.
Plattyng, *sb.* striking (or folding ?), B. 1542.
Play, A. 261.
Play-fere, play-fellow, companion, C. 45.
Playn, *adj.* even, clear, A. 178, 689; B. 1068; C. 439.
Playn, *sb.* A. 104, 122; B. 1216.
Playned, lamented, A. 53, 242.
Playneȝ, complains, C. 376.
Playnt, complaint, A. 815.
Plek, place, plot of ground, B. 1379. "*Pleckke* or plott, porculetum." (Prompt. Parv.) N. Prov. E. *pleck*. A.S. *plæc*.

"Se that the hare hathe be at pasture in grene corne, or in eny other *plek*."—(Quoted by Way from MS. Harl. 5086, fol. 47.)

Pleny, to complain, A. 549.
Plete, demand, plead for, A. 563.

Pleyn, mourn, C. 371.
Plontte, plant, A. 104.
Plow, plough, B. 68.
Plyande, pliant, C. 439.
Plye, A. 1039; B. 196, 1385.
Plyt, danger, fault, A. 647; B. 1494; C. 114. A.S. *pliht.*
Plyȝt, condition, A. 1075; B. 111.
Pobbel, pebble, A. 117.
Pole, pool, stream, A. 117.
Polle, poll, head, B. 1265. Du. *polle, pol,* head, top, crown.
Polmente, a kind of pottage, B. 628. O. Fr. *polment.* Lat. *pulmentum.* "*Pulmentarium* a *pulment.*" Nominale, MS.

> "His brother (Jacob) he fand give—
> and his tent
> To grayth a riche *pulment.*"
> (Cott. MS. Vesp. A. iii. fol. 21*a*.)

Polyce, Polyse, } polish, B. 1068, 1131, 1134.
Polyle, poultry, B. 57. Fr. *poule,* a hen; *poulet,* a chicken. Lat. *pullus.* "*Polayle,* bryddys or fowlys, Altilis." (Prompt. Parv.)
Pomgarnade, pomegranate, B. 1466. Cf. Lat. *malum granatum.* It. *granata.* Sp. *granada.*
Poplande, rushing, foaming, C. 319. N. Prov. E. *popple,* to tumble about with a quick motion. O.Sc. *pople,* to flow, rush.

> "The wawis of the wild see apone the
> wallis betes,
> The pure *populand* hurle passis it
> umby." (K. Alex. p. 40.)
> "And on the stanys owt thar harnys
> [he] dang,
> Quhil brayn and eyn and blude al
> *poplit* owt."
> (G. Douglas, vol. i. p. 167.)

Porchase, purchase, A. 439.
Porche, B. 785.
Pore, poor, A. 873.
Porfyl, hem, A. 216. Fr. *pourfiler,* to work upon the edge, embroider; *fil,* a thread. O.E. *purfle,* to overlay with gems or gold. "*Purfyll* or hemme of a gowne, bort." (Palsg.)
Porpre, purple, B. 1568.
Porros, B. 1772.
Port, gate, B. 856; harbour, C. 90.
Portale, A. 1036.
Portray, B. 700.
Poruay, Poruaye, } to provide, B. 1502; C. 36.
Possyble, A. 452.
Potage, B. 638.
Poursent, course, A. 1035.
Pourtray, B. 1271. Fr. *pourtraire.*
Pouer, power, B. 1654.
Pouer, Pouere, } poor, B. 615, 1074.
Poueren (*pl.* of *pouer*), poor, B. 127.
Pouert, poverty, C. 43.
Pouerté, C. 13.
Powdered, A. 44.
Powleȝ, pools, C. 310.
Poyned, trimmed, ornamented, A. 217.
Poynt, *sb.* particle, A. 891.
Poysoned, B. 1095.
Poyntel, a style, B. 1533.
Pray. *sb.* prey, B. 1297; *vb.* to plunder, B. 1624.
Prayse, A. 301.
Prece, press, B. 880.
Prechande, preaching, B. 942.
Precios, Precious, } A. 4, 216; B. 1282.

Prelate, B. 1249; C. 389.
Pres, press, A. 730; to press, A. 957.
Prese, praise, honour; "his *prese*, his *prys*," A. 419. Sp. *prez*, honour, glory. Fr *prix*, value, worth, price.

"Fra þan forth heild Sir Moyses
þis wandes bath in *pris* and *pres*."
(Cott. MS. Vesp. A. iii. fol. 36*a*.)

Prese, } *sb.* press, A. 1114; *vb.*
Pres, } B. 1249.
Presens, } presence, A. 389; B. 8,
Presente, } 1496.
Present, *vb.* B. 1217.
Presonere, prisoner, B. 1217.
Prest, ready, B. 147; C. 303. Ital. *presto*.
Prestly, quickly, B. 628.
Presyous, B. 1496.
Pretermynable, A. 596.
Preue, prove, A. 983; B. 704, 1748.
Prisoner, B. 1297.
Profecie, B. 1158, 1308.
Profere, A. 235, 1200.
Profert, B. 1463.
Professye, A. 821.
Profete, prophet, A. 797.
Proper, A. 686.
Propertéȝ, properties, A. 752.
Property, A. 446.
Prophete, A. 831; B. 1300.
Prosessyoun, procession, A. 1096.
Prouince, B. 1300.
Pruddest, proudest, B. 1300.
Prudly, proudly, B. 1379, 1466. See T. B. 857.
Pryce, chief, B. 1308.
Prymate, B. 1570.
Pryncipale, B. 1531, 1781.
Pryncipalté, dominion, B. 1672, 1738.
Priys, } value, worth, A. 272,
Prys, } 419, 755; B. 1117. See *Prese*.
Prysoun, C. 79.
Pryuely, B. 238.
Pryuy, A. 12; *pryuyest*, B. 1748.
Pulde, pulled, B. 1265.
Pulle, draw, B. 68.
Pure, *adj.* A. 227; B. 704; *vb.* B. 1116.
Purely, } A. 1004; B. 1660.
Purly, }
Purpre, purple, A. 1016.
Pursaunt, a sergeant, B. 1385. O.Fr. *pursuivant*.
Pursue, B. 1177.
Purtraye, B. 1465, 1536.
Puryté, B. 1074.
Pyche, pitch, fix, B. 477.
Pye, B. 1465.
Pyked, adorned, A. 1036.
Pykeȝ, pick, choose, A. 573.
Pyle, building, A. 686.
Pyle, to rob, B. 1270, 1282. Fr. *piller*, to rob.
Pylere, pillar, B. 1271.
Pyne, *vb.* to torment, B. 1095; *sb.* pain, A. 330. Du. *pijnen*, to torture.
Pyne=pynd, fasten, C. 79. A.S. *pyndan*, to shut in.
Pynkardine, ? *perre carnadine*, carnelian stone (Marsh), B. 1472.
Pyony, A. 44.
Pytosly, pitifully, A. 370.
Pyty, A. 1206.
Pyȝt, fixed, placed (*pret.* of *pyche*), A. 117, 228, 742; B. 785.

Quat, what, A. 293.

Quat-kyn, what kind of, A. 771.

Quauende, flowing, waving, B. 324.

Quayle, *sb.* quail, A. 1085.

Quayntyse, wisdom, craft, B. 1632. O.Fr. *accointer*, to make known; *coint*, informed, acquainted with. Lat. *cognitus*.

Qued, *sb.* evil, crime, ill, B. 567; C. 4. Du. *kwaad*, bad. Pl. D. *quat*.

Quelle, kill, A. 799; B. 324; subdue, C. 4. A.S. *cwellan*.

Queme, *adj.* pleasing, A. 1179. A.S. *cweman*, to please. Your *qweme* spouse, T. B. 634.

Quen, when, A. 40, 93, 232, 804.

Quenche, C. 4.

Quere, where, A. 65.

Query, A. 803.

Quest, C. 39.

Queþer-so-euer, whether-so-ever, A. 606.

Quikken, C. 471.

Quo, who, A. 747.

Quo-so, who-so, B. 1647; C. 5.

Quos, whose, B. 1648.

Quoynt, wise, A. 889; B. 160, 871; curious, B. 1459. See *Quayntyse*.

Quoyntis, clothing, B. 54. "*Quoyntyse*, yn gay floryschynge, or other lyke. Virilia." (Prompt. Parv.)

Quoyntyse, device, C. 39. See *Quayntyse*.

Quyk, } quick, living (*pl. quykeȝ*, Quik, } A. 1179; B. 567), B. 324.

Quyl, while, B. 627.

Quyte, requite, reward, A. 595; B. 1632.

Quyte, white, A. 220, 842, 844.

Raas=rase, rese, way, course, A. 1167. A.S. *ræs*, way, course, race. Sw. *resa*.

Rac, storm, vapour, B. 433. N. Prov. E. *rack*, driving clouds, clouds driven along by the wind.

"A *rak* and a royde wynde rose in her saile." (T. B. 1984)

Rachche, proceed, go, B. 619. A.S. *ræcan*, to reach, extend. O.H.G. *rechen*. N. Prov. E. *ratch*, stretch. Perhaps *rachche* is a softened form of *rayke* (Icel. *reika*, to go), to go. S.Sax. *ruchen*.

Rad, frightened, B. 1543. Sw. *raedd*, afraid. N. Prov. E. *rade*.

"In a *rad* haste." (T. B. 917.)

"Vn-to the gryselyche gost Syr Gauane is gone,
And rayket to hit in a res, for he was neuyr *radde*;
Rad was he neuyr ȝette, quoso ryȝte redus."
(The Anturs of Arther, p. 5; ix. 8, 9.)

Radde, advised, C. 406 (*pret.* of *rede*, to advise). See *Rede*.

Radly, readily, quickly. A.S. *rád*, ready, quick; *rádlice*, speedily.

"The sight of þat semely sanke in hir herte,
And rauysshed hir *radly* þe rest of hir sawle." (T. B. 462.)

Raft, bereft, took, (*pret.* of *reve*), B. 1142, 1431; taken, B. 1739. See *Reue*.

Rak, C. 176. See *Rac*.

Rakel, hasty, rash, C. 526. N. Prov. E. *rackle*.
Rakente, chain (?), C. 188. A.S. *raccenta*.
Rakke, C. 139. See *Rac*.
Ramelande, fetid, filthy, C. 279. Prov. E. *ram*, fetid; *rammely*, tall, rank; *ramel*, rubbish, dirt.
Randeȝ, paths, borders, A. 105. A.S. *rand*, *rond*, a border, rim,

Rank, strong, severe, B. 233. Fris. *rank*, long-grown, rank. Dan. *rank*, upright. See T. B. 1392, 1879.
Rankor, rancour, B. 756.
Rape, blow, B. 233. Sw. *rapp*.
Rapely, quickly, A. 363, 1168. O.E. *rape*, haste. O.N. *rápa*, cursitare. In T. B. *rape*=to hasten (818).
Rasch, A. 1167.
Rasp, B. 1545, 1724.
Rasse, summit, top, B. 446. N. Prov. E. *raise*, a mound, cairn. O.N. *reysa*.
Ratted, rent, ragged, B. 144; from O.E. *ratte*, to tear, rend. N. Prov. E. *rats*, pieces, fragments. Fris. *rite*, tear, pull.

> "Thane the Romayns relevyde that are ware rebuykkyde,
> And alle *to-rattys* oure mene with theire ristė horsses."
> (Morte Arthure, E. E. T. S. 2235.)

Rauþe, **Rawþe**, = ruth, pity, sorrow, A. 858; B. 233, 972; mercy, C. 21.
Raue, A. 363, 665.
Rauen, B. 455.
Rauyste, ravished, A. 1088.
Rawe, row, "vpon a *rawe*," in a row, in order, A. 545.
Raweȝ, rows, borders, A. 105.
Raw-sylk, B. 790.
Raxled, roused up, A. 1174. A.S. *ræscian*, to shake, rustle. O.N. *ruska*. Sc. *rax*, to stretch.
Ray, A. 160.
Raykande, going, flowing, A. 112; B. 382.
Rayke, go, B. 465, 671; C. 89. N. Prov. E. *rake*, to go about.
Raynande, raining, B. 382.
Rayn-ryfte, rain-fissure, B. 368.
Raysoun, reason, cause, A. 268; C. 191.
Raȝt, **Raȝte**, afforded, extended (*pret.* of *rache*), B. 561, 766, 1691. See *Rachche*.
Reame, realm, B. 1316.
Rebaude, ribald, B. 873. Fr. *ribald*, from O.H.G. *hrûpa*, a prostitute. (Burguy.)
Rebel, B. 455.
Rebounde, B. 422
Rebuke, A. 367.
Recen, tell, A. 827. A.S. *recan*.
Reche, reach, extend, B. 10, 1369.
Rech, **Reche**, reck, care, A. 333; B. 465. A.S. *récan*.
Reche = reke, smoke, B. 1009. A.S. *reác*.
Recorde, *sb.* A. 831; *vb.* B. 25.
Recoverer, recovery, B. 394.
Rede, *vb.* to counsel, advise, B. 1346; explain, B. 1578. A.S. *rædan*.
Redles, **Redeles**, without counsel, uncertain, fearful, B. 1197; C. 502.

Refete, feed, refresh, A. 88; C. 20.
Reflayr, smell, A. 46; odour, B. 1079. Fr. *flairer*, to smell. Prov. Fr. *flairar*, to smell, sniff.
Refrayne, B. 756.
Reget, A. 1064.
Regretted, A. 243.
Regioun, A. 1178; B. 760, 964.
Rehayte, cheer, B. 127. O.Fr. *rehaiter*.
Reiatéȝ, kingdoms, royalties, A. 769. O. Fr. *reiauté*=*reialté*, royalty.
Reken, beautiful, A. 5, 906; joyous, A. 92; merry, B. 1082; pious, B. 10, 738; wise, B. 756. See Wright's Lyrical Poems, p. 27. A.S. *recan*. O.S. *recon*, to order, direct. Pl.D. *reken*, right, straight, orderly.
Rekenly, nobly, princely, B. 127, 1318.
Rekken up, B. 2.
Relande, reeling, C. 270.
Rele, reel, roll, C. 147.
Reles, } cessation, A. 956; B.
Relece, } 760.
Releue, C. 323.
Relusaunt, shining, A. 159. O.Fr. *reluire*, to shine.
Relygioun, B. 7, 1156.
Relyke, B. 1156, 1269.
Reme, realm, A. 448, 735.
Reme, lament, cry, A. 858, 1181; C. 502. A.S. *hreman*.
Remembre, C. 326.
Remnaunt, remainder, A. 1160; B. 433.
Remorde, grieved, A. 364.
Remue, } remove, A. 427, 899;
Remwe, } B. 646, 1673.

Renay, reject, forsake, B. 105; C. 344.
Renge, } reign, B. 328, 1321.
Rengne, }
Rengneȝ, courses, B. 527. A.S. *ryne*, course.
Renischche, foreign, strange, B. 96. See *Runische*.
Renk, } a man, originally a warrior, B. 7, 96, 766,
Renke, } 969. A.S. *rinc*. O.N. *reckr*.
Renne, run, B. 527, 1392.
Renoun, A. 986, 1182.
Renowleȝ, renews, A. 1080.
Renyschly, fiercely, B. 1724. See *Runische*.
Reparde, kept back, A. 611.
Repayre, *vb*. A. 1028.
Repente, A. 662.
Repreue, reprove, A. 544.
Requeste, A. 281.
Rere, rise, B. 366, 423; C. 188; raise, B. 873; proceed, A. 160.
Rert, if not *rered*, raised=*ert*, powerful, A. 591. Cf. *ertid*. T.B. 2641, 4841.
Res, onset, assault, B. 1782. See *Raas*.
Reset, resting place, seat, abode, A. 1067.
Resonabele, } A. 523; B. 724.
Resounable, }
Resoun, A. 665, 716; B. 1633.
Respecte, "in respecte of," A. 84.
Respyt, A. 644.
Resse, "on resse," in course, A. 874. See *Raas*.
Restay, keep back, restrain, A. 716, 1168.
Restleȝ=restless, unceasing, B. 527.

Restore, A. 659; B. 1705.
Retrete, treat of, A. 92.
Reue, bereave, C. 487. A.S. *refian*, *reafian*. O.Fris. *ráva*.
Reuel, B. 1369.
Reuer, river, A. 105.
Reuerence, / Reverens, } B. 10, 1318.
Rewarde, A. 604.
Rewfully, sorrowfully, A. 1181.
Rewled, ruled, ordered, B. 294.
Reynyeȝ, reins, B. 592.
Reȝtful, rightful, B. 724.
Rial, royal, B. 1082.
Rialté, royalty, B. 1321.
Ridlande, dropping (as out of a sieve), oozing, B. 953. A.S. *hriddel*, a sieve; *hridrian*, to sift.
Riboudrye, ribaldry, B. 184.
Rigge, back, C. 379. A.S. *hrycg*.
Rifteȝ, pieces, fragments, B. 964.
Ring=rink, man, B. 592. See *Renk*.
Robbor, B. 1269.
Roborrye, B. 184.
Roche, rock, B. 537.
Rode, cross, A. 705; C. 96.
Rok, crowd, throng, B. 1514. Sc. *rok*. O.Sw. *rok*, cumulus.
Rollande, curly, waving, B. 790.
Rome=roam, go, C. 52.
Romy, roar, howl, B. 1543. A.S. *reomian*, to cry out. O.E. *rome*. Sc. *rame*. Sw. *raama*.
Ronk=rank, fine, A. 844; bold, A. 1167; C. 490; bad, B. 455, 760; full grown, B. 869; *sb.* boldness, C. 298.
Ronkly, fiercely, C. 431.
Rop, rope, C. 150.
Rop, gut, intestine, C. 270. N. Prov. E. *ropps*, the guts. A.S. *roppas*, the bowels, entrails, the *raps*. Cf. A.S. *rop*-weorc, the colic.

"Huervore he (the liar) is ase the gamelos (chameleon), thet leveth by the eyr, and naȝt ne heth ine his *roppes* bote wynd, and heth ech manere colour, thet ne heth non (of) his oȝen."—(The Ayenbite of Inwyt, E. E. T. S. p. 62.)

Rore, roar, cry, B. 390, 1543.
Rose, praise, B. 1371. Sc. *ruse*. Sw. *rosa*. Dan. *rose*, to praise.
Rot, / Rote, } root, A. 26.
Rote, *sb.* rot, decay, B. 1079.
Rote, lyre of seven strings, B. 1082. O.H.G. *hrotta*. M.H.G. *rotte*. W. *crwth*. Eng. *crowd*.
Roþeled, prepared, B. 59; rushed, hastened, B. 890. A.S. *hrathian*, to be quick. Or from Welsh *rhuthr*, a sudden gust, onset, assault. Lanc. *rhute*, passion. Sc. *ruther*, uproar.
Roþer, rudder, B. 419.
Roþun, rush, B. 1009. See *Roþeled*.
Roum, room, B. 96.
Roun=rune, discourse, C. 514. A.S. *rún*, a letter, character, mystery, council, conversation.
Rourde, sound, A. 112. A.S. *reord*, *reard*, speech, language.
Route, snore, C. 186. Fr. *router*. O.N. *rauta*, to roar, bellow.

"Dormiendo sonare, Anglice to *rowtyn*."
(MS. Bibl. Reg. 12 B. i. f. 88.)

Rownande, murmuring, A. 112.

Rowned, sounded, C. 64. A.S. *rúnian*, to whisper.

Rowtande, rushing, B. 354. "A *routond* rayn, T. B. 1986.

Rowte, company, band, host, B. 969, 1197, 1782.

Rowwe, row, C. 216.

Royl, royal, B. 790.

Roȝ, } rough, B. 382, 1724; C.
Roȝe, } 139, 147; roughness, B. 1545; C. 144.

Roȝly, roughly, B. 433. Is it an error for *rwly*, sorrowful?

Roȝt. cared for (*pret.* of *reche*), C. 460.

Ruchen, fettle, set in order, C. 101. M.H.G. *rechen*. O.S. *recon*. A.S. *recan*, to order, direct.

> "(He) *riches* him radly to ride and remowis his ost."
> (K. Alex. p. 172.)

> "[The king] Ricchis his reynys."
> (T. B. 1231.)

Ruddon, light, literally redness, B. 893. O.N. *rodna*, rubescere, erubescere; *rodi*, rubor, rubigo. Prov. E. *roaded*, *rody*, streaked.

Rudnyng, ? lightning, C. 139. See *Ruddon*.

Rueled, rushed, B. 953. O.N. *hrolla*. Dan. *rulle*.

Ruful, sorrowful, pitiful, A. 916.

Runnen (*p.p.* of *rinne*), run, A. 26, 874.

Runisch, strange, B. 1545. A.S. *rénisc*, hidden; from *rún*, a mystery.

Runyschly, fiercely, roughly, C. 191. *Renisch* or *runisch*, signifies not only strange but fierce, rough. N. Prov. E. *rennish*, *rinnish*, furious.

> "Than has sire Dary dedeyne and derfely he lokes;
> Rysys him up *renysche* and reȝt in his sete."
> (K. Alex. p. 100.)

Rurd, cry, noise, B. 390; C. 64. A.S. *reord*.

Ruþe, arouse, B. 895, 1208. See *Roþeled*.

Ruyt, hasten, endeavour, C. 216. Fris. *rite*, to pull.

Rwe, to pity, C, 176, 502; *vb. impers.* *rwe*, repent, B. 290, 561. A.S. *hreówan*, to rue, repent, grieve; *hreówian*, to be sorry for.

Rwly = ruly, sorrowfully, piteously, B. 390; C. 96.

Ryal, royal, A. 160; B. 786.

Ryally, royally, A. 987; B. 812.

Rybaude, ribald, C. 96.

Rybe, ruby, A. 1007.

Ryche, kingdom, A, 601, 722. A.S. *rice*.

Ryche, rich, A. 770.

Rydelande, drifting, C. 254. See *Ridlande*.

Rydelles, without counsel, uncertain, B. 969. See *Redeles*.

Ryf = rife, abundant, plentiful, A. 770, 844. A.S. *ryf*, frequent. O.N. *rifr*.

> "Forþi he hight (promised) þam giftes *riif*,
> Þat suld bring David of his liif;
> In feild and tun, in frith and felle,
> Saul soght David for to quelle."
> (Cott. MS. Vesp. A. iii. fol. 43*a*.)

Ryg, } rain, torrent, shower, B.
Ryge, } 354, 382. O.N. *hregg*. A.S. *racu*. N. Prov. E. *rag*.

Ryngande, ringing, B. 1082.
Rynk, man, C. 216. See *Renk*.
Rypande, searching, trying, B. 592. O.E. *rype*, to probe, plunder. A.S. *rypan*; N.Prov. E. to investigate.

> "Now if ye have suspowse to Gille or to me,
> Com and *rype* oure howse, and then may ye se who had hir."
> (Town. Myst. p. 112.)

See State Papers, i. 295.
Rysed, rose, B. 1778.
Ryth, a hound, mastiff, B. 1543. A.S. *riththa*, a mastiff.
Ryȝt, right, A. 622.
Ryȝtwys, righteous, right, A. 675; C. 490.
Ryȝtwysly, aright, A. 709.

Sacrafyce, Sacrefyce, B. 510, 1447; C. 239.
Sad, Sade, Sadde, sad, staid, solemn, A. 211, 887; B. 595; long, B. 1286; bitter, B. 525.
Sadele, saddle, B. 1213.
Sadly, soundly, heavily, C. 442.
Saf, safe, secure, A. 672.
Saf, save, except, B. 1749.
Saffer, Safyre, sapphire, A. 1002; B. 1469.
Sage, B. 1576.
Saghe=saw, word, A. 226. See *Saw*.
Sake, fault, A. 800; C. 84. A.S. *sacu*.
Sakerfyse, sacrifice, A. 1064; B. 507.
Sakleȝ=sakeless, innocent, faultless, B. 716. Sc. *sackless*. O.N. *saklaus*, innocent. See *Sake*.
Sakred, hallowed, B. 1139.
Sale, hall, palace, B. 120, 1260, 1722. A.S. *sal*. T. B. 1657.
Samen, *adv.* together, at once, A. 518; B. 400, 468; *adj.* B. 985. O.N. *saman*.
Samen, to consort with, B. 870. A.S. *samnian*, to assemble, collect.
Samne, assemble, B. 53.
Samned, assembled, B. 126, 361.
Samnes (*imp.* of *samne*), C. 385.
Sample, example, A. 499; B. 1326.
Sapyence, wisdom, B. 1626.
Sardiner, sardine stone, B. 1469.
Sardonyse, sardonyx, A. 1006.
Sarre (*comp.* of *sare*), sorer, more painful, B. 1195; *superl. sarrest*, B. 1078.
Sattle, settle, C. 409. N. Prov. E. *sattle*.
Sau, Saue, =saw, word, B. 1545.
Sauce, B. 823.
Saudan, sultan, B. 1323.
Saule, Sawle, soul, A. 461; B. 290; C. 325.
Saundyuer, sandever, glass-gall, B. 1036.
Sauter, psalter, A. 677.
Sauteray, psaltery, B. 1516.
Saue, A. 666.
Sauer, *vb.* savour, B. 825.
Sauerly, savourly, sweet, A. 226.
Sauor, Sauour, B. 510, 995, 1447; C. 275.
Sauyté, safety, B. 489.
Saw, Sawe, word, A. 278; B. 109. A.S. *sagu*.
Sayde=sadde, stedfast, B. 470.

Saym, fat, grease, C. 275. Prov. E. *saim*, seam, lard. W. *saim*.

Sayned, blessed, B. 746. A.S. *senian*. Ger. *segnen*, to bless.

> "Swa sal I *saine* þe in lif mine,
> Sic benedicam te in vita mea,
> And sal lift mi handes in name thine,
> Et in nomine tuo levabo manus meas."
> (Psalm lxii. 5.)

Saynt, A. 835.

Saȝ, } word, B. 1599, 1737. See
Saȝe, } *Saw*.

Saȝ, saw, A. 1021.

Saȝt, } *sb.* reconciliation, A. 1201;
Saȝte, } *adj.* at peace, A. 52. A.S. *saht*, peace; *saht*, reconciled; *sahtlian*, to reconcile.

Saȝtled, appeased, reconciled, B. 230, 1139.

Saȝtled, settled, restored, B. 445; became calm, C. 232.

Saȝtlyng, reconciliation, peace, B. 490, 1795.

Saȝttel, to be calm, patient, C. 529.

Scale, A. 1005.

Scape, escape, B. 62, 529, 928; C. 155.

Scarre=scare, *vb.* be frightened, B. 598, 838; scatter, B. 1784. N. Prov. E. *skair*, wild, timid. S.Sax. *skerren*, to terrify.

Scaþe, harm, ruin, wrong, sin, B. 21, 196, 569, 600, 1148.

Scaþe, to break, destroy, B. 1776. A.S. *scethan*, to injure, hurt, harm. *Sceththe*, injury, loss, guilt.

Scaþel, dangerous, C. 155. Goth. *skathuls*. O. H. G. *scadhal*, hurtful.

> "Lokez the contree be clere the corners are large;
> Discoveres now sekerly skrogges and other,
> That no *skathelle* (hurtful thing) in the skroggez skorne us hereaftyre;
> Loke ȝe skyfte it so that no *skathe* lympe."
> (Morte Arthure, pp. 137–8.)

Ascalphus, a *skathel* duke, T. B. 4067.

Scelt, spread, served (?), B. 827.

Schad, descended, B. 1690.

Schadowed, shaded, A. 42.

Schaftes, beams, rays, A. 982; C. 455. A.S. *sceaft*, dart, arrow.

> "(He) had on a mitre
> Was forged all of fyne gold, and fret fulle of perrils,
> Stiȝt staffulle of stanes that straȝt out bemes
> As it warþ schemerand *schaftis* of the schire sonne."
> (K. Alex. p. 53.)

Schalk, } man, fellow, B. 762,
Schalkke, } 1029; C. 476. A.S. *scealc*, a warrior, serving man. Goth. *skalks*. O.S. *scalc*. O.N. *skálkr*.

Schape, devise, form, C. 247; endeavour, B. 762; happen, C. 160. A.S. *scapan*, to appoint, shape, create. O.N. *skapa*.

Schauen, shaven, scraped, B, 1134.

Schawe, show, B. 1599.

Schawe, } grove, thicket, wood,
Schaȝe, } A. 284; C. 452. Prov. E. *scow*, *shaw*. O.N. *skógr*, Dan. *skov*, a wood.

Schede, depart, A. 411.

Scheldeȝ, shields (of a boar), B. 58.

Schende, ruin, destroy, B. 519.

A.S. *scendan*, to confound, shame, destroy.

Schended, accursed, C. 246.

Schene=sheen, *sb.* bright, beautiful, A. 166, 965; brightness, C. 440; *adj.* A. 203, 1145; B. 1076, 1310. A.S. *sceone*, beautiful; *scine*, splendour.

Schent, } destroyed, A. 668; B.
Schente, } 1029; ruined, B. 47, 580.

Schep, sheep, A. 801.

Schepon, stall, stable, B. 1076. A.S. *scypen*.

Schere, divide, separate, A. 107; purify, A. 165. A.S. *scéran*, to divide.

Schet, shut, C. 452.

Schin, shall, B. 1435. See "Liber Cure Cocorum," p. 29, l. 29.

"For in a slac thou shalle be slayn,
Seche ferlès *schyn* falle!"
(The Anturs of Arther, p. 12, xxiii. 13.)

Schome, shame, B. 1115.

Schomely, shamefully, C. 128.

Schonied, shunned, B. 1101.

Schor, shower, B. 227.

Schore, shore, A. 230.

Schorne (gold), purified, refined, A. 213. See *Schere*.

Schortly, quickly, hastily, B. 519, 600.

Schowte, shout, A. 877.

Schowue, shove, B. 44, 1029, 1740.

Schrewe, a wicked person, a wretch, B. 186; C. 77.

Schrewedschyp, wickedness, B. 580.

Schrowde, clothing, B. 47, 170. A.S. *scrúd*, garment, shroud.

Schrylle=shrill, clear, A. 80.

Schulder, shoulder, B. 981, 1690.

Schunt=aside, aslant, B. 605. O.E. *shunt*, to slip aside, withdraw. A.S. *scunian*, to shun. Du. *schuins*, slope, slant.

"He schodirde and schrenkys and *shontes* bott lyttille."
(Morte Arthure, p. 354.)

"ȝa werpes tham up (the ȝates) quoth the wee, and wide open settes,
If at ȝe schap ȝow to *schount* unschent of oure handes."
(K. Alex. p. 73.)

Schylde, to shield, A. 965; C. 440.

Schyldere, shoulder, A. 214.

Schym, bright, A. 1077. A.S. *scima*, a brightness. M.H.G. *schîm*. A.S. *sciman*, to glitter, shine. See T. B. 4974.

Schymeryng, *sb.* brightness, A. 80. A.S. *scimrian*, to shine. Du. *schémeren*, to dazzle. Sw. *skimra*, to glitter.

Schyn, shall, B. 1810. See *Schin*.

Schynde, shone, A. 80.

Schyr, } brightly, A. 28; bright,
Schyre, } beautiful, A. 42, 284; B. 553, 605, 1278; bare, B. 1690. Comp. *schyrrer*, A. 982. A.S. *scír*, *sheer*, pure, clear, bright. See T. B. 1269.

Sclade=slade, valley, green plain, A. 1148. A.S. *slæd*.

Sclaȝt, slaughter, B. 56.

Scoghe, scoff, or perhaps perverseness, backsliding, A. 610. A.S. *sceoh*, askew, perverse.

Scole, cup, B. 1145. O.N. *skál*. Dan. *skaal*.

Scolere, scholar, B. 1554.

Scomfyt, to discomfit, B. 1784.

Scope, scoop, C. 155.

Scorn, Scorne, } *vb.* B. 709; *sb.* B. 827.

Scoumfit, discomfited, B. 151.

Scowte-wach, sentinel, guard, B. 838.

> "Thane the price mene prekes and proves theire horsez,
> Satilles to the cete appone sere halfes;
> Enserches the subbarbes sadly thare-aftyre,
> And skyrmys a lyttille;
> Skayres thaire skottefers
> And theire *skowtte-waches*."
> (Morte Arthure, p. 206.)

Scoymous, particular, scrupulous, fearful, B. 21, 1148.

Scrof, rough, B. 1546.

Scrypture, writing, B. 1546.

Scue. See *Skewe*.

Scylle, wit, B. 151. It signifies also reason, cause. O.N. *skil*.

Scylful, wise, B. 1148.

Sech, Seche, } seek, A. 354; B. 29, 420.

Seele, joy, happiness, C. 242. A.S. *sél*, good, excellent. Cf. *unsell*, T. B. 1961.

Sege, seat, C. 93. Fr. *siége*.

Sege, siege, B. 1185.

Segg, Segge, } a man, servant, B. 93, 398, 549, 681. A.S. *secg*, a man, literally a messenger, speaker; from *secgan*, to say.

Segge, say, B. 621.

Segh, saw, A. 790.

Sekke, sack, C. 382.

Selcouth, a marvel, B. 1274. A.S. *sel-cúth*=*seld-cúth*, rare, seldom known.

Selden, seldom, A. 380. A.S. *seldan*.

Sele, happiness, bliss, C. 5. See *Seele*.

Selepe=slep, slept, C. 186.

Self, very, A. 1046; same, B 1769.

Selly, a marvel, C. 140; wonderfully, C. 353. A.S. *séllic*, *sillic*, worthy, wonderful; *séllice*, wonderfully.

> "For thou has samned, as men sais, a *selly* noimbre
> Of wrichis and wirlinges out of the west endis,
> Of laddis and of losengers and of litille thevys."
> (K. Alex. p. 59.)

See T. B. 1544.

Sely, fortunate, blessed, happy, A. 659; B. 490. See *Seele*.

Sem, seam, B. 555.

Semblaunt, appearance, cheer, A. 211, 1143; B. 131, 640.

Semblé, assembly, B. 126.

Sembled, assembled, C. 177.

Seme, seemly, A. 190; B. 549, 1810. O.Sw. *sæma*. Dan. *sömme*, to be fitting, bear one's self becomingly. O.N. *sæmr*, seemly.

Seme, to be fitting, become, B. 793.

Semed, A. 760.

Semely, Semly, Semlych, } seemly, beautiful, A. 34, 789; B. 209, 1442. Comp. *semloker*, B. 868.

Sengeley, ever, constantly, A. 8. A.S. *singallice*, perpetually.

Ser, Sere, } diverse, various, separate, B. 358; *ser kynde*, B. 507; *sere course*, B. 1418; *ser wyse*, C. 12.

Serelych, severally, separately, C. 193.

Sergaunt, a royal servant, a squire, B. 109.

Serges, wax tapers, B. 1489. Lat. *cerea.*

Seriaunte, sergeant, C. 385. See *Sergaunt.*

Serkyndeȝ, diverse kinds, B. 336.

Serlypeȝ, diverse, different, separate, A. 994.

Sermoun, discourse, speech, A. 1185.

Sertain, certainly, A. 685.

Seruage, bondage, B. 1257

Seruaunt, A. 699; B. 631.

Serue, avail, A. 331.

Serue, deserve, A. 553; B. 1115.

Seruyse, B. 1152, 1401.

Sese, cease, B. 523; *seseȝ*, let cease, C. 391.

Sesoune, season, B. 523.

Sessed, } took possession of, A.
Sesed, } 417; B. 1313.

Sete, } sat, A. 161; B. 1171.
Seete, } *pl. seten*, B. 1763.

Sete, seat, C. 24.

Seþe = seethe, boil, B. 631.

Seue, } = sewe, sew, a kind of
Seve, } pottage, B. 108, 825.

Sewer, the officer who set and removed the dishes, tasted them, etc., B. 639.

Sewrté, surety, C. 58.

Sexte, sixth, A. 1007.

Seyed, passed, B. 353.

"*Seyet* furth with sory chere."
(T. B. 2512.)

Seysoun, season, A. 39.

Seȝ, saw, A. 158, 531, 698; B. 209.

Side-borde, B. 1398.

Siue, sieve, B. 226.

Skarmoch, fight, skirmish, B. 1186.

Skaþe, harm, danger, sin, B. 151, 598, 1186. See *Scaþe.*

Skele, dish, B. 1405.

Skelt, scattered, spread, B. 1186, 1206. O.E. *skale*, to scatter. N. Prov. E. *scale*, to spread. See Hall, Richard III. f. 15. A.S. *scylan*, to separate, divide; *pret. scel.*

"Skairen out skoute wacche for *skeltyng* of harme."
(T. B. 1089, 6042.)

Skelt, hasten, run, B. 1554. Sw. *skala*, to scamper, scour.

Skete, quick, sudden, B. 1186; quickly, C. 195. See T. B. 13672. O.N. *skjótt.*

Skewe, sky, cloud, B. 1206, 1759. Sw. *sky*, a cloud. A.S. *scüa*, a shadow.

Skowte, look, search, B. 483. See T. B. 1089.

Skoymous, B. 598. See *Scoymous.*

Skwe, sky, B. 483.

Skyfte, devise, order, ordain, A. 569. A.S. *scyftan.*

Skyfte, shift, change, B. 709. Sw. *skifta.*

Skyg, scrupulous, careful, B. 21. Sw. *skygg*, shy. N. Prov. E. *sky*, to shun.

Skyl, } reason, wit, A. 312; *by*
Skyle, } *skylle*, rightly, reasonably, A. 674; ordinance, B. 709; meaning, B. 1554. See *Scylle.*

Skylleȝ, doubts, A. 54.

Skylly, device, purpose, B. 529.

Skyly, excuse, B. 62.

Skyre = shire = sheer, clear, B. 1776. See *Schyre.*

Skyrme, screams (?), B. 483.

> "Scho gaffe *skirmande* skrikes at all the skowis range."
> (K. Alex. p. 176.)

Or does it here signify to look about, like Prov. E. skime? O.N. *Skima*, to look about.

Skyualde, ordained, manifested, B. 529. Prof. Child suggests Somerset, *scaffle*, scramble, scuffle. See *Skyfte.*

Slade, valley, A. 141.

Slake, absolve (lit. to loosen), A. 942. A.S. *sleacian*, to slacken.

Slauþe, sloth, B. 178.

Slaȝt, slaughter, A. 801.

Slaȝte, stroke, A. 59; C. 192. A.S. *slagan*, to strike, beat, kill.

Sleke, assuage, lessen, B. 708. See *Slake.*

Slente = slant, a slope, declivity, A. 141. Sw. *slinta*, to slip.

Slep, slept, C. 466.

Sloberande, slobbering, drivelling, C. 186. *Slobber* is evidently formed from *slob*, *slab*, in the same way as *blubber* is formed from *blob*, *blab*, a drop. Cf. "*Slobur* or *blobur*, of fysshe and other like Burbulum." (Prompt. Parv.) O.E. *slab.* Prov. E. *slob*, thick, slimy. Ir. *slaib*, mud, ooze. O.N. *sluppra.* Dan. *slubbre*, to sip, sup. Du. *slobberen*, to hang loose and slack.

Slode, slid, A. 59.

Sloghe, slow, C. 466.

Sloue, slew, B. 1264.

Sloumbe, slumber, C. 186, 466. N. Prov. E. *sloomy*, dronish, slow; *sloum*, *sloom*, slumber. O.E. *slome*, *sleme*, to sleep. A.S. *sluma*, a slumber. O.N. *slæmi.* Cf. the modern phrase, "to slumber and sleep."

> "(Sire Telomew) cairys into a cabayne, quare the kyng ligges,
> Fand him *slomande* and on slepe, and sleely him rayses."
> (K. Alex. p. 176.)

Slow, slew, B. 1221.

Sluchched, muddy, dirty, C. 341. Prov. E. *slutch*, mud; *slotch*, a sloven; *slotching*, slovenly.

Slyde, fall, C. 466.

> "And *slydyn* uppon slepe by slomeryng of age." (T. B. 6.)

Slyke, slide, slip. O.N. *slikja*, to make smooth. See *Atslyke.*

Slyp, stroke, blow, B. 1264.

Slyppe, go, glide, make off, slip away, B. 985; fall, C. 186. A.S. *slipan.*

Slyppe, escape, B. 1785. Sw. *slippa*, to escape.

Slyȝt, slight, A. 190.

Slyȝt, wisdom, B. 1289; device, C. 130. O.E. *sleghe*, *sleȝe*, wise. O.N. *slægr.*

Smach, scent, smell, B. 461, 1019. A.S. *smæc.* Prov. E. *smatch*, flavour.

Smachande, smelling, savouring, B. 955.

Smartly, quickly, B. 711.

Smod, stain, filth, B. 711. Sc. *smot*, *smad.* O.Sw. *smuts*, spot, stain. Dan. *smuds*, dirty. Pl. D. *smuddern*, to dirty.

Smolderande, smouldering, smothering, B. 955.

Smolt, be at peace, quiet, B. 732. A.S. *smolt*, serene, clear. Prov. E. *molt*-water, clear exudation; *smolt*, smooth, clear. See *Smelt*, T. B. 1669.

Smolt*es*; so in MS., but ? an error for smolt*e* = smelt, B. 461.

> "A smoke *smulte* through his nase." (T. B. 911.)

Smoþe, smooth, A. 6.

Smoþely, quietly, B. 732.

Smylt, decayed (?), B. 226. Sw. *multna*, to moulder. Dan. *smuldre*, to crumble, moulder.

Snaw, snow, B. 222.

Soberly, quietly, A. 256; courteously, decently, B. 117, 799. 1497. See T. B. 248.

Sobre, gentle, A. 532.

Sodanly, suddenly, A. 1098; B. 1769.

Soerly, on error for *Soberly*, B. 117.

Soffer, suffer, A. 940.

Soffraunce, forbearance, C. 417.

Soghe, sow, C. 67.

Soghe, moan, C. 391. A.S. *swógan*, *swégan*, to make a noise, howl. O.S. *suógan*.

Sok, *sb.* suck, C. 391.

Sokored, succoured, C. 261.

Solace, A. 130; B. 870, 1080.

Solased, B. 131.

Solemne, Solempne, B. 1171, 1447; C. 239.

Solempnely, B. 37.

Solemneté, Solempneté, B. 1313, 1678, 1757.

Solie, Soly, throne, B. 1171, 1678. A.S. *sylla*, a chair; *salo*, a hall, palace.

Somere, B. 1686.

Sommoun, Somone, *vb.* B. 1498; *sb.* summons, A. 1098.

Sonde, sand, C. 341.

Sonde = sande, message, word, A. 943; messenger, B. 53, 781. A.S. *sánd*.

Sondeȝ-mon, messenger, B. 469.

Sone, soon, B. 461.

Sonet, Sonete, B. 1415, 1516.

Songen, *pl.* sang, B. 1763.

Sope, sup, B. 108.

Soper, supper, B. 107, 829, 997, 1763.

Sor, Sore, sorrow, A. 130; C. 242, 507; *adv.* sorely, A. 550; B. 290.

Sorewe, sorrow, B. 778.

Sorquydryȝe = surquedrie, presumption, arrogance, conceit, A. 309.

Sorsers, sorcerers, B. 1579.

Sorsory, sorcery, B. 1576.

Sorte, lot, C. 193.

Sorȝ, Sorȝe, sorrow, A. 352; B. 75, 563, 1080.

Soth, Soþe, true, truth, A. 482, 653; B. 515; *soþes*, truths, B. 1598. A.S. *sóth*.

Soþefast, faithful, B. 1491.

Sothfol, truthful, A. 498.

Soþly, Soþely, truly, B. 299, 654, 657.

Sotte, fool, sot, B. 581; C. 501. A.S. *sot*. See T. B. 1961.

Sotyle, subtle, A. 1050.

Soufre, sulphur, B. 954.

Soumme, company, C. 509.

Soun, sound, word, A. 532; C. 429; to sound, B. 973, 1670.

Sounande, sounding, A. 883.

Souped, supped, B. 833.

Sour, bad, vile, B. 192. Cf. "Soory or defowlyd yn *sowr* or filth. Cenosus." (Prompt. Parv.)

Souȝed, sobbed, sighed, C. 140. See T. B. 342. Prov. E. *sugh*, *sow*, *suff*, to murmur. O.Sc. *swouch*, a noise, sound. A.S. *swoeg*, a noise; *swógan*, to sound, howl. Du. *swoegen*, to pant, puff.

Souerayn, B. 93, 552.

Soyle, soil, earth, B. 1039, 1387; C. 443.

Soȝt, sought, A. 518, 730; *soȝt to*, reached, B. 510, 563; made for, C. 249; endeavoured, B. 1286.

Spak, quickly, C. 104; *spakest*, boldest, C. 169.

Spakk, spake, A. 938.

Spakly, certainly, surely, quickly, B. 755; C. 338.

Spare, spar, C. 104, 338. Sw. *sparre*. O.H.G. *sparro*.

Sparred, spurred, rushed, A. 1169.

Spec, speck, B. 551.

Special, } A. 235, 938; B. 1492.
Specyal, }

Sped, help, B. 1607.

Spede, prosper, B. 511; hasten, B. 551.

Spedly, quickly, B. 1729.

Sped-whyle, a short space of time, a moment, B. 1285.

Speke, spoke, B. 1220.

Spelle, tell, relate, A. 793.

Spelle, speech, A. 363. A.S. *spell*.

Spenned, folded, A. 49. O.N. *spenna*. A.S. *spannan*.

Spenned, allured, enticed away, A. 53. A.S. *spanan*. N. Prov. E. *span*, to wean from.

Spiritually, B. 1492.

Spitous, fell, abominable, B. 845.

Spitously, fiercely, angrily, B. 1220.

Sponne=spun, grew, A. 35.

Spornande, rushing, dashing, A. 363. O.E. *sporn*, *spurn*, to dash. A.S. *spurnan*.

> "Now aithir stoure on ther stedis,
> *Spurnes* out spakly with speris in hand." (K. Alex. p. 27.)

Spot, blemish, A. 12, 764.

Spote, place, spot, A. 13; B. 551.

Spotleȝ, spotless, pure, A. 856.

Spotty, to defile, A. 1070.

Spoyle, B. 1285, 1774.

Sprad, } spread (*pret.* of *sprede*),
Spradde, } B. 1607; C. 365.

Sprange, sprung, A. 13.

Sprawlyng, B. 408.

Sprete=sprit (as in bow-sprit), C. 104. A.S. *sprit*.

Sprude=spread, fasten, C. 104.

Spryngande, springing, A. 35.

Spuniande = spinnande, sticky, cleaving, B. 1038. *Pynnand* occurs in this sense in the Northern Romance of Alexander, p. 142.

> "Than vmbyclappis thaim a cloude and covirs all ovir,
> As any *pynnand* pik (pitch) the planets it hidis."

Spure=spere, ask, inquire of, B. 1606. Sc. *speer*. A.S. *spirian*. See T. B. 823.
Sputen=spouted, uttered, B. 845.
Sput=spat, vomited, C. 338.
Spyce, } A. 235, 938; *pl. spysez*,
Spyse, } A. 25, 35.
Spye, B. 780, 1774.
Spylt, destroyed, B. 1220.
Spyrakle, breath, spirit, B. 408.
Spysereȝ, spice-mongers, B. 1038.
Spyt, cruelty, A. 1138; vengeance, B. 755.
Spytously, B. 1285. See *Spitously*.
Stable, *adj*. A. 597; *vb*. B. 1334, 1652.
Stac (*pret.* of *steke*), closed, fastened, B. 439. See *Steke*.
Stad, } placed, fixed (*pret.* of
Stadde, } *stede*), B. 806, 983, 1506.
Stage, state, A. 410.
Stal, seat, B. 1506. A.S. *stal*, *steal*.
Stale, step, degree, place, A. 1002.
Stalke, A. 152.
Stalle, place, fix, B. 1334. A.S. *stælan*.
Stalle, *vb*. bring, place, A. 188; B. 1184.

"Lia he (Jacob) *stalle* until his bedd" (Cott. MS. Vesp. A. iii. fol. 22*b*.)

Stalworth, strong, B. 884; great, B. 983.
Stalworþest, bravest, B. 255.
Stamyn, threshold, B. 486.
Stanc, pool, B. 1018. N. Prov. E. *stank*. Gael. *stang*, a pool.

"*Stagnum*, a pounde, a *stanke*, a dam." (MS. Harl. 2270, f. 181.)

Standen (*p.p.*), stood, A. 519, 1148.
Stange, pool, B. 439. See *Stanc*.
Stape-fole, high, C. 122
Stare, *vb*. A. 149; B. 389.
Stare, star, B. 583.
Stared, shone, B. 1506.
Staren (*3rd pers. pl. pres.*), shine, A. 116. "*Staring* stone," T.B. 3037. Cf. "*Staryng*, or schynyng as gaye thyngys. Rutilans." "*Staryñ* or schynyñ and glyderyñ, niteo." (Prompt. Parv.)

"Many *starand* stanes strikes of thair helmes." (K. Alex. p. 28.)

"As ai stremande sternes *stared* alle thaire wedes." (*Ibid.*, p. 129.)

Start, A. 1159.
Statue, B. 995.
Staue, } =stow, place, B. 352,
Staw, } 360, 480.
Stayre, shine, B. 1396. See *Staren*.
Stayre, ladder, C. 513.
Stayre, steep, high, A. 1022. A.S. *stigan*, to ascend; *stæger*, a stair. O.E. *staire*, to ascend.

"A hundreth daies and a halfe he held be tha playnes,
Till he was comen till a cliffe, at to the cloudis semed,
That was so *staire* and so stepe, the storé me tellis,
Miȝt ther no wee, bot with wynges, winne to the topp."
(K. Alex. p. 164, l. 4828.)

"With that *stairis* he forth the stye that streȝt to the est." (*Ibid.*, 4834.)

Steke, fasten, shut up, close, B. 157, 352, 754, 884. N. Prov. E. *steek*. A.S. *stician*, to stick in. O.N. *steckr*, a fold.

Stel, stole, B. 1203.

Stele, approach stealthily, B. 1778. A.S. *stélan.*

Stele, a step (of a ladder), C. 513. See *Stale.*

> "This ilke laddre (that may to hevene leste) is charite,
> The *stales* gode theawis."
> (Poems of Wm. of Shoreham, p. 3.)

Stemme=stem, to stop, delay, B. 905. The same root occurs in *stammer*, stumble, etc. Sw. *stümma*, to dam.

Stepe, step, B. 905.

Stepe, } bright, B. 583, 1396.
Steppe, } S.Sax. *steap*, bright, brilliant. "Stepe ene." T. B. 3101. Cf. "eyen *stepe.*" Chaucer. C. T. Prologue, l. 201.

Stere, direct, A. 623; rule, C. 27.

Sterne, star, A. 115; C. 207. O.N. *stjarna.*

Sterne (of a boat), C. 149.

Sterre, star, B. 1378.

Stewarde, B. 90.

Steuen, voice, A. 188; sound, A. 1125; B. 1203, 1402; noise, B. 1778; command, B. 360, 463. A.S. *stefen.*

Stiffe, B. 983.

Stifly, firmly, B. 157.

Stik, fix, fasten, B. 157. See *Steke.*

Stille, dumb, B. 1523.

Stoffe, fill, B. 1184. See T. B. 2748.

Stoken, fastened, enclosed, shut (*p.p.* of *steke*), A. 1065; B. 360, 1199, 1524.

> "Sothe stories ben *stoken* up & straught out of mind."
> (T. B. 11.)

Stokke, } stocks, B. 46, 157.
Stoke, }

Stonde, stand, B. 1490.

Stonde, blow, B. 1540. A.S. *stunian*, to beat, strike. O.E. *stund*, to strike.

> "Quat! wyns (wenis) þou I am a hund,
> Wit þi stans me for to *stund.*"
> (Cott. MS. Vesp. A. iii. fol. 42*b*.)

Stonen, *adj.* of stone, B. 995.

Ston-harde, fast, B. 884.

Store, a great (number), A. 847.

> "A *store* man of strength and of stuerne will."
> (T. B. 538.)

Stote, stand, stop still, A. 149. Dan. *stötte*, stay, support. S. Sax. *stuten*, to stop. Sc. *stoit*, stumble. "*Stotyng*, Titubatus." (Prompt. Parv.)

> "Anone to the forest they found (go),
> There they *stoted* a stound."
> (Sir Degrevant, 225.)
>
> "Ffurth he stalkis a stye, by tha stille euys,
> *Stotays* at a hey strette, studyande hym one."
> (Morte Arthure, p. 290.)
>
> "Than he *stotays* for made, and alle his strenghe faylez."
> (*Ibid.*, p. 357.)

Stound, } a space of time, mo-
Stounde, } ment, A. 659; B. 1716; *in stoundes*, at times, B. 1603. A.S. *stund.*

Stounde, blow, and hence sorrow, A. 20. See *Stonde.*

Stour, conflict; *bale-stour*, death pang, C. 426. Cf. *dede-stoure*, death conflict. Hampole's Pricke of Conscience, 1820, 5812. O.N. *styr.*

"Son efter-ward, it was not lang,
Gain Saul þai gaf batail strang;
Þaa sarȝins þan þe king umsett,
In hard *stur* þai samen mett;
Ful snaip it was þair, *stur* and snelle,
The folk al fled of Israel."
(Cott. MS. Vesp. A. iii. fol. 43*b*.)

Stout, firm, stable, A. 779, 935; brave, B. 1184.

Stowed, placed, B. 113.

Stowned, troubled, astonished, C. 73. A.S. *stunian*.

Strake, struck up, sounded, B. 1402.

Strate, street, A. 1043.

Straunge, strange, B. 409.

Stray, A. 1173; B. 1199. See T. B. 6258.

Strayne, strain, A. 128; labour, A. 691; pain, B. 1540; trouble, C. 234.

Strayt, B. 880, 1199.

Strech, Streche, } stretch, A. 843, 971; B. 905.

Stremande, shining, A. 115. See extract under the word *Staren*.

Strenkle, scatter, B. 307.

Strenþe, strength, B. 1155, 1430.

Streny, strain, toil, labour, A. 551.

Streȝt, strait, A. 691; C. 234. Cf. streght, T. B. 351.

Stronde=strand, stream, river, A. 152; C. 254, 311.

"Midward þat land a wel springes,
Þat rennes out wit four *strandes*,
Ffiummes farand in fer landes."
(Cott. MS. Vesp. A. iii. fol. 7*b*.)

"Quen thai war passed over *strand*,
And raght apon þe toiþer land,
Witte yee þat þai war ful gladd."
(*Ibid.*, fol. 46*a*.)

Strot=strut, contest, chiding, A. 353, 848.

"O pride bicums unbuxumnes,
Strif and *strutt* and frawardnes."
(The Seven Deadly Sins, in Cott. MS. Vesp. A. iii.)

Stroþe, bold, fierce (?), A. 115.

Strye, destroy, B. 307, 1768; *stryed*, B. 1018.

Stryf, A. 248.

Stryke, pass, go, A. 1125. A.S. *strican*.

Strynde=strond, stream, C. 311.

Stryuande, striving, C. 311.

Stud=stede, place, B. 389, 1334.

Sturnen, strong, B. 1402.

Styf, Styffe, } strong, A. 779; C. 234; *styfest*, strongest, B 255.

Styfly, fast, firmly, B. 352, 1652.

Styke=stryke, walk, go (?), A. 1186.

Stykked, fixed, placed, B. 583. See *Steke*.

Stylle, secret, A. 20; B. 589, 706; quiet, B. 1203; quietly, B. 486. See T. B. 1773.

"State from þe slyth kyng *styllé* by night." (T. B. 988.)

Stylle, secretly, B. 806, 1778.

Styngande, stinging, B. 225.

Stynkande, stinking, B. 1018.

Stynst, a mistake for stynt, stop, A. 353.

Stynt, stop, B. 225, 381, 1261; stopped, C. 73. A.S. *stintan*.

Styry, stir, move, B. 403, 1720.

Stysteȝ=stynteȝ, stops, B. 359.

Styȝe, path, C. 402. A.S. *stig*.

Styȝe, ascend, climb, B. 389. A.S. *stigan*, to ascend.

Styȝtle, place, order, fix, B. 90; C. 402. A.S. *stihtan*, to arrange, dispose. See T. B. 1997.

"Unstithe for to stire or *stightill* the the Realme." (T. B. 117.)

Sued, followed, B. 681.

Suffer, } A. 554.
Suffre, }

Suffraunce, endurance, patience, C. 3, 529.

Suffyse, A. 135.

Sulp, } defile, pollute, B. 15, 550,
Sulpe, } 1130, 1135. O.E. *sulwe*, to defile, soil. M.H.D. *besulwen*. O.N. *söla*, to pollute. Prov. Ger. *sulpern*, unclean, to defile. The word *sulp* (*solp*) occurs in the Romance of K. Alexander, ed. Stevenson, but the editor renders it "*to swallow*"!

"Oure inward enmys ilkane we inwardly drepis,
That is to say alle the sin, at *solp* may ȝe (the?) saule."
(K. Alex. p. 146.)

Sulpande, defiling, A. 726.

Sumkyn, of some kind, A. 619.

Sumoun, to summon, A. 539.

Sum quat, some sort of, B. 627.

Sum-while, formerly, C. 57.

Sunderlupes, severally, C. 12.

Suppe, B. 108; C. 151.

Supplantor, A. 440.

Sure, A. 1089.

Sum, one, "*al & sum*," one and all, A. 584.

Surely, B. 1643; C. 315.

Sustnaunce, B. 340.

Sute (?) A. 203, 1108.

Sv̇e = sue, follow, go after, A. 976.

Swalt, died, A. 816, 1160. See T. B. 1200, 4687. See *Swelt*.

Swaneȝ, swans, B. 58.

Swange (*pret.* of *swenge* or *swinge*), toiled, worked, A. 586. A.S. *swingan*, to dash, to labour.

Swange, flowed, A. 1059.

Swangeande, flowing, rushing, A. 111. See T. B. 13024.

Swap, blow, B. 222. A.S. *swipian*. O.N. *svipa*, to shake. O.E. *swepe*, *swappe*, to beat. See T. B. 1889.

"He swynges out with a swerd and *swappis* him to dethe.
(K. Alex. p. 38.)

"With a swinge of his sworde *swappit* hym in þe fase." (T. B. 1271.)

Sware, square, A. 837; B. 1386.

Sware, answer, A. 240; B. 1415. O.N. *svara*. See T. B. 1200.

Swarme, B. 223.

Swart, black, C. 363.

Swat, } sweated (*pret.* of *swete*),
Swatte, } A. 586, 829.

Swayf, blow, literally, a sudden movement. See *Swayue*.

"Than Alexander . . . . .
Swythe swyngis out his swerde and his *swayfe* feches,
The nolle of Nicollas, the kyng, he fra the nebb partis."
(K. Alex. p. 28.)

Swayne, swain, servant, B. 1509.

Swayue, swims. T. B. 2358. Dan. *swæve*, to wave, move, flutter.

Swe, follow, A. 892; ran, B. 956.

Sweande, flowing, B. 420.

Sweft, swift, C. 108.

Swelme, heat, C. 3. A.S. *swell*, a burning; *swélan*, to burn, *sweal*.

"[He] lete assuage, or he sware (spoke), the *swelme* of his angirs." (K. Alex. p. 21.)

Swelt, die, perish, B. 108; C. 427; destroy, B. 332. A.S. *sweltan*. O.N. *svelta*.

Swemande (*pres. part.* of *sweme*), afflicting, B. 563. A.S. *swima*, a stupor. S. Sax. *sweamen*, to grieve, vex.

"Whan this was seide, his hert began to melt
For veray *sweme* of this *swemeful* tale."
(Lydgate's Minor Poems, p. 38.)

"Sum swalt in a *swym* with outen sware more." (T. B. 1200.)

Sweng, *sb.* toil, labour, A. 575. A.S. *sweng*, a stroke, blow. See *Swange*. See T. B. 1271.

Swenge, hasten, rush, dash out, B. 109, 667; C. 108, 250, 253.

"He *swynges* out with a swerd and swappis him to dethe." (K. Alex. p. 33.)

A.S. *swingan*, to swing, dash.

Swepe, glide, A. 111; hasten, B. 1509. See T. B. 342. O.E. *swippe*, to pass quickly. O.N. *svip*, a rapid movement; *svipa*, to whip, do quickly, turn.

Swepe, to seize, C. 341. A.S. *swipian*, to take by violence.

Swer, swore, B. 69, 667.

Swete, life; *to lose the swete*=to die, C. 364. *Swete* may here signify *sweet*, the word *life* being understood.

"And alle at lent ware on loft loste ther the *swete*." (K. Alex. p. 105.)

"——— the brande es myne awene
Many swayne, with the swynge [struck], has the *swete* levede." (Morte Arthure, p. 281.)

"All the kene mene of kampe, knyghtes and other,
Killyd are colde dede and castyne over burdez
Theire swyers sweyftly has the *swete* levyde." (*Ibid.* p. 309.)

Swetter, sweeter, C. 236.

Sweuen, dream, A. 62. A.S. *swefen*.

Swey, go, walk, B. 788; came, C. 429. See T. B. 2512. O.N. *sweigia*. Dan. *sveje*, to bend. N. Prov. E. *swey*, to swing; *sweigh*, to press. See *Swe*.

Sweyed, swayed, C. 151.

Sweȝe, go, C. 72; drove, C. 236.

Swolȝe, swallow, C. 250, 363; kill, B. 1268.

Swone, swoon, A. 1180. A.S. *aswunan*.

Swowed, swooned, C. 442. S. Sax. *swowen*, to swoon.

Swyed=sweyed, followed, B. 87.

Swyere, squire, B. 87,

Swypped, escaped, B. 1253. See *Swepe*.

Swyre, neck, B. 1744. A.S. *sweora*.

Swyþe, firm, strong, A. 354; C. 236; great, B. 1283; very, B. 816; many, B. 1299; quickly, A. 1059; B. 354; greatly, B. 987. A.S. *swith*, strong, great; *swithe*, very, greatly.

Swyþe, burn, scorch, C. 478 (*pret.*

swath). N. Prov. E. *swither*, to singe; *swidden*, to scorch. O.N. *svitha*.

> "Mi Gode, als whele set þam,
> Als stubble bi-fore wind lickam
> Als fire that brennes wode swa;
> Als lowe *swiþand* hilles ma."
> (Ps. lxxxii. 15.)

Syence, B. 1454, 1599.

Syfle, blow, C. 470. *Syfle* sometimes signifies to *whistle*. It may be connected with the Prov. E. *suffe*, to pant, blow. A.S. *siofian*, mourn, lament.

Sykande, sighing, B. 715. A.S. *sycan*, to sigh.

Syked, sighed, C. 382.

Sykerly, surely, C. 301. O.Fris. *sikur*. Ger. *sicher*, sure.

Syle, to glide, go, proceed, B. 131. See T. B. 364, 1307. Prov. E. *sile*, to go. O.N. *sila*.

> "With that the segge all himselfe *silis* to his chambre."
> (K. Alex. p. 5.)

See T. B. 364.

Sylueren, silver, B. 1406.

Symbale, B. 1415.

Symple, A. 1134; B. 746.

Sympelnesse, A. 909.

Syn, since, C. 218.

Syngne, sign, B. 489, 1710.

Synglerty, singularity, singleness, A. 429.

Synglure, uniqueness, A. 8.

Syngnetteȝ, signets, A. 838.

Synne, after, B. 229.

Syre, lord, B. 1260.

Syt, Syte, } sorrow, sin, B. 566, 1257: C. 5, 517. O.N. *sút*.

> "Jacob wen he was mest in *siit*,
> God lighted him witouten *liit*."
> (Cott. MS. Vesp. A. iii. fol. 27*b*.)

> "This tre in forbot haf I laid,
> If þou sa bald be it to bite,
> Þou sal be ded in sorou and *site*,
> And if þou haldes mi forbot,
> Þou sal be laverd ouer ilk crot."
> (*Ibid.* fol. 52*b*.)

Syþe, time, A. 1079; B. 1169, 1417, 1686. A.S. *sith*.

Syþen, afterwards, A. 13, 643, 1207; B. 998; since, A. 245.

Sytole, citole, guitar, A. 91.

Syȝ, Syȝe, } saw, A. 308, 788, 985; B. 985.

Syȝt, Syȝte, } sight, A. 226; B. 552, 1710.

Ta, take, arrest, C. 78. "Ta me," take, arrest me. Tatȝ, take, B. 735. (Cf. O.E. *ma*= make.)

Tabarde, coat. It sometimes signifies a short coat or mantle, B. 41. Fr. *tabar*. Ital. *tabaro*.

Tabelment, A. 994.

Taborne, tabour, B. 1414.

Tached, fixed, fastened, A. 464.

Takel, C. 233.

Tale, tale, message, B. 1437.

Talent, will, pleasure, C. 416. See T. B. 464.

Talle=tuly (?), B. 48.

Tan, taken, B. 763.

Tatȝ, take, B. 735. See *Ta*.

Tayt, agreeable, lively, B. 871. O.N. *teitr*.

> "The laddes were kaske and *teyte*."
> (Havelok the Dane, 1841.)

> "Ther mouhte men se the boles beyte,
> And the bores with hundes *teyte*."
> (*Ibid.* 2331.)

Tayt, fear, B. 889.

> "Brynges furtho, [as] sayd the boke, bestes out of noumbre,
> And trottes on toward Tyre with *taite* at thaire hertes."
> (K. Alex. p. 42.)

Teche, teach, B. 160.
Teche, mark, sign, B. 1049.
Teche, fault, B. 1230; device, B. 943. Fr. *tache*.
Tede, an error for *tene*=tēn (?), B. 1634.
Tee, go, B. 9, 1262; C. 87.

> "Let hym *tegh* to þe tempull."
> (T. B. 2541.)

A.S. *teon*. Cf. *teght*, T. B. 1786.
Telde, tent, B. 866. A.S. *teld*.
Telded, raised, B. 1342. See T. B. 6075.
Telle, raise, excite, B. 1808. Du. *tillen*, to lift up.
Teme, approach, A. 460; B. 9; C. 316. See T. B. 3306. It seems to be connected with the A.S. *geteman*, to bear witness; *teama*, to cite, summon. In Laȝamon *teman* signifies to go, proceed, approach, vol. i. p. 53, l. 1245.

> "Albion hatte that lond;
> Ah leode ne beoth thar nane,
> Ther to thu scalt *teman* [wende]
> & ane neowe Troye thar makian."

Teme, team, C. 37.
Teme, theme, C. 358.
Tempest, C. 231.
Temple, A. 1062.
Tempre, moderate, B. 775.
Temptande, tempting, B. 283.
Tender, A. 412; B. 630.
Tene, *sb.* anger, sorrow, A. 332; B. 283, 687, 1137; C. 90; *adj.* angry, B. 1808; *vb.* punish, B. 759. A.S. *teonan*, *tynan*, to anger; *teona*, wrong, mischief.
Tenfully, sorrowfully, bitterly, B. B. 160.
Tenor, C. 358.
Tenoun, A. 993.
Tent, Tente, } attend, care for, B. 676, 935; C. 59, 498; heed, A. 387.
Terme, term, A. 1053; B. 1393.
Terne, lake, B. 1041. N. Prov. E. *tarn*. O.N. *tjörn*.
Teuel (or *tenel* ?), enclose, or ? *undermine*, B. 1189.
Þacce, blow, C. 325. A.S. *thaccian*, to stroke.
Þayreȝ, theirs, B. 1527.
Þaȝ, though, A. 134.
Þede, country, A. 711. A.S. *theód*.

> "I sett ȝowe ane ensample ȝe se it alle day,
> In thorps and in many *thede* ther ȝe thurȝe ride,
> At ilka cote a kene curr, as he the chache walde,
> Bot as bremely as he baies, he bitis never the faster."
> (K. Alex. p. 62.)

Þede, vessel, B. 1717. Prov. E. *thead*, a strainer used in brewing. "*Thede*, bruares instrument, qualus." (Prompt. Parv.)
Þeder, thither, B. 461.
Þef, thief, A. 273.
Theme, A. 944; C. 358.
Þen, Þenne, } than, A. 134.
Þenkande, thinking, C. 294.
Þerue, unleavened, B. 635. Prov.

E. *therf*, *tharf*, *thar*. A.S. *theorf*, *therf*.
Þester, darkness, B. 1775. A.S. *theostru*. See T. B. 2362.
Þewe, virtue, B. 1436 ; C. 30 ; ordinances, B. 544, 755.
Þewed, virtuous, B. 733.
Þewes, thieves, B. 1142.
Þikker, oftener, C. 6.
Þirled, pierced, B. 952.
Þo, the (*pl.*), B. 635 ; those, A. 557.
Þole, suffer, A. 344 ; B. 190 ; C. 6. A.S. *thólian*, to suffer, endure.
Þonc, *sb.* thank, A. 901.
Þonkke, *vb.* thank, B. 745.
Þore, there, A. 562.
Þorpe, city, B. 1178. O.N. *thorp*.
Þorȝ, through. See *Þurȝ*.
Þoȝ, though, A. 345.
Þoȝt, seemed, A. 153 ; B. 562.
Þoȝt, imagination, B. 516.
Þrad, reproached, tormented, B. 751. A.S. *threagan* (*pret. threáde*, *p.p. thread*), to blame, vex, torment.
Þrange, pierce, A. 17. See *Þrenge*.
Þrast, stroke, thrust, B. 952.
Þrat, vexation, torment, C. 55. A.S. *threat*, threat ; *threatian*, to vex, distress.
Þratten (3*d pers. pl. pret.*) threatened, B. 937.
Þrawe, to reach, B. 590.
Þrawen, close, thick, B. 1775.
Þrenge, press, crowd after, follow, B. 930 ; pass, C. 354. A.S. *thringan*, to press, crowd, throng. O.N. *threnga*.
Þrep, contradiction, B. 350. N. Prov. E. *threap*, *threpe*, to dispute. A.S. *threapian*, to reprove, chide.

"*Withoutyn threp* more."
(T. B. 1127.)

Þrepyng, *sb.* strife, B. 183. A.S. *threapung*.
Þret, Þrete, } threaten, A. 561 ; B. 680, 1728.
Þretty, thirty, B. 751.
Þreuenest, wisest, noblest, B. 1571.
Þro, anger, B. 754 ; C. 6 ; angry, A. 344. N. Prov. E. *thro*, keen, eager. O.N. *thrá*.

"Be þou noght in þi hert so *thra*."
(MS. Harl. 4196. fol. 94.)

Cf. "his *throo* hert," T. B. 147. "A *throo* (bold) knight." *Ib.* 1482.
Þro, good, A. 868.
Þro, sharply, quickly, B. 220. A.S. *thred*.
Þro, thoroughly, B. 1805.
Þroble, press, B. 879.
Þroly, fiercely, quickly, B. 180, 514.

"*Throly* he thoght in his hert."
(T. B. 209.)

Þrong, Þronge, } *sb.* crowd, B. 135, 504, 754.
Þrongen (3*d pers. pl. pret.* of *thringe*), crowded, pressed, B. 1775.

"Mony thoughtes full thro *thronge* in hir brest."
(T. B. 470.)

Þrublande, pressing, B. 504. See *Þroble*.
Þrwen, Þrowen, } thrown, B. 220, 504.
Þrych, through, A. 17. O.Sc. *throuch*.

Þryd, Þryde, Þrydde, } third, A. 833; B. 249, 300, 1639.

Þryeȝ, thrice, B. 429.

Þrynge, press, B. 180; follow, B. 1639. See *Þrenge*.

Þrynne, three, B. 606, 1727.

Þryuande, good, pure, B. 751. See T. B. 1482.

Þryue, prosper, thrive, B. 249; C. 521.

Þryuen, prudent, wise, A. 868, 1192; grown up, adult, B. 298; *þryuenest*, wisest, noblest, B. 1639.

Þryȝt, thrust, pressed, thronged, A. 670, 706, 926; B. 135; Cf. *thriccing* of hondys. T. B. 1522. A.S. *thryccan* (*pret. thrycte*), to thrust, press, tread on.

Þurȝ, through, A. 670.

Þykke, closely, B. 504.

Þyȝe, thigh, B. 1687.

To, toe, C. 229.

To-cleues, separate, B. 1806.

To-corue (*3d pers. pl. pret.*), slit, ript up, B. 1250.

Token, betoken, B. 1557.

To-kerue, divide, B. 1700.

Tole, Tool, } tool, B. 1108, 1342.

Tolk, Tolkke, Tulkke, } man, B. 687, 757. *Tolk*, like *segge*, signified originally a speaker, an interpreter. O.N. *túlka*, to explain, interpret; *túlkr*, an interpreter, a mediator. See T.B. 63.

Tom, (1) leisure, A. 134; opportunity, B. 1153; interval, C. 135; (2) time, A. 585. O.Sw. and O.N. *tóm*. "*Toom* opportunitas." (Prompt. Parv.)

"Tharfore þis *tyme* I may noght cum
Telle þi lord I haue no *tome*."
(MS. Harl. 4196, fol. 105.)

In T. B. 1088, we have *tomly*.

To-marred, spoilt, B. 1114.

To-murte, crushed to pieces, C. 150. See *murte*, T. B. 6128.

Tonne (or toune ?), conceive, B. 655.

Top, head, C. 229.

Topace, topaz, B. 1469.

Tor, tower, A. 966.

Tor, hard, A. 1109. O.N. *tor*. Sans. *dus*, hard, difficult. Cf. O.E. *torfer*, hardship, T. B. 81.

"But this tyme is so *tore*."
(T. B. 645.)

To-rente, To-rent, } rent asunder, A. 1136; B. 368; C. 96.

To-riuen, torn away, A. 1197.

Tormenttour, B. 154.

To-rof (*pret.* of *to-riue*), burst, B. 964; C. 379.

Torreȝ, towers, A. 875.

Toter, totter, C. 233.

Toteȝ=totȝ, toes; Cf. *gotȝ*=goes, etc., B. 41.

To-torne, torn, B. 41.

Totȝ, goes, A. 513. Sw. *tota*.

Tour, tower, B. 216.

Tourneȝ=turns, devices, B. 192.

Tow, two, B. 866.

"*Two* pyllers he pight in a place low."
(T. B. 310.)

To-walten, overflowed (*3d pers. pl.*), B. 428.

Towche, to relate, deliver a message, speak, A. 898; B. 1437

"Litille kyngis there come . . . . .
Touches titly thair tale and tribute him askis."
(K. Alex. p. 31.)

Towche, *sb.* touch, C. 252.
Towe, C. 100.
Towen, drawn, A. 251.
Toȝe, tough, B. 630.
Toȝt, firm, binding, A. 522.
Tra, high (?), B. 211, or (?) *tor*, great, difficult of access.

"This castel es o luve and grace,
Bath o socur and o solace,
Apon the mathe it standes traist;
O fede ne dredes it na fraist;
It is hei sett upon þe crag,
Trai and hard wituten hag."
(Cott. MS. Vesp. A. iii. fol. 55*a*.)

Tramme, tackle, gear? C. 101. In the northern Romance of Alexander, p. 5, *tramme* signifies an instrument (optical).

"He toke *trammes* him with to tute (look) in the sternes."

Tras=trace, path, course, A. 1113. "*Trace*, a streyght way, *trace*." (Palsg.)
Trasches = trauses or trossers, drawers or trousers? B. 40.
Trauayle, *sb.* labour, C. 505; *vb.* A. 550; C. 498.
Trave=trawe, believe, B. 587.
Trauerce=traverse, B. 1473.
Traw, Trawe, } =trow, believe, suppose, A. 282, 295; B. 655, 1335, 1686. See T. B. 298.
Trawande, believing, B. 662.
Trawþe, Trauþe, } truth, A. 495; B. 63, 667; belief, 1490, 1703.
Trayled, B. 1473.
Traysoun, treason, B. 187.
Trayþly, Trayþely, } certainly, surely? B. 907, 1137. If *trayþly* be derived from *trauth*, *truth*, the meaning here assigned to it may be correct; but the sense of *fiercely*, *fearfully*, would suit the context better.
Traytoure, B. 1041; C. 77.
Tre, wood, B. 1342.
Trendel, roll, A. 41.
Trés, yards (of a ship), C. 101.
Tresor, Tresore, } treasure, A. 237, 331, B. 866.
Tresorye, treasury, B. 1317.
Trespas, B. 48.
Trespast, B. 1230.
Trestes, trestles, B. 832.
Trichcherye, treachery, B. 187.
Troched, ornamented? An architectural term of uncertain meaning, B. 1383.
Tron, Trone, } went (*pret.* of *tryne*), A. 1113; B. 132; C. 101. See *Trynande*.
Trone, throne, A. 1055.
Trot, *sb.* pace, step, B. 976.
Trow, believe, B. 1049.
Trumpen, trumpets, B. 1402.
Trussed, deposited, B. 1317. See T. B. 1819.
Trwe, true, A. 460.
Tryed, select, trusty, B. 1317. O.E. *trie*, choice. See T. B. 695.
Tryfled = trayfoled, ornamented with knots, B. 1473. Fr. *tref-filier*, a chain maker.
Trynande, going, walking, B. 976. Dan. *trine*, to go.

"Than the traytoure treunted the Tyesdoy thar aftyre,
Trynnys in with a trayne tresone to wirke."
(Morte Arthure, p. 326.)

"The trays (path) of the traytoure be *trynys* fulle evenne,
And turnys in þe Treyute, the traytoure to seche."
(*Ibid.* p. 339.)

"They *tryne* unto a tente whare tables whare raysede."
(*Ibid.* p. 267.)

Tryste, trusty, A. 460; *vb.* to trust, C. 324.

Trysty, trusty, B. 763.

Tryȝe, to trust in, rely upon, A. 311. N. Prov. E. *trigg*, firm, faithful. Sw. *trygg*, safe, sure.

Tuch, cloth, B. 48. Ger. *tuch.* Cf. Eng. *tuck* and *tucker*.

Tulkke, man, soldier, B. 1189, 1262. See *Tolk.*

"The Tothyr was a *Tulke* out of Troy selfe." (T. B. 63.)

Tulket=tulked, sounded, B. 1414. The original meaning of *tulk* is to speak, explain (O.N. *túlka*), hence to utter, sound.

"The Tebies *tulked* (addressed) us with tene (anger)."
(K. Alex. p. 83.)

Tult, threw, pitched. B. 1213; C. 252. See *Tilt*, in T. B. 914, 3704. A. S. *tealtian*, to tilt, shake.

Tuyred, destroyed, B. 1234.

Twayned, separated, A. 251.

Tweyne, two, B. 674, 1749.

Twynande, entwining, B. 1691. Sw. *twinna*, to twine.

Twynne, two, A. 251; B. 1047.

Twynne, separate, B. 402.

Tyd, quickly, B. 64, 1213; C. 100, 229. A.S. *tid, tidlice.* Sw. *tida*, frequently.

Tyde, time, B. 1393.

Tykel, uncertain, B. 655.

Tylle, to, B. 1064.

Tymbre, B. 1414. "Tymbyr a lytyl taboure, timpanellum." (Prompt. Parv.)

Tylte, overturn, B. 832; tumble, C. 361.

"*Tylude* ouer borde."
(T. B. 3704.)

Tynde, branch, A. 78. A.S. *tine.* O.E. *tind*, a tine, tooth, prong, fork.

Tyne, lose, A. 332; destroy, B. 775, 907. O.N. *tyna.*

Tynt, lost, B. 216. See T. B. 1208.

Type, overturn, C. 506.

Typped, extreme, C. 77.

Tyraunte, B. 943.

Tyrauntyré, tyranny, B. 187.

Tyrne, flay, B. 630. Du. *tornen*, to rend, rip up.

"And so thai did al bidene and sum oure douth sloȝe,
Tuke out the tuskis and the tethe and *ternen* of the skinnes."
(K. Alex. p. 140.)

Tyt, quickly, A. 728. N. Prov. E. *tite*, soon. Cf. *tytly*, T. B. 1094. See *Tyd.*

Tyþe, tenth, B. 216.

Tyþynge, tiding, B. 458, 498; C. 78.

Tytter, sooner, C. 231. N.Prov.E. *titter.* See *Tyt.*

Tyxt, text, B. 1634; C. 37.

Tyȝed, tied, A. 464; B. 702.

Tyȝt, Tyȝte, } described, A. 1053; give, B. 1153; endeavour, B. 1108; near, A. 503. See T. B. 1358. A.S. *tihtan*, to draw.

U = o = of, A. 792.

Vch, Vche, Vcha, } = ilk, ilka, each, every. A. 33, 117.

Vchon, each one, A. 546.

Vglokest (*superl.* of *vgly*), most horrid, dreadful, B. 892. See *vgsome*, horrible, T. B., 877.

Vmbe, about, B. 879, 1384; C. 309. A.S. *ymbe.*

"Grete toures full toure all þe toune *vmbe.*" (T. B. 320.)

Vmbe-brayde, accost, B. 1622. See *Brayde.*

Vmbe-grouen, overgrown, B. 488.

Vmbe-kest, look about, B. 478.

Vmbe-lyȝe, compass, surround, B. 836.

Vmbe-pyȝte, surrounded, A. 1052.

Vmbre, rain, B. 524. Cf. *ymur*, in T. B. 897. Lat. *imber.*

Vmbe-schon, shone about, C. 455.

Vmbe-stounde, Vmbe-stoundes, } at times, sometimes, C. 7, 122.

Vmbe-sweyed, encircled, B. 1380.

Vmbe-walt, surrounded, B. 1181.

Vnavysed, unadvised, thoughtless, A. 292.

Vnblemyst, unblemished, A. 782.

Vn-brosten, unburst, B. 365.

Vnblyþe, dismal, B. 1017.

Vncheryst, uncherished, uncared for, B 1125.

Vnclannesse, uncleanness. B. 30, 1800, 1806.

Vnclene, B. 550, 1713.

Vncler, indistinct, C. 307.

Vnclose, disclose, B. 26, 1438.

Vncortoyse, uncourteous, A. 303.

Vncouþe, Vncowþe, } unknown, B. 414, 1600, 1722.

Vnder, the third hour of the day, A. 513. A.S. *undern.* Goth. *undaurns.*

Vnder-nomen, understood, perceived, C. 213.

Vnder-stonde, understand, A. 941; C. 122.

Vnder-ȝede = under-ȝete, understood, B. 796. A.S. *undergitan*, to perceive.

Vndyd, destroyed, B. 562.

Vnfayre, bad, B. 1801.

Vnfolde, B. 1563.

Vnfre, unfortunate, B. 1129.

Vngarnyst, unadorned, B. 137.

Vnglad, sorry, C. 63.

Vngoderly, bad, wicked, B. 145, 1092.

Vnhap, misfortune, B. 143, 1150; misery, B. 892. See T.B. 1402.

Vnhappen, unfortunate; and hence bad, B. 573.

Vnhaspe, disclose, B. 688.

Vnhole, badly, B. 1681.

Vnhonest, vile, B. 579.

Vnhuled, uncovered, B. 451. See *Hile.*

Vnhyde, disclose, A. 973.

Vnhyle, disclose, B. 1628. See *Hile.*

Vnknawen, unknown, B. 1679.

Vnkyndely, wickedly, B. 208.

Vnmard, undefiled, B. 867.

Vnmete, unmeet, unfit, A. 759.

Vnneuened, unnamed, B. 727. See *Neuen.*

Vnnynges, signs, C. 213. A.S. *unnan*, to give, grant, permit.

Vnpynne, to unpin, unfasten, A. 728.

Vnresounable, unreasonable, A. 590.

Vnryȝt, wrong, B. 1142.

Vnsmyten, B. 732.

Vnsounde, wicked, evil, bad, B. 575; C. 527; misfortune, wretched state, C. 58. See T. B. 495.

Vnsoundely, badly, B. 201. See T. B. 1826.

Vnstered, unmoved, B. 706.

Vnstrayned, untroubled, A. 248.

Vnswolȝed, unhurt, B. 1253. See *Swolȝe*.

Vnþank, } wrath, displeasure, B.
Vnþonk, } 183; C. 55.

Vnþewe, fault, vice, B. 190. See *Thewe*.

Vnþryfte, folly, wickedness, B. 516, 1728.

Vnþryftyly, unwisely, badly, B. 267.

Vnþryuandly = unthrivingly, badly, B. 135. See T. B. 4893.

Vntrwe, untrue, A. 897; B. 456; unfaithful, B. 1160.

Vntwynne, separate; and hence destroy, B. 757.

Vnwar, foolish, C. 115.

Vnwaschen, unwashed, B. 34.

Vnwelcum, B. 49.

Vnworþelych, unworthy, B. 305.

Vnwytté, unwise, foolish, simple, C. 511.

Vpbrayde, literally to raise; and hence to utter loudly, rebuke, C. 430. See *Brayde*. In the sense of to utter, speak, we find *upbrayde* used in the following passage.

> "Again my brether haue I bene
> Oft-sith lightly for to tene,
> Wit flitt, wit brixil, strive and strut;
> Myn euen cristen haue I hurt,
> And oft unsaght o him I said,
> And of his lastes (faults) gane upbraid."
>
> (Cott. MS. Vesp. A. iii. fol. 156.)

Vp-caste, spoken, B. 1574.

Vp-folden, up-folded, B. 643.

Vp-lyfte, uplifted, B. 987.

Vpon, open, B. 453.

Vp-rerde, upreared, B. 561.

Vp-ros, uprose, C. 378.

Vpryse, C. 433.

Vp-set, raised, C. 239.

Vp-so-doun, upside down, C. 362.

Vp-wafte, uprose, B. 949.

Vpynyoun, opinion, C. 40.

Vrnementes, ornaments, B. 1284.

Vrþe, earth, A. 442.

Vrþely, earthly, A. 135; B. 35.

Vsage, B. 710.

Vsched, B. 1393, *to vsched* = ?*touched* = *towched*, approached. See B. 1437.

Vse, B. 11.

Vsle, } ashes, cinders, B. 747, 1010.
Vslle, } A.S. *ysle*, ashes. O.N. *usli*, fire. "Isyl, of fyre. Favilla." (Prompt. Parv.) Prov. E. *isle*, *easle*, embers; *eizle*, ashes.

Vtter, out, B. 42; without, B. 927.

Vt-wyth, without, outside, A. 969.

Vus, us, B. 842.

Vȝten, the morning, dawn, B. 893. A.S. *uhta*.

> "Hi sloȝen and fuȝten
> þe niȝt and þe *uȝten*."
>
> (K. Horn, 1424.)

Vale, A. 127; B. 673.
Vanyté, B. 1713; C. 331.
Vanyste, vanished, B. 1548.
Vayle, avail, A. 912; B. 1151, 1311.
Vayment, exhibition, show, B. 1358.
Vayn, A. 811; B. 1358.
Vayned, brought, A. 249. See *Wayned*.
Venge, avenge, B. 199, 559; C. 71.
Vengeaunce, B. 247, 1013.
Venkkyst, }
Venquyst, } vanquished, B. 544, 1071.
Venym, venom, filth, B. 574; C. 71.
Veray, }
Verray, } true, A. 1184, 1185; truly, C. 333; very, C. 370.
Verayly, verily, B. 664, 1548.
Vered, veered, raised, A. 254.
Vergyne, virgin, A. 1099.
Vergynté, }
Vergynyté, } virginity, A. 767; B. 1071.
Vertue, A. 1126.
Vertuous, precious, B. 1280.
Vessayl, vessel, B. 1713.
Vesselment, vessels, B. 1280, 1288.
Vesture, B. 1288.
Veued = weued, passed, A. 976. See *Weue*.
Vilanye, C. 71.
Vilté, filth, vileness, B. 199. O.Fr. *vilté*.
Violent, B. 1013.
Voched, prayed, A. 1121. Fr. *voucher*.
Vouche, resolve, B. 1358.
Vouched, vowed, C. 165.
Vowe, C. 239.
Voyde, do away with; B. 744; destroy, B. 1013; C. 370; depart, B. 1548.
Vus, use, or ? drink, B. 1507. We may, however read, and thus preserve the alliteration, *bus* = *bous* = *bouse*, to drink deeply. Du. *buysen*.
Vycios, vicious, B. 574.
Vyf, wife, A. 772.
Vygour, A. 971.
Vyl, vile, evil, B. 744.
Vylanye, crime, sin, B. 544, 574.
Vyle, defile, B. 863.
Vyole, vial, B. 1280.
Vyolence, B. 1071.
Vyrgyn, A. 426.
Vys, }
Vyse, } face, A. 254. O.Fr. *vis*.
Vyueȝ, wives, A. 785.

Wach, watch, B. 1205.
Wade, A. 143, 1151.
Waft, closed, B. 857. A.S. *wefan*, *wæfan*, to cover. O.N. *vefa*.
Wafte, move, lift up, raise, B. 453. O.N. *veifa*, to raise, move, swing. *Waft*, B. 857, in the sense of *closed* may be of the same origin with *wafte*,
Wage, endure, A. 416.
Wage, wave, B. 1484. A.S. *wágian*.
Wake, watch, B. 85; C. 130. A.S. *wæccan*. O.N. *vaka*.
Waken, raise, arouse, awake, A. 1171; B. 323, 437, 891, 933, 948; C. 132; O.N. *vakna*.

"Wyndis at hir wille to *wakyn* in the aire." (T. B. 404).

Wakker (*comp.* of *wayke*), weaker, B. 835.
Wale, }
Walle, } *vb.* discern, A. 1000; choose, select, B. 921; C. 511; *adj.* noble, choice, B.

1734. Sc. *wale*. See T. 386, 4716. Ger. *wählen*, to choose, select. O.N. *val*, electio, optio, delectus.

"O mister was ther wimmen tuin,
Þat ledd þar liif wit sike and sin,
Ffor þai had husing nan to *wale*,
Þai lended in a littel scale."
(Cott. MS. Vesp. A. iii. fol. 48*a*.)

"Of choys men syne, *walit* by cut (lot), thai tuke
A gret numbyr, and hyd in bylgis dern."
(G. Douglas, vol. i. p. 72.)

"Awai þan drou him son Davi,
Bot Saul dred him mo forþi,
And of a thusand men o *wal* (worth)
He made him ledder and marscal."
(Cott. MS. Vesp. A. iii. fol. 43*a*.)

"That worthy had a wyfe *walit* hym seluon." (T. B. 105.)

Walkyries, witches, fate-readers, B. 1577. O.N. *valkyriur*; *f.pl. Parcæ*. Dan. *valkyrier*.

Wallande, boiling, bubbling up, A. 365. A.S. *weallan*, to boil up.

Walle-heued = well-head, spring, B. 364.

Walt, Walte, } rolled, turned, B. 501, 1734. Prov. E. *walt*. *welt*. A.S. *wealtian*, to roll. O.N. *vella*.

"Hit *walt* up the wilde se."
(T. B. 4633.)

Walter, roll, flow, B. 415, 1027; C. 142. O.Sc. *welter*, *walter*. Dan. *vælte*, to roll. See *Walt*.

Walteręʒ, an error for watterez = waters? C. 263.

Walterande, swimming, C. 247.

Walteʒ, pours, rushes, flows, B. 364, 1037. See *Walte*, T. B. 3699, 4632.

Wame, belly. See *Wombe*.

Wamel, to wamble, C. 300. O.N. *vambla*. Dan. *vamle*, to wamble, to create or cause a squeamishness or loathing. "*Wamelyn'* in the stomake. Nauseo." "*Wamelynge* of the stomake, Nausia." (Prompt. Parv.)

Wan (*pret.* of *wynne*), got, reached, A. 107; B. 140.

Wap, a step, C. 449. O.N. *vapp*. It is generally explained by a blow, stroke, which was probably its original meaning.

"The werld wannes at a *wappe* and the wedire gloumes."
(K. Alex. p. 141.)

"It (worldly wealth) wites away at a *wapp*, as the wynd turnes."
(*Ibid.* p. 181.)

See T. B. 207, 6405.

Wappe, to strike, knock, B. 882.

War, aware, A. 1096; crafty, B. 589. A.S. *wær*, wary. O.N. *var*.

War, Ware, } guard, beware, B. 165, 545, 1133. A.S. *wárian*.

Warded, guarded, C. 258. A.S. *weardian*, to guard.

Ware, were, A. 151.

Warisch, protect, B. 921.

Warlaʒe, wizard, B. 1560. See *Warlow*.

Warlok, prison, C. 80.

Warlow, a monster, C. 258. A.S. *wér-logu*, a liar, a faith-breaker.

"Þe warlaʒ was wete of his wan atter." (T. B. 303.)

Warne, bid, C. 469.

Warnyng, *sb.* B. 1504.

Warpe, Warpen, } cast, hurl, B. 444; ejaculate, utter, A. 879;

B. 152, 213. O.N. *varpa*. A.S. *weorpan*, to throw, cast.

Warþe, a water-ford, C. 339. A.S. *warth*, *waroth*, the shore.

Wary, curse, B. 513. A.S. *wærgian*, to curse.

Waryed, accursed, B. 1716.

Wassayl, B. 1508.

Wast, } destroy, B. 326, 431,
Waste, } 1178. A.S. *wéstan*.

Wasturne, a wilderness, B. 1674. *Wasterne* signifies a desert place, from the A.S. *wéste*, desert, barren, and *ærn*, a place.

"Methoughte I was in a wode willed myne one,
That I ne wiste no waye whedire that I scholde,
Ffore wolueȝ and whilde swynne, swykkyde bestez
Walkede in that *wasterne* wathes to seche."
(Morte Arthure, p. 270.)

Wate=wot, know, A. 502. A.S. *witan* (*Ic wát*, *þu wást*, *he wát*).

Water, stream, A. 107, 139; river, B. 1380.

Wauleȝ, shelterless, from the A.S. *wáh*, a wall (?), C. 262. We should perhaps read wanleȝ= wonleȝ, hopeless, from the A.S. *wén*. O.N. *von*. O.E. *wone*, hope.

Wawe, wave, A. 287; B. 382; C. 142. A.S. *wæg*.

Wax, increase, B. 521.

Waxlokes, waves (?), B. 1037.

Wayferand, wayfaring, B. 79.

Waykned, weakened, B. 1422. O.N. *veikr*. A.S. *wác*, weak; *wácan*, to become weak.

Wayle, select, choice, B. 1716. See *Wale*.

Waymot, passionate, C. 492. A.S. *weamod*.

Wayne, give, B. 1504; gain, recover, 1616, 1701. The original meaning seems to be that of gaining, getting. O.Fr. *gaagnier*. In some O.E. works *wayne* is used like our word *get*.

"Than past up the proude quene into prevé chambre,
Waynes (*i.e.* puts out her head) out at wyndow and waytes aboute."
(K. Alex. p. 33.)

Wayte, look into, search, B. 99; be careful, B. 292; look about, B. 1423; inquire, B. 1552. See T. B. 876. "*Waytyn* or *aspyyn*, observo." (Prompt. Parv.)

Waȝeȝes, *waȝes*, waves, B. 404.

"Girdon ouer the grym *waghes*."
(T. B. 1410.)

See *Wawe*.

Webbe, cloth, A. 71.

Wedde, A. 772; B. 69.

Wedded wyf, B. 330.

Weddyng, A. 791.

Wed, } garments, weeds, A. 748,
Wede, } 766; B. 793. A.S. *wæd*.

Wed, } become mad, B. 1585. A.S.
Wede, } *wédan*, to rave, be mad.

Weder, storm, B. 444, 948.

Weder, weather, B. 1760.

Wela-wynnely, very joyfully, B. 831. A.S. *welig*, rich, bountiful; *wyn*, pleasure, joy.

Welcom, } B. 813.
Welcum, }

Welde, govern, rule, wield, B. 195, 835; use, employ, possess, B. 705, 1351; C. 16. A.S. *wealdan*, rule, exercise, possess.

Welder, ruler, C. 129.

Welo, joy (*pl. wele3*), A. 14, 154, 394; B. 651; C. 262. A.S. *wela*.
Welgest, worthiest, B. 1244. A.S. *welig* (*welga*), rich, wealthy.
Welke, walked, A. 101.
Welkyn, welkin, the sky. A.S. *welcn*, *wolcen*. O.Sc. *walk*, a cloud.
Welle-hede3, springs, B. 428.
Welt, revolved, C. 115. See *Walter*.
Welwed, faded, C. 475. A.S. *wealwian*.

"The grond stud barrant, widderit dosk or gray,
Herbis, flowris and gersis *wallowyt* away."
(G. Douglas, vol. i. p. 378.)

Wely, joyous, happy, A. 101. A.S. *welig*.

"*Welli* make, Laverd, and noght ille,
To Syon in þi gode wille."
(Ps. i. 20.)
"Þan was þar never suilk a hald,
Ne nan in *welier* in werld to wald."
(Cott. MS. Vesp. A. iii. fol. 55*b*.)

Wem, } spot, blemish, A. 1003.
Wemme, } A.S. *wem*.
Wemle3, spotless, without blemish.
Wenche, woman, B. 974, 1250; concubine, B. 1716. A.S. *wencle*, a maid. S. Sax. *wenchell*, a child.
Wende = wened, thought, A. 1148; C. 111.
Wene = ween, believe, A. 47; B. 821; C. 244. A.S. *wénan*.
Wene, doubt, A. 1141.
Weng, avenge, B. 201.
Wenyng, supposition, C. 115.
Wepande, weeping, C. 384.
Weppen, weapon, B. 835.
Wered, guarded, protected, C. 486. A.S. *weren*. Ger. *wehren*, defend.
Werke3, labours, B. 136.
Werp (*pret.* of *warp*), threw, B. 284.
Werre, war, B. 1178.
Wers, worse, B. 80.
Werte, root, herb, C. 478. A.S. *wyrt*.
Weryng, wearing, age, B. 1123. "*Weryn* or wax olde, febyl, veterasco." (Prompt. Parv.)
Wesch, washed, A. 766.
Westernays, wrongly, A. 307. See Note on this word, p. 106. ? wiþer-ways, wrong-wise.
Wete, wet, A. 761.
Weue, pass, A. 318.
Weued, cut off (?), B. 222.
Wex (*pret.* of *wax*), became, A. 538; B. 204.
We3e, weigh (anchor), C. 103; carry round, B. 1420, 1508. A.S. *wegan*, to weigh, carry.
We3te, weight, B. 1734.
Wham, whom, A. 131.
Whate3 = wat3, was, A. 1041.
What-kyn, what kind of, B. 100.
Whichche = hutch, ark, B. 362. "*Hutche* or *whyche*, cista, archa." (Prompt. Parv.) A.S. *hwæcca*.
Whyle, moment, B. 1620.
Wite, blame. See *Wyte*.
With-dro3, withdrew, A. 658.
With-nay, refuse, deny, A. 916.
Wi3t = wight, quickly, C. 103. See *Wy3t*.
Wlate, to abhor, hate, detest, B. 305; to be disgusted at, B. 1501. A.S. *wlættian*.
Wlatsum, hateful, abominable, B. 541.

Wlonc, } beautiful, A. 122, 1171;
Wlonk, } B. 606, 793, 933; C. 486; good, A. 903. A.S. *wlanc.*

Wod, } mad, enraged, B. 204,
Wode, } 1558; foolish, B. 828; fierce, strong, B. 364; C. 142. A.S. *wód.*

Wodbynde, woodbine, C. 446.

Wodder (*comp.* of *wode*), fiercer, rougher, C. 162.

Woghe, wrong, sin, A. 622. A.S. *woh.*

Wolde=walde, perform, do, A. 812. See *Welde.*

Wolde, would, A. 772.

Wolen, woollen, A. 731.

Wolle, wool, A. 844.

Wombe, belly, B. 462, 1250.

Won, } *sb.* dwelling, abode, A.
Wone, } 32, 1049; B. 140, 928; woneȝ, A. 917, 924; *vb.* to dwell, A. 404, 298; B. 875. A.S. *wunian.* O.Fris. *wona.*

Won=wone, custom, usage, B. 720. A.S. *wune.*

Wonde, fear, hesitate, B. 855. A.S. *wandian.*

Wonde=wande, delay, cease, A. 153.

> "[I wole] for no dethe *wonde.*"
> (T. B. 591.)
>
> "I wille noghte *wonde* for no werre,
> To wende whare me likes."
> (Morte Arthure, p. 292.)
>
> "Sua did þis wiif I yow of redd,
> Sco folud Joseph ai þar he fledd,
> And for sco foluand fand a spurn,
> Sco waited him wit a werr turn,
> Hirself in godds gram and gilt,
> And almast did him to be spilt;
> How sco broght him to the fand (trial),
> Fforth to telle wil I noght *waand.*"
> (Cott. MS. Vesp. A. iii. fol. 25*a.*)

Wonder, *adj.* wonderful, A. 1095; B. 153.

Wonderly, wonderfully, B. 570; C. 384.

Woned=waned, decreased, B. 496. A.S. *wanian,* to decrease.

Wonen (*pret. pl.*) got, B. 1777.

Wonne, pale, wan, C. 141. A.S. *wonn,* wan.

Wonne, got, A. 32.

Wonnen, begotten, B. 112.

Wonnyng, dwelling, B. 921. See *Won.*

Wont, be wanting, B. 739.

Wony, dwell, abide, live, A. 284; B. 431; C. 462. See *Won.*

Wonyande, dwelling, living, B. 293.

Wonys, dwells, A. 47.

Worche, *vb.* work, labour, A. 511.

Worcher=worker, maker, B. 1501.

Worchyp, honour, B. 1802.

Worded, spoken, uttered, C. 421.

Wore, were, A. 142, 232; B. 928.

Worme, reptile, B. 533.

Worre, weaker, literally, worse, B. 719. O.N. *verr.* Sw. *värre.* O.Sc. *war.* O.E. *werr,* worse.

Worschyp, honour, A. 394.

Worteȝ, herbs, A. 42. See *Werte.*

Worþe, to be, C. 22.

Worþely, } worthy, A. 47,
Worþelych, } 846, 1073; B.
Worþly, } 471, 651, 1298,
Worþlych, } 1351; beautiful;
Worþyly, } C. 475.

Worþloker, more worthy (*comp.* of *worþelych*), C. 464.

Wost, } knowest, A. 293, 411;
Woste, } B. 875. See *Wot.*

Wot, know, A. 47, 1107; C. 129.

Wote, knows, C. 397.

Woþe, hurt, harm, B. 855. This word occurs under the forms *quathe*, *wathe*, and seems to be related to O.E. *qued.* Low Ger. *quat*, bad. O.E. *wathe*, bad; *wathely*, badly.

"Ffor *woþe* of þe worse." (T. B. 1223.)

Woþe, path, A. 151, 375. A.S. *wáth*, *wáthu*. O.E. *wathe*, a way, path. See extract under the word *Wasturne*.

Wowe, } Woȝe } wall, A. 1049; B. 832, 839, 1403, 1531. A.S. *wáh*. "*Wowe* or wal, murus." (Prompt. Parv.)

Wrache, vengeance, B. 204, 229; C. 185. A.S. *wrec*, *wracu*.

Wrak (*pret.* of *wreke*), avenged, B. 570.

Wrake, vengeance, B. 213, 235, 718, 970, 1225.

Wrakful, angry, bitter, B. 302, 541.

Wrang, wrong, A. 15; B. 76; wrongly, A. 488, 631; bad, C. 384.

Wraste (*pret.* of *wreste*), raised, uplifted, B. 1166, 1403; thrust, 1802; C. 80.

Wrastel, } Wrastle, } wrestle, B. 949; C. 141.

Wraþe, become angry, B. 230; C. 74; make angry, B. 719.

Wraȝte, wrought, A. 56.

Wrech = wrache, vengeance, B. 230.

Wrech, } Wreche, } Wrechche, } wretch, B. 84, 828; C. 113.

Wrech, wretched, C. 258. A.S. *wrec*, wretched. With *wrech* and *wretched*, cf. *wik* and *wikked*.

Wrek, } Wreke, } avenged, B. 198.

Wrenche, device, B. 292. A.S. *wrence*.

Wro, passage; literally, corner, A. 866. O.Sw. *wraa*. Dan. *vraa*.

Wroken, (*pret.* of *wreke*), banished, exiled, A. 375. A.S. *wrecan*, to exile, banish.

Wrot (*pret.* of *wrote*), grubbed up, C. 467. A.S. *wrótan*, to turn up with the snout; *wrót*, a snout.

"With wrathe he begynnus to *wrote*,
He ruskes vppe mony a rote
With tusshes of iij. fote."
(Avowynge of Arthur, xii. 13.)

Wroþe, fierce, B. 1676. A.S. *wráth*, wroth, enraged.

Wroþeloker (*comp.* of *wroþely*), more fiercely, angrily, C. 132.

Wroþely, } Wroþly, } angrily, fiercely, B. 280, 949; C. 132.

Wroþer (*comp.* of *wroþe*), fiercer, C. 162.

Wroȝt, } Wroȝte, } wrought, worked, A. 525, 748.

Wruxeled, raised, B. 1381. *Wrixle* = change, turn, occurs in T.B. 445.

"Þis unwarnes of wit *wrixlis* hys mynd."

Wryst, B. 1535.

Wryt, B. 1552.

Wryþe, turn, A. 350, 488; wriggle, B. 533; toil, A. 511; bind, thrust, C. 80. A.S. *writhan*, to writhe, bind, twist. "*Writhen* like a wilde eddur." T.B. 4432.

Wunder, B. 1390.

Wunnen, won, B. 1305.

Wyche, B. 1577.
Wyche-crafte, B. 1560.
Wyddere, wither, C. 468.
Wydowande(*wyndowande*), withering, dry, B. 1048; *wyndowand* = burnt up. N. Prov. E. *winny*, to dry, burn up.
Wyke, member, part, B. 1690. O.N. *vik*.
Wykke, } wicked, B. 908, 1063.
Wyk, } A.S. *wican*, to become weak, to yield. O.N. *vikia*.
Wykket, } wicket, gate, door, B.
Wyket, } 501, 857.
Wyl, } wandering, C. 473; for-
Wylle, } lorn, B. 76. O.N. *villa*, error; *villa*, to lead astray, beguile. Phrase, *wille o wan*, astray from abode, uncertain where to go; *wil-sum*, *wil-ful*, lonely, solitary, desert.

"So I *wilt* in the wod."
(T. B. 2359.)

"Adam went out ful *wille* o wan."
(Cott. MS. Vesp. A. iii. fol. 7*a*.)

"All wery I wex and *wyle* of my *gate*."
(T. B. 2369.)

"Sone ware thay *willid* fra the way
the wod was so thick."
(K. Alex. p. 102.)

"Sorful bicom þat fals file (the devil)
And thoght how he moght man *bi-wille*;
Aguins God wex he sa gril,
Þat alle his werk he wend to spil."
(Cott. MS. Vesp. A. iii. fol. 6*b*.)

"His suns þat (we) of forwit melt,
Al þe werld bituix þam delt;
Asie to Sem, to Cham Affrik,
To Japhet Europ þat *wilful* wike:
Al þer þre þai war ful rike."
(*Ibid.* fol. 13*a*.)

Wyldren = wyldern (?), waste, wilderness, C. 297. A.S. *wild*, wild, and *ærn*, a place(?). See *Wasturne*.

"In *wildrin* land and in wastin,
I wil tham (the Israelites) bring of
þair nocin;
Bot wel I wat he (Pharaoh) is ful thra,
Lath sal him think to let þam ga."
(Cott. MS. Vesp. A. iii. fol. 33a.)

Wylsfully, wilfully, B. 268.
Wylger, wild, fierce, B. 375. See extract under the word *Note*.
Wylle, forlorn, B. 76. See *Wyl*.
Wylnes, apostacy, B. 231.
Wylneȝ, desirest (2*d pers. sing.* of *wylne*), A. 318. A.S. *wilnian*.
Wyly, curiously, craftily, B. 1452. A.S. *wile*, a device.
Wyndas, windlass, C. 103.
Wyndowe, B. 453.
Wynne, joyful, A. 154. A.S. *wyn*, pleasure, delight.
Wynne, obtain, get, A. 579; B. 617. A.S. *winnan*. See T.B. 1165.
Wynnelych, gracious, B. 1807, Cp. *wynly* = dexterously, 1165.
Wyrde, fate, destiny, A. 249, 273; B. 1224. Sc. *wird*. A.S. *wyrd*.
Wyrle, flew, B. 475.
Wyschande, hoping for, wishing, A. 14.
Wyse, manner, A. 1095; *wyses*, B. 1805.
Wyse, } show, appear, A. 1135,
Wysse, } B. 1564; direct, send out, B. 453; instruct, C. 60. A.S. *wissian*.
Wyst, } knew, A. 376; B. 152.
Wyste, }
Wyt, wisdom, B. 348; C. 129.
Wyt, know, learn, B. 1319, 1360. A.S. *witan*.

Wyte, blame, B. 76; C. 501. A.S. *witian.*

Wyte, pass away (?), C. 397. A.S. *witan.*

Wyter, true, truly, B. 1552. O.N. *vitr*, wise, prudent.

"& her ice wile shæwenn ȝaw
Summ þing to *witter* tàkenn."
(Ormulum, vol. i. p. 115.)

"Ne þe nedder was noght bitter
Þan, þowf he was ever *witter;*
Ffor of alle, als sheus þe boke,
Mast he cuth o crafte and crok."
(Cott. MS. Vesp. A. iii. fol. 5*b.*)

Wytered, informed, B. 1587.

Wyterly, truly, B. 171, 1567. Dan. *vitterlig*, known, manifest.

Wyþe, gentle, soft, C. 454. A.S. *wéthe*, soft, pleasant.

Wyþer, contrary, opposite, A. 230; adverse, hostile, C. 48. S.Sax. *witherr*, adverse, evil. A.S. *witherian*, to oppose, resist. Cf. *wetheruns* = *wetherings*, enemies, T.B. 5048.

"Ga, *witherr* gast, o bacch fra me."
(Ormulum, vol. ii. p. 41.)

Wyþerly, fiercely, angrily, B. 198; C. 74.

Wyth-halde, withhold, B. 740.

Wythouten, without, A. 390.

Wytles, foolish, B. 1585; C. 113.

Wytte, meaning, B. 1630; wit, A. 294; *wytteȝ*, devices, B. 515.

Wyȝ, } Wyȝe, } person, being, A. 131, 579; B. 545. A.S. *wiga*, a warrior, soldier; *wig*, war.

Wyȝt, quick, quickly, B. 617; C. 103. O.E. *wight*. Sw. *vig*, active.

Wyȝtly, quickly, B. 908.

"He waites vmbe hym *wightly.*"
(T.B. 876).

Ydropike, dropsical, B. 1096.

Yle, isle, A. 693.

Ylle, bad, evil, C. 8.

Ynde, blue, A. 1016; B. 1411.

"Þe toiþer heu neist (to grennes)
for to find,
Es al o *bleu*, men cals it *ynd.*"
(Cott. MS. Vesp. A. iii. fol. 53*a.*)

Yow, you, A. 287.

Yor, your, A. 761.

Yre, anger, B. 775, 1240.

Yþe, wave, B. 430; C. 147. A.S. *ythu*, a wave, flood. S. Sax. *uthe*.

"Þe roghe *yþes.*"—T. B. 1045.

Yȝe, eye (*pl. yȝen*), A. 254, 302.

Ȝare=yare, plainly, accurately, A. 834. A.S. *gearo*, ready, prepared, accurate.

Ȝark, *adj.* select, B. 652; prepare, B. 1708; *vb.* to grant, B. 758. A.S. *gearoian*, to prepare, make ready. See T.B. 414.

Ȝarm, cry, B. 971. As the character ȝ in these poems always represents *g* or *gh*, *ȝarm* is evidently not derived from the A.S. *cyrm*, noise, retained in O.E. *charm*, a humming noise, the cry of birds, etc., but is from the Welsh *garm*, shout, outcry; *garmio*, to set up a cry, from which the A.S. *cyrm*, is itself derived.

Ȝate, gate, A. 1034.

Ȝe, ye, A. 381.

Ȝede (*pret.* of *go*), went, A. 526, 1049; B. 432.

Ȝederly, quickly, soon, B. 463. O.N. *gedugr*, exceedingly. The adjective *ȝeder* does not occur in the poems, but was not unknown to O.E. literature. It occurs in the glossary to the Romance of King Alexander, ed. Stevenson, but is left unexplained by the editor.

"Then bownes agayn the bald kyng, baldly he wepis,
That he so skitly suld skifte and for his skars terme;
So did his princes, sais the profe, for pete of himselfe,
With ȝedire ȝoskinges and ȝerre ȝette out to grete." (p. 172.)

"*Ȝedire ȝoskinges* = great (frequent) sobbings."

Ȝelde, yield, perform, B. 665.

Ȝellyng=yelling, outcry, B. 971. A.S. *geallian*, to yell. "*Ȝellyn'* or hydowsly cryin', Vociferor." (Prompt. Parv.)

Ȝeme, protect, guard, B. 1242, 1493. A.S. *géman*, to care for, take care of.

Ȝemen, yeomen, A. 535.

Ȝender, yonder, B. 1617.

Ȝep, Ȝepe, } quick, active, bold, B. 796, 881. A.S. *gæp*.

"So yonge & so *ȝepe*." T.B. 367.

Ȝeply, quickly, B. 665, 1708. See T. B. 414.

Ȝer, Ȝere, } year, A. 483, 588.

Ȝerne=yearn, desire, A. 1190; B. 66, 758.

Ȝestande, B. 846. If from the A. S. *gæston*, "afflicted," we may render this term "afflicting," but if, as is more probable, it is from the A.S. *gist*, froth, yeast, we may explain it as "frothing," "overflowing." Cf. the phrase, "the *yesty* waves."

Ȝete, offer, give, A. 558. O.E. *yate* (*pret. yatte*). O.N, *géta*.

"He *yatte* hir freli al hir bone (prayer)."
(Cott. MS. Vesp. A. iii. fol. 47*a*.)

Gate, in T. B. 979, seems to mean a request.

"And he hir graunted þat *gate* with a good wille."

Ȝete, yet, A. 1061.

Ȝeȝed, spoke, B. 846. Prov. Ger. *gaggen*, to stutter, gabble.

Ȝif, if, B. 758.

Ȝise, truly, yes, C. 117.

Ȝisterday, yesterday, B. 463.

Ȝokke, yoke, B. 66.

Ȝolden, restored, B. 1708.

Ȝolpe, *vb.* boast, B. 846. A.S. *gilpan*.

Ȝomerly, sorrowful, lamentable, B. 971. A.S. *geomor*, sad; *geomorlic*, doleful. Cf. *ȝomeryng*, T. B. 1722.

Ȝon, yon, A. 693; B. 772.

Ȝonde, yonder, B. 721.

Ȝong, Ȝonge, } young, A. 412, 474; B. 783.

Ȝore, before, A. 586. A.S. *geara*.

Ȝore-fader, forefather, A. 322.

Ȝore-whyle, ere-while, B. 842.

Ȝornen (*3rd pers. pl. pret.*), ran, B. 881. A.S. *ge-yrnan*, to run.

Ȝyrd, go, hasten, A. 635. The original meaning of *ȝyrd* is perhaps a sudden sting, blow, hence to strike, then to start forward. Goth. *gasd*, a sting, goad. Lat. *hasta*. O.E. *gird*, to strike.

"*Gird* out the grete teth of the grym best." (T.B. 177).

MSS. AND BOOKS THAT EDITORS ARE WANTED FOR.

Among the MSS. and old books which need copying or re-editing are:—

ORIGINAL SERIES.

English Inventories and other MSS. in Canterbury Cathedral (5th Report, Hist. MSS. Com.).
Maumetrie, from Lord Tollemache's MS.
The Romance of Troy. Harl. 525.
Biblical MS., Corpus Cambr. 434 (ab. 1375).
Purvey's Ecclesie Regimen, Cot. Titus D 1.
Hampole's unprinted Works.
þe Clowde of Unknowyng, from Harl. MSS. 2373, 959, Bibl. Reg. 17 C 26, &c. Univ. Coll. Oxf. 14.
A Lanterne of Liȝt, from Harl. MS. 2324.
Soule-hele, from the Vernon MS.
Lydgate's unprinted Works.
Boethius, A.D. 1410, &c.; Pilgrim, 1426, &c., &c.
Vegetius on the Art of War. (Magd. Oxf. 30, &c.)
Early Treatises on Music: Descant, the Gamme, &c.
Skelton's englishing of Diodorus Siculus.
The Nightingale, and other Poems, from MS. Cot. Calig. A 2, Addit. MS. 10,036, &c.
Boethius, in prose, MS. Auct. F. 3. 5, Bodley.
Penitential Psalms, by Rd. Maydenstoon, Brampton, &c. (Rawlinson, A. 389, Douce 232, &c.).
Documents from the early Registers of the Bishops of all Dioceses in Great Britain.
Ordinances and Documents of the City of Worcester.
Chronicles of the Brute.
T. Breus's Passion of Christ, 1422. Harl. 2338.
Jn. Crophill or Crephill's Tracts, Harl. 1735.
Burgh's Cato.
Memoriale Credencium, &c., Harl. 2398.
Book for Recluses, Harl. 2372.
Lollard Theological Treatises, Harl. 2343, 2330, &c.
H. Selby's Northern Ethical Tract, Harl. 2388, art. 20.
Hilton's Ladder of Perfection, Cott. Faust. B 6, &c.
Supplementary Early English Lives of Saints.
The Early and Later Festialls, ab. 1400 and 1440 A.D., Cotton, Claud. A 2 Univ. Coll. Oxf. 102, &c.
Select Prose Treatises from the Vernon MS.
Jn. Hyde's MS. of Romances and Ballads, Balliol 354.
Metrical Homilies, Edinburgh MS.
Lyrical Poems from the Fairfax MS. 16, &c.
Prose Life of St. Audry, A.D. 1595, Corp. Oxf. 120.
English Miscellanies from MSS., Corp. Oxford.
Miscellanies from Oxford College MSS.
Disce Mori, Jesus Coll. Oxf. 39; Bodl. Laud 99.
Alain Chartier's Quadrilogue, &c., Univ. Coll. Oxf. 85.
Mirrour of the blessed lijf of Ihesu Crist, Univ. Coll. Oxf. 123, &c.
Pilgrimage of the Soul, A.D. 1400, prose, Univ. Coll. Oxf. 181, &c.
Poem on Virtues and Vices, &c., Harl. 2260.
Maundevyle's Legend of Gwydo, Queen's, Oxf. 383.
Book of Warrants of Edw. VI, &c., New Coll. Oxf. 328.
Adam Loutfut's Heraldic Tracts, Harl. 6149-50.
Rules for Gunpowder and Ordnance, Harl. 6355.
John Watton's englisht Speculum Christiani, Corpus Oxf. 155, Laud G. 12, Thoresby 530, Harl. 2250, art. 20.

EXTRA SERIES.

Erle of Tolous.
Sir Eglamoure.
Ypotis.
Emare.
Lyrical Poems, from the Harl. MS. 2253.
Le Morte Arthur, from the unique Harl. 2252.
Sir Tristrem, from the unique Auchinleck MS.
Miscellaneous Miracle Plays.
Sir Gowther.
Dame Siriz, &c.
Orfeo (Digby, 86).
Dialogues between the Soul and Body.
Barlaam and Josaphat.
Amis and Amiloun.
Ipomedon.
Sir Generides, from Lord Tollemache's MS.
The Troy-Book Fragments once cald Barbour's in the Cambr. Univ. Library and Douce MSS.
Gower's Confessio Amantis.
Poems of Charles, Duke of Orleans.
Carols and Songs.
Songs and Ballads, Ashmole MS. 48.
The Siège of Rouen, from Harl. MSS. 2256, 753. Egerton 1995, Bodl. 3562, E. Museo 124, &c.
Jn. Hart's Methode to read English, 1570.
Octavian.
Ywain and Gawain.
Libeaus Desconus.
Avntures of Arther.
Avowyng of King Arther.
Sir Perceval of Gallas.
Sir Isumbras.
Partonope of Blois, Univ. Coll. Oxf. 188, &c.
Pilgrimage to Jerusalem, Queen's, Oxf. 357.
Other Pilgrimages to Jerusalem, Harl. 2333, &c.
Horæ, Penitential Psalms, &c., Queen's, Oxf. 207.
St. Brandon's Confession, Queen's, Oxf. 210.
Scotch Heraldry Tracts, copy of Caxton's Book of Chivalry, &c., Queen's Coll. Oxford, 161.
Stevyn Scrope's Doctryne and Wysedome of the Auncyent Philosophers, A.D. 1450, Harl. 2266.

The Founder and Director of the E. E. T. Soc. is Dr. F. J. Furnivall, 3, St. George's Sq., Primrose Hill, London, N.W. Its *Hon. Sec.* is W. A. Dalziel, Esq., 67, Victoria Road, Finsbury Park, London, N. The Subscription to the Society is 21*s.* a year for the *Original Series*, and 21*s.* for the *Extra Series* of re-editions.

Early English Text Society.

ORIGINAL SERIES.

The Publications for 1893 (*one guinea*) *are*:—

100. Capgrave's Life of St. Katharine, ed. Dr. C. Horstmann, with Forewords by Dr. Furnivall. 20*s*.
101. Cursor Mundi. Part VII. Essay on the MSS., their Dialects, &c., by Dr. H. Hupe. 10*s*.

The Publications for 1894 (*one guinea*) *are*:—

102. Lanfrank's Science of Cirurgie, ab. 1400 A.D., ed. from the 2 MSS. by Dr. R. von Fleischhacker. Part I. 20*s*.
103. The Legend of the Cross, from a 12th century MS., &c., &c., ed. Prof. A. S. Napier, M.A., Ph.D. 7*s*. 6*d*.

The Publications for 1895 (*one guinea*) *are*:—

104. The Exeter-Book (Anglo-Saxon Poems), re-edited from the unique MS., by I. Gollancz, M.A. Part I. 20*s*.
105. The Prymer, or Lay-Folks' Prayer-Book, Cambr. Univ. MS., ab. 1420, with Facsimiles, ed. H. Littlehales. Part I. 10*s*.

The Publications for 1896 (*one guinea*) *are*:—

106. Richard Misyn's Fire of Love, 1534, & Mending of Life, 1535 (from Hampole), ed. Rev. R. Harvey, M.A. 15*s*.
107. The English Conquest of Ireland, A.D. 1166-1185. 2 Texts, about 1425, 1440, Part I, ed. Dr. Furnivall. 15*s*.

The Publications for 1897 (*issued: one guinea*) *are*:—

108. Child-Marriages and Divorces, &c. Depositions in the Bishop's Court, Chester, 1561-6, ed. Dr. Furnivall. 15*s*.
109. The Prymer, or Lay-Folks' Prayer-Book, Part II, ed. Hy. Littlehales. 10*s*.

The Publications for 1898 (*ready: one guinea*) *are*:—

110. The Old English Version of Bede's Ecclesiastical History, Part II, § 1, ed. Dr. T. Miller. 15*s*.
111. The Old English Version of Bede's Ecclesiastical History, Part II, § 2, ed. Dr. T. Miller. 15*s*.

The Publications for 1899 *and* 1900 *will be chosen from*:—

Queen Elizabeth's Englishings of Boethius, Plutarch, &c., ed. Miss Pemberton. 15*s*. [*Finisht*.

Minor Poems of the Vernon MS., Part II, ed. Dr. F. J. Furnivall. [*At Press*.

The Craft of Nombrynge, the earliest English Treatise on Arithmetic, ed. R. S. Steele, B.A. [*At Press*.

Jacob's Well, edited from the unique MS. by Dr. A. Brandeis. [*At Press*.

Vices and Virtues, from the unique MS., ab. 1200 A.D., ed. Dr. F. Holthausen, Part II. [*At Press*.

An Anglo-Saxon Martyrology, edited from the 4 MSS. by Dr. G. Herzfeld. [*At Press*.

The Exeter Book (Anglo-Saxon Poems), re-edited by I. Gollancz, M.A. Part II. [*At Press*.

George Ashby's Active Policy of a Prince, A.D. 1463, ed. Miss Mary Bateson. [*At Press*.

Prayers and Devotions, from the unique MS. Cotton Titus C. 19, ed. Hy. Littlehales, Esq. [*Copied*.

Sir David Lyndesay's Works. Part VI and last, ed. W. H. S. Utley. [*At Press*.

The Lay Folks' Catechism, by Archbp. Thoresby, ed. Canon Simmons and Rev. H. E. Nolloth. [*Text set*.

EXTRA SERIES.

The Publications for 1893 *are*:—

LXIII. Thomas a Kempis's De Imitatione Christi, englisht ab. 1440, and 1502, ed. Prof. J. K. Ingram, LL.D. 15*s*.

LXIV. Caxton's Godeffroy of Boloyne, or Siege & Conqueste of Jerusalem, 1481, ed. Dr. Mary N. Colvin. 15*s*.

The Publications for 1894 (*one guinea*) *are*:—

LXV. Sir Bevis of Hamton, Part III. ed. Prof. E. Kölbing, Ph.D. 15*s*.

LXVI. Lydgate's and Burgh's Secrees of Philisoffres, ab. 1445-50, ed. R. Steele, B.A. 15*s*.

The Publications for 1895 (*one guinea*) *are*:—

LXVII. The Three Kings' Sons, from the unique MS., ab. 1500 A.D. Part I, the Text, ed. Dr. F. J. Furnivall. 10*s*.

LXVIII. Melusine, the prose Romance, from the unique MS., ab. 1500, ed. A. K. Donald, B.A. Part I. 20*s*.

The Publications for 1896 *will probably be*:—

LXIX. Melusine, the prose Romance, from the unique MS., ab. 1500, ed. A. K. Donald, B.A. Part II. 10*s*.

LXX. Promptorium Parvulorum, c. 1440, from the Winchester MS., ed. Rev. A. L. Mayhew, M.A. 20*s*.

The Publications for 1897 *and* 1898 (*to be ready in* 1896) *will be chosen from*:—

The Towneley Plays, re-edited from the unique MS. by G. England, Esq., and A. W. Pollard, M.A. [*At Press*.

Lydgate's Assembly of the Gods, ed. Prof. Oscar L. Triggs, M.A. [*At Press*.

The Chester Plays, Part II, re-edited by George England, Esq. [*At Press*.

Hoccleve's Regement of Princes, 1411-12, ed. Dr. F. J. Furnivall. [*At Press*.

Hoccleve's Minor Poems, II, from the Ashburnham MS., ed. I. Gollancz, M.A. [*At Press*.

Lichfield Gilds, ed. Dr. F. J. Furnivall; Introduction by Prof. E. C. K. Gonner. [*Text done*.

Extracts from the Rochester Diocesan Registers, ed. Hy. Littlehales, Esq.

The Owl and Nightingale, 2 Texts parallel, ed. G. F. H. Sykes, Esq. [*At Press*.

The Three Kings' Sons, Part II, French collation, Introduction, &c., by Dr. L. Kellner.

Deguilleville's Pilgrimage of the Life of Man, 3 prose Versions, 2 English, 1 French, ed. G. N. Currie, M.A.

Robert of Brunne's Handlyng Synne (1303), and its French Original, ed. Dr. F. J. Furnivall.

The Coventry Plays, re-edited from the unique MS. by George England, Esq.

☞ *The Large-Paper Issue of the Extra Series is stopt, save for unfinisht Works of it.*

www.ingramcontent.com/pod-product-compliance
Lightning Source LLC
Chambersburg PA
CBHW020053030726
47498CB00006B/1763

* 9 7 8 3 3 3 7 3 9 5 5 1 3 *